BLOOD OF AENARION

A TYRION & TECLIS NOVEL

More William King from the Black Library

• TYRION & TECLIS •

Book 1: BLOOD OF AENARION
Book 2: SWORD OF CALEDOR (December 2012)
Book 3: BANE OF MALEKITH (December 2013)

• GOTREK & FELIX •

GOTREK & FELIX: THE FIRST OMNIBUS
(Contains books 1-3 in the series: *Trollslayer,
Skavenslayer* and *Daemonslayer*)

GOTREK & FELIX: THE SECOND OMNIBUS
(Contains books 4-6 in the series: *Dragonslayer,
Beastslayer* and *Vampireslayer*)

GOTREK & FELIX: THE THIRD OMNIBUS
With Nathan Long
(Contains books 7-9 in the series: *Giantslayer,
Orcslayer* and *Manslayer*)

• SPACE WOLF •

SPACE WOLF: THE FIRST OMNIBUS
(Contains books 1-3 in the series: *Space Wolf,
Ragnar's Claw* and *Grey Hunter*)

SPACE WOLF: THE SECOND OMNIBUS
With Lee Lightner
(Contains books 4-6 in the series: *Wolfblade,
Sons of Fenris* and *Wolf's Honour*)

More High Elf action from the Black Library

DEFENDERS OF ULTHUAN
SONS OF ELLYRION
By Graham McNeill

• TIME OF LEGENDS: THE SUNDERING •

By Gav Thorpe
Book 1: MALEKITH
Book 2: SHADOW KING
Book 3: CALEDOR

AENARION
An audio drama

A WARHAMMER NOVEL

BLOOD OF
AENARION

A TYRION & TECLIS NOVEL

WILLIAM KING

BLACK LIBRARY

For my brother Eddie King, 1960-2010.
You'll be missed, big man.

A BLACK LIBRARY PUBLICATION

First published in Great Britain in 2011 by
The Black Library,
Games Workshop Ltd.,
Willow Road, Nottingham,
NG7 2WS, UK.

10 9 8 7 6 5 4 3 2 1

Cover illustration by Raymond Swanland.
Icon by Nuala Kennedy.

A CIP record for this book is available from the British Library.

UK ISBN13: 978 1 84970 090 0
US ISBN13: 978 1 84970 091 7

See the Black Library on the internet at
www.blacklibrary.com

Find out more about Games Workshop
and the world of Warhammer at
www.games-workshop.com

Printed and bound by CPI Group (UK) Ltd, Croydon, CR0 4YY

THIS IS A dark age, a bloody age, an age of daemons and of sorcery. It is an age of battle and death, and of the world's ending. Amidst all of the fire, flame and fury it is a time, too, of mighty heroes, of bold deeds and great courage.

THESE ARE BLEAK times. Across the length and breadth of the Old World, from the heartlands of the human Empire and the knightly palaces of Bretonnia to ice-bound Kislev in the far north, come rumblings of war. In the towering Worlds Edge Mountains, the orc tribes are gathering for another assault. Bandits and renegades harry the wild southern lands of the Border Princes. There are rumours of rat-things, the skaven, emerging from the sewers and swamps across the land. And from the northern wildernesses there is the ever-present threat of Chaos, of daemons and beastmen corrupted by the foul powers of the Dark Gods.

AN ANCIENT AND proud race, the high elves hail from Ulthuan, a mystical island of rolling plains, rugged mountains and glittering cities. Ruled over by the noble Phoenix King, Finubar, and the Everqueen, Alarielle, Ulthuan is a land steeped in magic, renowned for its mages and fraught with blighted history. Great seafarers, artisans and warriors, the high elves protect their ancestral homeland from enemies near and far. None more so than from their wicked kin, the dark elves, against whom they are locked in a bitter war that has lasted for centuries.

PROLOGUE

*79th Year of the Reign of Aenarion,
the Cliffs of Skalderak, Ulthuan*

FROM HIGH ATOP the cliffs of Skalderak, Aenarion looked down on the camp of his enemies. The Chaos worshippers' fires blazed in the darkness, more numerous than the stars. There were hundreds of thousands of his monstrous foes down there and even if he killed every last one of them, more would come.

He was going to die. The whole world was going to die. There was nothing anyone could do to stop it. He had tried, with all his enormous strength, with all his deadly cunning, with power greater than any mortal had ever possessed, wielding a weapon so evil it was forbidden by the gods, and still he had failed to stop the forces of Chaos.

Their armies surged across Ulthuan, crushing the last resistance of the elves. Howling hordes of blood-mad beastmen smashed through the final defences. Armies of mutants overwhelmed the last guardians of the island-continent. Legions of daemons revelled in the ruins of ancient cities.

After decades of warfare, Chaos was mightier than ever, and his people were at the end of their strength. Victory was impossible. He had been mad to think it could be otherwise.

He cast his gaze back to his own camp. Once he would have deemed his own army mighty. Hundreds of dragons slumbered amid the silk pavilions spread out across the mountaintop. Tens of thousands of heavily armoured elf warriors awaited his command. They would throw themselves into the attack once more if he gave the order, even though they were outnumbered more than twenty to one. With him to lead them they might even win, but it would be a fruitless victory. The Chaos army at the foot of the cliffs was only one of many. There were other armies, equally great and many greater, scattered across Ulthuan and, for all he knew, the rest of the world. They could not all be beaten by the forces at his disposal.

He turned and strode back inside his pavilion. It was futile to contemplate the size of the enemy force.

He unsheathed the Sword of Khaine. It glowed an infernal black, casting out hungry shadows that dimmed the hanging lanterns within the great silk tent. Red runes burned along a blade forged from alien metal. The Sword whispered obscenely to him in a thousand voices, and every voice, whether commanding, entreating or seductive, demanded death. It was the most powerful weapon ever forged and still it was not enough. It was heavy in his hand with the full weight of his failure. For all the good it had done him, he might as well have kept using Sunfang, the blade Caledor had made for him back when they were still friends.

The Sword was killing him by inches, bleeding away his life a droplet at a time. Every hour aged him like a day would age another elf. Only the unnatural vitality he had acquired when he passed through the Flame of Asuryan had enabled him to survive this long and even that would not last forever.

If the Sword was not fed lives it feasted on him instead. It was part of the devil's bargain he had made when he had still thought it was possible to save the world, when he had still thought that he was a hero.

Morathi stirred in her sleep, one arm thrown out, casting off the silken coverlet, leaving one perfect breast revealed, a strand of her long curly black hair caught between her lips as she writhed in some erotic dream. The potions still worked for her. She could still find sleep, no matter how troubled. The drugs had long ago ceased to work for him even when taken in dosages that would have killed anyone else.

Wine had no savour. Food had no taste. He lived in a world of moving shadows, far less vivid than the one he had known as a mortal. He had given up much to save his people – his ideals, his family, his very soul.

Kill her. Kill them all.

The Sword's ancient, evil voices kept whispering in his head. In the quiet of the night he could still ignore them. There had been times when the mad bloodlust was upon him when he could not, and he had committed acts that made him burn with shame and wish that the wine still worked so that he could find forgetfulness in it.

Had there been time enough left, the day would come when he would no longer be able to resist the Godslayer's urging, and nothing within his reach would be safe. If the daemons did not end the world, he would do it himself.

He laughed softly. Phoenix King they called him now. He had passed through the sacred flames and come out the other side, not burned but stronger, faster, more alive than any mortal should be. He had offered himself as a sacrifice to save his people when the gods had rejected all others, and they had taken his flesh and his agony as their offering and sent him back transformed to do their work.

He had died and been reborn the day he passed through the Flame of Asuryan, and he had caught glimpses of things that had blasted his sanity. He had seen the vast damaged clockwork of the ordered universe and that which lay beneath it and beyond.

He had looked upon the Chaos that bubbled around everything for all eternity. He had seen the smile on the face of the daemon god who waited to devour the souls of his people. He had witnessed that god's kin use worlds for their playthings and populations for their slaves. He had glimpsed the great holes in the fabric of reality through which their power and their servants poured in to conquer his world.

He had seen eternities of horror and he had come back reshaped, remade, reborn to fight. He had tried then with all his new-found might to save his people from the tide of daemonic filth engulfing the world.

At first he thought he could win. The gods had gifted him with power beyond that of any mortal. He had used it to lead the elves to victory after victory but every triumph had cost them irreplaceable lives and for every foe that fell two more came to take their place.

He had not realised then that it was all a black cosmic joke. He was only slowing down the destruction of his people, making it more painful by drawing out the agony.

He had taken the Everqueen as his wife and she had borne him two perfect children, a promise of a brighter tomorrow, or at least a pledge that there still would be a tomorrow. He had believed that then, but his family been taken from him by the daemons and slaughtered. In the end he had not even been able to protect his own kin, and their loss had ripped the heart from him.

It was then that he had sought out the Blighted Isle and the Godslayer. It was a weapon never meant to be drawn from the Altar of Khaine but he had drawn it. If the gods had given him strength, the Sword had made him all but invincible. Where he walked daemons died. Where he led, victory was inevitable. But he could not be everywhere and with every day the forces opposed to him grew stronger and those who followed him grew fewer and fewer.

The evil of the Sword had seeped into him and changed him, making him angrier and less sane as the odds against him mounted. His closest friends had shunned him and the people he was pledged to save had drifted away, leaving only hardened embittered remnants, elves as angry and deadly as himself, a legion of warriors almost as mad and twisted as the foes they faced. They too had been changed by the baleful influence of his unholy weapon. He had taught his people too well how to make war.

A mood of black despair had come upon him, and at that darkest period of his life he had found Morathi. He glanced at her beautiful sleeping form, loathing her and wanting her at the same time. What he had with her he could not call love. He doubted he was capable of any tender emotion any more, even with a woman less twisted than his current wife. This was a mad, sick passion. In Morathi's caresses he had found some respite from his troubles and in their wild love-making he had found distraction from his cares.

She had brewed potions that for a time had let him sleep and made him almost calm. And she had borne him a son, Malekith, and taught him that there was still some spark of feeling within him yet. He had found something to fight for once more and returned to the fray, if not with hope, at least with determination. But now, at long last, he could see that it was over, that his enemies would win, and that his people were doomed to death and an eternity of damnation.

A GLOW IN the air warned him. Long, sharp-edged shadows danced away from him. He turned, sword raised ready to strike, and only at the last heartbeat did he stay his hand.

'Aenarion, can you hear me?' asked a voice of eerie quietness that seemed to be carried on some dismal breeze from the desolate margins of the world.

Caledor stood there, or at least his image did, a glowing translucent ghost, cast across long leagues by the force of the mage's magic. Aenarion studied his former friend. The mightiest mage in the world looked half-dead. His body was wasted, his cheeks were sunken, his face looked like a skull. His features were schooled to impassiveness by the power of his will but terror glittered in his eyes. It was never far from the eyes of any of the elves now.

'Aenarion, are you there?' The image flickered and Aenarion knew that all he had to do was wait and the image would vanish as the spell collapsed. He did not want to talk to the one who had turned his back on him, who had walked away from the doom he felt that Aenarion was leading their people towards.

He bit back words of anger and reined in the rage burning in his breast. In his more lucid moments he knew that Caledor had done the right thing, taking some remnant of the people out from under the shadow of the Sword and the doom that Aenarion carried within him.

'I am here, Caledor,' Aenarion said. 'What do you wish of me?'

'I need your aid. We are besieged by land and sea.'

Aenarion's laugh was bitter. 'Now you need my help! You turned your back on me but you do not scruple to seek my aid when you need it.'

Caledor shook his head slowly and Aenarion could see the weariness eating away at him. The mage was at the end of his tether. His last resources of strength were dwindling. Only willpower was keeping him going. 'I never turned my back on you, my friend, only on that cursed thing you carry and the path you set your feet upon.'

'It comes to the same thing. I saw the way that would save our people. You, in your arrogance, refused to follow.'

'There are some roads it is better not to travel even if they are the only way to escape death. Your way would make us worse than the things we face. It would merely be a different kind of defeat. Our enemies would win in the end either way.'

In his heart of hearts Aenarion agreed but he was too proud to admit his folly. Instead he gave vent to his bitterness and anger. 'Accursed you have called me, accursed till the end of time, and all of my seed to be accursed. And yet you dare ask for my aid?'

'I did not curse you, Aenarion. You cursed yourself when you drew that blade. Perhaps you were accursed before that. I know you were always chosen by destiny and that in itself is a sort of curse.'

'Now that you need my help, you seek to twist your words and give them a honeyed meaning.'

Anger passed across Caledor's features. His lips twisted into a sneer. 'The world ends and yet your pride must be salved. It is more important to you than life, the life of our people. You will not aid me because of harsh truths I once spoke. You are like a child, Aenarion.'

Aenarion laughed. 'I have not said I will not aid you. What is it you seek?'

'There is only one way to save our world. We both know it.'

'You intend to put your plan into effect then, to sing your spells and try and banish magic from the world.'

'That is not what I seek and you know it.'

'Morathi says that will be the effect of what you do.'

'I doubt your wife knows more of the ways of magic than I do.'

'Now who is mad with pride, Caledor?'

'The gates of the Old Ones are open. The winds of magic blow through them like a hurricane. They carry the energy that causes the humans to mutate and lets the daemons dwell here. Without that energy they must leave our world or die. This is truth. We have constructed a mighty network of spells to channel that energy, to drain it away, to use it for our own purposes. All we need do now is activate it.'

'We have been over this a hundred times. Too much could go wrong.'

'We are dying, Aenarion. Soon there will be none of us left to oppose Chaos. We have tried your way. It has not worked. The forces of Chaos are stronger now than they were the day you passed through the Flame.'

'That is not my fault, wizard.'

'No, but it is the truth.'

'So you seek my permission to try your plan?'

'No.'

'No?'

'We have begun.'

'You dare to do this when I have forbidden it?'

'You are our leader, Aenarion. We are not your slaves. The time has come for a last throw of the dice.'

'*I* will decide when that is to be.'

'It is too late for anything else, Phoenix King. If it is not done now, it will not be done at all. The forces against us will be too strong. Perhaps they already are.'

'If you have decided to defy my will, why bother telling me?'

'Because the daemons sense our purpose and try to stop us, and we do not have the strength to prevent them.'

'So you want me and mine to protect you, in spite of your defiance.'

'We are all one people. This will be the last stand of the elves. If you do not wish to be there, that is your choice.'

'There will be other battles.'

'No. This will be the last. If our spell goes wrong the fault lines beneath Ulthuan will be torn apart, the continent will sink, drowning our enemies. Perhaps the whole world will end.'

'And yet you will still proceed.'

'There is no other choice, Aenarion. You told me once that mine was the counsel of despair and that you would find another way to win this war. Have you done so?'

He wanted to cast the mage's words back into his teeth but he was too proud and too honest to do so. He shook his head.

'Will you come to the Isle of the Dead? We need you.'

'I will consider it.'

'Do not consider too long, Phoenix King.'

Caledor put his hands together and bowed and vanished. Morathi's eyes snapped open and she screamed.

* * *

HE TURNED TO look at his wife. She stared at him as if looking at a ghost.

'You are not dead, thank all the gods,' she said.

'Apparently not,' he said.

'Do not joke about such things, Aenarion. You know I see the future and tonight in my dreams I had a vision. A battle is coming. If you take part in it you will die.'

'So?'

'If you leave my side, you will die.'

He stared at her hard, wanting to ask her how she knew and not daring to because he feared the answer and what he would have to do if she gave it.

Morathi had studied the ways of their enemies for a very long time, and, he suspected, far too closely. There were times when he was not sure where her true loyalties lay. He only knew that she looked at him, as he looked at her, with a mixture of lust, respect, hatred and anger. It was a potent, heady brew that had fuelled many memorable days and more memorable nights.

'Everyone dies,' he told her.

'I will not,' she said with certainty. 'And your son Malekith will not. And if you listen to me, you will not either. If you go today you forfeit immortality. Stay with me and live forever.' She stretched out her hand in entreaty. It seemed for a moment as if she were actually going to beg. She would not ever do that. And yet...

'That is not possible,' he said quickly, to break the spell of the moment.

'You are the Phoenix King. Anything is possible for you.'

'Whatever else I am, I am a warrior, and today may be the last battle the elves ever fight.'

'You are going to help that fool Caledor with his insane plan.' She was angry now. Rage did not make her ugly. It made her more beautiful and more dangerous. He stared at her, unintimidated. She had never frightened him. He suspected that intrigued her. He was probably the only one her rage had never daunted.

'It is the only way we can win this war. I know that now,' he said calmly, because he knew that would goad her more.

'And I say to you, if you go, you will die.'

He shrugged and began donning his armour. As he fastened the clasps, he spoke the words that activated its dormant power. Titanic fields of protective magic shimmered into place around him. Potent spells amplified his already enormous strength. It was a barrier between himself and her that he wanted at that moment though.

She walked towards him, arms outstretched in entreaty. 'Please stay with me. I do not want to lose you forever.'

As ever he was astonished by her beauty. He doubted there had ever been a woman as lovely as Morathi. At the same time, he was untouched by her loveliness. It had no hold over him. It never had. And he knew that in some way that was the secret of the power he held over her. Other elves might be driven mad with longing and lust for her. He was not. There was a coldness in him that she could not touch but nothing could stop her trying.

He pulled on his gauntlets and reached out and touched her cheek with his armoured hand. He could not feel the softness of her skin but that was not so different from the normal way of things. He felt neither pleasure nor pain as much as normal mortals did after he passed through the Flame.

'I will return,' he said.

She shook her head with absolute finality. 'No. You will not. You are a fool, Aenarion, but I love you.'

The words hung in the air. It was the first time she had ever said them.

She stood there waiting for him to say something, obvious entreaty in her eyes. He knew how much it cost her to say such words. Not to hear any response must be humiliating to one of her enormous pride.

There was nothing he could say or wanted to. He had only ever loved one woman and she was dead, along with the children she had borne him. Nothing could change that fact. Nothing ever would.

Morathi was merely wicked and she had drawn him into her wickedness. Even now she was trying to prevent him from going forth to face his foes. At that moment he felt certain that she was numbered among his enemies and the enemies of his people, and she would be forever.

Kill her, whispered the Sword.

He would be doing the elves a service if he struck her down. He stared at her for a moment, certain that she knew what he was thinking, and just as certain that at that moment she did not really care what he did.

She moved closer as if daring him to strike. He reached out with one hand, jerked her to him and crushed her lips against his, putting all his lust and rage and hatred into one long and brutal kiss. She responded in kind, writhing against his metal-encased form until he thrust her away, her naked body bleeding in a dozen places from pushing against the edges of his armour.

He smiled at her savagely, turned on his heel and left the pavilion without another word. He thought he heard her crying as he left. He told himself he did not care.

INDRAUGNIR STOOD BEFORE him like a living mountain. The span of the dragon's wings blocked out the sky. His head arched downwards on the titanic column of his neck. Aenarion looked into his strange glittering eyes and saw a ferocity and anger there that matched his own. The dragon sensed his fey mood and responded with a bellow. The other dragons took up his war cry until the mountains around them echoed as if to the sound of thunder.

Horns rang out summoning the elves to war. Dragon riders rushed forth to greet the dawn, clutching their long spears, strapping on their glittering armour, making the air shimmer with the enchantments on their gear. Grooms attached saddles and harnesses to the dragons' necks. The air stank of sulphur and leather and the deadly gaseous breath of the great beasts.

All eyes were upon him now. His whole army watched him. All of them were grim, scarred elves with hard eyes and a cruel set to their mouths. All of them had suffered in this long war. All of them were consumed with a mad hatred of their enemy that Aenarion understood only too well. All of them knew they had been summoned forth for some mighty effort. Enormous ranks of ground troops formed up beyond them. They would be useless in the coming battle. They would not be able to travel to the Isle of the Dead fast enough to take part. They expected him to speak. The magic of the dragon armour carried his calm measured tones to the furthest units of the assembled army.

'You have followed me far. Some of you must follow me a little further. We must ride far and fast and only those mounted on dragons will be swift enough to follow me. The rest of you must remain here and guard my queen.'

He saw anger and pride war in the faces of the infantry and cavalry. They knew he had already lost one wife and they would not let him lose another. These troops had followed him through hell and they loved him in their cold, cruel way. 'Those of you who stay must guard this place and endure. After today you may be the last elves in the world. You will need to follow my queen and my son and rebuild our kingdom come what may.'

They heard the knowledge of his own death in his voice at the same moment as he heard it himself. He had given them implicit instructions for the succession. These veterans would see they were carried out. He turned his attention to the dragon riders, the elite of the elite, the greatest warriors of the elves. He paused for a moment and let his gaze sweep over them all, meeting the eyes of every soldier. As he did so Indraugnir roared again, and the other dragons took up the chorus till the mountains echoed.

'Today will be our last battle. Today, for better or worse, this war ends,' he shouted, and his voice carried even over the bellowing of the dragons. 'Today we go forth from this place to victory or to death. Gird on your armour. Make ready your lances. We ride!'

AENARION LEAPT INTO the saddle and tugged the reins. Indraugnir threw himself into the sky, his enormous leathery pinions beating the air with a crack like a storm hitting the sails of an ocean-going ship.

The roar of the wind was loud in his ears as they gained altitude, the great line of dragon-borne elf warriors taking their place in formation until a huge arrowhead filled the sky behind him. For the first time in a long time, wild joy filled him. This might be the last dawn he ever saw but there were still wonders in this world that could stir his heart and make it beat faster.

'To the Isle of the Dead,' he shouted and the wind carried away his words so that only Indraugnir could hear him.

He did not need to know the direction in which they should fly. In the distance an eerie glow filled the sky, rivalling the dawn. His elven senses told him that there a great confluence of magical energies gathered. Caledor had lit a beacon that would attract the attention of anything with the slightest sensitivity to magic and there were things out there that could sense the casting of the faintest spell at a distance of a thousand leagues.

Their journey carried the dragons over mountains and forests, plains and seas. He had time to take in the wild beauty of the land he had sworn to protect for one last time. Even marred by the monstrous hordes of Chaos, it was lovely. As the leagues and hours rushed by, the land beneath him came alive with monsters and mutants and daemons all racing towards the place where the most powerful spell ever woven was being cast.

As they approached the Isle of the Dead, horror and wonder filled his mind in equal measure. Thousands of crude ships filled the sea, delivering legions of monsters to the shores of the island.

Hundreds of thousands of twisted beings filled the beaches beneath him, some the size of elves, some the size of dragons and every size and shape in between. Here and there things raised hands or claws or a staff to the sky and a futile bolt of magical energy blasted skyward to strike a dragon impotently. At this range and height there was nothing their foes could do to harm them. Those flying Chaos creatures that dared to rise and challenge them were blasted from the sky by the power of dragon-breath or elven magic.

Ahead of him now, he could see the great open-roofed temple where Caledor had chosen to work his ritual magic. The air above it shimmered with power. Already the sky was changing colour, clouds becoming yellow and gold and crimson and sapphire as they swirled like a great whirlpool in the air. Multi-coloured lightning flickered. The winds became stronger, slowing the flight of even a dragon as mighty as Indraugnir.

Aenarion swooped lower. He saw lines of apprentice wizards standing in geomantic formation around the centre of the temple, chanting words of power, feeding their strength to the archmages who stood at the point of each column, all adding a tiny morsel to the overall pool of energy.

At the centre of it all stood Caledor and his circle of the greatest of all elven magii. Each was limned with an aura of awesome power. From their outstretched hands, writhing bands of energy fed the ever-more complex enchantment growing in their midst. The force of magic at the centre of that web was already so great that nothing unprotected could survive there for long. He sensed that the spell was spinning on the edge of being out of control. Something mighty enough to shatter the world was being shaped down there. Nothing like this had ever been attempted before and Aenarion doubted anything like it would ever be attempted again.

The daemons were drawn to it like sharks to blood. The clever ones must know that what was being done here was not for their benefit. The less clever ones just wanted to reach this great trove of power.

A seemingly endless horde of Chaos worshippers surrounded the place, brandishing the banners of the four great Powers they worshipped: Khorne, Slaanesh, Tzeentch and Nurgle.

Each of the armies was led by a greater daemon sworn to those powers, chosen representatives of the daemon gods. They were mighty beyond the understanding of mortals. They had led their forces to countless victories in countless places. The fact that they were all gathered here argued that the daemonic leaders understood quite as well as he did exactly how important this place was, that the fate of the world would be decided by what happened here today.

He took in the battleground at a glance, understanding the play of forces on it instinctively. The elves were doomed. Their foes were too numerous and too powerful. Nothing could stop the forces of Chaos triumphing today. The best that might be achieved was that they be delayed long enough for Caledor to finish working his spell.

So be it, Aenarion thought. If the only road to victory is by way of death, we will take it.

Kill, whispered the Sword.

Aenarion raised his blade and the first wing of dragons peeled off and descended on the advancing Chaos hordes. They swept over the teeming multitude, breath of fire cleansing the tainted earth. The Chaos worshippers were packed so closely together there was no way to avoid the flames raining down from the sky. They died in their thousands, like a column of warrior ants marching into a pool of burning oil.

Wave after wave of dragons descended. Legion after legion of Chaos worshippers died. The smell of scorched flesh rose to reach even Aenarion's nostrils as he circled high above the battlefield.

The winds grew stronger. The columns of fire above the temple grew brighter. In the distance the earth erupted as towers of magic sprang into being in answer to the spells of Caledor and his fellow mages. As far as the eye could see fingers of swirling magical light stabbed into the sky, illuminating the darkening land and revealing the great crowds of Chaos monsters racing towards the site of battle. All over Ulthuan the same thing was happening as Caledor's vortex came to life.

Clouds obscured all of the sky now. Below him it was dark as night save where the hellish illumination of the glowing columns lit their surroundings or the dazzling flash of some mighty polychromatic lightning bolt split the sky. The geomantic pattern the elf mages had been arranged in was plain now, a great rune made of flesh and light visible from the sky through which Aenarion flew. The terror and the wonder of it filled his heart.

This was a sight worth seeing even if it cost the life of the world.

In the distance the sea boiled with ships and huge monsters. All sensed that the hour of final battle was at hand. The screaming, chanting horde surged up the stairways of the shrine. The Isle of the Dead was never meant to be a fortress but a holy place. The makeshift defences of the elves were smashed by the rampaging daemon worshippers.

Chaos sorcerers on glowing disks of light rode the skies, howling incantations as they tried to breach the spell walls protecting the shrine. One by one, the barriers fell, for there were not enough elven mages left to maintain them. Too many were committed to the creation of the vortex.

As he passed over, Aenarion saw mighty banners fluttering over enormous moving towers. Each bore the sign of the greater daemons who were the generals and champions of the besieging force. Even in the shadow of the gigantic spell Caledor was weaving, Aenarion sensed the power of these deadly creatures. They were the mightiest of their kind, hardened by millennia of constant warfare in the hells they came from. Normally they would have been the deadliest of enemies, but on this day, in this place, they seemed to have managed a truce in order to crush the one threat remaining to their domination of this world.

The dragons swooped and slew like great birds of prey. Hills of smouldering corpses rose on the way to the temple but it did not matter. No matter how many they killed more came on, rushing forwards to inevitable death as to the embrace of a lover. Now the dragonfire began to weaken as the dragons reached the end of their resources. Flocks of winged daemons surrounded individual dragons and smashed them from the skies.

They could not prevent the great horde reaching the outer defences of the temple and engaging the thin lines of desperate elf soldiers waiting there.

A terrible wave of agony and terror rippled out from the temple. For a moment, the huge spell at the centre of it trembled and threatened to collapse. Aenarion swooped lower and saw that one of the archmages had fallen along with all the apprentices who had been linked to him. The power of the spell had burned the life out of him. The whole mighty edifice Caledor was creating threatened to collapse like a palace hit by an earthquake.

Somehow the mage at the centre of it all managed to stave off the disaster and continue. The structure of the spell stabilised and the ritual went on. Aenarion was not sure how much longer it could endure.

How many of the archmages could die before Caledor was unable to constrain the forces he had unleashed and destruction rained down on them all? For better or worse, Aenarion thought, it would all be over soon.

Four gigantic forms made their way to the temple, each surrounded by a bodyguard of potent worshippers. The greater daemons who led the Chaos horde were vying to see which would be the first to reach Caledor and end the threat he posed. The greatest enemies of all wanted to be in at the kill.

Ahead of them the first wave to reach the walls of the temple looked as if they were about to break through and interrupt the ritual. If they were not stopped, they would succeed.

He dropped Indraugnir into the middle of the melee. They landed on top of a massive self-moving siege engine within which the living essence of a dozen daemons was bound. The dragon took the great battering ram in his claws and beat skyward, lifting it and sending it toppling backwards to crush a hundred foes beneath its weight. It lay there broken, like a beetle turned on its back. Indraugnir smashed into the press of bodies, tearing foes asunder with his claws, searing them with his fiery breath, snapping twisted Chaos monsters in half with his jaws.

A group of elf soldiers tried to fight their way towards the embattled Phoenix King but died before they could reach him, overwhelmed by the sheer number of their foes. Aenarion leapt from Indraugnir's back, like a swimmer diving into a sea of monstrous flesh. His blade flickered faster than mortal eyes could follow, smashing through the bodies of his enemies as if they were made from matchwood. A beastman leapt at him, jaws snapping; he caught it in the air one handed, and sent it flying a hundred yards with a flick of his arm. It cartwheeled through the air to splatter against the walls of the shrine.

Aenarion cleaved through his opponents, killing everything within reach, his blade sending pulses of black light over the battlefield, the red runes glowing ever stronger as it drank life. His enemies died in their hundreds and then their thousands. Nothing could stand against him, and seeing his unleashed wrath his foes turned to flee.

FOR A MOMENT, Aenarion thought he had turned the battle but then the air in front of him shimmered and a hole appeared in the fabric of reality. A figure of horror emerged, towering twice as high as any beastman, monstrous wings snapping on its back. A huge vulture-like head, gazed down with eyes that held more than elven wisdom. The appearance of this greater daemon, this mighty Lord of Change, halted the rout.

'Long have I wanted to meet you, Phoenix King. Now the hour of your death is at hand.' The daemon's voice was high-pitched and shrieking and it would have broken the nerve of a less bold warrior than Aenarion just to listen to it.

'What is your name, daemon,' Aenarion said, 'so I can have it etched on my victory stella that all may know who I conquered?'

The daemon laughed. There was madness in its mirth that would have blasted the sanity of most mortals. 'I am Kairos Fateweaver and I will send your soul to Tzeentch so he may use it as a bauble for his pleasure.'

It stretched out its taloned hands and ravening streamers of multi-coloured light flashed towards Aenarion. Whatever they touched, living or unliving, warped and changed. Beastmen devolved into protoplasm, hardened stone ran like water. Aenarion raised his blade in front of him and the ribbons of light parted on either side of him.

He pushed forward, like a swimmer against a strong tide.

The Lord of Change bellowed its rage and fury and invoked another spell, but by the time it was complete Aenarion was upon it, and the black blade bit home into its flesh. Where the weapon struck, chunks were hacked away and ectoplasm swirled forth in a choking cloud. The daemon screamed, unable to believe that anything could cause it so much pain. Its mighty taloned hands reached out to grip Aenarion.

Such a feast, whispered the voices in his head. *More.*

Sparks flickered where the daemon's grip bit into Aenarion's breastplate. The Lord of Change was a being of awful magical energies and not even the potent spells woven into the elf's armour could completely resist it. The talons bit flesh and drew blood as they sought out the Phoenix King's heart.

Aenarion stifled his own cry of pain, and, knowing he had only one chance to live, struck a blow with the black blade, piercing the daemon's head and striking its jewelled brain. It exploded into a thousand pieces. The force of the blast hurled him through the air to land sprawling on the steps of the temple. He felt ribs break on impact.

Behind him the Vortex surged, and a high-pitched keening roar filled his ears. The air stank of ozone. A thousand voices screamed in unison as death overtook them. Another archmage had fallen. Who could it be, Aenarion wondered? Rhianos Silverfawn? Dorian Starbright? Undoubtedly it was someone he had known and now did not have the time to mourn.

He glanced around him dazedly and caught sight of another gigantic figure slaying the last guardians of the doorway beyond which Caledor and his mages still struggled to maintain their spell. The warding spells could not stop it. The guardians were not even trying to. They were throwing themselves willingly onto the monster's claws, and greeting death as they would a newfound lover. There was something obscene about the way they went to meet their doom.

Aenarion's heart sank. He knew this four-armed creature. It had taken all his strength to kill it once and now here it was again. This was N'Kari, the Keeper of Secrets, one of the deadliest of all the servants of the Gods of Chaos, the leader of the forces of Slaanesh, Lord of Pleasure.

'I see I must slay you again,' Aenarion shouted to get the daemon's attention. 'Or will you escape your just doom by some new trick as you appear to have done in the ruins of Ellyrion?'

N'Kari laughed its beautiful woman's laugh, and the wind bore its pungent erotic aroma to Aenarion's nostrils. Normal mortals would have been bemused, but Aenarion was hardened against any temptation it might have borne.

'Arrogant mortal, I let you live once so I might experience the sensation of defeat. Now I am gorged on ten thousand souls and I am invincible. Be honoured! Your soul will learn agony and ecstasy under the lash of the Dark Prince of Pleasure once I send it to meet him.'

N'Kari sprang, and its huge crab-like claw snapped together where Aenarion had been standing a moment before. It was a feint, and it caught Aenarion with its other hand. Aphrodisiac poisons poured from its nails. Its cloying perfumed breath filled Aenarion's nostrils. For a moment, he was dizzy and his legs threatened to give way beneath him.

'Now is the moment of ultimate pleasure,' said the Keeper of Secrets. 'You will fall to your knees and adore me before you die, Phoenix King.'

Aenarion lashed out with his blade, slashing the creature's chest. Such was the daemon's power that the flesh tried to knit behind the blade as it passed, but nothing could resist the fatal power of the Sword, and after a moment, N'Kari's flesh smoked and burned.

'I do not fear you or that blade you carry,' said N'Kari, but there was an odd strain in its voice.

'I will teach you to do so before this day is much older,' said Aenarion. Rage filled the daemon's eyes at his mockery. The massive claw swung round and gripped Aenarion's chest. It closed. Aenarion felt the weakened armour buckle and his ribs snap.

'You will not defeat me again, mortal.'

Aenarion reached out with his hand into the cavity the black blade had made. He pulled forth the daemon's still pulsing heart and raised it before him.

'No,' bellowed N'Kari. Aenarion closed his fist, crushing the heart. The daemon spasmed as if the organ being pulped were still within its chest. Poisonous blood dripped over Aenarion's mailed fist, burning through the armour and threatening to make his hand useless. Aenarion forced its own blood into the daemon's eyes, blinding it, then he raised the blade once more and drove it into N'Kari's shattered chest.

Ectoplasm poured forth as the daemon sought to evade the killing power of the sword. Tiny fragments of its essence flickered through the air towards the Vortex and vanished. As they did so, some of the chanting sorcerers moaned in ecstasy and died.

Aenarion reeled. His left hand was burned and useless now. His chest was a fiery cauldron of agony. The pain mingled with an odd pleasure caused by the effects of the daemon's blood.

More. More. More. The voices in his head were crazed with demented passion now. The Sword was feasting on essences stronger than any it had known in a long time and it was enjoying its meal.

A monstrous giggling form loomed over him. The smell of excrement and rotting flesh overcame the scent of everything else. He looked up to see the towering figure of a Great Unclean One, mightiest of the servants of the plague lord, Nurgle. It was the largest of the daemon princes by far. It loomed over him like a living mountain of filth, its vast flabby belly rippling in time to its idiot laughter.

'Two of my peers have fallen to you, Phoenix King, and I would not have thought that possible.' The daemon's voice was deep and rich and humorous. Its tone was conversational. The cruelty of its gaze belied the warmth of its manner. 'Still I, the Most Amiable Throttle Gurglespew, shall do my humble best to claim the victory.'

The Great Unclean One vomited forth a mass of maggots and bile onto him. The creatures began to burrow their way into Aenarion's flesh through the gaps in his armour, and force themselves into his eyes and mouth through the open visor of his helmet. He tried to keep his mouth closed but they wriggled up his nostrils and into his ears. They found gaps in his armour and squirmed across his flesh.

Each of the maggots had a tiny face that was a perfect copy of the features of the massive daemon that had belched it forth. All of them tittered with an insane mirth that was a high-pitched echo of the greater daemon's. They bit and gnawed at him and every bite was infected. He felt even the fires of the Phoenix within him gutter as his life force was drained away.

A wave of fire passed over him, hotter than the heart of a volcano, brighter than the sun. The tiny daemons vaporised under the incandescent barrage. Aenarion, who had passed through the Flame of Asuryan, remained standing. Through the blaze he saw Indraugnir blast the greater daemon of Nurgle with flames and then rend its putrid flesh asunder with its mighty talons.

Aenarion cheered his companion on as it tore its foe to pieces, reducing the greater daemon to a foul-smelling stinking pool of sewage on the ground. Indraugnir raised its head to the sky and let out a long bellow of triumph.

An explosion of dragon flesh and dragon blood smashed into Aenarion's face. An enormous gash appeared in the dragon's side and a burning axe emerged from it. Indraugnir toppled backwards, a huge hole carved in its flank. Its triumphant cry died in its throat.

Aenarion's heart sank. Before him was a Bloodthirster, a greater daemon of Khorne, perhaps the deadliest creature in all creation save for the Blood God himself. It was a massive thing with mighty wings and a monstrous animal head. Its eyes blazed like falling meteors. Its huge form was encased in runic armour of bronze and black iron. It radiated an aura of power greater than that possessed by any living creature Aenarion had ever faced.

The Bloodthirster struck again, with the force of a thousand thunderbolts, and Indraugnir bellowed and was still. Only its tail gave one last reflexive twitch and all life seemed to go out of it. Aenarion's awareness narrowed until it contained only himself and the daemon. They were like the last two living things moving in the ruins of a dead world.

Kill it. Kill it. The voices chorused in his head. They sounded even more demented than ever as they advised him to use his waning strength against this all but invincible opponent.

Limping painfully Aenarion forced himself to confront the last and mightiest of his foes.

It tossed back its head and laughed at the sight of him. He understood its mirth. His body was broken, his armour shattered, his flesh seared by the dragon's cleansing flame. Poisons and disease spores raced through his bloodstream. It was a race between them and loss of blood to see which killed him first. That was if the final greater daemon did not do their work for them.

He staggered towards it, holding his blade at the ready with both hands. The daemon sprang forward in a cloud of fire and brimstone. Its weapons lashed out and Aenarion twisted to avoid the blow. It caught Aenarion in his already wounded arm, breaking armour, shattering bone, sending the Phoenix King flying through the doorway of the temple to land amid the last few surviving wizards who still chanted the spell.

Aenarion looked around, appalled. So few mages were left. They had given up their lives to create the Vortex. At the centre of the chamber, near that towering whirlwind of unleashed magical power, only a few of the archmages remained, with Caledor standing on the central rune frantically trying to complete his spell even as the effort killed him.

The greater daemon roared with triumph. 'I am victorious,' it said in a voice like the blast of a thousand brazen trumpets. 'Only I remain and soon this world will be mine to do with as I will. I will take this power you have so conveniently collected and use it to reshape the face of this creation.'

Aenarion forced his broken body to move and staggered between the Bloodthirster and its prey. It stared at him with burning eyes. 'You cannot live through this, Phoenix King.'

'I do not need to live,' Aenarion said quietly. 'I only need to kill you.'

'That is not possible, mortal. I am Hargrim Dreadaxe and I am invincible. Never have I known defeat.' The Bloodthirster pounced like a tiger leaping on a deer. Its speed was almost too fast for mortal eye to follow. Its power was all but irresistible.

Aenarion unleashed the last of his carefully husbanded strength. A mighty blow arced downwards. The Sword howled in triumph as it smashed through eldritch armour, bit into unearthly flesh, shattered bone and ribs and cleft the daemon from head to groin. It fell to earth chopped almost in two, leaving Aenarion standing over its swiftly evaporating form.

'There is a first time for everything,' Aenarion said.

THE PHOENIX KING turned to stare at the wizards. He was near the end of his strength and he remembered Morathi's prophesy. Once again his wife's predictions had proven to be correct. He would die soon.

Only Caledor stood now, his form incandescent with power.

Thunder boomed. Lightning jumped from peak to peak. The great towers of light blazed brighter than the sun. Caledor's flesh shrivelled and turned black until only something like a mummified corpse stood there, still chanting. Then even that desiccated husk blew apart, turning to ashes on the howling wind, leaving only the afterglow of the mage's spirit, standing there, imprinted on Aenarion's retina like the image of the sun seen through closed eyes.

Aenarion leaned on his sword, unable to move his broken body. Pain burned every nerve ending. His ragged breathing rasped through broken lips. Something gurgled deep within his chest as his lungs filled with blood. He had taken more punishment than even his mighty frame could endure. He had been smashed, poisoned, blasted with fire and magic. He had defeated four of the mightiest daemons ever to blight creation. His army was all but dead. His friends were dead. And still the spell was not complete.

They had rolled the dice and they had lost. The last gamble of the elves was over and all that remained was to pay the price of failure. He threw back his head and laughed.

They had tried and there would be none left to witness their failure. He considered throwing himself into the still half-formed Vortex and offering himself up as a sacrifice as he had once done before the Flame of Asuryan but he knew that this time it would not work. There was nothing left to be done, except to return to the fray and slay what he could until he was pulled down into death.

Yes, whispered the voices. *Go! Kill until the world itself ends.*

A moment of awful silence came. The Vortex spun and danced before him, about to fall like a child's top that had run out of energy. Aenarion watched fascinated and horrified as it began to collapse. Then the fading image of Caledor stabilised. The ghost turned to the Vortex and continued its spell. Shimmering figures appeared around him as if summoned by his will. Aenarion recognised them as the ghosts of the dead archmages. Somehow, something of them still survived in this place. Even in death something now bound them to it.

The spirits of the other archmages joined in the ritual, walking one by one into the Vortex and vanishing. Aenarion peered at them through fast dimming eyes. He could see them becoming frozen, trapped in the awful centre of the spell as they continued the ritual.

Something within him told him what was happening, that the ghosts were giving themselves up for all eternity to hold together the spell they had woven.

No! The voices in his head shrieked. He felt the chorus of mad hatred build up in his head, threatening to overpower his will. *Destroy it! Destroy them all! Destroy the world!*

The chant was seductive. He wanted to obey it. Why should anyone else live when he was dying? What did he care whether the world went on, if he could not be in it, ruling it?

He walked slowly towards the centre of the Vortex. The ghost of Caledor stood before him and made a gesture for him to stop. The archmage shook his head, and pointed at the blade. It howled within Aenarion's grasp, urging him to cut down Caledor and then leap into the Vortex, slashing all around him. By doing so, he would undo everything, slay the entire world by unleashing all the pent up magic the mages had struggled so long and so hard to control.

He was tempted. He could end everything, kill everyone, and the blade could feast upon the death of an entire planet. Part of him wanted to do it, to end all life even as his own life ended. If he was to die, why not take everything else with him?

He stood there, gazing at the ghost of the elf who had once been his friend. Caledor's spirit sensed the struggle within him but there was nothing it could do to either aid or hinder. The decision was Aenarion's own, or it was the Sword's.

That thought at last made Aenarion stir. He was his own master. He had always gone his own way. He had not bowed to his people, to Chaos, to the gods of the elves. In the end he would not bow to the Sword. It howled in frustration as if it sensed his decision and fought against it.

Caledor smiled and waved farewell, and turned and walked into the place where he would be trapped for all that remained of eternity.

Slowly, Aenarion turned his back on Caledor and the Vortex and walked away. The Sword fought him every step of the way.

OUTSIDE, ALL WAS howling madness. Lightning lashed down from the sky. Time flowed strangely within the range of the Vortex's influence. The daemons were vanishing, turning back into the stuff of Chaos that had formed them. Their worshippers aged before his eyes, years passing in seconds, putrefying flesh falling away from corpses even as they fell. Piles of bones formed everywhere.

Aenarion stood and watched. Even the elves caught within the range of the newborn Vortex were ageing. He gestured for the survivors to flee and they obeyed.

Aenarion knew he was dying from the wounds and the poisons burning in his veins. He knew he had to leave, to return the Sword to the place from whence it came. He could not risk it falling into the hands of anyone else. Not so near the heart of the Vortex. Not with the possibility of some daemon or creature of evil finding it. He knew now why the gods had not wanted any to wield it.

He looked upon the corpse of Indraugnir. 'It is a pity you cannot help me now, old friend,' he said.

One great eye opened, and the dragon tried to bellow. Instead of its usual proud roar, its voice was a mere hiss, but it forced itself upright on weakened legs, and stood there tottering as its heart's blood pumped forth.

'One last flight then,' said Aenarion and the dragon nodded as if in agreement. 'We take the blade back to the Blighted Isle and drive it so deeply into the altar that no one will ever be able to take it out again.'

Aenarion forced himself into the saddle on the dying dragon's back and strapped himself in. He took one last look about him at this place of destruction. Strange magic flowed all around him. The shadowy outlines of ghosts were visible in the ruins of the temple working on some great mystical pattern, performing the rites of some vast incomprehensible ritual. He tugged on the reins and the dragon leapt into the sky, soaring through the swirling clouds, climbing towards the sun.

The winds of magic howled beneath Indraugnir's wings as he and his dying rider flew into legend.

N'KARI THE KEEPER of Secrets looked out from within the newly born Vortex and watched Aenarion depart. He was lucky to be alive and he knew it. The weapon the Phoenix King had carried was potent even beyond the imagining of daemons.

Never in all his aeons-long existence had N'Kari experienced anything like this. He was reduced to the barest nub of sentience, a thing little greater than a maggot or a human, barely aware of its own existence. He had only just managed to escape from Aenarion by casting himself within the roaring magical energies summoned by the elven archmages and hiding there. And he was barely a shadow of what he had been. The Sword had weakened him greatly, in some way he still did not quite understand.

Still, all he had to do was escape and his power would regrow as it always did.

He willed himself elsewhere, trying to plunge into the great Realm of Chaos to bathe in its eternally renewing energies. Nothing happened. He could not escape.

Rage and something else he did not quite recognise filled his mind. Perhaps it was fear. He was trapped within the huge spell the elves had cast. It was preventing him from departing this world for his own.

Even now, some vague sense of self-preservation warned him to keep still, to do nothing, to gather his strength. Around him were beings of awful power, the ghosts of the archmages who had given their lives to weave this spell. They were weaving it still.

His encounter with Aenarion had left him so weakened that he would have no chance if one of those terrible ghosts were to turn its attention on him and the small flaw in the vast matrix of spells he occupied. They could squash him from existence with the barest effort of their will.

It was painful and humiliating for N'Kari to admit his plight to himself, but it had been a long time since he had enjoyed these sensations and he determined to make the best of it.

Now he needed a plan, a way to escape from this enormous trap of a spell without the ghosts noticing him. He needed to wait and husband his power and let his strength regrow until he was himself again.

He did not doubt that it was possible, that he would get out of this place. He was a daemon. Time had little meaning for him, even the strangely altered flow of time within the Vortex. As long as he was careful and did not draw attention to himself he would survive, and he would work out a way to be free.

Then he would enjoy another sensation – vengeance on Aenarion and all of his blood.

CHAPTER ONE

There are those who express wonder that Aenarion was never told that Morelion and Yvraine, his children by the Everqueen, survived. It might have changed the whole course of elven history if he had known. Perhaps he would never have visited the Blighted Isle and drawn the Sword of Khaine. He might never have met Morathi. Malekith might never have been born.

Such speculation is fruitless. What happened, happened. The Sword was drawn. The elves of Nagarythe followed Aenarion into its shadow and into damnation. And the world was saved.

Perhaps because Aenarion was never told that his children were alive.

Many scholars think that once the Sword was drawn, Oakheart and those princes in his confidence were right to keep the knowledge of the children's survival from Aenarion. They point out what happened to those elves who followed the Phoenix King, and what happened to Malekith who was to become known as the Witch King. By keeping the children apart from their father, they kept them safe from the Sword's baleful influence.

And thus, from Yvraine, the elves of Ulthuan still have an Everqueen unsullied in her purity, for which we should all give thanks.

Perhaps those who kept the secret from Aenarion had other reasons. Scholars point out that given the ambitions that Morathi had for her son,

Malekith, it is unlikely the children would have survived long in Nagarythe where they would easily have been within her grasp. Aenarion's second wife has become famous for her knowledge of poisons, potions and malefic sorcery. Who knows how long Morelion and Yvraine would have lived had she known of their existence?

Whatever their reasons, by their actions, Oakheart and the princes ensured the survival of Aenarion's line in two main branches – one line has given us all the succeeding Everqueens unto the present generation. The other line has blessed and cursed Ulthuan with many heirs of Aenarion's brilliant, tainted blood. In part, they, like their great ancestor, have given the elves as much cause to curse them as to be grateful.

– *Prince Iltharis*, A History of the Blood of Aenarion.

10th Year of the Reign of Finubar,
Arathion's Villa, Cothique

TYRION SAT ON the edge of the wall of his father's villa, legs dangling, enjoying the sense of danger. Behind him lay a twenty-foot drop and the one in front of him was even steeper, for the ground sloped away downhill. If he fell from here he might break a limb on the rock-strewn ground below.

The late winter sun burned bright in the clear blue sky. It was cold this high in the mountains of Cothique. His breath came out frosted and he felt the chill through the thin cloth of his tattered tunic and his patched woollen cloak. In the distance, he could see a troop of mounted figures riding up-slope towards the hilltop villa.

Strangers were rare in this part of Ulthuan. Very few people ever came to visit them. Most were passing hunters dropping off part of their kill as a tithe for hunting on his father's lands. One or two were highland villagers who came to consult his father about a sickness in their family or on some minor matter of magic or scholarship.

Things had been different when his mother was alive, or so Thornberry claimed. The house had been busy then when his parents had arrived to occupy it for a summer season or two, escaping from the heat of the lowlands. Sorcerers and scholars from all over

35

Ulthuan had come to visit it along with his mother's rich relatives. People had liked his mother and were prepared to travel to even this remote place to visit her.

Tyrion was in no position to know. She had died during the difficult birth of himself and his brother and he had never known a world with her in it. There was one thing of which he was sure – none of the locals except his father could afford a horse, let alone a warhorse.

Tyrion's eyes were keen as an eagle's and he could see that the strangers were mounted on steeds even larger than his father's, caparisoned in a way he had only seen illustrated in books. Most of them were carrying lances. He could not imagine what else that long pole with its fluttering pennon might be.

The truth was he did not want it to be anything else. He wanted them to be knights, glamorous warriors such as he and his brother were always reading about in their father's old books. He wondered if this were somehow connected with his birthday, which was tomorrow, although his father appeared to have forgotten yet again. He felt somehow that it was. It seemed right.

He sprang up, balanced on the thin lip of the wall, then walked along it to the roof of the stables, arms held out from his sides to maintain balance. He let himself in through the large hole in the slates and dropped down onto the support beam. The dusty, musty smell of the old building filled his nostrils along with the warm animal scent of his father's horse. He ran along the beam, grabbed the rope he had left knotted round the edge and jumped.

This was always the best part, the long swing to the ground, the dizzying sense of speed as he careened downward and let go, landing rolling in the bales of hay. It always made him smile.

He raced out of the stable, past the startled Thornberry. The wrinkled old elf woman watched him with a look almost of embarrassment on her face, as if young Tyrion's energy somehow baffled and upset her.

'Strangers coming,' Tyrion yelled. 'I am going to tell father.'

'Hush, young Tyrion,' said Thornberry. 'Your brother is sick again. You will wake him.'

'My brother is already awake.'

Thornberry raised an eyebrow. She did not ask how Tyrion could know that. Tyrion could not have answered her anyway. He had no idea how it was possible that when he was in close proximity to his brother he could sometimes tell whether he was asleep or awake, happy or sad or in great pain. To tell the truth it always seemed strange to him that others could not. Maybe it was something to do with them being twins.

'He is now – with you making all that noise,' said Thornberry. Her tone was grumpy and she was trying to make her face stern but her gaze, as always, was kind. Nonetheless, as always she managed to make him feel guilty.

He raced upstairs, and ran into his father's chambers.

HIS FATHER HELD up a hand for silence. He was standing over his workbench, peering at something through the eyepiece of a magna-scope. 'Hush, Tyrion, I will be with you in a moment.'

Tyrion stood there almost bursting from his desire to give the news but he knew his father was not to be hurried when he was about his studies. To occupy himself he gazed round the room, taking in his father's huge library of books and scrolls, so beloved of Teclis, the jars full of pickled monster heads, and odd chemicals and weird plants from the jungles of Lustria and the rainforests east of Far Cathay.

His gaze was drawn as ever, and no matter how much he tried to avoid it, to the gigantic, terrifying suit of armour that stood on its wire frame in the corner. It looked for all the world like some monstrous golem waiting to be animated. His father claimed that this armour had been forged in the magical furnaces of Vaul's Anvil for their legendary ancestor Aenarion and that it was broken and dead now, needing magic to bring it back to life and grant it power and make it once again fit to be worn by a hero. Tyrion was not entirely sure of the truth of this but he hoped it was the case.

It was discoloured around the chest and arms where his father had repaired the ancient damaged metalwork with his own hands. In those places the armour did not have the patina of age it had elsewhere.

It was his father's life work to make the armour whole again. He had dedicated a lifetime of scholarship to it, ever since he had inherited it from his father, who had inherited it from his father before him and so on back into the mists of time. Family lore had it that the armour had been presented to their ancestor Amarion, by Tethlis himself, as a reward for saving the life of his son. It was their family's most precious heirloom.

As far as Tyrion knew his father was the first of his line who had tried to remake the armour. So far his efforts had proved fruitless. There was always just one more thing needed, one more piece of rare metal, one more fabulous rune to be re-discovered and re-inscribed, one more spell to be re-woven. Many times Tyrion had heard his father claim that this time, he would do it, and always he had been disappointed. It had cost his father his not-inconsiderable fortune and his life's energy and it was still not complete.

Tyrion studied his father now and realised how frail he was. His hair was fine as spun silver and white as the snow on the peak of Mount Starbrow. A mesh of wrinkles spun out from his eyes to cover most of his face. The purple veins stood out thinly on his hands. Tyrion looked at the smooth skin of his own hands and saw the difference at once. A life of failure had aged his father prematurely. Prince Arathion was only a few centuries old.

'Tell me what you came to say, my son,' said his father. His voice was calm and gentle and remote but not without a certain mocking humour. 'What brought you into my workroom without even knocking?'

'Riders are coming,' Tyrion said. 'Warriors mounted on warhorses.'

'You are certain of that?' his father asked.

Tyrion nodded.

'How?' His father believed that observations had to be tested and justified. It was part of his method of scholarship. 'Not just book learning' were his watchwords.

'The horses were too large to be normal mounts and the riders carried lances with pennons on them.'

'Whose pennon?'

'I do not know, father. It was too far away.'

'Might it not have been more useful, my son, to wait until you could see it? Then you might have been able to tell me more about who the strangers were and what their purposes might be.'

As always Tyrion could not help but feel that he was somehow a disappointment to his gentle, scholarly father. He was too loud, too boisterous, too active. He was not brilliant like Teclis.

His father smiled at him.

'Next time, Tyrion. You will do better next time.'

'Yes, father.'

'And fortunately I have a spyglass here in my study that will allow me to find out the information you missed, despite the fact these aged eyes are not as keen as yours. Run along now and tell your brother. I know you are dying to give him the news.'

TECLIS LAY IN the great four poster bed, covered in piles of threadbare, patched blankets. The room was so shadowy that it was impossible to see how moth-eaten the bed's canopy was and how old and rickety the room's furnishings were.

Teclis coughed loudly. It sounded as if a bone had come loose inside him and was rattling round in his chest. He twisted in the tangle of covers and looked up at his brother with bright feverish eyes. Tyrion wondered if this time Teclis was really going to die, if this illness would be the one that would finally claim him. His brother was so weak now, so feeble and so full of pain and despair.

And selfishly Tyrion wondered what would happen to him then. He felt the echoes of his brother's pain and his weakness. What would happen when Teclis went on the dark journey? Would Tyrion too die?

'What brings you here, brother? It is still light out. It is not yet reading time.'

Tyrion looked guiltily at the copy of Maderion's *Tales of the Caledorian Epoch* that lay on the chipped table beside the bed. He walked over to the windows. The drapes were fusty and smelled of mould. Cold air whistled in through gaps in the shutters, despite the torn shreds of sacking he had stuffed into the gaps. There was no place in the old villa where Teclis could escape the cold that seemed to leech all vitality from him.

'We have visitors,' said Tyrion. Interest flickered in Teclis's eyes and for a moment he seemed a little less listless.

'Who are they?' The tone was a dry echo of their father's, as was the question itself. Tyrion wondered at the resemblance. For all his weakness Teclis was very much their father's son, in a way that Tyrion never felt himself to be.

'I don't know,' he was forced to admit. 'I did not wait to check their heraldic banners. I merely ran in with the news.' He could not keep the sullenness from his voice even though he knew his brother did not deserve it.

'Father has been subjecting you to inquisition again, I see,' said Teclis and was wracked by another long, horrible paroxysm of coughing. Laughing was sometimes a mistake in his case.

'He makes me feel stupid,' Tyrion confessed. '*You* make me feel stupid.'

'You are not stupid, brother. You are just not like him. Your mind runs in different channels. You are interested in different things.' Teclis was trying to be kind, but he could not keep a certain satisfaction from his voice. His twin was eternally conscious of his physical inferiority. His sense of intellectual superiority helped balance that. Normally it did not trouble Tyrion but today he felt unsettled and insecure. It did not take much to put him off-balance. 'Battles and weapons and such are what interest you.'

The tone of his brother's voice let him know exactly how unimportant he considered such things in the great scheme of things.

'One of the riders at very least is a warrior. He carried a lance, and his armour shone brightly in the sun.'

At first Tyrion thought he was making up the latter detail but even as he said it he realised it was the truth. He had observed more than he thought. It was a pity his father had not questioned him about that detail.

'And what of the other riders?' Teclis asked. 'How many were there?'

'Ten with lances. One of them without.'

'Who would that be?'

'I don't know, a squire perhaps or a servant.'

'Or a mage?'

'Why would a mage come here?'

'Our father is a wizard and a scholar. Perhaps he has come to consult him and the warriors are his bodyguard.'

Tyrion saw that Teclis was twisting events to suit his own views and fantasies. He wanted one of those riders to be a scholar and the others, the warriors, to be in the inferior position. It stung. He felt like he should say something but he could not think what, then Teclis laughed.

'We really are country mice, aren't we? We sit in our rooms discussing strangers who may or may not be coming to visit us. We read of the great battles of the Caledorian Age but some horsemen in search of a night's shelter are a source of great commotion to us.'

Tyrion laughed, glad that he was not going to have to argue with his brother. 'I suppose I could go and ask them what they want,' he said.

'And rob us of a delightful mystery and the anticipation of its solution?' Teclis asked. 'We shall have those soon enough.'

Even as he said the words, the great gate bell rang. There was something ominous in its tolling, and Tyrion could not help but feel that it heralded some massive change, that for some as yet unknown reason, their lives would never be the same after today.

THE GREAT BELL tolled again, as Tyrion raced down into the courtyard. He got to the gate at the same time as Thornberry. They stood facing each other for a moment, each waiting to see what the other would do.

'Who goes there?' Tyrion shouted.

'Korhien Ironglaive and Lady Malene of the House of Emeraldsea and her retinue. We have business with Prince Arathion.'

'And what would that business be?' Tyrion asked. He was overwhelmed by the glamour of those names. His father had talked of Korhien. House Emeraldsea were kinfolk of his mother's, merchant princes of the great city state of Lothern, where the twins had lived when they were small children. What could they possibly want here?

'That is for me to discuss with Prince Arathion, not his doorkeeper.' The elf's voice sounded impatient. There was definitely something martial about it. It had the clarity of a great bronze horn intended to ring out over a battlefield.

'I am not his doorkeeper, I am his son,' Tyrion replied to show he was undaunted, even though he was a little.

'Tyrion, open the gate,' said a gentle voice from behind him. Tyrion turned, surprised to see his father there. He was wearing his finest over-cloak as well, and a torque of intricately worked gold on which were set certain blazing mystical gems. 'It would not do to keep our guests waiting. It is uncouth.'

Tyrion shrugged and put his shoulder against the bar of the gate. It raised easily for he was very strong for his age. He stepped back as the gates swung open and found himself looking up at the mounted strangers. One of them was the tallest elf male Tyrion had ever seen, as tall and broad as he was, with a great axe over his back and a sword strapped to his side. In his hand he did indeed hold a long lance. Over his shoulders was a cloak made from the hide of a white lion. Tyrion was thrilled. He had never met a member of the Phoenix King's legendary bodyguard before. What could such a one want here?

Beside the White Lion was a female elf in a beautifully woven and cowled travel gown. Her expression was haughty, her amber-eyed stare piercingly direct. She wore a number of glowing amulets that marked her out as a mage. A lock of long raven-black hair emerged from beneath the cowl of her cloak.

Behind them a group of riders sat, mounted on caparisoned horses. All of them wore the same tabard and had the same emblem on the pennons of their lances; a white ship on a green background. A line of spare mounts and pack mules straggled out behind them. It looked like quite an impressive expedition.

Before Tyrion could say anything the White Lion had planted the lance in the earth of the gateway, vaulted down from the saddle, strode across the courtyard and swept his father off his feet in a massive hug. Much to Tyrion's surprise his father did not object, he was laughing merrily. It was the first time Tyrion had ever seen such a thing.

He glanced at the woman to see if she was as wonderstruck as he, and noticed that her expression was sour and disapproving. She looked around the courtyard as if she were inspecting a pigsty. Her horse was smaller than the warriors' but even more beautifully accoutred. She caught him watching her and frowned. He met her gaze though and held it till she looked away.

'Korhien, you old warhound, it is good to see you,' said Father.

'And you, Arathion,' said the warrior, slapping his father's back with a force that Tyrion feared would do him injury. His father winced under the impact but made no protest. It suddenly occurred to Tyrion that Korhien and his father were friends. It was a novel concept. In all the years of his childhood, Tyrion could not recall his father showing affection to anyone or anything, even his sons. 'How long has it been?'

'Not since you retired here, after Alysia...' Korhien said, and the way his expression changed showed he knew he had made a mistake even as he spoke. He closed his mouth. A wave of sadness flashed across his father's face and he looked away into the distance.

'Lady Malene,' said his father at last. 'Welcome to my home.'

'So this is where my sister died,' said the woman. 'It is not a very... prepossessing place.'

Another faint shock rippled through Tyrion's chest. This woman was his aunt. He studied her even more carefully now, wondering just how much she resembled his mother. Now that he looked closely he saw that some of her features bore a resemblance to Teclis's and even to those he saw in the mirror. She was staring at him just as hard. There was hostility in that gaze and something else he could not make out, curiosity perhaps.

She held out her hand and looked at him again. It occurred to him that she was a lady who was not used to mounting or dismounting a steed without aid. He felt tempted to go and help her, but something in him rebelled against it and after a moment, he realised why.

It would be servants who would aid this woman, and he was most definitely not her servant. She saw the knowledge strike him, and she smiled coldly, dismounted gracefully and strode over to where he stood. She walked all around him inspecting him the way a mountain housewife might inspect a calf she was thinking of buying. Tyrion did not like the way she did it.

'Do you like what you see?' he asked.

'Tyrion,' his father said, his tone disapproving. The warrior laughed. The elf woman's response surprised him.

'Yes, very much,' she said. 'Although its manners could be improved.'

Korhien laughed at that too. Tyrion felt his face redden. He clenched his fists defiantly, not used to being mocked by any but his father or Teclis. Then he saw the funny side and laughed himself.

'You look like her when you laugh,' Malene said, and there was a sadness in her voice that reminded him of his father sometimes. 'Alysia was always a merry soul.'

Alysia had been his mother's name, and it was obvious from Malene's tone that she missed her. It occurred to him that perhaps this proud, cold woman might be something like he would become if Teclis died, and he found he had a certain sympathy for her then.

'Are we going to stand out here in the dust all day?' asked Korhien, 'Or are you going to ask us in and ply us with some of the fine old wines in that cellar of yours you always boasted about.'

'Of course, of course,' said his father. 'Come in, come in.'

It was the first time Tyrion had ever heard about fine old wines in their cellar. It was certainly turning out to be an interesting day. The riders still sat on their horses, impassive, as if waiting to charge. There was a sort of menace in their stillness.

'Perhaps your retainers would care to join us,' his father added. 'It seems like a very large party for a social visit.'

Tyrion did not miss the quick look of warning that flashed between Father and Korhien.

'The roads grow dangerous again,' Korhien said. Tyrion sensed that he would like to have said something else but was constrained by the presence of the others.

What was going on here?

CHAPTER TWO

THE SITTING ROOM was damp and fusty and cold, and Tyrion could tell that the Lady Malene was less than impressed. For the first time he felt ashamed of his father and his home.

Looking at her raiment woven from silks and magical cloths he could not even name, Tyrion saw for the first time how very shabbily he and his father were dressed. For so long he'd had nothing to compare his family to other than the local villagers who were, he now realised, simple mountain folk.

It was obvious that Korhien and Malene belonged to a very different order of people, and one to which he felt he and his father did not. Perhaps his father once had, but, if so, no longer.

Lady Malene sniffed the air and looked at the chipped wooden armchairs. They were not padded or cushioned and he guessed that was something else she was not used to. Korhien laughed. 'I have been in army camps that were more prepossessing, Arathion. Not much chance of you going soft out here.'

'Be seated, I will soon have the fire lit,' said Father, and he was good as his word. He exited the chamber and returned with some of their precious supply of winter logs. He tossed them into the fireplace any old way and lit them with a word of power.

Each log erupted simultaneously into blue mystical flame when he spoke. Sparks flickered and faint popping sounds filled the air as the sap within ignited. Tyrion looked at his father in amazement. It was the most, and the most obvious, magic he had seen him use in years. He wanted to run and tell Teclis but was kept frozen to the spot by curiosity, a desire to see what extraordinary thing might happen next.

Thornberry brought in a clay bottle of wine and three goblets on an ancient-looking bronze tray. She seemed uncomfortable but tried not to show it, keeping her face stone-like in its lack of expression. She placed the wine on the low table and retreated from the room as quickly as she could.

His father gestured for the guests to be seated. 'There will be food soon.'

Tyrion wondered at this as well. His father must have given instructions for the food to be prepared which was something of a wonder in and of itself. Often he forgot to eat for days at a time, and, when Thornberry was not there, Tyrion had to cook for himself and Teclis.

Korhien and Malene sat while his father poured the wine. Tyrion went over to the fire and stood with his back to it, luxuriating in the unaccustomed heat.

'To what do we owe the honour of this visit?' his father asked eventually.

'It is time,' said Korhien. 'The twins are almost of the age to be presented at the court of the Phoenix King.'

'It is their right,' said Lady Malene. 'And their duty. They are of the Blood of Aenarion.'

'Yes, they are,' said his father. He sounded oddly sharp and looked more combative than Tyrion had ever seen him. His father was never aggressive to anyone. 'I am wondering why House Emeraldsea has chosen to send its fairest daughter and its greatest ally at court to collect them.'

Tyrion felt another shock. Collect them. What did his father mean? He could tell from Malene's expression she had not expected this response either. She had the look of a woman who people did not talk to in that tone. Korhien too was looking at Tyrion's father oddly but not without admiration.

'What do you mean?' Malene asked eventually.

'I mean for the past fifteen years or so, House Emeraldsea has shown little enough interest in my sons. And yet today, here you are, reminding me of my paternal duty to have them presented before the Phoenix Throne in the company of a troop of armoured warriors. I am curious as to why.'

'They must be presented,' said Korhien. 'You know the law as well as I do, Arathion. They are of the Blood.'

'And if they are to be presented at court, I must see that they do not disgrace our family,' said Malene.

His father let out a soft laugh. 'I thought it must be that.'

'Why must we be presented at court, father?' Tyrion burst out, unable to contain his curiosity.

His father looked at him, as if noticing for the first time that he was there. 'Leave us, Tyrion, your aunt and I have much to discuss. I will tell you what you need to be told later.'

His father sounded stern, and what he was saying was unfair, but there was such a look of pain in his eyes when he spoke that Tyrion did not have the heart to argue with him or question him. He stalked to the door and closed it behind him, resisting the urge to slam it although the temptation was very great.

'THINK,' SAID TECLIS. His voice sounded even more husky and rasping than usual. His cough was worse, but there was a feverish interest in his eyes now. He sat upright in his bed, a blanket draped round his shoulders like a cloak. 'Try and remember, what else did they say?'

Tyrion shook his head. 'I have told you all of it.'

He drew his cloak tighter around him. After the warmth of the sitting room downstairs, Teclis's room seemed colder than ever. Perhaps he should carry Teclis down and let him sit by the fire for a while. He knew better than to suggest it though. His brother would never agree. He did not like his weakness to be exposed before strangers.

'You are sure she said we are to be presented to the Phoenix King?'

'Yes.'

'I suppose it makes sense. We are potential inheritors of the Curse, after all.'

Tyrion laughed. 'The Curse? The Curse of Aenarion? Be serious!'

'The Archmage Caledor claimed that all of those of the Blood of Aenarion could inherit his curse and be touched by Khaine, god of murder.'

'Surely that only applies to those like Malekith, born after Aenarion picked up the Godslayer and was tainted by its power.'

'You would think, wouldn't you? But such were not Caledor's words. And if you think about it, it would make no sense. Malekith has been sterile since he passed through the Flame. He has never had any children.'

'Why? I do not believe you are cursed by Khaine nor I, for that matter.'

Teclis gestured at his wasted form and raised one eyebrow. 'I think it is possible.'

'I don't think you are cursed.'

'How many elves ever get sick, Tyrion? How many are as feeble as I am?'

Tyrion tried to laugh the matter off. 'I hardly think that qualifies you as a threat to the Realm.'

'It does not matter what we think, Tyrion. It matters what the Phoenix King and his court think.'

'We are being presented there so they can inspect us for the taint of Khaine?'

'I believe so.'

'That does not seem fair.'

'They may be right.'

'You cannot mean that, brother!'

'Aenarion was unique. He did things no elf ever did before and very few even attempted afterwards. He passed through the Flame of Asuryan unaided and unprotected. He drew the Godslayer from the Altar of Khaine. There was something different about him, something that allowed him to wield the power of the gods, and for them to act through him. Who is to say that difference is not passed on through his blood. Caledor Dragontamer certainly thought so, and he was the greatest mage this world has ever known.'

'How do you know all this?' Tyrion asked. He knew the answer already but as usual the full extent of his brother's learning astonished him.

'Because while you roam abroad, I have nothing better to do than read, when I have the energy.'

'Yes, but what you read, you always remember. I wish I could do that. With me it always slips in one ear and slides out the other.'

'Unless it's to do with war or heroes,' said Teclis. 'Anyway, don't you think it unusual that Lady Malene and Lord Korhien came to visit us this way?'

'What do you mean?' Teclis gave him a warning look.

A draft of air hitting his back told him that someone had just opened the door to Teclis's room. Tyrion turned and saw the Lady Malene standing there. She did not look embarrassed to be intruding. She matched their stares and then marched right into the chamber without waiting to be invited.

'You would be Teclis,' she said. 'The cripple.'

'And you would be Malene, the rude.' Teclis replied.

She laughed. 'Well said, boy.'

'You may address me as prince. It is my title.'

'That has yet to be determined. I will know what to call you after you have stood before the Phoenix Throne.'

'Why don't you start practising now?' Teclis said. 'We can pretend that we are all well-bred elven nobles together.'

Malene stared at him for a long moment, obviously taking in the difference between his haughty manner and his wasted form and being forced to reassess the situation. 'Indeed, Prince Teclis, why don't we do that,' she said at last.

'Very good, *Lady* Malene. And further let us make an agreement that I won't enter your chamber without knocking if you don't enter mine.'

Tyrion thought his brother might be pushing things a little too far but Malene laughed and nodded in agreement. For some reason she seemed pleased with Teclis's insouciance. 'I am pleased to make your acquaintance and will bid you good day then, Prince Tyrion, Prince Teclis.'

As the door closed behind her, Teclis gestured for Tyrion to lean closer.

'She has come here to kill us,' he whispered.

'Kill us?' Tyrion asked.

'Or have us killed, by the redoubtable Korhien.'

'No.' Tyrion was quite certain this was not the case.

'Be assured of it. If she thinks we may prove to be tainted by Khaine, we will have an accident on the road to Lothern. Why else did they come?'

'You are being over-dramatic,' said Tyrion. He simply did not want to believe what Teclis was saying. 'Why would they want to do that?'

'Perhaps because House Emeraldsea has ambitions to seat its own candidate on the Phoenix Throne and it does not want the embarrassment of being associated with two tainted princes.'

'We are not princes yet,' said Tyrion. 'You heard what Lady Malene said.'

Teclis laughed sourly till his mirth ended in a fit of coughing that brought tears to his eyes. 'I must sleep now,' he said. 'Good night to you, brother.'

'Isha smile on you, Teclis,' said Tyrion hating the irony of the words even as he gave the traditional farewell. His brother was one of those that the goddess had most definitely not smiled upon. 'May you live a thousand years.'

DISTURBED BY TECLIS'S suspicions, Tyrion padded through the house. He reached the head of the stairs. From his vantage point he saw his father and Korhien sitting by the fire, a chessboard between them. Looking at the big warrior, Tyrion found it impossible to imagine him being involved in stealthy murder, in anything dishonourable at all. Such would not be Korhien's way, Tyrion felt certain. If there was killing to be done, he would do it face to face, weapon to weapon.

Korhien leaned forward and moved a silver Gryphon. His father stroked his chin and contemplated his response. Tyrion padded down the stairs, luxuriating in the unaccustomed warmth of the sitting room, and moved quietly over to the board so as not to disturb the concentration of the players. He took in the position at a glance.

His father was playing gold with his usual cautious, reasoned approach. He was already on the defensive, despite having the advantage of the first move. Playing silver, Korhien had a formation of Archers massed on the right flank, and was mounting a strong attack on Father's Everqueen with his Everqueen's Dragon supported by his Gryphon riders and a Loremaster attacking down the long diagonal. His father's hand hovered over his King's Gryphon which would be a mistake.

'Your doorkeeper disapproves of your strategy,' said Korhien with a booming laugh when he noticed Tyrion's expression.

'Then I had better pay attention,' said Father. 'Tyrion is the best player in this house.'

Korhien raised an eyebrow. 'Is that so? Better than you? Better than this brilliant but sickly brother I have yet to meet?'

'Better than you,' Tyrion said, nettled by the way Korhien's words seemed to disparage Teclis.

'Are you challenging me, doorkeeper?' Korhien asked.

'I could beat you from my father's position.'

'Oh ho, you are a cocky one. I would say I have your father well beaten.'

'It looks that way now perhaps, but there are some glaring weaknesses in your tactics.'

'I don't see them,' said Korhien.

'Tyrion, if you please.' Father rose from his seat and gestured for Tyrion to sit down. 'If you are going to make such outrageous claims, you should be able to provide us with proof.' His father was smiling though. Tyrion guessed he was not enjoying being beaten even by his friend. Few elves enjoyed defeat in anything.

Tyrion sat down and confidently moved an Archer two squares forwards, on his Phoenix King's flank.

'What?' said Korhien obviously amused. He picked up his Gryphon and skipped it over Tyrion's Archer into a position where it threatened a Loremaster. Tyrion contemplated the board. As always, he played quickly, by instinct, seeming to feel the strengths and weaknesses of the pieces and the complex web of forces woven by their placement and interaction.

He moved another Archer forwards, clearing space to bring his own Loremaster and Phoenix King into play, building a flanking position of his own. The exchange of pieces Korhien planned occurred and by the end of it he had gained an Archer, but was looking at the board thoughtfully. He clearly sensed that the balance of power was changing. He was a good enough player to understand what Tyrion was doing but he had not quite grasped the young prince's plan yet.

He maintained his own attack, but Tyrion blocked it, with a cunning combination of Loremaster and Archers used to block the long diagonal that was Korhien's main line of attack. A few moves later, Tyrion began his own attack. By the end of it, Korhien was laying his

Everqueen on her side to show that he had resigned. He laughed loudly, seemingly delighted.

'Are you always this good, doorkeeper?'

'Yes, he is,' said Father, with a pride which surprised Tyrion. 'Better actually, since he would not have made the mistakes I did in the opening.'

'I must see if this was a fluke,' said Korhien. He picked up one gold Archer and one silver Archer in his huge hands, placed them behind his back and asked Tyrion to choose one. Tyrion chose silver this time and the game began. He won this game in forty-two moves and a third, in which he started as gold, in thirty. He could see that Korhien was impressed.

'Your father is an excellent chess player and I am considered one of the best at court, and yet you have bested us without much trouble. You are not at all what I expected, doorkeeper.'

'What did you expect?'

'Not you,' said Korhien clearly not wanting to say any more.

'Another game,' Tyrion suggested.

'No, I have had quite enough defeats for one day.' He said it with a smile though. There was no sourness in this Korhien. Tyrion liked him.

TYRION SHRUGGED AND, well pleased, made his way outside. He was surprised to find that there was still some daylight left. It was the first time he could ever recall there being a fire in the grate before night-fall, no matter how cold it got in the mountains. He drew his cloak around him and thought about his chess games against the older warrior. Korhien was a better player than both his father and Teclis, which was not what he would have expected at all.

He felt flushed with his small victory and filled with restless energy, so he went out through the small postern in the main gate and began to run, slowly at first, just to warm himself up, and then faster and faster, vaulting over the rocks and bounding down the treacherous trail with careless disregard for life and limb.

It was dark by the time he returned, and he still was not tired, not even breathing heavily. The huge greater moon was in the sky. The lesser moon was a small green spark in a different quadrant. It seemed like a good omen. He was even more surprised to find Teclis warming himself in front of the fire in the sitting room, talking with Korhien. The chessboard was in front of them. Tyrion took in the board at a glance. Korhien was winning. Teclis saw him noticing this and gave a sour grimace. He did not like being beaten, which was why he did not often get the chance to play with his brother.

Teclis looked up sardonically as Tyrion entered. 'Where is father?' Tyrion asked.

'He is closeted with the Lady Malene,' said Teclis. 'Apparently they have much to discuss.'

There was a warning note to his voice. Teclis suspected that something was going on and he wanted Tyrion to know this too.

'I hear you have been winning again at chess, brother,' Teclis said, changing the subject. He, at least, did not sound at all surprised when he said it. 'It is not something I seem to be able to manage against Lord Korhien here. How do you do it? Win, I mean.'

Tyrion studied the board. 'You could win from this position.'

'Pray explain to me how?'

Tyrion looked at Korhien. 'May I?'

The warrior laughed. 'I am not sure I am going to enjoy this, but go ahead.'

'Get used to being beaten by my brother; he does not like to lose,' Teclis said.

'That is a useful trait in a warrior,' said Korhien. Tyrion proceeded to demonstrate how Teclis could win.

'How do you do that?' Teclis asked again.

'How can you not? It just seems very obvious to me.' It was true too. Tyrion really could not understand why his cleverer brother could not see what was so clear to him.

'In what way?' Korhien asked. There was a sharpness to his tone that Tyrion could not quite understand. He gave more thought to his response than he normally would.

'Certain squares are more important than others, most of the time. Certain combinations of moves fit together. There are always weaknesses in every position and always strengths. You play to minimise the weaknesses and maximise the strengths.'

'Those are sound general principles,' said Korhien, 'but they do not really explain anything.'

Tyrion felt frustrated. He understood how Teclis must feel when his twin tried to explain the principles of working magic to him. 'It's like I can see the way the patterns will work out. I see the ways all of the pieces potentially interlock. It's like when I look at the maps of battlefields in old books...'

'What?' Korhien asked even more sharply.

'There are certain obvious lines of attack on every battlefield. Places where troops should be placed. Places where they should not be. Hills with clear fields of fire for archers out over the rest of the field. Flat areas where cavalry can advance quickly. Woods and swamps that can guard flanks. You can see these things when you look at the maps.'

'*You* can,' said Teclis, stifling a yawn.

'Blood of Aenarion,' muttered Korhien. It was Tyrion's turn to stare hard at him.

'What do you mean by that?' he asked.

'They say Aenarion could do the same thing. See the patterns on a battlefield.'

'Anybody can, if they take the trouble to think about these things,' Tyrion said.

Teclis laughed again.

'It is not often I hear my brother laud the virtues of thinking,' he said, by way of explanation. 'You should be applauding.'

'Anyone can look at a map and say something. The trick is to be correct,' said Korhien. Tyrion shrugged. He went over to the book shelf and picked up a copy of *The Campaigns of Caledor the Conqueror*. He opened it to a well-thumbed page and then walked over to where the warrior sat.

'Look,' he said. 'Here is an example of what I mean. Here are Caledor's dispositions against the druchii General Izodar. See the way he has placed his war machines to cover the approaches to Drakon Hill. Notice also the way the main strength of his cavalry is placed out of sight here behind this range of hills but with easy access to the defile that will allow them to emerge onto the field of battle at his signal.'

'Yes, everyone knows about this, though. It was a fine trap, one of Caledor's greatest victories.'

'Yes,' said Tyrion. 'But he made mistakes.'

'Oh ho, you do not lack for confidence, do you doorkeeper? The

Conqueror was the greatest general of his age. His record is one of more or less unbroken victories. You look at a map of one of his greatest triumphs and claim he got it wrong.'

'No. I do not. He won. No one can fault that. I said he made mistakes.'

'An important distinction,' admitted Korhien. 'So, by all means, explain to me the mistakes he made, doorkeeper.'

'Look where he placed the bulk of his cavalry. In full view, close to the enemy, and when the battle started, they closed too quickly with the druchii right flank. It could easily have spoiled the trap.'

Korhien smiled. 'Your analysis is flawless, but you have failed to consider one thing.'

Tyrion was not offended to hear his theory so casually dismissed. He sensed that here was a chance to learn something about a subject that intrigued him from one who possessed some expertise in it.

'What have I missed?' he asked.

'I doubt Caledor wanted to place his cavalry there, or that he gave the order for that early charge.'

'Then why did it happen?'

'Because Prince Moradrim and Prince Lelik were rivals, and they both wanted the glory of breaking the enemy. They insisted on being where they were. Then one of them charged and the other, not being able to endure the possibility of his rival grabbing all the glory, followed suit.'

'Why did Caledor allow that? He was the Phoenix King, he was in charge. Why would they disobey him?'

Korhien's mighty laugh gusted around the sitting room.

'Once you have spent some time around our glorious aristocracy, you will not have to ask me that, doorkeeper.'

'Indulge my curiosity and answer me now.'

'Because our princes are a law unto themselves and their warriors swear service to those princes, not direct to the Phoenix King. They follow the leaders from their homeland, not some distant king.'

'That is not what our laws say,' said Teclis.

'I am sure you have read enough, Prince Teclis, to know that what the laws say should happen and what actually does are not always the same. In the heat of battle, when sword rings on sword, and the battle-shout echoes over the field, warriors follow their usual loyalties and instincts, not the law. And princes often crave glory more than the common good. It is not unknown for them to think they know better than their commanding general. Sometimes it is even the case, for the warrior on the spot often sees things invisible to the general on the hill.'

Tyrion nodded. He could see the sense in what Korhien was saying. It was something he had suspected himself when reading the descriptions of these old battles. It was nice to have it confirmed by one who knew what he was talking about.

'Why don't our historians mention this?' Teclis asked.

'Because they dwell at the courts of princes, and their pens and paper are paid for by the treasuries of those princes. Have you ever read a chronicle in which one historian blames one ruler for defeat and praises another for almost snatching victory from the jaws of defeat? Then gone to another scroll and had a different historian say exactly the opposite? It happened to me so often when I was young my head hurt.'

'I've had that experience,' said Tyrion.

'My brother's head often hurts when he tries to read,' said Teclis.

'I meant I have read two conflicting views,' said Tyrion. This was serious and he was in no mood for Teclis's flippancy.

'I suggest that when it happens next, you check where the historians were living when they wrote their tomes, or who their patron was. A bronze bracer will get you a golden torque that they have some connection with the court of the prince they are praising and there is some enmity between them and the ruler they are disparaging.'

'You are a very cynical elf, Lord Korhien,' said Teclis. He sounded more admiring than condemnatory. He was a very cynical elf himself.

'There are honest historians,' said Tyrion.

'Yes,' said Korhien. 'And those who believe themselves to be honest, and those who are in the pay of no prince because they are sponsored by the White Tower or dwell at the court of the Everqueen, and those who have their own estates. But it's odd how often those who dwell in Avelorn praise the wisdom of the Everqueen, and those who live at Hoeth dwell on the excellence of the Loremasters – except the ones they have a personal feud with, of course. And those who are independently wealthy tend to find previously unsuspected virtues among their ancestors and relatives.'

'I see you are corrupting my sons with your cynicism, Korhien, and undermining their simple faith in scholarship.' The twins' father had entered the chamber unnoticed while the brothers listened to the White Lion.

'I am simply pointing out that all scholars bring their own biases to their work. It is inevitable, part of elven nature. You know this better than I do, my friend.'

'To my cost,' said their father with some bitterness.

'How goes the great work anyway?' Korhien asked.

'Slowly as always, but I am making progress.'

'May I see it?'

'You may.' Father gestured for Korhien to follow him. Tyrion helped Teclis up and supporting his brother on his shoulder, they made their way to their father's chambers. By the time they made it up the stairs, Teclis was breathing heavier than Tyrion had after running for hours. Tactfully Korhien pretended to ignore his eel-like walk, the way his body twisted first one way and then the other as he moved.

'Where is Lady Malene?' Korhien asked.

'She has retired to her chamber for the moment. She has many letters to write.'

'Have you finished the business she came to discuss with you?'

'I have told her I will consider it,' Father responded. There was an undercurrent of tension to the words that Tyrion caught but did not understand.

'I suggest that you do,' said Korhien. Again, there was that note of warning in his voice.

CHAPTER THREE

'I SEE YOU have made progress,' said Korhien. He walked around the suit of armour, inspecting it but not touching it. The metal suit somehow dwarfed him while simultaneously giving the impression of having been made for someone about his size.

'Not as much as I would have liked,' said Father. He eyed the armour the way he would have gazed upon a personal enemy with whom he was about to fight a duel. Tyrion had never seen him look at it this way before. Maybe the presence of Korhien reminded him of something.

As usual Teclis was gazing at it in awe. His magesight was far better than Tyrion's and he had often helped their father trace the runes on the armour and the flows of magic they were intended to contain. He even claimed to have sometimes seen the faintest flickers of power within it, a thing which had at first intrigued Father but which he had never witnessed himself.

Looking at the three of them now, Tyrion felt excluded, a blind man listening to three artists discussing painting, or a deaf man reading about musical composition.

Korhien looked at the suit once more. 'When do you think you will be done with it?'

'Who knows,' Father responded. 'I have given up trying to predict that. There have been so many false dawns and broken promises with this.'

'It is a pity. It looks fine, and would put fear into the heart of Ulthuan's foes whether Aenarion wore it or not.'

Father glared at his friend. 'Aenarion wore it. I am certain.'

Korhien nodded soothingly, obviously aware he had touched a nerve with his quiet musing, even if he had not intended to.

'The spells woven around this armour are old indeed,' said Teclis. Korhien shot him an amused glance.

'I am sure the Council of Loremasters will take your word for that, Prince Teclis.'

'They ought to, if they are not fools,' said Teclis.

Korhien laughed outright.

'One son criticises the battle-plans of the greatest of our generals, the other is prepared to dismiss our most learned sorcerers as fools if they do not agree with his assessment of an artefact. Your children do not lack for confidence, Arathion.'

There was no malice in his tone, and yet there was a warning there that Tyrion did not quite know how to interpret.

'They have been brought up to speak their minds,' said Father.

'You have made them in your own image then, which is only to be expected, I suppose. I am not sure it will serve them well in Lothern.'

Tyrion caught his breath. Father had said nothing yet about them being sent to the great seaport. Had Father already agreed to their going? Tyrion supposed he did not have much choice in the matter. If the law required them to be presented because they were of the Blood of Aenarion, presented they would be.

'When?' Tyrion asked. His father shot another venomous glance at Korhien and then at Tyrion.

'Very soon,' said Father. 'If I choose to permit it. There are still details to be worked out.'

Tyrion looked at Teclis and smiled. He could sense his brother was as excited as he was by the prospect of seeing one of the greatest of all high elf cities once more, a place where they had not been since they were both small children.

There would be libraries there to consult and they would look upon wonders. They would see the Sea Gates, and the Lighthouse and the Courts. There would be soldiers and ships and tournaments. There would be the palaces of their mother's family and their own old house. A whole vast dizzying prospect danced before his eyes. Korhien sensed their excitement too and laughed with them, rather than at them.

'There are many things to be discussed,' said Father. 'Before you go. If you go.'

He sounded saddened by the words even as he said them. 'Before *we* go,' said Tyrion. 'You are not coming with us?'

'I have been presented at court,' said Father. 'I do not feel any great need to meet a Phoenix King and his courtiers again. And I have work to do here. You will be back soon enough.'

He did not look at them as he said this but there was a faint catch to his voice. He turned towards the armour and began to tinker with the scales on the left upper arm.

'If you will excuse me,' he said. 'I will need to get on with it.'

'Of course,' said Korhien quietly. 'Come, lads, let us leave your father in peace.'

Teclis pushed himself painfully up from his chair and limped over to Father, his body writhing as he moved. He laid a hand on Father's shoulder and whispered something in his ear. Tyrion wished that he could bring himself to do the same, but he felt sure that Father would not have accepted it from him. Instead he waited for Teclis and then helped him along the corridor to his room.

TYRION LAY IN bed, staring at the ceiling, tired and excited. All around him he sensed the presence of the strangers in the house. Some of them were still awake, talking in low voices so as not to disturb the others. Tyrion, who knew every night noise of their very quiet house, was disturbed by the sound. He had read of ship's masters who knew there was something wrong with their vessels because of a faint, unfamiliar creaking. He suddenly understood how that could be.

He made himself relax. His breathing became deeper and slower and he closed his eyes. He became aware that a vast weight pressed down on him. He felt as if all of the breath was being crushed from his lungs. He had to force air into them. He tried to sit up but his body was weak and would not obey him. He burned as with a dreadful fever and ached all over as human victims of plagues were said to.

He opened his eyes but the room was unfamiliar to him. There was a bell on the table for summoning assistance and a flask of the cordial his father had prepared to ease his sickness.

He reached for it, but his limbs felt wasted and numb. They refused to obey him with their customary alacrity. He forced more air into his lungs but it was a struggle. He opened his mouth to call for help but he could not force the words out. He knew he was dying and there was nothing he could do about it.

Suddenly his eyes snapped open and he was back in his own room, his own body. It had been a dream, but not just any dream. He got up from the bed and raced through the house to where Teclis lay, burning with fever, struggling to breathe, desperately reaching for his medicine. Tyrion moved over to the bed, poured some of the cordial and helped his brother to drink.

Teclis swallowed the medicine like a drowning man, a look of strange revulsion on his face that Tyrion understood. What must it be like to feel like you are drowning and have to force yourself to drink?

'Thank you,' said Teclis at last. His breathing had become more regular. The rasping sound coming from his chest had died away. His eyes were no longer bright with panic.

'Shall I call father?' Tyrion asked.

'No need. I am all right now. I think I shall sleep.'

Tyrion nodded. His brother looked terribly frail and wasted in the beams of moonlight coming in through the gap in the shutters.

'I shall sit a while,' he said. Teclis nodded and closed his eyes. Tyrion watched silently and wondered whether his twin was dreaming about being him. He hoped so.

It would be the only experience of good health Teclis was ever likely to have.

TYRION MOVED SILENTLY through the house, unable to get back to sleep now that he was awake. Night noises seemed determined to keep him up. Downstairs he could hear his father and Korhien talking quietly of old times as they sat beside the dying fire. Lady Malene was locked in her chamber. Teclis had finally drifted into fitful slumber.

Tyrion found himself inevitably drawn to his father's work room, filled with curiosity as he sometimes was, and half-lost in a waking dream of adventure and glory and things that might yet come. Visions of grim knights and silken princesses and mighty kings filled his mind along with great ships, huge dragons, proud warhorses. He saw himself in palaces and on battlefields. He pictured jousts and sword fights and all manner of adventures with himself as hero. Sometimes Teclis was with him, a proud mage from the storybooks.

Beams of moonlight came in through the crystalline window, illuminating the huge armoured suit that was his father's life's work. Not for the first time, Tyrion thought how strange it was that this room should have windows of precious crystal when Teclis's did not. When he was younger such thoughts had never troubled him. The world was the way it was and he had neither required nor expected any explanations from it. Now he found himself questioning things more and more.

In the moonlight the armour looked like a living warrior, tall and lithe and deadly. He approached it as he would a great cat he was hunting, padding in on silent feet till he stood before it, looking up at the massive helmet, measuring himself against the titanic figure of the elf who had once occupied it and finding himself insignificant and all his dreams of glory tiny, meaningless, insect things.

At this moment Tyrion had no trouble believing his father's theories. It seemed perfectly possible that Aenarion had once worn this damaged armour. Even without the magic that would give it life, there was a power about the thing. Its simple presence spoke of an earlier, more primitive age when mortal gods strode the earth and made war with foes the likes of which no longer existed in the modern world.

The metalwork was beautiful but it lacked the sophistication and loveliness of much later elven armour. It had been forged by masters in an age of war. The elves who had made it had other things on their mind than the creation of an object of beauty. They had been making a weapon for the solitary being who stood between their world and utter destruction.

'What were you like?' he asked himself, trying to picture Aenarion, to imagine what it must have been like to walk the world in that ancient time of blood and darkness. It was impossible to imagine a being of flesh encased in this suit of armour. It was easier to picture a creature of living metal such as some claimed the Witch King now was. Yet Aenarion had lived and breathed and fathered children, from one of whom Tyrion was descended. There was a link of blood and bone and flesh between himself and the one who had once worn this armour.

He reached out and touched it as if by doing so he could reach across the ages and touch his distant ancestor. The metal was cold beneath his hand and there was no life in it, no sense of presence other than that the armour itself possessed.

He felt obscurely disappointed. There was no echo down the ages from the avatar of the godhead who had saved his people. And he felt obscurely relieved that he had disturbed no ancient ghost, felt no ancient power. Perhaps it was true as some scholars now claimed that the great magics had departed from the world and that the high elves were but pale shadows of what they had once been.

He stood there for a long moment, enjoying the cold and the odd sense of being linked with ancient glories and terrors that could not touch his life. It was thrilling to imagine the time of Aenarion but he was happy too that he would not have to confront the horrors the first Phoenix King had been called upon to face. He was safe within the walls of his father's house and nothing could touch him.

Somewhere off in the night something screamed, a hunting cat that had found prey perhaps or maybe one of the monsters that sometimes made their way down from the Annulii. A trick of the moonlight made it seem as if a mocking smile twisted the armour's helmet-face and for a moment Tyrion thought of ghosts and deadly destinies.

Then he shook his head and dismissed his fears and padded softly to his own bed.

N'Kari dreamed. He relived the ancient days of glory when he had led the horde of Chaos that had come so close to conquering Ulthuan. He saw himself lolling on a throne made of the fused bodies of still-living elf-women and giving orders for the sacrifice of a thousand elf-children. He saw himself storming ancient cities of carved wood and putting them to the torch. He relived inhaling the scent of the burning forests as if it were incense as he devoured the souls of the dying. He saw again his first battle with Aenarion in the burned-out ruins of that ancient city and found himself once again facing that terrible blade. Something about that image brought him, shuddering, back into the present.

All around him the fabric of the Vortex flowed in a way that would have been incomprehensible to anyone but a daemon, a mage or a ghost. It was like being trapped in an infinite labyrinth of light.

He needed to escape. He needed to break out of this place.

He forced himself to think, to concentrate on his plans. It was too easy to lose track of time in this place, to lose himself in his far too vivid dreams. He had slowly become himself again. Over the long millennia he had gathered power. He had found holes in the fabric of the Vortex. He knew where it was deteriorating. He knew where he could break out when the time came.

The time was almost right. The stars were in the correct position. The power was within his grasp. Soon he would escape from this sterile, dull, haunted place and write his name in blood on the pages of history.

He would take vengeance on all of the line of Aenarion.

CHAPTER FOUR

'WHAT DO YOU know of the Art?' Lady Malene asked.

She had knocked this time before entering Teclis's chamber. She still looked around distastefully though, then went over to the windows and threw the shutters open, letting in fresh air and the unaccustomed sunlight.

It was morning then, Teclis thought. He had lived through another night.

'Just what I have read in my father's books of theory and what I have picked up from talking to him. He will not let me read his spellbooks yet.' Teclis coughed and could not stop coughing. His lungs felt full of something and made a horrible wheezing sound.

Malene looked at him with distaste. She was not used to being around the infirm. Few elves were. It made him want to limp away and hide.

'One of the things your father and I have been talking about is your education,' she said at last. 'He feels that you would be better apprenticed to one such as I than to him. He says your gifts are more suited to an active school of magic. You are sixteen today. You are of an age to begin proper study of the Art. If you wish to be taught.'

Teclis looked at her with wonder. He tried to push himself upright.

The effort made his shoulder ache and left him feeling exhausted. Even that could not dim his excitement. Was it possible that Malene really would teach him to work magic? He forced himself to look her in the eye and say, 'I want to learn all you can teach me.'

'That may take a very long time,' she said.

'We are elves. We have time.'

'I am not sure you do.'

'You do not want to waste your time teaching one who might not live to be grateful for it, is that it?' Teclis could not keep his bitterness from showing. He felt as if someone had shown him a treasure he had desired all his life and then snatched it away.

Lady Malene shook her head. 'No. I will teach you what I can, in whatever time you have to learn it, once the Seers have pronounced you fit to be taught.'

'So I must await their permission?' He could not keep the sourness out of his voice. Another barrier between himself and his heart's desire. 'That is not fair.'

He wanted so hard to be a mage. He knew he could never be like Tyrion, swift and strong and certain, but he felt he had it in himself to be a mage like his father. He could see the winds of magic perfectly when they blew and felt the tug of power whenever his father used the slightest of cantrips.

'There are certain secret societies and cults who believe that one of the Blood will draw the Sword of Khaine and bring about the end of the world,' she said this as if she was imparting a great secret.

'It won't be me. I want to be a mage. What use have I for a sword?'

She smiled at that and her face was lovely for a moment but then it became serious again. 'The Art can be a terrible weapon and a mage under the Curse of Aenarion can be a terrible foe.'

Teclis cocked his head to one side. 'There have been such then?'

'Of course.'

'How is it that I never read of them?'

Lady Malene's smile showed her amusement at his arrogance. 'So in your sixteen years, you have become acquainted with everything written in seven millennia of asur history? You are quite the scholar.'

Teclis felt his face flush and he started to cough again. The spasm wracked his body painfully. He realised how foolish and arrogant he must sound to Lady Malene, when really he was just frustrated. 'I have not. But I want to. Where can I find these books?'

She reached out and ruffled his lank hair. It was a gesture of affection that surprised and touched him as well as embarrassed him. He was not used to such things. He looked away. 'You will not find them here, or in any library outside of the Tower of Hoeth. It's the sort of knowledge that the Loremasters keep to themselves.'

'You have been to Hoeth?'

She nodded.

'You have seen the library?'

'I have seen the parts of it I was allowed to see.'

'Allowed?'

'The library is a vast, strange place, like the Tower itself. There are sections that some people never see and yet others can visit every day. Sometimes, a mage will find a chamber full of books just once in his life and never be able to find the way back. The library is part of the Tower and the Tower has a mind, of sorts, of its own.'

'It sounds wonderful and terrible at the same time,' said Teclis.

'I do not think the mages who built the Tower entirely understood what it was they were creating. I think the spells they cast had unforeseen consequences. It is often the way with magic.' She sounded a little sad when she said that, as if she had direct personal experience of such a thing. 'A thousand years in the building, a millennium of work by hundreds of the greatest mages of the elf people. Webs of geomantic power spun within webs of geomantic power, monstrously powerful spells layered upon monstrously powerful spells, built in a place that was already sacred to the God of Wisdom and a font of awesome power. It is the greatest work of the elves, I think it will most likely endure after we have gone. I sometimes think that it will endure the wreck of the world and that it was intended to do so.'

'What do you mean?'

'I believe the Tower is a vault as well as a repository of knowledge. When the elves are gone, it will still be there, preserving our knowledge, all that we are, all that we were, all that we will be. There was never a place like it built before and there never will be again. Bel-Korhadris, its architect, was the greatest geomancer since Caledor Dragontamer and I doubt there are any living now who can fully compass his design or his intention.'

Her words started a great blaze burning in Teclis's heart. A desire to look upon this place and to walk through its library and penetrate its secrets, insofar as he might, filled him. He had never heard of any-where so attractive. He wondered if they might take him there, even in the meanest capacity, as a sweeper or scribe or a warden. He felt like he would do anything required to look upon this place and be part of it.

'My father never talked of the Tower as you do,' he said. He had never heard anyone talk of any place with such passion. She sounded like his father when he talked about the dragon armour of Aenarion or Tyrion when he talked about warfare.

'All elves who see it, see it slightly differently. All elves who go there experience it slightly differently. I am not so sure your father's experience was as pleasant as mine. Or it may be that he does not like to talk about it the way I do. Some people are secretive that way. In general I do not speak of my time there much. It is odd that I feel compelled to discuss such a thing with you, Prince Teclis. I wonder why that is?'

Teclis could not answer because he did not know. He did feel that in Lady Malene he had found a kindred spirit. Perhaps she felt the same. 'Why did you ask me what I know of the Art?'

'Because there is a very great power within you. I can sense it, your father has sensed it, any mage with the Sight can sense it. If you live and are not accursed you may become a very great wizard one day.'

'Will I get to see the Tower of Hoeth?'

'Most assuredly.'

'That would make me very happy,' said Teclis and once more he fell into a long fit of coughing until he felt like he was almost unable to breathe.

'Poor child,' said Lady Malene. 'Not much has given you happiness, has it?'

'I do not want your sympathy,' Teclis said at last. 'Only your know-ledge.'

'I may be able to give you more than that.'

'Really?'

'I may be able to help you with what ails you.' Teclis looked at her disbelievingly.

'That would be a gift beyond price,' he said.

'Well, it is your birthday after all.'

'Yes, it is,' he said, surprised. He had not expected to live to reach sixteen years of age.

'I make no promises,' she said. 'I will see what I can do.'

She left the room. For the first time in a very long time, Teclis felt like crying. It was odd. He had thought there were no tears left in him.

'I HAVE A birthday gift for you, doorkeeper,' said Korhien. Tyrion looked at the giant warrior, not sure whether he was being mocked. He glanced around the courtyard but all of the soldiers who had come with Lady Malene were busy about their own business. If this was a joke no one could see him being the butt of it.

Korhien loosed the belt and scabbard at his waist, folded the leather strap neatly and handed the equipage over to Tyrion.

'What do you want me to do with this?' Tyrion asked.

'It is yours,' said Korhien. 'Unsheathe the blade.'

Tyrion's heart leapt as he obeyed the White Lion. He drew the longsword from its scabbard. It was a true elven blade, long and straight and keen edged and it glittered in the mountain sunlight. Runes were etched in the metal. A blue sunstone inscribed with a dragon glinted from the pommel. He held it easily in his hand although it was heavier than he had imagined such a thing would be.

'I cannot take this,' said Tyrion, although he very much wanted to keep it. He was too proud to accept such an expensive and beautiful thing from a stranger. It was a charity he did not require. He might be poor but he was of a most ancient lineage. His father had taken the time to instil that knowledge in him.

He slid the blade back into the scabbard and presented it, hilt first, scabbard held over his left forearm back to Korhien. Tyrion felt the wrongness of his words even as he said them. He knew that in some way he was insulting Korhien but at the same time he did not want to be beholden to any elf for something as important as his first sword.

Korhien seemed to understand.

'Keep it for a season and if you do not want it, return it to me in Lothern. You are going to need it now, for how else I am going to give you a lesson with it? That will be my birthday gift to you if your pride will not allow you to accept more than a loan of the sword.'

Tyrion smiled back. It was a compromise his pride was prepared to accept and his father would too. And he really, really wanted the sword. It fitted in perfectly with his image of himself and his unspoken dreams of glory. 'Very well. I thank you for your loan.'

'Don't be so quick to thank me, doorkeeper. I mean to repay you for your lessons in chess-play,' Korhien added. 'Your father has told me you have not been schooled with a sword.'

Tyrion shrugged. He did not want to say there were no swords in the house. It seemed shameful to admit that his father had sold them for the money needed to continue his research. 'I know how to use a bow and a spear well enough,' Tyrion said.

'I am sure you do,' said Korhien seriously. 'But the sword is the weapon you will be called on to use in Lothern, if you have any cause to use a weapon there at all.'

Tyrion did not need to ask why. Duels were not fought between asur nobles with spear or bow, not unless the situations were very unusual.

'So when do we begin?' Tyrion asked.

'No time like the present.'

Tyrion shrugged and unsheathed the sword and fell into the stance he had always imagined wielding it. Korhien looked at him puzzled.

'I thought you told me you had no training with a sword.'

'My father has never given me any. Swords were not his weapon when he was in the levies. He says he is more likely to cut himself with one than any enemy.'

Korhien walked around him, inspecting his stance. 'That is nothing less than the truth. Your father was the worst sword-bearer I have ever seen. Better to have no training at all than be taught incorrectly. That said, who has been teaching you?'

'No one,' Tyrion said.

'Why did you choose that stance, that grip?'

'It just seemed right.'

'It most assuredly is, perfect for fighting one-handed with that blade, and without a shield.' The big warrior looked at him thoughtfully. 'A moment if you please.'

He walked away and returned. He returned with his enormous axe. 'I would not normally allow another to bear this weapon, but show me how you would hold this axe.'

Tyrion shrugged and took the weapon, holding it two-handed across his body, feet apart, left in front of right.

'Like you had been training with it for years,' Korhien muttered. He seemed perplexed.

'You say you can use a bow. Show me!'

'I thought you were going to teach me how to use a sword,' Tyrion said.

'Time enough yet for your first lesson,' said Korhien. 'For the moment, indulge me.'

Tyrion brought his bow and strung it, strapped on his quiver and aimed at the target he had set up on the western wall of the villa. He breathed easily and loosed three arrows one after the other, placing them easily in the central ring he had made. They were not difficult shots and yet Korhien seemed impressed. A small crowd of warriors had begun to gather around them. They had begun to talk quietly among themselves.

'Technique with a bow... perfect,' he said, as if he had a list in his head and he was checking something off against it. 'Spear now.' He handed Tyrion one from the rack. 'Cast it at the target.'

Tyrion smiled and turned, throwing the spear as part of the same motion he had taken the weapon. He was showing off now and he knew it. The spear landed in the central ring of the target and buried itself there, among the arrows. Korhien's eyes narrowed.

'I think I have seen enough,' he said.

'Enough for what?' The warrior considered his answer for a long moment, as if undecided as to what he should actually say.

'Enough for me to see that you will not be as difficult to teach as your father.'

'I am glad to hear that. Shall we begin?'

'Are you so anxious to learn how to kill?' Korhien asked.

It was a serious question, and Tyrion sensed that more depended on his response than at first appeared. He decided, as he inevitably did, that honesty was the best policy.

'I already know how to kill,' he said. 'I am anxious to learn to use a sword.'

'Who have you killed?'

'I have killed deer,' said Tyrion, a little embarrassed now.

'Killing another elf, or even an orc or a human, is not the same thing,' said Korhien.

'In what way?' Tyrion asked, genuinely curious. He did not doubt for a moment that Korhien possessed personal knowledge of this subject.

'For one thing they are intelligent beings who know how to fight. They will try to kill you in turn.'

'I have killed mountain lions and monsters come down from the Annulii.'

'Monsters?'

'Mutated creatures with the forms of animals all mixed together, or so the other huntsmen assured me.'

'You take me aback, doorkeeper. I came here expecting sheltered and scholarly princes, like their father once was, not someone who speaks quite so casually of killing.'

'Is it a bad thing?' Tyrion asked, well aware that his father found him coarse, violent and unruly, and was often embarrassed by his behaviour.

'Not in the world we live in,' said Korhien.

Tyrion was relieved. He had already discovered that Korhien's good opinion was important to him, and he felt the big warrior was capable of teaching him about those things that were important to him, not just to Father and Teclis. He had long ago outstripped the local hunters in his ability with bow and spear.

'You said you were going to teach me how to use a sword.'

'And I am an elf of my word,' said Korhien. 'I thought I would need to begin by telling your father's son which end of a sword was which, and which parts were used for doing what, but I suspect that in your case this might prove redundant. So let us move on to the practice swords.'

'Wooden swords,' said Tyrion, disappointed.

'Everyone has to start somewhere, even you, doorkeeper. Do you have some around here?'

'In the stables, on the rack.'

'Typical... of your father I mean... to keep them there.'

Tyrion laughed at the obvious truth of what Korhien was saying and went to fetch them. The wooden swords were much more like clubs than real blades. They had handles and cross-hilts but where the blades would have been on a real sword were circular wooden poles.

Korhien weighed them in his hands critically and said, 'These will do, to begin with, anyway.'

He handed one to Tyrion and then saluted; unconsciously Tyrion mimicked the moment. It was Korhien's turn to laugh.

'Did I do something wrong?' he asked, face flushing.

'No, doorkeeper, you did not.'

'Then why did you laugh?'

'Because like everything you do connected with fighting you do it so well.'

He took up a guard stance, and Tyrion mimicked it too.

'Try and hit me,' Korhien said.

Without any further prompting, Tyrion sprang forward. Korhien parried his blow, but did not riposte. Tyrion kept attacking, lunging and swinging. At first he was not trying too hard, not wanting to take a chance of accidentally hurting Korhien as he had done with Teclis and local hunters when he had tried using the wooden swords on his own. Soon he realised that Korhien was having no difficulty parrying him and he speeded up his attack, striking with greater force and precision.

'Surely you can do better than this, doorkeeper,' Korhien taunted.

'Indeed,' Tyrion murmured but did not allow himself to be provoked. He kept on attacking, looking for weak spots in Korhien's defence, areas where his guard came up too slowly, where his responses were a beat behind. To his surprise, he did not find any. He kept on attacking, and Korhien kept on parrying, and then suddenly the sword was knocked from his hands. When he replayed the action in his mind, he saw the trick that Korhien had used, and was surprised that he had not thought of it himself.

'That was embarrassing,' said Tyrion.

'In what way?' Korhien said.

'In that you disarmed me so easily after I could not lay a blow on you.'

'Trust me, doorkeeper, you did not do so badly. There are elves with a century of practice who have done worse than your first efforts here.'

'My father, for one,' said Tyrion sourly.

'No. Elves who would kill your father in the first passage of blades.'

Tyrion found this talk of anyone killing his father disturbing. It made him uncomfortable, and it must have showed on his face.

'It's something you need to know, doorkeeper. Anyone you fight will be someone's father or mother, someone's son or daughter or brother. That's what makes it difficult. That's why some elves, like your father, to his credit, never really learn.'

'Why do you say to his credit?' Tyrion asked.

'Because the loss of any elf life is something to be mourned.'

'Even dark elves?'

Korhien nodded even if he could not bring himself to say the words. 'There are not so many elves left in the world, doorkeeper. The loss of any one of us is a grievous loss to our people.'

'It's a pity Malekith's subjects do not feel the same way.'

'Who is to say they do not?' said Korhien. 'We are all still kin after all, even after all these centuries of Sundering.'

'Perhaps someone should tell them that,' said Tyrion.

'Perhaps you are right,' said Korhien. 'Or perhaps they already know.'

'It has not stopped them from raiding us.'

'Nor us them, doorkeeper. It's worth remembering that it takes two sides to make a war.'

'You do not sound much like I expected a warrior to sound,' said Tyrion.

Korhien laughed. 'I am sorry to disappoint.'

'That is not what I meant.'

'What did you mean?'

'You talk less of glory and more of reasons.'

'I have heard too many people talk about glory, doorkeeper, and usually they meant their own. Normally when you hear an elf talking about glory and the spilling of blood, they mean their glory and your blood.'

'You are doing it again.'

'I am telling you this, doorkeeper, because I suspect you will turn out like me,' Korhien's voice was softer now and sadder. 'I suspect you will end up spilling a lot of your blood and other people's for causes not your own, in places you would rather not be.'

'Why?' interrupted Tyrion, now genuinely curious and quite

excited. He did not think turning out like Korhien would be such a terrible thing.

'Because you are already very good with weapons and you will become very much better unless I am greatly mistaken. And our rulers have need of warriors, our world being the sort of place it is.'

Again, Tyrion suspected he was missing something. He did not find the idea that there was a place where an elf like him might be needed as saddening as Korhien appeared to. He found it hopeful. It meant that there might yet prove to be something he could do with his life, and there would be people who were not disappointed with him.

'Do you really think I could be a White Lion like you?' Tyrion asked. He had promoted himself in his own imagination, he realised, and he felt as if he were overstepping the mark.

'You will be whatever you choose to be, doorkeeper. You have that in you. I suspect it is your destiny to be something more than me. You are of the Blood of Aenarion, after all.'

'Is that why you are really here?' Korhien considered his answer very carefully and seemed to come to a decision.

'Yes,' he said. He threw his arm around Tyrion's shoulder and took him to one side, out of earshot of the other soldiers. It looked like a casual thoughtless act, but Tyrion knew that it was not.

'My brother thinks they will kill us if we turn out to be cursed.' Tyrion felt as if he had truly overstepped the mark this time, particularly given what Teclis suspected. Korhien's eyes widened. Tyrion guessed he had never expected to hear this.

'He might well be right. Or you may find yourself in some isolated tower or dungeon.'

'Would you kill us?' Tyrion asked, feeling the sword heavy in his hand, not sure of what he planned to do if he got the wrong answer. He knew that if he wanted to Korhien could kill him quite easily for all that they were of the same size and strength. Korhien was silent for a very long time.

'No,' he said eventually.

Tyrion was uneasily aware that Korhien had taken the question very seriously and was giving a truthful answer. 'I would not. But they would find others who would try.'

'Why do you say that?'

'Because I am sure you would not prove so easy to kill, doorkeeper.'

'They might be right to kill us if we are truly accursed, as Malekith was.'

'They might be. If you were. I do not think you are.' Korhien smiled again and there was genuine humour in it. 'This is a very morbid conversation and I am sure your aunt would be very disturbed to know we have had it.'

'She shall not hear of it from me,' said Tyrion.

'Nor from me,' said Korhien. It felt as if they were partners in a conspiracy, and Tyrion knew in that moment he had found another person in the world he could trust.

'We should return to our lessons. You have a long way to go yet before you are a blade master,' said Korhien. He never seemed to doubt for a moment that Tyrion would become one. Nor at that moment, did Tyrion. He picked up the wooden sword with the sudden seriousness of a boy who had just found his vocation.

CHAPTER FIVE

LADY MALENE ENTERED the room. She carried a glass beaker of a clear sapphire liquid in her hands. She walked carefully as if unwilling to take the risk of spilling a drop. Teclis struggled upright. The effort made him dizzy. The room seemed to tilt sideways for a moment before righting itself.

When she reached the bedside Malene handed the container to Teclis.

'Drink,' she said.

'What is it?' Although he was starting to trust her, Teclis was still unwilling to drink anything she had prepared without question.

'It is a mix of aqua vitae and sunroot. I have woven several spells into it.'

Teclis looked at it dubiously. 'What will it do?'

'Help your body resist the infection currently raging through it.'

'My father's potion already does that.'

'Your father's potion does not. It soothes your nervous system and boosts some of your body's resistance to disease. It lets you breathe easier and by taking the strain off your lungs, it makes it easier for your body to fight the disease in it. It does not do anything else to help you.'

'You are claiming you know more about these things than my father?' Teclis knew he was simply putting off the moment when he had to drink the potion. He realised it was not because he feared it might poison him, but simply because he was afraid of disappointment. What if it did not work as well as he hoped it would?

'I hate to puncture your childish illusions but your father is an artificer, not an alchemist. He knows a lot about making and repairing weapons and armour but comparatively little about medicinal herbs.'

'And you do know, of course,' said Teclis with as much sarcasm as he could muster.

'Actually, yes. Better than your father at least and very much better than you. I did not notice any volumes on herb lore or advanced alchemy in your library.'

'I will have to take your word for that.'

'I would advise you to do so, if you wish to recover your health.'

Teclis grimaced. He did not like being told he had to do anything. He was naturally contrary that way.

'What is the matter, Prince Teclis? Are you afraid I am going to poison you?'

Teclis stared at her. 'Do I need to be?'

'What exactly do you mean by that?'

'What exactly are you doing here with your soldiers and your over-muscled lover?'

Lady Malene cocked her head to one side and stared at him. He met her gaze and for a long time neither of them looked away. A slow smile, almost of understanding, crossed her face. 'Are you jealous?'

Teclis was annoyed because he had not realised that he was, in part, until she had asked him. He knew how ludicrous that must look to her and beyond all things he disliked being made to look ludicrous.

'Answer my question, please.' It sounded more imploring than he would have liked. Normally he was better at controlling his expression than this.

'I have come to take you to Lothern.'

'Why?'

'So that you may be presented to the Phoenix King and then, most likely, to the Priests of Asuryan.'

'Why?'

'So that you may be judged and found untainted by the Curse of Aenarion.'

'What if I am not so judged?'

'You are worried that you might be found to be cursed?' She sat down on the bed beside him, still holding her flask of medicine.

'Would you not be, if you were me?'

'I suspect I would, Prince Teclis, but I am in no position to know. I am not a descendant of Aenarion.'

'There are times when I wish I were not. There are times when I think I am accursed, that I must be, to have turned out the way I have.'

'If your illness is your only manifestation of the Curse, you have nothing to fear.'

'I fear my illness,' he said.

'I meant from us, from the Council of Mages, from the Phoenix King's personal magii, from the Priests.'

'What if you do see a reason to be worried, some echo of the doom of Aenarion down all the long centuries? What will happen then?'

'I do not know, for certain.'

'Feel free to speculate.'

'You are a very odd youth, Prince Teclis.'

'I would not know. I do not have much to compare myself to. Only my brother, Tyrion, and comparisons with him are invidious.'

'Why? Because you lack his health, his charm, his beauty?'

It was all rather too close to the truth for his liking.

'Please do not hold yourself back to spare my feelings,' said Teclis. Malene laughed.

'You have your own charm, and you have wit and more to the point you have very great potential in the Art. You are also much cleverer.'

'Do not make the mistake of underestimating my brother.'

'I do not. The fact that you are brilliant does not make him a fool.'

'I think you will find he is quite brilliant in his own way.'

'And what way is that?'

'Show him anything to do with warfare and he understands it at once, instinctively. Play him at any game, any, and you will be beaten.'

'Korhien says that he is... gifted beyond any young warrior he has ever met. I suspect you will prove to be the same when it comes to magic. I am not sure that is such a good thing.'

'Why?'

'Because the ones who are exceptional are the ones who are feared. Aenarion was exceptional. Malekith was too. There have been others. Prince Saralion, the Plaguebearer, the Daemonologist Erasophania. They are the ones who bring doom.'

'There are others of the line of Aenarion who were exceptional too and they did great good,' said Teclis, aware of how desperate he sounded. 'The healer Xenophea. Lord Abrasis of Cothique who found a way to stabilise broken waystones. I could name a dozen more.'

'Then let us hope you are one of those.' She smiled again and it came to Teclis that Lady Malene, whatever else she might be, was not his enemy. She did not mean him any harm, simply because of who he was, or who she was.

That did not mean she would not turn on him if he turned out to be cursed, of course.

'Do you think I could be?'

'Yes. Now will you drink this medicine? Or should I pour it out?'

'You would not poison me, would you?'

'If I was going to, would I tell you?'

'I bow to the logic of your argument.' Teclis drank the medicine and grimaced.

'It tastes foul,' he said.

'Next time I will add some peppermint.'

'I doubt that would improve the flavour.'

'No, but it would really give you something to complain about.'

'How long before I feel the effects?'

'Give it an hour to start working and then a couple of hours after that to take effect. By that time you should be dead.'

Teclis shot her a black look.

'You are not the only one with a dark sense of humour, Prince Teclis,' she said.

Teclis laughed. He was already starting to feel better.

* * *

THE SITTING ROOM was quiet and the fire was still on. Tyrion was amazed. It had burned the whole time the visitors had been here. Such extravagance was unheard of in his experience. Their father stood as far away from it as possible, in a corner of the room, as if he felt too guilty to enjoy the heat. Tyrion felt pleasantly tired. His muscles ached. He had spent all day sparring with the wooden swords, first with Korhien and then with the warriors of Lady Malene's retinue. He had loved it. He felt like he was finally getting to do what he wanted to do.

Teclis sat near the fire, wrapped in a blanket. He looked more alert than he had in quite some time. It looked like he was passed the crisis of his latest illness and would live. The medicine Lady Malene had prepared for him seemed to have done its work.

Tyrion was glad. He went and stood beside his brother, hands outstretched towards the heat. The embers burned orange amid the ashes, and small blue flames danced over them. Here and there they took on an alchemical green tinge as something strange within them, some trapped magic perhaps, caught fire.

'You are going to Lothern with your aunt,' Father said.

'Both of us?' Tyrion asked.

'Both of you.'

'Why?' Teclis asked. He always wanted to know why.

'Because you must present yourself before the Phoenix King. It is an honour that those of our line have long had to endure.'

'Did you?' Teclis asked.

'Most assuredly.'

'What will happen?' Tyrion asked.

'You will see his Exalted Highness, and he will be very gracious to you and tell you how much Ulthuan owes to those of our blood. Then, most likely, you will be taken aside and sent to be examined by a cabal of sorcerers and priests and seers to determine whether your lives have been bent by the Curse. For this you will be sent to the Shrine of Asuryan.'

'They did this to you?' Tyrion asked.

'Yes. They do it to every descendant of Great Aenarion. There are all sorts of prophesies concerning those of our blood, some of them good, some of them bad. Sometimes, the seers present have visions concerning the future of those before them and speak as the compulsion of prophesy comes upon them.'

Tyrion did not much like the sound of this. He pictured something vaguely shameful and sinister here, and he did not like the idea of being singled out in such a way because of who he was, and from whom he was descended. Teclis, on the other hand, was fascinated. He had known a little about the process from his reading, of course, but his father had never spoken of it.

'Do they cast spells?' he asked.

'Divinations of all sorts,' said father. 'From the simplest to the most complex. I did not recognise them at the time but I came to know what they were latterly.'

'Was there any prophecy made about you?' Tyrion asked.

'They said I was marked for greatness by fate,' said their father sourly. He gestured around the barren sitting room in the cold and tumbledown mansion. His expression was ironic. 'They said my children would cause me great pain.'

Tyrion's face fell. Teclis took on the blank expression he always thought masked his feelings. Their father laughed.

'You did. Your mother died the night you were born and that was the greatest pain of my life. But you have never caused me any other pain, either of you, only sleepless nights. You have both been good boys as far as you are capable.'

It was not exactly a resounding declaration of pride or love. Their father could not bring himself to look at them while he talked. Instead he kept staring at the portrait of their mother above the fireplace.

'I am not sorry,' he said very quietly and almost apologetically, and it took Tyrion a long moment to realise that he was talking to her about them being born. The curious idea struck him that Prince Arathion could have avoided a great deal of pain simply by never having fathered them. He was a wizard. He knew ways of preventing conception if he wanted to.

Or perhaps fate would have taken a hand and seen they were born anyway. After all, what was the point of a prophecy if it was not going to come true?

Perhaps it was simply that their father had not known what form the pain they were going to cause was going to take. He wondered if Prince Arathion would have made the same decision if he had known it was going to cost him his wife. He wondered what it would be like to live with that notion, and only at the end did it strike him that his parents had conceived the pair of them anyway, even knowing it would have terrible consequences.

How little he knew of this quiet, unworldly elf with whom he had shared a house for all of his life.

Father shook his head and looked from Teclis to Tyrion and back again. 'The two of you are going away and there is little I can give you save my blessing. I wish that there were more.'

'You have given us enough,' said Tyrion.

'I do not think so, my son. And you cannot know that, for you have never seen Lothern as it truly is, only through the eyes of a very small child. It is a wonderful place but it can also be a terrible one for such as you. It is a place of jealousy and malice as well as wonders and greatness. The Lady Malene has promised me she will look after you but I am not sure how far she will be capable of that.'

'What will happen to us if they decide we are accursed?' Teclis asked. He had always been better at divining the current of their father's thoughts than Tyrion.

'You are not accursed,' said Father.

'What will happen if they find us so?'

Their father smiled, thin-lipped. 'You have always been very quick of understanding, Teclis. It has gratified me.'

Tyrion felt a stab of jealousy. 'Of course, there is the possibility that they might find you so, even if it were not true. Politics can be a nasty business among the elves. I am glad you understand this.'

'And you still have not answered my question,' said Teclis gently.

'I do not know the answer, my son. I would like to believe the best.'

'But...'

'But I fear that something terrible might be done.'

'We are not cursed,' said Tyrion. He believed that as well and he did not like the way this conversation was developing. This might be the last night they spent with their father in a long time and he would prefer it to be a happier memory than this.

'Of course you are not, and I am sure you will both make me very proud.'

'We will do our best,' said Tyrion.

'We will pass their tests,' said Teclis.

'Once you do, Teclis, Lady Malene will begin your instruction in the ways of magic. I would do it myself but I have the great work to continue.'

Tyrion looked at his unworldly father and wondered how unworldly he really was. He had certainly chosen the best way to deflect Teclis from his line of questioning. His twin's face glowed with pleasure. He had for a very long time wanted to begin his studies in the Art and now it seemed like they were to begin.

'And Tyrion, Korhien Ironglaive has offered to see that you learn the ways of the warrior. He says you have a great gift for it and few elves know as much about these matters as he does. Pay attention to what he tells you. I have heard it said that he is quite possibly the greatest warrior in Ulthuan. I am no expert on these things but I have heard it from the lips of those whose business it is to know.'

Tyrion's heart leapt. He could think of nothing he would like more than to learn how to be a warrior under Korhien's tutelage. Prince Arathion smiled, seeing the happiness written on his sons' faces.

'I shall miss you both,' he said. 'Having you both here has been the light of my life.'

The twins were both too excited to notice the sadness in his voice although Tyrion was to remember it well in years to come.

'We shall miss you too,' he said with all the sincerity of a youth of sixteen who sees only excitement and good fortune ahead of him.

'I bid you both good night,' said their father and returned to his workroom. The light burned there long into the night.

'LOTHERN,' SAID TECLIS as if he could not quite believe the word. 'It's not Hoeth, but it's a start. It has one of the greatest libraries in all Eataine. And Inglorion Starweaver and Khaladris have mansions there.'

'The Sea Guard are there,' said Tyrion. 'Perhaps I will be able to find a place in one of the regiments. Who knows some day I might even become one of the White Lions, if the opportunity to win glory presents itself.'

Teclis looked as happy as Tyrion could ever remember him being. 'At last, I will have my chance to see a bit of the world before...'

He did not finish his sentence. He did not have to. Tyrion knew he was thinking about his illnesses and the possibility of death. That always lay over his brother like a shadow even when he was in his brightest moods.

'Maybe we will be able to get on a ship,' said Tyrion, playing to his brother's fantasies, 'and go to the Old World and the Kingdoms of Men.'

'Cathay and the Towers of Dawn,' said Teclis naming a place they both knew he would never see. Teclis laughed. He was happy and that was infectious. Tyrion could not remember the last time he had heard honest mirth from his brother. The laughter stopped as suddenly as it came.

'In truth, I will be happy just to see Lothern again,' he said. 'Just to see... there have been times when that seemed a wish beyond all fulfilling.'

'What do you think will become of us?' Tyrion asked, just as suddenly serious. He felt as if their lives had just come to some vast shadowy crossroads. It was like being a traveller lost in the dark in the mountains, who realises suddenly he is standing on the edge of a precipice with no idea how deep it is. Soon they would be leaving the only home they had ever known and voyaging to a land of strangers.

'I don't know,' said Teclis. 'But we will face it together.'

It came to him then that his brother was not as confident as he sounded, that he was seeking reassurance, as much as making a statement.

'Yes, we will,' Tyrion said, smiling. With the confidence of youth he could not imagine anything that could tear them apart. 'You will be a great wizard.'

'And you will be a great warrior.' Teclis sounded as sure as if he could see it with his own eyes.

Tyrion hoped he would live to do so.

IT WAS ALMOST time, N'Kari could feel it. The ancient spells were weakening. The terrible ghosts were weary. Something was happening. Somewhere far off at the very edges of this great net of magic, something was beginning to unravel. The world was changing once more. In recent centuries the flows of dark power had become ever stronger. Something was happening out there in the worlds beyond worlds, something that was drawing the forces of Chaos to this mudball planet once more.

Perhaps the ancient dormant gates in the Uttermost North were awakening. Perhaps it was merely the whim of the Powers that they would return to this place and amuse themselves for a time. It did not matter to N'Kari what it was. It was the results that counted for him.

He sniffed with nostrils that were not nostrils and drew tainted magic into lungs that were not lungs. He had waited in the centre of this web of power for thousands of years, keeping still, drawing no attention to himself, accumulating tiny amounts of magic whenever he could, when he knew that it would not draw attention to his presence.

He had become familiar with the strange lines of the spell, and the even stranger paths left by an ancient race that lay underneath them. It was obvious that the master wizards among the elves had known about the presence of the ancient ways beneath the fabric of time and space made by this world's original masters. They had incorporated elements of them into their grand design. It was both a strength and a weakness.

The strength lay in the fact that they could tap into the energy wells of the Old Ones, use their ancient grids to strengthen their own magic.

The weakness lay in the fact that the Paths of the Old Ones were corrupt and slowly unravelling and letting elements of the Realms of Chaos, the Daemon Realms in which N'Kari had been spawned, seep into them.

N'Kari had fed on that corrupted energy and regained a small fraction of his original strength. In a sense he had done the elves a favour he had never intended. He had helped maintain their construct by consuming a great deal of the Chaotic magical energy seeping into it. He had helped lessen the corruption of the ancient spell although he was sure that the ghostly wizards would not see things that way.

He had projected his consciousness to various points along the interstices of the Vortex where the waystones stood. He had mapped the whole huge system. He knew it as well or perhaps better than any of the elf wizards did. He knew where it was strong and where the protective spells held good. He knew where it was weak and the ancient defences were crumbling.

He moved a part of his mind now to the area he had selected. It was a waystone that looked out from a mountain top down into a hidden valley. It was a long way from anywhere inhabited on Ulthuan and no one had come to it for many centuries to perform the rites that would strengthen it.

The waystone itself was crumbling. Lichen had grown in the channels of the carved runes, despite the spells that should have prevented its growth and burned it away. The very pattern of the stone was eroded by wind and weather and that was important, for the shape of the stone was as much a part of the spell as the flows of magical energy around it, or the runes chiselled into it. Every aspect had been part of its design, every element contributed something to what it did.

Now it was like a rusty nail from which a heavy picture hung. It was slowly bending and slipping from its original position and it would not hold for much longer. All it would take would be for something to give it a nudge, to apply a little bit of extra pressure and that part of the spell would collapse. The barriers that contained the vast energies of the Vortex would be punctured. Things could get into it, and, more importantly from N'Kari's point of view, things could get out of it.

He knew he would have to be careful. The ghosts still watched over their handiwork and would repair it where they could. They would notice the collapse of any small part of it and if they thought any sentient entity was behind it, particularly any entity trapped within their realm, they would destroy it.

The greater daemon knew there would be only one chance to do what needed to be done. At best if it failed it would mean spending many more centuries acquiring the energy for another attempt at escape.

At worst it would mean complete and utter destruction. N'Kari knew that if the patterns of energy that made up his consciousness within the Vortex were destroyed, he would be destroyed forever. He had no physical form to anchor him and his connection to the Realms of Chaos was still blocked by the intricate wards of the Vortex.

He was only going to get one chance. He had better do it right. He shifted the focus of his consciousness to the furthest extent that he could, somewhere out in the deep ocean of the lands that had once been part of Ulthuan but had now sank beneath the waves.

Overhead he sensed a storm being born. He measured the vast swirls of air, the huge pattern of wind and moisture and energy that was waiting to be unleashed, and he reached out as subtly as he could from within the Vortex, feeding it dark energies, setting up currents and systems that would drive it in a certain direction.

The storm began to move inland, gaining energy as it went, driven from within by elementals of dark magic that steered it towards the distant mountain top.

Soon, thought N'Kari. Soon.

CHAPTER SIX

Eastern Ulthuan, 10th Year of the Reign of Finubar

TYRION COULD SMELL the sea. The air tasted different; saltier, fresher. The wind was cooler and damper. Gulls drifted overhead. Just the sound of it and the sight of the white birds made him smile. He felt as happy as he ever had in his life.

He was mounted on a horse. He was riding down from the mountains and, within hours, he would catch a ship to the greatest city in Elvendom. He felt in some ways as if his life had finally begun.

As soon as the thought struck him, he felt guilty about his father and about his brother. He rode back along the small column to where Teclis lay stretched out on a bolster in the back of a wagon. The tented canvas cover of the wagon was drawn back and his twin lay looking up at the sky. They had hired it from one of the villagers who dwelled near his father's villa and used it for taking his produce into town to market. The elf would come into town in a few days and collect it.

'Isn't this wonderful,' Tyrion said unable to contain his enthusiasm.

'If you can call having your bones jarred on this wooden instrument of torture wonderful then I suppose it is,' Teclis said. He was smiling though and he looked better than he had in months. Tyrion had worried that the hardships of travel might finish off his brother but the potions Lady Malene had brewed really seemed to have improved his health. More than that, the prospect of travel and of learning magic seemed to have eased his troubled spirit and made life more endurable for him. Tyrion suspected it had given Teclis a reason to live. He felt grateful to Lady Malene for that at least.

He glanced ahead. The sorceress was riding side by side with Korhien Ironglaive. The two of them exchanged secret smiles but there was nothing sinister in them. They looked like the lovers which Tyrion supposed they were. It was hard to imagine what the open-handed and hearted warrior and the stony-faced mage-woman saw in each other, but they obviously saw something.

Tyrion wondered how Father was getting on. He was not concerned for his welfare. Prince Arathion was quite capable of looking after himself without any help from his sons and his work would keep him from being lonely. It was just strange to think of him wandering about the empty villa with only Thornberry for company.

It made Tyrion uneasy. Sometimes monsters came down out of the mountains. Maybe one of them could get over the wall. He told himself not to be foolish. His father was a mage. He was capable of handling any monster that might find its way down to their home.

Teclis had raised himself up on one elbow and was looking over the side of the wagon into the distance. 'I think I see the sea,' he said. Tyrion followed his pointing finger. They had just crested the brow of a hill and below them there was indeed a wide slice of shimmering blue starting where the green land ended.

The land was starting to change around them. It looked much more heavily cultivated and they had passed the fields worked by yeomen and many glasshouses where enchanted fruits were grown in magically controlled environments.

It was the richest and most fertile place Tyrion knew although he would have been the first to admit that his experience of such places was limited. Here and there on the higher grounds were mansions of such a scale that their father's house could be easily fitted into one wing. Indeed, it seemed little better than some of the yeomen's cottages they had passed. Tyrion was used to his father being the richest property owner in the area where he had grown up. Once again, he realised now that compared to the elves of even this small town, his father was very poor indeed. It was odd to realise how small his life had been and how large the world was. Exciting too.

On many of the buildings green paper-lanterns hung outside windows or on verandas. People were beginning to prepare for the Feast of Deliverance, the great festival that celebrated the return of spring and the saving of Aenarion's children from the forces of Chaos by the Treeman Oakheart. Alongside the streets stood little carved models of the Treeman, a creature that looked like a friendly cross between an elf and a massive oak. All elves had reason to be grateful to him. Without his intervention, there would be no Everqueen. Every spiritual leader of the elves since that time had been descended from Aenarion's daughter, Yvraine. Tyrion had a more personal reason to be grateful. He was descended from Aenarion's son, Morelion.

He rode back to where Teclis lay. His brother grimaced. He was tired and the strain of the long day's ride showed in his face. 'We will be in town soon and aboard ship after that.'

'I look forward to it,' said Teclis. 'I can't imagine anything could be worse than this.'

A FEW FISHING boats rode at anchor in the harbour along with a vessel that dwarfed them like a whale alongside dolphins. It was an elven clipper, part trading vessel, part warship, long and sleek and three-masted. It had a huge eagle head carved on the prow. There was a massive ballista on the aft deck and near the prow. Sailors swarmed through the rigging and moved across the deck with purpose. A set of planks had been laid from the midships to the pier, wide enough for horses to be led up.

The messenger bird Lady Malene had sent must have got through for they were expected. The ship's mistress waited at the docks to greet them. Much to Tyrion's surprise she reported to Lady Malene and not to Korhien; she seemed to find the enchantress a much more important figure than the White Lion. The flags fluttering from the ship's masts bore the same device as the bodyguard wore on their tabards. House Emeraldsea owned this ship and the lady was the highest ranking representative of the House present.

'Are we ready to depart, Captain Joyelle?' Malene asked. She cocked her head to one side and sniffed the air. 'I smell a storm coming in and there is magic on its winds.'

The ship's mistress nodded. She was even taller than Lady Malene and if anything looked sterner. Tyrion was starting to wonder if all the women of Lothern were so hard-faced when he noticed some of the female sailors were staring at him. They were younger and much prettier. As was his habit, he smiled back. Some of them met his gaze boldly. Others looked away shyly. It seemed that sailor women were not so different from the hunter-girls of the hills with whom he had experience.

'The *Eagle of Lothern* is ready to sail, Lady Malene. We can catch the tide if Captain Korhien and his men can get their horses aboard quickly.'

The horses looked restive. They had obviously been aboard ship before and had not much enjoyed the experience but they were elven steeds and they obeyed their riders. One by one they allowed themselves to be led up the gangplanks and lowered by a small winch into the hold. It seemed that all had been made ready for them, for the mangers were full of fodder and the act of eating seemed to settle the beasts.

Tyrion noticed that the captain too was staring at him as he helped Teclis up the ramp. At first he thought he had committed some sort of faux pas by not asking permission to board. No one else had, but presumably they were already known to the ship's mistress. Then the thought crossed his mind that perhaps she was unsettled by the sight of Teclis. His brother's infirmity often had that effect on his fellow elves. They were not used to the sight of illness. When he glanced back the captain had stopped staring and said something to Lady Malene in a low voice.

The mage nodded agreement and then walked over to them.

'The captain has had cabins assigned to you.'

'What else was she saying?'

'Nothing of any great importance,' said Lady Malene, a little too casually. Tyrion remembered Teclis's suspicions about her. He thought about the upcoming voyage. How many people would notice anything or say anything if they were to vanish over the side during the voyage south to Lothern? He told himself not to be so suspicious. There was almost certainly an innocent explanation for the mage's attitude.

Nonetheless, he resolved that he would keep his eyes open and the door barred. Despite his fears he could not keep his heart from soaring when the ship raised anchor and headed out of port a couple of hours later. The sun was sinking behind the mountains, and he could not help but think about his father once more.

He wondered if any of those tiny lights on the mountainside belonged to their home and he wondered how long it would be before he saw it again.

'THIS IS COSY,' said Teclis. He looked around the cabin thoughtfully. It was tiny, like all such chambers on ships. There was just room enough for a couple of narrow bunk beds and a couple of sea chests. Between them the twins did not have enough to fill even one. There was a tiny porthole that let in some moonlight.

'Two of the junior officers gave this up so we would have a place to sleep, or so Korhien told me,' Tyrion said. 'It seems we are honoured guests. The rightful owners are sleeping on the deck.'

'I am not sure that I would rather not be there myself,' said Teclis. He did not sound too good.

'Are you all right?' Tyrion asked looking closer. His brother looked sick again. He had gone a nasty shade of green.

'I have not felt right since I got aboard this accursed vessel. There's something about the way it sways that makes me feel very uncomfortable.'

'Seasickness,' said Tyrion. 'I've heard some people get it.'

'And I am one of them, and you are not. What a surprise! Normally I am so healthy and you are so feeble!'

'If you don't like it here, I can ask for us to be allowed to sleep on deck. This is more sheltered if rough weather comes though.'

'Isha's Blessing – don't talk to me about rough weather. This is bad enough.'

'It should only be for a few days, if we get decent winds, and there's no reason we should not. Apparently they blow southerly at this time of year.'

'You are becoming quite the sailor, brother.'

'I've been listening to the sailors. I intend to learn what I can on this voyage. You never know when it might come in useful.'

'My plan involves lying on my back here and hoping my stomach settles and the room stops spinning.'

'I think they call this a cabin.'

'They can call it what they like as long as it stops moving!'

Tyrion sprang into the upper bunk. The ceiling seemed very close above his head. It felt odd just to be lying there, with the boat gently rocking up and down as it moved. Aside from his nights camping with the hunters, he had never spent the night away from their father's villa before. This was the first time he had ever slept in an actual bed that was not his own. The strangest thought of all was that even as he lay there, he was getting further and further away from home and closer and closer to Lothern, a city they had not seen since they were very small children.

It occurred to him then that this was what made ships such a swift way to travel. A boat did not move any faster than a horse, really. It could just keep on moving through the night if it needed to as long as there was someone on watch. Ships never got tired and they kept steadily moving towards their goal.

He was thinking that there was a lesson to be learned from this somewhere, when he drifted off to sleep.

TYRION WAS WOKEN by the rays of the sun beaming in through the cabin window and the sound of Teclis being noisily sick into the bucket beside his bunk. The smell was overpowering in this tiny cabin.

He lowered himself from the top bunk, being careful to avoid landing with his foot in the bucket. He waited for Teclis to finish and then tossed the contents out through the porthole. It took him a fair bit of time to unscrew the handles that held it in place, and he decided to leave it open to let the stink escape.

'I was thinking that perhaps I should try flying next,' said Teclis. 'My head will probably fall off. Every mode of transportation I have tried so far has been worse than the last.'

'You will get used to this. It might take a few days but your body will get over it.'

'I sincerely hope so.'

'You want to take a turn on deck and see if perhaps we can find some breakfast?'

'A walk on deck, yes. Breakfast? What daemon possessed you to suggest such an infernal torture?'

'Well I am hungry.'

'And doubtless, as always, you will eat enough for the both of us.'

'I will try, if I can find some food.'

He helped Teclis up onto the deck. Many of the crew were already up and about. They worked away, scrubbing and sanding the planking and coiling ropes. They clambered over the rigging, making adjustments to the sails on the orders of the ship's officers. One of them sat in the crow's nest, another stood watch by the great figurehead on the prow. It seemed like the seas around a ship took a great deal of watching.

As they came up out of the stairwell, Tyrion was aware that they were being stared at again. It was not just Teclis who was attracting the looks either, it was him. It made him feel uncomfortable even though he made a point of smiling at everyone when he caught their eye. He was used to being looked at by women but the males were giving him odd looks too.

He looked around for Korhien or Malene but neither were visible. One or two of the soldiers were on deck, sharpening their weapons and chatting casually and trying hard not to look completely idle amid this bustling hive of activity.

'Where can we get something to eat?' Tyrion asked. One of the soldiers jerked his thumb in the direction of a small chamber behind him. Tyrion saw a firepit and a cauldron bubbling away within.

'I might have known you would be close to where the food was,' said Tyrion.

'Spoken like an old campaigner,' said the elf. 'We will make a soldier out of you yet.'

'I hope so,' said Tyrion.

Tyrion entered the ship's cookhouse. 'Could we have something to eat?' he asked. 'Please.'

The cook smiled and tossed him two bowls and a package of ship's biscuits wrapped in a large leaf. Tyrion held out the bowls and the cook ladled out some form of spicy fish stew into them. Tyrion handed one bowl to Teclis and took the other for himself and they made their way back onto the deck.

Tyrion was surprised to find the stew was good, and that the biscuit was nutritious and filling.

'There is some sort of enchantment in it,' said Teclis. 'Like with waybread.'

'I suppose they need to keep the crew fit,' said Tyrion. 'You want yours?'

'I don't feel like eating.'

'Take the soup, at least. I would not want you dying of starvation before we get to Lothern.'

'It would be a mercy,' said Teclis.

'Don't even joke about it.'

One of the sailor girls was watching them closely. Tyrion smiled at her. She smiled back and then looked away shyly. She was the prettiest girl on the ship for sure.

'I see you are going to be breaking hearts again,' said Teclis. Tyrion had shared some of the details of his experiences with the hunter-girls with his brother.

'Such is never my intention,' Tyrion replied.

'The gap between intention and consequence is as large as that between heaven and hell,' said Teclis.

'Who are you quoting now?'

'No one. I just made that up.'

'Are you contemplating a career as a philosopher then?'

'It would be useful to have something to fall back on if I fail as a mage.'

'I doubt that is going to happen.'

'You never know. My life has not been conspicuous for its successes so far.'

The twins stood on the deck for a long time, watching the life of the ship around them. Tyrion found it all infinitely fascinating. Teclis seemed to find it just tiring.

CHAPTER SEVEN

TYRION STOOD ON the prow of the great ship, staring out over the bird of prey's head carved there. A school of flying fish erupted from the water nearby. The sight of them flickering silver in the sunlight before they vanished once more beneath the waves made him smile.

The wind filled the sails and the vessel seemed almost to skim over the sea. Green flags with the insignia of House Emeraldsea fluttered in the wind.

Sailors leapt from mast to mast and clambered over the rigging in response to commands given by the ship's mistress. To Tyrion, it was all incomprehensible and all very exciting. So far he had loved every moment of it. He liked the feel of the hard wooden deck beneath his bare feet. He liked the salt smell of the sea.

Laughing, he leapt up and caught a cable, and pulled himself up to a crossbar. When he had first started doing this the ship's officers had been worried that he might fall and break his neck but it had swiftly become obvious that he was far more at home in the rigging than most sailors and far more agile than any of them.

None of the sailors objected as long as he did not get in their way. He clambered all the way to the crow's nest high atop the second mast. The figures on deck looked tiny beneath him. It felt far more exposed than being atop a hill of similar height. For one thing, hills did not sway with the movement of a ship.

The wind tugged at his linen shirt. Gulls perched just out of reach. He swung himself out onto the spar and then ran out along it to where the gulls sat. Seeing him coming, they fluttered away, circling over the ship, cawing mockingly at him. He wished that he could fly so that he could follow them.

He shaded his hand with his eyes and glanced off into the distance. Huge shapes moved beneath the clear water, perhaps whales, perhaps some of the legendary monsters that were said to haunt this part of the sea. So far none of them had paid any attention to the ship, for which he was grateful.

Some leagues away he thought he could see islands. Sometimes. Sometimes they were there. Sometimes not. A faint shimmering covered the waves, as far as he could see. It resembled a heat haze but it was not. To his eyes it looked tinged with magic, more than that he could not say.

Far below him, Teclis waved. Tyrion leapt out into space, grabbed a dangling rope and slid down it with dizzying speed, laughing aloud until his feet hit the deck. He sprang forward exuberantly, performed a handspring and landed upright beside his brother.

'What were you looking for?' Teclis asked. He lounged on a wicker deckchair, looking even sicker than usual. Despite all the good Lady Malene's potions had done him, the voyage did not agree with him. He still suffered from seasickness worse than any dwarf.

'I don't know,' Tyrion replied. 'But whatever it is I think I will have trouble finding it. There is some enchantment on these waters, stronger than the glamour that covers the Annulii.'

Teclis laughed at him. 'Perceptive as ever, brother. You are looking on the effects of one of the most potent and far-reaching spells ever cast. Bel-Hathor and his mages wove magic here to hide Ulthuan from the humans. Believe me, any confusion you are feeling would be increased a thousand-fold if you were one of them. When they enter the weave of this spell they get lost and turned around by a labyrinth of spells and eventually, if they do not starve, or run aground, they find themselves back out on the open ocean.'

'I believe you.'

'Good. You ought to.' He made a face and for a moment looked as if he was going to be sick again. Somehow he controlled the impulse. 'By all the gods, I hate this.'

'YOU ARE NOT enjoying this voyage?' They had been at sea two days now, and Tyrion was growing concerned about his twin's health. His seasickness had not improved over the long days of their sailing. The smell of stale vomit hung constantly over their cabin. They spent a good deal of time on deck, as they were doing now.

'Let us say I cannot wait to begin my magical studies so that I can learn a charm against seasickness,' Teclis responded.

'I am astounded by your towering ambition. It is nice to know I have a brother who aims so high in life. Seven thousand years of elf magic to learn from and the biggest thing driving you to master this ancient and terrible lore is your desire to avoid seasickness.'

'If you had been as sick for as long as I have you would understand why I feel that way. Lady Malene's potions had only just helped me get over my last illness.'

Tyrion immediately felt guilty about his joking manner. He had never endured a moment's illness in his life. Seasickness did not affect him in the slightest nor had he expected it to.

For Teclis things were different. Perhaps they always would be. He himself had spent most of the voyage learning the ways of the sea from sailors who looked at him as if he were a young god when they were not giving him superstitious looks. Teclis had spent his daytime sleeping on deck, trying to keep from vomiting and being looked down on by everyone who passed him, save the few among Korhien's riders who also suffered from the same malady.

'You always wanted to go on a ship,' he said eventually.

'I still do,' Teclis responded. 'But only once I have achieved immunity to this vile plague. In the few brief instants I have not been heaving what I have eaten over the sides I have greatly enjoyed this voyage.'

'Do you think we will see pirates?'

'I was just starting to feel better. Why did you have to say that?'

'Because I have heard stories that these are dangerous waters, full of Norse raiders and human pirates and dark elf sea marauders despite all the spells that are supposed to keep them out. We might meet some that have gotten lost.'

'This might seem like an adventure to you, Tyrion, but what I am I supposed to do if we are attacked by pirates – be sick all over them?'

'That might prove to be a very effective defensive strategy.'

'There are times when I doubt that you understand military matters quite as well as you pretend you do.'

'Don't worry. If we are attacked, I will protect you.'

'And who is going to protect you?'

'I think I can manage to protect myself, brother. Never doubt it.'

'Look over there.' Tyrion followed his brother's gesture. Korhien and Lady Malene strolled hand in hand across the deck towards them. It seemed Tyrion was not the only one enjoying this sea voyage.

'Greetings, young princes,' said Korhien, sounding more than usually amiable.

'Good afternoon to you both,' said Teclis.

'It is,' said Lady Malene. 'There is something to be said for the fresh sea air, I always find.' She looked at Korhien as if sharing some secret joke. Korhien smiled.

'It is invigorating,' he said.

'I find it so,' said Tyrion, wondering why the two of them looked as if they wanted to laugh at him. They had just spent a long time in their cabin below. They had not been enjoying a lot of the fresh sea air. Suddenly he realised what they had been up to and looked away.

'This is a wonderful ship,' said Teclis. 'Very fast.'

'It is one of many House Emeraldsea owns,' said Lady Malene.

'How many?' Teclis asked. He always liked to pin things down exactly.

'Thirty or so. They sail and they trade and they explore. Sometimes we use them to raid the coast of Naggaroth.'

'Thirty ships, is that a lot?' Tyrion asked.

'It is,' said Korhien. 'A significant contribution to our fleets in wartime. There are very few Houses in Lothern who can match that number and only Finubar's House exceeds it.'

'Well, he is the Phoenix King,' said Teclis.

'We were just talking about pirates,' said Tyrion. 'Do you think we shall see any?'

'My brother is keen to try his hand at fighting them,' said Teclis sardonically.

'There is no need to worry my young friend,' said Korhien. 'If we are attacked, Lady Malene will protect us.'

'She will?' said Tyrion.

'Oh yes, like many a mage of Lothern she started her career of wizardry aboard ship.'

'Is that true?' asked Teclis. As ever, mention of any aspect of magic got his attention instantly.

Lady Malene nodded. 'Most mages of Lothern spend half their lives aboard ship.'

'Why?' Teclis asked.

'Summoning winds, protecting them from monsters, blasting enemy ships with spells when the need arises and preventing enemy wizards doing the same to our vessels.'

To Tyrion that sounded like just about the most exciting use of wizardry he had ever heard. It almost made him want to study it himself, despite his total lack of any gift for the Art. 'You can summon winds?' he asked.

'Yes.'

'Why not do it now?'

'Because there is no need,' Malene replied. 'We have a fair wind driving us as fast as we can sail naturally, and I see no need to tire myself out to make us go faster. If any pirates do show up, I will need my strength for then.'

Tyrion saw it at once, 'Of course,' he said.

'Of course, what?' Teclis asked.

'Better to bind the winds then than for travel. With a mage aboard capable of doing so we could sail against the wind, or increase our manoeuvre speed.'

Korhien beamed like a teacher proud of a prize pupil. 'I told you he was quick on the uptake,' he said to Lady Malene.

'Show my brother the military possibilities of anything and he grasps it instantly,' said Teclis. 'Unfortunately he is not so quick on the uptake for anything else.'

'He is quick about all he will need to be quick for,' said Korhien. 'Nothing more need be asked of him.'

'I would not be so quick to make such statements if I were you,' said Lady Malene. 'Who knows what Prince Tyrion's destiny will require of him?'

Tyrion laughed. 'I doubt it will be anything too exalted.'

The others looked at him as if they did not believe that. He noticed the pretty young sailor girl had been listening to all of this from nearby. She looked away when she saw him notice her. He wondered if she was really as shy as she pretended or whether this was simply a way of getting his attention.

He resolved that before the day was much older, he would find out.

'WHAT IS THIS called?' Tyrion asked, pointing to the large sail above them.

The sailor girl smiled. They stood alone high on the central mast of the ship, perfectly balanced as was the way of elves. They swayed slightly with the motion of the ship, but both of them were perfectly at ease, as if they were standing on dry ground, not above a drop that would shatter their bodies if they were to accidentally fall to the deck sixty feet below.

'This is the topsail,' she said.

'And what are you called?'

'Karaya.'

'I am Tyrion.'

'You are Prince Tyrion,' she said. 'You are the nephew of Lady Malene. We were sent all this way to pick you up. You must be a personage of some importance.'

'Really?'

'A trading Eagle is not normally dispatched to a small fishing port in Cothique for matters of no consequence. We should be sailing to the Old World or Cathay. Instead, we are off the coast of Ulthuan carrying a cargo of warriors and horses.'

'I had not realised I was so valuable,' said Tyrion.

The girl smiled at him. 'House Emeraldsea thinks so.'

'You have a pretty smile,' he said.

'And you have strange and lovely eyes,' she said. He found the intensity of her look somewhat disturbing. It reminded him of a question he had been wanting to ask for a while.

'Why does everyone look at me so oddly?' he asked. The girl looked startled. It was obviously not what she had been expecting him to say. The mood of the moment was broken.

'You really don't know?'

Tyrion shook his head.

'I hate to strike such a blow to your vanity but it is not just because they are overwhelmed by your sheer physical beauty.'

'I do find that hard to believe,' said Tyrion.

Karaya smiled.

'It's because you look like a statue.'

'Are we talking about my chiselled good looks?'

'No. We are talking about the fact that you look like the statue of Aenarion in Lothern harbour. That's why the whole crew spend so much time staring at you.'

'No!'

'Yes. The resemblance is uncanny.'

'You mean aside from the fact that the statue is six hundred feet tall and I am not.'

'You will have a chance to judge for yourself soon. We will arrive in Lothern in the next few days if the winds are fair.'

Tyrion noticed dark clouds gathering in the distance. He wondered if a storm was coming in.

From below an officer bellowed an order and Karaya jumped to obey.

'Perhaps we can continue this discussion later,' said Tyrion.

'Perhaps,' the sailor girl replied. 'There are other things I would like to discuss too.'

N'KARI FELT HIS storm being birthed. He felt like howling with glee. The first part of his plan was under way. The weather was shaped to his will. Now he needed to make sure the other elements were in place.

Carefully, with infinite patience, he extruded tiny filaments of himself through the waystones. He was not yet powerful enough to break out physically but he could send out a message to every elf with even the slightest sensitivity to such things and blend their dreams with his own. He would prepare the world for his coming and make sure the first recruits were ready for his army.

Mages across the face of the world would sense something, for their gift would make them sensitive to his magic. That would not be such a bad thing. Some of them would provide him with excellent recruits.

He invoked the name of Slaanesh and sent thistledown splinters of dream out from the waystones into the night. Borne by the winds of magic, they floated over Ulthuan and touched the dreams of those they were drawn to.

In southern Cothique, a group of orgiastic cultists was touched by magic. As they lay naked and spent from their ritual lovemaking, they felt an odd desire enter their minds, to go to a certain place at a certain time and make themselves ready for the rise of a new prophet who was about to enter their world.

In the Shadowlands, a group of dark elf infiltrators learned that if they headed eastwards, they would find something of great use to their master. It seemed to them that Morathi herself had appeared naked in their dreams with the instructions and promised them the ultimate reward of her person if they obeyed.

In Saphery, an archmage who had long dabbled in the ways of the Dark Prince of Pleasure dreamed that he would learn a great secret if he ventured to the western waystone of the realm.

In Lothern, the greatest assassin in the world dreamed of rebellion against his master and a life of luxury among the enemies he had been raised to hate. He woke beside the sleeping wife of a friend and covered his stolen eyes with a hand covered in the flayed skin of elves.

All across Ulthuan, the dreams of wizards and the sensitive were troubled, and visions entered their mind that carried the promise and the threat of the power of Slaanesh's greatest follower.

TECLIS HAULED HIS painful way up onto the deck, one shoulder rising, the other falling with every step. It was dark. The night sky was full of stars and the beams of the moon fell on his face. The sound of the waves lapping against the sides of the ship was oddly relaxing. The wind was cool on his skin. At night, he felt stronger, and he suffered the seasickness less. He felt more able to limp around and less self-conscious about his infirmity with most of the crew save for the nightwatch and the officer in charge asleep.

His dreams had been dark, troubled things, full of images of walls closing in and four-armed daemons stalking innocent elves and flaying them alive while they screamed in what might have been agony or ecstasy or some combination of both. In any case, the image was disturbing enough to make him want to leave the little cabin and come up into the fresh air.

There was a splash and a plopping sound and he saw something silver wriggling on the deck in front of him. At first, he was startled and a little scared but he saw it was a flying fish. It had leapt from the water and was now spasming on the deck as if drowning in air. He felt a stab of sympathy. He knew what that felt like. He lifted the fish, ignoring the slimy wriggling between his fingers, limped to the edge of the deck and dropped it back over the side into the ocean.

He looked out onto the black waters and saw the moon reflected in them. He saw his own reflection as a shadowy, broken outline in the rippling waves. It made him look even more ill-made than usual.

He heard someone moving behind him and turned to see the girl who was always following Tyrion about. He smiled at her. She looked at him oddly for a moment, and he thought she was going to speak but she walked away, unwilling to meet his gaze, receding into the night.

He turned away himself so as not to show his hurt. He schooled his features to cold composure and told himself he did not care anyway. It was a hard thing to be ugly and a cripple among the elves. They did not like to look upon things less beautiful and less perfect than themselves. In his father's villa, with only his family and Thornberry, he had been shielded from that, but he was starting to realise how isolated his life was going to be among what were supposedly his own people. He wondered for a moment whether that was why his father had retreated there.

Tyrion was going to have it easier now. He was good-looking even among elves and he was good-natured, easy going and charming. His sunny disposition would always win him friends and admirers.

What is going to become of us, he asked the Moon Goddess. What is going to become of me? There was no answer. The waves rolled on. The sea was empty, a vast dark mirror to the sky.

It was a long time before he slept and, once again, his dreams were dark.

CHAPTER EIGHT

THE WIND GREW stronger, ruffling Tyrion's hair with invisible fingers and making the sails crack as they fluttered. The sea was choppier, white caps of foam appearing atop waves that grew larger and larger. The ship rose and fell more as it cut into them. From the east, purple clouds streamed across the sky, covering the sun and overhauling the ship with surprising swiftness.

Tyrion watched with interest. The sailors reacted with practised discipline, tying things down, making sure everything was in place. In the hold, one of the horses whinnied in fear, catching something in the air. The rest of the steeds became uneasy. Tyrion could hear them moving restlessly. One by one the soldiers went down into the hold and began to whisper softly to their animals, calming them.

Slowly it dawned on Tyrion that there really might be something to be uneasy about. The wind was blowing ever more strongly. The gulls perched on the masts were taking to the air. The *Eagle of Lothern* turned slightly, setting a new course towards the coast. Tyrion was no sailor but he wondered at the wisdom of this. A storm might drive them onto the rocks, run them aground, break the ship up.

'What is going on?' he asked Korhien. The White Lion stood near him on the prow of the ship watching the onrushing clouds. He turned to face Tyrion, stretched ostentatiously as an elf without a care in the world. He looked as if he was contemplating simulating a yawn.

'Big storm coming in. The captain is looking for a safe harbourage although I doubt she will find one on this stretch of coast.'

'Is that wise? Might we not run aground?'

'Your guess is as good as mine. I am just going with what Malene told me. I think it's because you are here. Normally they would run before the storm but they don't want to take any chances with the Blood of Aenarion being onboard.'

Tyrion was not sure whether Korhien meant they were not taking any chances because they valued the lives of himself and Teclis or whether they feared the curse. Perhaps it was a little of both.

'What should we do?' Tyrion asked. Korhien laughed.

'Not a lot we can do, doorkeeper. Neither of us are sailors. We can offer up a prayer to the sea gods and trust in the fact that the captain knows what she is doing.'

Tyrion smiled.

'You don't look too worried, doorkeeper.'

'I wanted to find adventure. It looks like adventure has found me.'

'You have a good attitude. Let's hope that your first adventure is not your last.'

'I am going below to check on my brother,' Tyrion said.

'I THINK I had better close the window,' said Tyrion. Huge waves were already splattering against the side of the vessel and water was sopping onto the floor. He was very conscious of the *swoosh* of the sea against the hull.

'I think you will find that sailors call it a porthole,' said Teclis. 'They can get very sniffy if you call it a window.' He mimicked the tone with which Tyrion had earlier explained the ways of sailors to him with uncanny accuracy. It was a gift he had.

'Window, porthole, big round thing with bullseye glass panes – whatever it's called I had better close it.' Tyrion wrestled with the handles. The wetness was making them slippery and the increased motion of the ship was making it difficult to force the porthole into place. Eventually he managed to. Turning, noticed Karaya standing in the door.

'I was just sent down below to make sure the port was closed,' she said. 'Glad to see it is.'

Tyrion nodded and she ran off up the stairs again. Teclis lay on his bed. His face looked strained and Tyrion could tell he was doing his best not to moan.

'Spit it out,' he said. 'You know you want to.'

'I suspect the gods have found a new way to torture me. This is worse than normal seasickness – which is quite a feat.'

'You are not in the least green. And you are not throwing up.'

'That is because I am too frightened to.'

'Really?'

'Not everyone is so stupid that they feel no fear.'

'You are afraid?'

'Terrified.' Tyrion wondered why he almost never sensed his brother's emotions when he was close enough to see him. Was it because he did not need to know them then?

'What are you afraid of, brother? Getting wet?'

'Where do I start? Sinking? Being struck by lightning? Running aground? Being attacked by a maddened sea monster?'

'Why not all of them at once?'

'Why do I feel that you are not taking my distress entirely seriously?'

'We are safe, brother. The crew have been through these storms a thousand times. This ship was built to endure these things.'

'Ships still sink, brother, despite the best intentions of their builders. Crews make mistakes. Monsters get hungry.'

Tyrion shrugged. 'There is nothing I can do about any of these things.'

'You know how to swim.' Tyrion felt like telling him that under the circumstances that would not make too much difference. He doubted anything could live in a sea like this if the ship went down. Saying that would not improve his brother's mood though.

'Don't worry if the ship goes down, I will save you.'

'How? We will both be stuck in this cabin. The ship will be a coffin for both of us.' Now Tyrion sensed Teclis's fear. It was becoming so intense his own heart was starting to pound. He was feeling a little uncomfortable. Normally nothing much frightened him. It was not part of his nature to let fear rule him. He had never really experienced anything like the terrors he had read about in books save as an echo of Teclis's fears.

'Would you be happier on deck?'

'I think I would.'

'It might be easier to be swept overboard.'

'We can rope ourselves to the railings, the way real sailors are supposed to.'

'You sure?'

'I would rather be above than trapped down here.' Tyrion understood. Spending your last few moments watching a small cabin fill with water would not be a good way to leave the world.

Tyrion helped his brother up the stairwell. He was not sure this was a very clever idea. He was confident he was sure-footed enough not to be swept away. He was not so sure about his twin. Teclis could barely walk at the best of times.

Nonetheless it appeared the decision had been made.

THE RAIN SPLATTERED onto the deck, huge droplets hitting the wood and bouncing with a flicker that reminded Tyrion of miniature lightning bolts. White foam surged over the prow of the *Eagle of Lothern* and added to the slick wetness underfoot.

He left Teclis near the afterdeck and went to find some ropes. The sailors looked tense and ready for action, like soldiers getting ready before a battle. Their enemies were the sea and the storm. The officers bellowed last minute instructions. Down below the horses whinnied in panic and it struck Tyrion what a cruel trial this must be for them. How unnatural for creatures reared to race across an endless plain to be imprisoned within a bobbing wooden box as it was battered from all sides by mighty waves.

The ship rose and fell through the long swells. He swayed to keep his balance as he moved. He was surprised to see Lady Malene come on deck and ask permission to join the captain on the afterdeck. He was even more surprised when the officer beckoned for him and Teclis to come up and join them. Malene nodded to emphasise this and the twins went to join the officers. The wind had risen to a dull roar now. The waves smashed against the ship. The decks creaked. The sails boomed and cracked.

'If you are going to remain on deck, lash yourself to something,' said Lady Malene. He could see that she was already lashed to the railings. 'Particularly Teclis. We do not want to lose you overboard.'

He cinched his brother to a banister, making sure the knots were tight and in the style he had observed the sailors using, then he stalked across the deck, sure-footed as a big cat.

No one seemed to want to question them about why they had not stayed below. No one minded that they were on the aft-deck, the sacred space reserved for officers and mages. It seemed that on this ship at least they were regarded as personages of some importance.

Lightning flickered in the distance, and the sullen boom of thunder rippled in its wake. Somewhere down below a horse whinnied in terror and tried to kick its way out of a stall. A rider shouted words meant to be reassuring but which just sounded panicked.

Suddenly the rain intensified. Within heartbeats Tyrion was soaked to the skin and looking at everything as though through a thick, grey mist. The ship heeled to the right as it struck a wave at the wrong angle. The roll was disturbing, as if some great monster had risen from the sea beneath the ship and was trying to push it over. That was not an image he wanted in his head.

The captain yelled something to the steersman, who twisted the great wheel that guided the ship. In response to bellowed instructions, sailors overhead did something to the sails, Tyrion was not sure what. The vessel righted itself. The prow rose like a bucking horse. Tyrion felt himself begin to slide back down the deck. He looked around to make sure that Teclis was still held fast. His twin stood by the rail, clutching it as if it were the only thing that stood between him and watery death, and yet despite this, his gaze was riveted to Lady Malene.

Tyrion followed his look and understood why. An aura of power played around the sorceress, its nimbus visible even to Tyrion's sight. Tyrion was not sure what she could do against the unleashed fury of the storm, but he sensed enormous power pooling within her.

The rain lashed his face, and his eyes stung with salty tears. It was difficult to tell where the rain ended and the sea spray started. It was hard to remember that only a few minutes ago the waters had seemed relatively calm and he could see all the way to the horizon.

The ship's timbers creaked and groaned now and he realised that something, somewhere was putting the hull under enormous stress. The wind and the waves roared like angry daemons.

The worst of it was that he had no idea of how likely things were to go wrong. It seemed entirely possible to him that the whole ship could break in two at any instant, or that the power of the waves could swamp the vessel, filling the hold with water and sending them to the bottom like a stone.

He glanced at the captain and at Lady Malene and then at the rest of the officers. They looked tense but not worried and he decided that it would be best to take his cue from them.

Part of him realised that they were in the same position as him. Even if they knew the vessel was about to break up, it would do them no good to panic. It helped that they remained calm. The sense of authority radiating from them affected the crew, who went about their duties with a will. If the officers had seemed frightened, the crew might panic as well, and in that panic the whole ship could be lost.

There was a lesson in the duties of command here that was not lost on Tyrion. He filed it away in his memory for future reference, swearing that he would remember the demeanour of the captain and the mage if and when he was ever in a similar situation.

Lightning erupted in the sea in front of them, so brilliant that it was blinding. Someone, somewhere, screamed and Tyrion wondered whether the bolt had hit the ship. An instant later thunder bellowed like an angry god overhead. A huge gust of wind and a giant wave hit the ship simultaneously. Water crashed over the deck and surged towards Tyrion like a moving wall.

DESPITE THE RAGING seas, despite the swaying deck, despite the lightning flare and the thunder roar, only one thing held Teclis's attention – Lady Malene. She had begun working magic almost as soon as the storm started, a slow, subtle weaving that most elves would never have spotted but which was obvious to Teclis with his peculiar sensitivity to the flows of power.

He watched, fascinated. He had never seen anyone work magic like this before. His father was a wizard, for sure, but his craft was the slow, subtle assembly of runes and flows of power that went into making and moulding things. It was rare he had ever seen his father do anything that was not directly connected with the armour of

Aenarion, and even that was usually small, trivial stuff like the making of light or fire.

This was something of an entirely different order. He was not sure what Lady Malene was going to do but he was sure it was going to be something much greater than anything he had ever seen Prince Arathion cast.

Malene summoned more and more of the winds of magic to her. She pulled power from the very air surrounding her and moulded it with gentle, small motions of her hands and body.

Teclis watched, understanding instinctively what was happening. He was tempted to copy it the way a child copies the action of a parent but he was sufficiently conscious of what was happening to know that any interference on his part might prove disastrous. Instead he made himself watch and memorise, hoping that at some point in the future he might be able to recreate what she was doing.

As the storm intensified, Lady Malene wove her spells. Teclis moved as close as the ropes binding him to the ship's railings would allow so he could hear what she was saying over the howling of the wind. There was magic in the words and in her voice. They were laced with power and his magic-attuned senses caught what she was saying in a way his hearing alone never could have if she was merely speaking words.

He saw the relation between her words, her gestures and the flow of the winds of magic. She was the still centre and she was doing something that manipulated the forces around her. Something about her mind and her spirit anchored the whole structure of spell-work she was creating.

Even as he watched, she made a gesture like a fisherwoman casting a net, and a lattice of power, complex and tight, flew forth from her hands.

It enmeshed the *Eagle of Lothern*, bolstering its timbers and strengthening them against the storm, aiding it to cut through the water. The ship, which had been heeling before the wind, righted itself. The timbers creaked but held. He sensed that in some way Lady Malene was communing with the vessel. It was bound to her as she was bound to it.

An enormous wall of water smashed over the prow and raced towards them. Teclis saw Tyrion brace himself for impact. Lady

Malene gestured and the waters parted in front of her, sloughing off over the afterdeck, leaving Tyrion standing a little bemused at being hit only by spray.

No sooner had she completed weaving that spell than she began another, summoning sentient vortices, forming the wind into air elementals, calming their anger and directing them about the ship as if they were a second crew. The sails billowed outwards but did not rip or tear or drive the ship down. Some of the elementals ran before the ship, shielding it from the worst buffeting of the storm; others gathered the fury of the wind and harnessed it, sending the vessel scudding along like a cloud over the angry sea.

Teclis was no longer frightened. He no longer worried that the ship would go down. He understood that Malene was completely the mistress of the situation and as long as she remained so, the *Eagle of Lothern* was safe.

Here was something he understood, could do. This woman was capable of teaching him it. Chance or fate, whatever anyone might choose to call it, had placed her in his path and he was determined to make the most of the opportunity. For long hours he watched fascinated, as she as much as the captain and crew brought the ship through the worst of the storm.

As suddenly as it had come upon them, the storm passed, leaving the sea calming in its wake as it raced off inland towards the mountains where it could continue to wreak havoc. The ship continued to sail its course, moving on steadily towards its goal, the only sign it had ever been captured in the storm's embrace the pools of water left puddling on the deck.

Lady Malene looked a little tired but also triumphant. Perhaps the oddest thing and certainly the one that impressed itself most on Teclis in that moment was that, though everyone around her was soaked to the skin, she was absolutely dry. Neither the sea nor the storm seemed to have touched her.

'That was the worst storm I have seen in a long, long time,' said Captain Joyelle.

'Yes,' Malene said. 'And there was dark magic in it. I fear that it may serve some fell purpose before it is done.'

The captain nodded and was silent, unwilling to discuss the matter further.

Lady Malene turned and looked at Teclis knowingly. 'You saw all of that, didn't you?'

He nodded. 'It was very impressive.' The words were an understatement but they were all he could think to say. 'I have read about such things but I never thought to witness them.'

'You will witness far more impressive things before you are done, unless I miss my guess,' she said. 'Work them too.'

'I hope so,' he said. She smiled at him again and walked off the deck and down the stairs below. The looks of the captain told him that now she was gone, he and Tyrion were no longer welcome on the command deck either. He did not really care. He went below himself and for the first time in a long time, he did not feel sick.

THE STORM BLEW in from the east. It toppled trees and blew off roofs and hurled the seas around Ulthuan forwards in great churning waves. Enormous winds drove brutal, black thunderclouds before it. Savage rains poured down as if intending to drown the world.

The storm roared through the mountains of Ulthuan, passing over a carved stone so ancient it was crumbling. The runes on its face, despite their magical protections, were all but obscured by the millennia-long erosion of the elements.

As if tossed by the hand of a wicked god, a bolt of lightning surged down and struck the ancient waystone. Sparks flew and the stench of ozone and something else filled the air. Thunder roared and then died away and for a moment there was eerie silence. Then it seemed as if the thunder's growl was answered from deep within the earth.

The tip of the mountain shook. The ancient stone danced and then toppled. As it fell ancient spells became undone and things erupted outwards onto the mountain top, winged things that beat up into the stormy night, laughing and cackling.

A moment later a massive claw emerged, and then an arm, then a deformed bestial head and finally a monstrous androgynous body. Two additional arms pushed it from the ground.

N'Kari looked down from the mountain top for a long moment. He breathed air as he had not breathed it in six thousand years. He looked down the slopes of a great mountain illuminated by the hellish flicker of lightning. Overhead winged things soared and cackled on the storm winds. He raised one clenched fist in a gesture of triumph and defiance.

With his escape from the Vortex full cognisance of what he was and who he had been came crashing in on him. In the Vortex, he had been a pallid ghostly thing, his mind and memories dull, his passions shadowy, his desires weak and suppressed. Now that he had regained physical form once more, his emotions were stronger, as if they needed glands and hearts and blood and bone and organs to give them their full strength.

He remembered a great deal he had forgotten and felt once again the titanic towering passions that were his birthright.

He smiled, showing his fangs, and then with an impulse of his will changed his shape to something more resembling an elf, albeit one horned and fanged whose long nails were talons and whose eyes glowed like bloody fire.

In this world his will was constrained by foolish rules and the magic he worked would have to be done in accordance with them. So be it. The knowledge of what was necessary was instinctive to him. He could feel the constraints that hemmed him in in the way a man would feel walls surrounding him or the tug of gravity on his body. It took him mere moments to work out what was needed and then he inscribed a circle in the ground with his claw.

Now, he thought, I will take vengeance. It was time to locate his prey. He reached out with his mind and formed a vision of Aenarion as he had been at the height of his power.

He could recall the slightest detail of his foe and recollect him on a scale that was unimaginable to the weak minds of mortals. He remembered the exact pattern of Aenarion's spirit and the genetic markers that had flowed in his blood and which would flow in the blood of all of those descended from him.

As the lightning blasted the ground about him, he pricked the flesh of his hand with one of his talons. A drop of his magical blood flowed forth. He flipped it into the air and ignited it with a word. It became a mote of energy, a pulse of magic that he could shape to his will.

He imprinted the genetic rune that he remembered upon it and then summoned more magical energy. As he did so the original mote divided and replicated like an amoeba, again and again and again as more power flowed into it. Soon N'Kari was surrounded by clouds of tiny motes of light, swarming around him like fireflies. With another gesture he sent them racing away from him to seek out the ones he was looking for.

The motes flew across Ulthuan fast as sunbeams, seeking the few remaining possessors of the marks that N'Kari sought. They flashed around them invisibly and then hurtled back across the vast distances to their master.

As they returned, they swirled around him once more, each of them bearing an image of the being they had found. Visions of faces and places danced in his mind. He saw young women waiting to be married, wizards in their laboratories, princes in their palaces, a pair of twins little more than children riding aboard a ship. All of them bore the unmistakeable imprint of Aenarion's blood.

Now, N'Kari knew the locations of his prey and his tiny pets, following an invisible magical scent, would always be able to find them again.

He smiled to himself revealing very sharp fangs. One of those he was looking for dwelled not too far from here. It would not take him long to begin his revenge. Within the passing of a moon, he swore he would have wiped all of the line of Aenarion from the face of Ulthuan. He would make this world pay for all of the long millennia of his incarceration. He roared with the ecstasy of it.

He began work on another spell, one that would reach out to all those whose dreams he had touched and who were vulnerable to his influence. It would draw those he needed to him and it would let him sense their presence.

He would need followers, an army of them if he was to achieve his goal and he would need other things, daemons to follow him and slay his enemies on his command. He would need worship to nourish him and souls on which to feed.

His great bellow echoed for scores of leagues and those who heard his voice above the crack of thunder shuddered.

CHAPTER NINE

Lothern, 10th Year of the Reign of Finubar

AT FIRST IT was a day like any other. They followed the coastline of Ulthuan as it grew steadily more rugged. The breeze was strong, the weather warmer than Tyrion was used to. It had been getting steadily hotter as they made their way south.

In the mountains of Cothique, winter was still present but here in the south it felt like spring. Tyrion sat on the highest cross-spar on the ship and watched the sun spring over the horizon and the day grow ever warmer. The sea and the sky were of almost matching blue. In the distance, he could see more and more ships, converging from every point on the horizon, all of them heading towards the same goal.

There were mighty elven warships and larger, slower but still sleek cargo clippers. There were ungainly looking vessels that he guessed must belong to humans. There were small fishing boats and huge galleons and every size of sea-going craft in between. He felt as if the *Eagle of Lothern* was becoming part of a great crowd of pilgrims all heading towards the same holy spot. He had been keeping his eyes open for pirates but this interested him just as much. He would not have guessed there were so many ships in the world. Just the vessels he could see and count probably held as many people between them as the population of a city in Cothique.

It was not long before he caught sight of what he was waiting for. On the horizon, rising like the masts of a ship heaving into view, he caught sight of first one huge tower and then another. They were tall and slender, tipped by elongated minarets and swirling spires. Flags fluttered on their tips. He looked over at the sailor occupying the crow's nest. It was Karaya, the pretty one who he had seen many times before. He had not had a chance to talk to her since the storm.

'Lothern?' he asked.

'Your eyes are very good,' Karaya said, once she lowered her spyglass. 'Yes, those are the towers of Lothern. We shall pass through the sea gate this evening – wind, weather and the favour of the gods permitting.'

Tyrion grinned at her. 'The last time I was here, I was a small child. I don't remember much about the place.'

'I am surprised you could forget,' she said with a teasing smile. 'Lothern is the greatest seaport in the world, the greatest city of the elves as well. And I am not just saying that because it's my home. I have seen many cities here and in what the humans call the Old World and in Naggaroth too, although I went there only to burn them.'

'You have seen the land of the Witch King?' Tyrion asked, envying her all of her experiences. He got up and walked along the cross-spar until he reached the crow's nest then dropped in beside her. Their bodies were very close. She did not object. 'What was it like?'

'Cold and bleak and harsh and full of people who did not like us very much. Their hospitality was execrable and we did not stay for long.'

Tyrion laughed. 'I have heard that said.'

'It is nothing but the truth. We would give Malekith and his people a warmer welcome if they chose to come visiting us.'

'I do not think that is very likely.'

'Nor do I. Their land was empty. There were few dark elves to see. I think the druchii are dying out more quickly even than our people.'

'I had heard that Lothern was a lively place.'

'That it is,' she said. There was sadness in her voice. 'But even Lothern is not as populous as it used to be, and it is by far the most populous city in Elvendom.'

'I look forward to seeing it.'

'You will be made welcome there.' She reached out and touched his arm. It was as if a sudden electric shock passed between them. 'Whatever your business is.'

'I am to be presented to the Phoenix King.' He leaned forward, moving his head closer to hers. Their breaths seemed to mingle in the air before them.

'Then you have nothing to fear. There was never a fairer nor more open-handed ruler than Finubar. He is from Lothern you know. The first Phoenix King ever to come from our city and our land. It is a sign of the times.'

'How so?' He looked directly into her eyes.

'You have the strangest eyes,' she said. 'There are gold flecks in them, the colour of the sun.'

'You have very lovely eyes,' he said. 'Like the sea.'

She pulled back a little as if suddenly aware of their closeness. 'You asked me about the times.'

'I did,' he said, knowing that delay before gratification was part of this game.

'Our land grows in power and wealth and influence in proportion to the growth of our trade with the humans. I do not doubt it is the richest city in Ulthuan.'

'Surely wealth isn't everything,' Tyrion said. It was what his father would have said and it seemed right to him.

'No,' the sailor agreed. 'But it counts for a lot. It takes a heap of money to pay for our fleets and build our ships and equip our armies. It is not something to be despised.'

She sounded almost defensive and Tyrion could guess why. The elves of Lothern were often looked down on by the inhabitants of the other elven lands. They were seen as money-grubbing merchants, not proud warriors or noble wizards. Now did not seem like a good time to mention this though.

'It takes a mountain of gold to fight a war,' said Tyrion. 'Caledor the Conqueror said that, and he was one of the greatest generals who ever lived.'

'And he was right. Although it takes swords and spells also.'

'I am going to be a warrior,' said Tyrion.

'I do not doubt it. You have the look of one,' she said. 'You will be made a White Lion at least, if Master Korhien has his way. He is very proud of you.'

Tyrion laughed. He was pleased and flattered to be told this. 'That would be a great honour.'

'It would be, but if it's battle you want you should join the Sea Guard of Lothern. My brother is one and he has fought in many frays.'

'I will be happy to join any company of warriors,' said Tyrion. 'It is what I have always wanted to do.'

'Isha rewards those who follow their dreams, or so I have heard say.'

'I sincerely hope so,' said Tyrion. He stared into the distance intently. He could hardly wait to reach the city. At that moment, it felt as if he only needed to stretch out his hand and whatever he wanted would fall into it.

He reached out for her and pulled her to him. Their lips touched. They shed their clothes swiftly. Soon their naked bodies moved in time to the motion of the ship and the gulls were not the only things who cried out.

'LOOK AT THAT,' said Tyrion barely able to keep the wonder from his voice. To their left, the titanic tower of Lothern lighthouse loomed out of the sea. Its lights already blazed even as the sun started to slide below the horizon.

Ahead of them were the vast sea gates of the city, open at this moment to let ships pass through into the harbour beyond them. They were enormous things, cut out of the huge sea walls of the city, large enough for a tall-masted ship to sail through with room to spare.

'You sound happy,' said Teclis. 'And have sounded so since you climbed down from the crow's nest.'

'I am always happy,' said Tyrion.

'Then you sound even happier than usual.'

Tyrion did not doubt that Teclis knew what had happened between him and the sailor girl. He could sometimes sense such things.

'I am happy to see Lothern,' said Tyrion.

'Of course,' said Teclis sourly. 'That must be it.'

All around them ships moved in stately order towards the gate. There were human vessels with elf pilots aboard to guide them through the correct channels and to give the signals that would prevent the mighty siege engines on the walls from opening fire.

There were elven trading vessels returning from every part of Ulthuan and beyond. Fresh painted, gleaming clippers that traded along the coast moved alongside battered-looking vessels that had made the long haul from the Old World, Araby, Cathay and beyond. Ships from Lothern traded with every part of the planet. There was no sea into which they did not venture, no land they were afraid to visit.

When they emerged from the maze of channels that lay beyond the gate, Tyrion could see the vast harbour. It was large enough to shelter all the fleets of every nation. Even without the sea walls it would have provided a safe haven and deep water anchorage for visiting vessels. The walls sheltered it from the worst of weather as well as all incoming marauders. In the centre of the harbour, upon a plinth as large as a small island, the gigantic statue of Aenarion glowed in the last light of the sunset.

Tyrion looked at it, seeing it as if for the first time. It was a titanic figure, a hundred times the height of a normal elf and carved so brilliantly as to appear almost alive. It was a very disturbing thing for him to gaze upon.

He heard Teclis gasp as he looked at it.

Looking up at the statue of the first Phoenix King, Teclis felt only wonder. It was an astonishing work of art. It captured in full the grandeur of Aenarion and his nobility and his tragic loneliness. The huge stone warrior leaned on a great sword around which flames seemed to writhe. He gazed outward, the line of his vision passing far over the heads of the viewers as if he was looking into the distance and seeing things further and higher than any mere mortal might view.

'Do you think he really looked like that?' Tyrion asked. He sounded genuinely curious.

'They say this statue was made from drawings and paintings saved from before his fall. Those who knew him say it was accurate. Even Morathi remarked it was a likeness to the life, or so the historian Aergeon claims.'

'I don't see the supposed resemblance,' said Tyrion. He sounded piqued. It took Teclis a moment to realise what his brother was talking about. He glanced from the statue to Tyrion and then back to the statue.

'You do look like him,' Teclis said eventually. 'A lot like him.'

'I don't see it.' Tyrion shook his head for emphasis.

'Then you are the only one.'

'His chin is nothing like mine and his ears are a different shape.'

Teclis laughed. 'Those are very small differences.'

'Not to me. They are as clear as day.'

'You have the great privilege of staring at yourself in the mirror for hours every day – such being your vanity, of course – you can spot the small differences that might be invisible to the eye of lesser and less beautiful mortals like myself.'

'They are not small differences,' said Tyrion. He sounded genuinely troubled now. Teclis wondered what was really disturbing him.

Surely it could not be something so simple as the fact that there was a physical resemblance between himself and the first Phoenix King? That was something that would please most elves; should, in fact, please him. He was the one who had always dreamed of being a legendary hero like Aenarion.

Perhaps that was it. Perhaps he was being confronted by the reality of what that really meant carved in stone, a hundred times life size.

Aenarion did not look like the common idea of a hero. His brow was furrowed in thought, and there was a haunted look about his eyes that the sculptors had somehow caught. He did not look merely bold or complacently self-confident or simply brave. He looked lonely and a little lost and burdened by the weight of an awesome responsibility.

Looking on that proud handsome face brought things into focus for Teclis. Here was an elf who had carried a burden too great for any mortal to bear for longer than anyone could be expected to carry it, who had faced daemons within himself as well as outside, who had carried on when all seemed lost and who had, in the end, given his life to save the world and his people. Perhaps Tyrion was coming face to face for the first time with the reality of what it meant to be a hero, and he was finding it not quite what he had expected.

'Is that the Sword of Khaine?' Tyrion asked.

Or perhaps Tyrion felt no such thing, Teclis thought wryly. He now seemed merely curious about a sword. A glance at his brother showed he was still in a thoughtful mood and had changed the subject to try and distract himself.

'No. That blade is never represented anywhere.' said Teclis. 'This sword is Sunfang.'

'The first blade? The one Caledor forged for him in the fires of Vaul's Anvil? The one that blazed with fire and could shoot jets of flame like a dragon?'

'The very same.'

'Do you think it is an accurate representation?'

'Again the historians say yes. The elves took care about these things in those days.'

'Whatever happened to it?'

'No one knows. They say Aenarion gave it to Furion, one of his favoured commanders. It remained in his family for generations. They say Malekith coveted it and schemed to get it on many occasions. They say it was carried off by Nathanis, the last of Furion's line on his great ship, *Farwind*, and was never seen again, for the ship never returned. They think it was lost somewhere on the coasts of the Old World, but no trace of it was ever found.'

'You think the blade still exists?'

'It might.'

'It was made by Caledor. Surely the spells he wove would endure for as long as the Vortex does, at very least.'

'It might be at the bottom of the sea. Or in some dragon's hoard. Or in Malekith's treasure vaults for all we know.'

'It would be something to find it though, would it not?' Tyrion sounded excited and the grim mood that had fallen on him when he looked at the statue of Aenarion was lifting.

'It would indeed. If it still exists it would be one of the few fully functioning artefacts created by Caledor in the world. It would be a thing well worth studying.'

'I was thinking more of using it as a weapon.'

'Naturally! Of what possible use could it be to study the handiwork of the greatest mage that ever lived? Better to bang people over the head with it instead.'

'It is the purpose it was made for.'

'The sheer literal-mindedness of your response is irrefutable.'

'Anyway, I was thinking more of blasting them with its flames. That would be a useful power on the battlefield.'

'There might be something about it that would allow our father to complete his work. If the spells on the sword still function, they might give some clue as to how to remake the armour. They were both made by the same elf. They would both carry the same type of magic.'

Teclis could see that idea really caught Tyrion's imagination. With that thoughtful look on his face he resembled Aenarion more than ever, although a bright, merry Aenarion, not nearly so grim. Perhaps Teclis thought, that was what Aenarion had looked like when he was young.

They continued to look at the statue in silence and in wonder, as they passed into the waters beyond. At some point, the sailor girl Karaya came down and joined them. She did not seem compelled to say anything either.

AROUND THE EDGES of the harbour were many more giant statues all on the same scale as that of Aenarion and all of them sharing something of his statue's power and pride and dignity.

On the western edge of the docks, a massive new statue was rising. Scaffolding still surrounded it. Masons laboured away unremittingly. At the moment it was faceless and somewhat shapeless, but Tyrion knew that within the next few decades it would take on the aspect of Finubar. The statue had only just begun to rise at the start of his reign, a mere ten years ago. It would be some time until it was completed. But what did that matter, Tyrion thought? If there was one thing that elves did not lack it was time.

Vessels lying at anchor crowded the harbour. Many were tied up at the long piers belonging to the great mercantile houses. The flags of their owners flew over ship and warehouse alike. Off to the west, on a walled complex of islands shut off from the rest of the city and accessible only through a series of bridges, walls and small forts was the Foreigners' Quarter, the only part of the city where the humans were allowed to dwell and to wander freely without special permission from the Phoenix King or his representatives.

'I can remember when that place was only the size of a fishing village,' said Karaya. 'Now they say there are almost as many humans living there as there are elves in the city. It will not be long before we are outnumbered in our own land.'

'The humans breed quickly.'

'It is not just that. More and more of them come here every year, seeking to trade. They bring us their goods. They buy our wares and the goods our ships bring in from the far corners of the world.'

'What could they sell us that we could possibly want?' Tyrion asked.

'They bring dwarf-made clockworks from the Worlds Edge Mountains. The dwarfs still refuse to trade with us directly. They bring gold and silver and gems that cannot be found here on Ulthuan. They bring ores and wool and tobacco. They bring preserved meats and grains and books of lore.' She seemed to be working her way through a long list.

Tyrion laughed. 'I believe you. I had not thought there were so many things they had that we could want.'

'I can tell you come from the old kingdoms of Ulthuan, Prince Tyrion. No one from Lothern could possibly think that way.'

In the early dusk, the ship glided towards an enormous warehouse over which the Emeraldsea flag fluttered, propelled by a gentle magical breeze Lady Malene had conjured. The crew dropped anchor. Guards in house colours waved to the arriving sailors.

Gangplanks were run down from the side and longshoremen with hooked staves and hooked knives ran aboard when given permission. The ship's captain bowed to Lady Malene. The horses of Korhien's guard were raised from the hold using levered cranes and dropped kicking onto the pier. Their riders stood nearby waiting to gentle them with words and softly spoken charms. Korhien observed the whole operation with satisfaction. Tyrion noticed that others watched from nearby, and ran off when they saw him watching.

'What was that about?' he asked.

'All of the houses spy on each other. The watchers saw Lady Malene and you and ran off to report to their masters.'

'What possible consequence could our appearance here have?' Tyrion asked.

'Twins of the Blood of Aenarion? It could have incalculable consequences. Who knows what gifts you might possess or what importance you may have in the future?' He seemed to be talking as much to himself as Tyrion and he looked very thoughtful. 'Also Lady Malene and myself are both personages of some consequence in the city, believe it or not.'

Tyrion smiled at the big warrior. 'That I can believe.'

He turned around looking for Karaya to say goodbye, but she was already gone, without taking leave, after the manner of elf maids and strangers they met a-journeying.

THEY TOOK THE road from the docks, joining the evening traffic making its way into the great city. They rode alongside wagons full of silk bales, and fish on ice, and piled high with fruit. They passed vendors selling everything from snacks to bits of jewellery.

The escort bantered with passing traders, purchasing bits of fruit to eat. A fresh-faced elf maid offered Tyrion a peach, causing the warriors to whistle knowingly. Tyrion accepted with all the good grace he could muster and fumbled for his purse.

'A gift,' said the girl, touching his hand gently. Tyrion was glad, for he had no money to offer her anyway.

The inner gates of the city lay ahead. Soldiers in the tabards of the Sea Guard of Lothern watched them enter. It was obvious from their manner that they knew most of the elves coming in, and were known by them in turn. Their easy manner altered perceptibly as the group rode up and Korhien's white lionskin cloak became visible. They stood taller, looked sterner, and saluted smartly. The White Lion responded in kind.

It occurred to Tyrion then that there was being known and being known. The guards knew who Korhien was in a different way from the friendly manner in which they acknowledged the local traders.

The White Lion was obviously an elf of some consequence. It was only natural, he supposed; Korhien was one of the Phoenix King's elite guard. It was more than that though – people looked at him with awe and his name was whispered among strangers as they passed along. It had never occurred to him that Korhien was famous.

He wondered if Malene or any of the others were too but got no hint of it from the demeanour of the people around them. He noticed that he was coming in for a lot of attention as well, then he realised it was his resemblance to that statue in the harbour that was the cause of the attention. He wondered if ever he would be judged here for himself.

They rode beyond the inner walls. Immediately there was a sense of age and beauty. Lampposts lit by incandescent magic kept the night at bay. Long streets wound up tree-clad hills. Many flights of stairs ran up the steeper slopes. There were palaces with towers and spiked minarets. There were fountains everywhere. It seemed like a legion of sculptors had been kept busy for many ages of the world beautifying the city. There were statues of mages and warriors and kings, as well as people he did not recognise but guessed were lawmakers and orators and poets. He pointed out these wonders to his brother; stone worked to look life-like, auras of glamour and ancient warding sorceries protecting the work from the ravages of time and weather.

'It's amazing,' he told Teclis, as they passed a row of towering warriors garbed like Korhien. 'Just think of the work that went into this.'

'Think of the ego and the pride,' said his twin.

'What do you mean?'

'You don't think these were put up just to beautify the streets, do you?'

'What other purpose could they have?'

'Your brother is right, doorkeeper,' said Korhien riding up beside them. 'These statues and fountains were all put up for political reasons. They represent the power and the wealth of the people who paid to have them created. They praise the ancestors of those people, or in many cases the living elves themselves.'

Tyrion laughed.

'I am serious, doorkeeper. Politics is a serious business in Lothern, although you are right to laugh at it. Every one of the statues on the pedestals on the roof of that palace represents a glorious ancestor of the occupants. It reminds the mass of the citizens of the power and greatness of the family, just in case its members have not performed any worthy deeds lately.'

Teclis squinted at Korhien with something like respect. He obviously had never expected to hear such words coming from the White Lion's mouth.

'Not everyone who wields a blade is brainless, Prince Teclis,' said Korhien with the elaborate courtesy with which he always treated Teclis and which Tyrion suspected concealed a genial contempt. 'You will soon find that out in this place. You will need to, if you are to live and prosper here.'

'I would settle just for living at the moment,' said Teclis. 'This odious beast has half-killed me on the ride.'

'Not much further, prince,' said Korhien. 'Soon you will have a bed for the night. In the bosom of your loving family.'

There was a subtle irony in his tone that Tyrion could see Teclis appreciated.

'Where do you come from, Lord Korhien?' Teclis asked. There was an edge to his voice but he was curious too.

'I was born in a barn in the mountains. My father was a freeholder. My mother was the local archery champion. No ancient high blood there, I am afraid. Well, no more than any other elf.'

'You are allied to Emeraldsea though, aren't you?'

'I am allied to Lady Malene,' said Korhien with a wink. 'She is my only entanglement with House Emeraldsea. My loyalty is to the Phoenix King. As is only right for an elf of my position.'

Why was there tension between the two of them, Tyrion wondered? Perhaps his twin sensed a rival for his loyalty. Tyrion had never looked at the matter in that light before. Perhaps Teclis feared being abandoned in this vast city with its palm trees and roof gardens and endless streets full of echoing, half-empty palaces.

Now they were away from the gates, the crowd had thinned out and the streets seemed much emptier. Some of the houses, not too far from the main thoroughfare, had patched and crumbling roofs. Some of the people who gazed at them out of half-shuttered windows had a lean and hungry look to them, although as far as Tyrion knew there was no hunger or famine in Ulthuan.

What then could they be? Were they diseased? Was it true that some of the human plagues could jump to elves? He had heard some of the mountain villagers claim such things, that humans should never have been allowed into Lothern, and should be sent packing back to their homelands.

For himself, Tyrion was curious to see one of the semi-legendary savages. He knew he would find the opportunity soon. They were mostly associated with the dark elves who kept them as slaves and occasionally allied with their daemon-worshipping medicine men. As he had seen, many of them lurked down by the harbour, living in the area of land set aside for them and quarantined from the rest of the city. He found himself unwholesomely curious about them.

They turned a corner and entered a massive plaza. On one side of the square was a huge mansion, made from green-tinged stone, topped with emerald towers. Flags with the emblem of a mighty elf warship on them fluttered above the entrance. Gigantic lanterns set atop corner towers lit the entire street with a green-tinted light.

'You're home,' said Korhien. 'This is the Emeraldsea Palace.'

Tyrion felt overwhelmed by awe. The building was on the scale that he had imagined a city would be built. It looked large enough to house the population of an elven town, and unlike many of the surrounding buildings it did not seem deserted. Small armies of people seemed to come and go from it. Korhien caught his look.

He rubbed thumb and forefinger together. 'Lothern is built on the wealth of its merchants. House Emeraldsea is one of the wealthiest of the merchant houses.'

He rode closer and spoke so quietly that Tyrion was not sure he caught the actual words, 'And the most hated.'

Tyrion knew better than to ask about that now. He resolved that he would have some questions for Korhien later.

CHAPTER TEN

When they passed through the great gates of the House they entered a different world. Green paper-lanterns hung everywhere, illuminating a courtyard that contained a pool the size of a small lake. In that pool were fountains carved in the shape of dolphins and sea-drakes and other legendary creatures of the ocean. Around the courtyard, the mansion rose a full five storeys high.

Retainers in the livery of the House went about their business. Richly dressed elves strolled around discussing tonnages and rates of interest and market prices. Even though the hour was getting late, they conducted business with the intensity of farmers haggling over sheep at a morning market.

Tyrion had no idea what was meant. For all he knew these serious-looking elves could be discussing magic spells. Some of them paid attention to him, particularly the women. They stared quite openly. He smiled and was smiled at in response. The male elves noticing this sometimes glared, sometimes smiled knowingly.

'I see you are going to be popular,' said Lady Malene, riding close to him.

'What makes you think that?' he asked, although he already knew the answer.

'I think you'll find out for yourself soon enough,' she said. 'For the moment, let me enjoy your country-born innocence. I am sure the ladies here will.'

He was conscious of the fact that elf girls in Cothique considered him good-looking, but there was very little to compare himself to: his father, Teclis and the uncouth villagers. But he lacked the sophistication and polish of these city-bred elves. He was not nearly so well-dressed or so well-groomed. It had never occurred to him that the mere fact that he looked different might be considered a point of attraction, not a strike against him. It was something to bear in mind.

Live and learn he told himself. If he was going to survive and thrive here, he was going to have to, and he saw no reason not to enjoy himself at the same time.

Retainers helped the riders dismount, and led away their horses to the stables. The warriors who had escorted them noticed acquaintances around them and shouted greetings and went their separate ways. Soon, only Tyrion and Teclis, and Lady Malene and Korhien were left, standing together in a small group near one of the fountains.

Korhien looked around at them. He smiled broadly. 'I must go soon and present myself to Finubar. He will want to know I have returned.' He leaned forward and kissed Malene. He stretched out his hand and clasped Tyrion's arm just below the elbow. Tyrion returned the gesture. He was surprised. It was the grip that warriors used for comrades and for friends. He bowed to Teclis and then turned and strode away.

Tyrion paused for a moment and considered what had just been said. He had known Korhien was a White Lion, but it was one thing knowing that and another hearing him speak so casually of reporting to Finubar. Tyrion wondered what he was going to tell the Phoenix King about himself and Teclis.

From under the arched walkway at the west end of the palace, Tyrion noticed a small group of extremely well-dressed young elves were studying him. They wore the long loose robes favoured by the upper class at leisure, all trimmed with silk and gold.

They were attempting to look nonchalant but he sensed that they were more interested in him and his brother than they would have cared to admit. He smiled easily and waved at them. They did not wave back. He laughed, honestly not caring, and noticed that Lady Malene was watching him from the corner of her eye. A young elf girl in the tunic of a retainer approached. The girl looked at Tyrion as if seeing a god.

'Yes, indeed,' Malene said. 'You will get on very well here.'

The girl whispered something to her. She looked suddenly a lot more serious. 'Your grandfather will see you now,' she said. 'You would do well to watch your manners around him. He is not as tolerant as I am.'

'WELCOME TO MY home,' said Lord Emeraldsea. He did not look very welcoming, Tyrion thought. He looked as if he were inspecting a couple of very dubious cargoes he was considering investing in.

'Thank you for having us here,' said Tyrion, with all the politeness he could manage. Teclis murmured something inaudible.

Lord Emeraldsea sat at a huge desk piled high with documents awaiting his inspection and signature. His study was on the topmost floor of the house. Out of his window, he had a fine view of the harbour below. His balcony held a bronze telescope on a metal tripod. Tyrion guessed he took a proprietorial interest in the ships arriving in the harbour.

Lord Emeraldsea was tall and thin and quite the oldest elf that Tyrion could ever remember seeing. Blue veins were visible in the ancient hands that toyed with a small set of scales. His hair was the colour of spun silver, his eyes cold and grey as the northern sea before a storm.

It took Tyrion a moment to accept the fact that this was his grandfather. In the elf's manner there was no real suggestion of any familial relationship. There was distance, the implication of hostility, perhaps a suggestion of contempt or dislike.

Lord Emeraldsea rose from his hard wooden chair, walked round the desk and stood before them. He walked with a very straight back and the same air of command Tyrion had noticed in Captain Joyelle. There was something in Lord Emeraldsea's manner suggestive of the sea. He was very tall, taller even than Tyrion. For the first time in a very long time, Tyrion experienced the sensation of being looked down upon. Cold eyes measured him, calculated his worth and placed it on the scales at the back of his grandfather's mind.

'You do look like him,' he said, and Tyrion had no doubt as to who *he* was. 'You look a little like my poor daughter too. I am pleased to see that you have grown up into such a fine figure of an elf.'

He strode over to Teclis and loomed over him. 'I wish I could say the same for you.'

'Why don't you try, out of politeness,' said Teclis with poisonous sweetness.

Lord Emeraldsea looked taken aback. Tyrion could tell he was not used to being mocked. His smile was wintery and not without humour. Like many people before him he was being forced to reassess his opinion of the sickly young elf standing before him. The two of them locked gazes and the air fairly crackled between them. Here were two elves of very different ages and enormously strong wills.

'You look like my daughter,' Lord Emeraldsea said. 'And like your father. But you seem somewhat... firmer of character.'

Tyrion wondered what his grandfather meant by that. In any case, Lord Emeraldsea did not seem displeased to discover that Teclis was not some sort of feeble half-wit. 'I like that, lad, but don't push my goodwill too far.'

'I am a prince,' said Teclis.

Lord Emeraldsea's stare was cold, a captain looking at a disrespectful cabin boy. 'That remains to be determined. We will know soon enough if you are blessed or cursed by the Blood of Aenarion.'

There was a strong emotion in his voice when he said that that Tyrion did not recognise at all. He followed the old elf's gaze to the wall behind him and saw that he was looking at a portrait of their mother. He looked back at Lord Emeraldsea's lined face and he knew then the emotion was grief. Lord Emeraldsea caught Tyrion's glance and for a moment there was flicker of genuine emotion between them.

'It's an ill thing for a parent to outlive a child,' Lord Emeraldsea said. Tyrion could see that took Teclis off guard. His mouth shut just as he was about to say something sardonic again. Perhaps he understood that their appearance here must be difficult for their grandfather.

'My other daughter tells me that you have a gift for sorcery. Let us hope you live long enough to enjoy the use of it.'

Tyrion wondered if there was threat implicit in his grandfather's words. Perhaps it was only a warning. They were in a place now inhabited by elves that would kill you if you provoked them. Tyrion was grateful for one thing. No one would ever call his brother out to duel because of rudeness. There would be no honour in it. Perhaps the old elf was merely making a reference to Teclis's sickliness.

Lord Emeraldsea returned to his desk and sat down. He lifted a quill, sharpened the end with a small knife, dipped it in his inkwell and made an inscription on one of his scrolls, as if acknowledging the delivery of a cargo with a receipt.

'Rooms have been prepared for you,' he said. 'Go to them.'

It was clear they had been dismissed. A servant appeared from somewhere to show them out. Tyrion had no idea how she had been summoned.

'THIS IS VERY nice,' said Tyrion, looking around the chamber.

Very nice was something of an understatement; the apartment they had been installed in seemed as large as their father's villa and considerably more luxurious. It had windows of polished crystal. Murals depicting sea-scenes covered the walls of the reception chamber and numerous busts of proud-looking elves stood on columns in the alcoves.

There was a small library of books, mostly about the sea and ancient lands. The furnishings were lovely and lovingly crafted. A small table of Sapherian dragonwood sat in the middle of the reception room. A number of carved chairs were placed around it. They were well-upholstered and comfortable in a way that nothing had been back home.

Tyrion had taken the bedroom that overlooked the street outside. It contained a large bed, and more books, a mirror and paintings of ships and sea battles executed by a painter with a gift for detail. The bed was massive and draped with a gauze curtain for keeping out night-biting insects. There was a balcony with a fine view of the street two storeys below. When he stood on it he had wondered if this was how the Phoenix King felt when he looked down on his subjects.

Teclis was installed in the bedroom that faced the inner courtyard. It was quieter and cooler and smaller. There was a painting of a sea-wizard summoning a wind to propel a ship across the ocean. It was the presence of this painting more than anything that had influenced his brother's choice. Teclis lay on the bed exhausted, but his gaze was bright, and Tyrion could tell he had absorbed everything about their surroundings, and would remember it.

'What do you think?' Tyrion asked. He was excited. There were chambers in the apartment he had no more than glanced at. Teclis even had his own sitting room which Tyrion had not seen yet. Apparently it had a mirror in it. This was luxury indeed.

'I think our relatives are very rich,' Teclis replied.

'As ever, brother, your powers of observation astonish me.'

'I wonder why they feel so compelled to show interest in us now. They paid no attention whatsoever for nearly sixteen years.'

'I am guessing the fact that we are summoned to the court of the Phoenix King may have something to do with it.'

'Of course, Tyrion, but why did Lord Emeraldsea send Lady Malene and her riders and a White Lion? Why draw attention to our presence this way?' He appeared to have been giving the matter some thought since their ride through the city.

'Why not?' said a girl's voice from the door.

Both twins looked around. A young elf maiden stood there, garbed in a simple but expensive gown of greenish silk trimmed with cloth of gold. Her hair was elaborately coiffed. Her features were extraordinarily beautiful. 'Everyone knows about you anyway, or will do soon. You are our kin. Whatever we do and however we treat you, it will be talked about.'

'Hello,' said Tyrion, smiling.

'I thought it was polite to knock,' said Teclis.

'I thought it was impolite to be ungrateful to your hosts,' said the girl seemingly unabashed by his tone.

'So we are supposed to be grateful to you?' said Teclis, caustic as ever.

'My name is Tyrion,' said Tyrion. 'The rude, ungrateful one is my twin, Teclis. And you, our impolite host, would be...?'

He said it without malice and both Teclis and the girl laughed.

'I am Liselle. I am your cousin. I came up to welcome you but the door was open and I overheard you speaking. I was wondering what you were like, so I listened.'

'We don't have a lot of experience with great houses, I am afraid,' said Tyrion. He did not feel at any disadvantage because of this. He would learn his way around. But he felt the need to explain the situation so there were no misunderstandings.

'So I gathered,' said Liselle. She walked over and looked up at him. Her eyes were a very beautiful shade of green. Her skin was very pale, her beauty willowy. Tyrion reached out and moved a strand of her hair that had come loose as if it was the most natural thing in the world. She did not object. Teclis stared.

'Has your curiosity been satisfied?' he asked.

'Not yet. I have never met twins before. You are not what I expected. I thought you were supposed to be identical.'

'Not all twins are identical. Those are quite rare.'

'There have been only twenty-five recorded pairs of identical twins in elven history,' said Teclis. 'Out of three hundred and fifteen recorded births of twins.'

It was the sort of thing he would know. His knowledge of the obscure facts of genealogy was incredible and he forgot nothing. Liselle looked less than impressed. She kept looking up into Tyrion's eyes.

A handclap announced another visitor. Tyrion saw Lady Malene standing in the doorway. 'Liselle, pray give our guests some time to settle in before disturbing them with your curiosity.'

'She was not disturbing us,' said Tyrion.

'Ah, but she will,' said Lady Malene. 'Liselle, if you would be so kind as to leave us alone for a moment. There are things I need to talk about with your cousins.'

'Yes, mother,' said Liselle, departing with good grace.

'WHAT IS YOUR wish, mistress?' the chief cultist asked. He was a tall, stately elf of considerable dignity. He had emerged from the group of twenty or so naked elves gathered in the grove of pleasure.

N'Kari wore the form of a beautiful elf maiden with hooves instead of feet and small curling horns emerging from her head. Her appearance and sensuous aura caused lust and a desire to obey in dedicated followers of the Lord of Pleasure.

And these were certainly all elves who followed the Way of All Pleasures. She had sensed their corruption from afar, smelled their decadence like the odour of a rich and corrupt night-blooming orchid. She had surprised them and filled them with wonder and terror by materialising at their orgiastic rites to celebrate their devotion to Slaanesh.

These were some of those who had been summoned by N'Kari's original dream-spell who had made their way into the mountains seeking to answer its call. N'Kari smelled her spell on them like the last lingering remnants of some old perfume. Their rite had already provided a morsel of sustenance, and before this night was over they would provide a great deal more.

N'Kari studied their leader closely in the light of the moons. 'I require your obedience,' she said.

She sensed their confusion. These elves had been playing a dangerous game, performing rites of pleasure for their own gratification, thinking that there was no price to be paid, that nothing would come in answer to their summons. They had discovered they were wrong and they were at once exalted and terrified by what they had done.

'We are your slaves, mistress. We live only to abase ourselves at your feet and give our lives for your slightest pleasure.' At the moment, the elf believed this. He had no choice under the impact of N'Kari's presence. The nodding of heads, licking of lips and shining bright eyes of the rest of the cultists told of their agreement.

N'Kari looked upon them and found everything to her liking. She needed an army to work her vengeance, and here she had the core of one. It was a small start to be sure but it was a beginning on which she could build, and she would make the elves of Ulthuan tremble when they heard her name before it was over.

'What is your name?' N'Kari asked.

'Elrion, great mistress.'

'And your purpose?'

'I exist only to obey you, great mistress,' said Elrion.

'I know,' replied N'Kari. 'Come now. We have matters to attend to nearby. There are those I have ancient business with.'

CHAPTER ELEVEN

'You are in a different world now,' said Malene. She glanced around to make sure the door was shut and spoke a Word. Tyrion felt as if the lightest of breezes had passed over him. Teclis cocked his head to one side, suddenly intensely curious. 'There are some things you need to know and some words that need to be spoken plainly.'

'And you are going to speak them,' said Teclis.

'I am, and I will thank you not to use your haughty tone with me, Prince Teclis. I like you but I expect you to treat me with the same respect I extend to you. We are not on the ship any more, not on a journey. Things are more formal here.' She sounded almost as if she regretted that fact.

Teclis looked surprised, not so much at her manner but by the admission she liked him. He was not used to that. He smiled, suddenly looking very young and intensely vulnerable.

'You are guests in this house. I would ask you, Tyrion, to remember that. Some of your cousins are at a dangerous age and you are a very handsome youth. I am sure you will find plenty of opportunities for amorous adventure outwith the confines of your immediate kinswomen.'

'I'll try and remember that,' he said.

'You would do well to do so. Your grandfather does not like the harmony of his household disturbed.'

'We did not ask to be here,' said Teclis. He was back to his usual sullen self now.

'No, but the Phoenix King requested the pleasure of your company and here you are. We must now see to it that you are suitably prepared for entering the royal presence.'

'What do you mean?'

'We must see that you do not disgrace us in his presence.'

'You mean to teach us manners?' There was an edge to Teclis's voice. He sounded as if he was getting ready to unleash his temper again.

'I intend that you should learn protocol.'

'I am already familiar with how one addresses the Phoenix King,' Teclis said with superlative arrogance.

'There is a difference between knowing what to say and knowing when and how to say it.'

'On formal occasions he is addressed as Blessed of Asuryan. Under some circumstances, most notably when haste might be required, he is to be called Chosen One, or simply Chosen. On high holy days, he is known as Fireborn. The last sentence of any address on such days is always: Watch over us Vessel of the Sacred Fire. Normally a simple sire will do if you are addressed in conversation.'

Lady Malene looked impressed. 'How many different forms of address are there?'

'Twenty-one. Shall I recite them?'

'No. I am sure you will astonish me with that phenomenal memory of yours. Tyrion, can you match your brother's scholarship?'

Tyrion was sure she already knew the answer to that, but she was making a point.

'I am afraid not. I have never had much of a gift for it,' he said.

'You will need to learn them. You will need to know the titles of all the officials at court. You will need to know how to respectfully address his Sacred Majesty under every circumstance that might arise. You will need to learn the same things concerning the Everqueen for that matter.'

Tyrion groaned. 'When am I ever likely to meet the Everqueen?'

'Don't worry, brother, I will help you,' said Teclis.

'That's what I am worried about,' said Tyrion. 'It will be as much fun for the both of us as me teaching you how to use a sword.'

'There are times when the right words and the right manner are as useful as being able to use a blade,' said Lady Malene. 'And they can be as deadly under the right circumstances.'

She sounded very serious. Tyrion looked abashed. She laughed.

'Be grateful you did not grow up surrounded by this protocol, Prince Tyrion. You at least have had some time in which to be free of it.' She sounded as if she envied him, which surprised Tyrion.

After a moment, she said, 'There are some clothes in the wardrobes. They will be a poor fit but wear them for the moment. In a few minutes, the house tailors will visit you and see you are more suitably accoutred. Your grandfather wishes you to be dressed as is fitting for your station. So do I, for that matter.'

After she had gone Tyrion looked in the wardrobe. The most beautiful clothes he had ever seen hung there. He felt almost embarrassed when he put them on. Looking at himself in the mirror was like looking at a stranger.

There was another knock on the door. The tailors had arrived.

THE WOMAN STARED at Tyrion and then walked around him, studying him with intense, more-than-professional interest. She walked over to where Teclis sat and gestured for him to stand. She nodded to herself twice, made some notes in a wax tablet with her stylus and then produced a cord of silk in which regular knots had been set. She used this to measure Tyrion's chest size, his waist and the length of his leg. She nodded approvingly then went over to Teclis and did the same thing although she seemed less pleased with the results. All of this having been done, she left the room.

A male elf entered this time, placed a piece of parchment under each of Tyrion's feet, and drew a line around them in charcoal. He too measured Tyrion's thigh and ankle girth, did the same for Teclis and then left.

A jeweller arrived and used small copper rings to take the measure of their fingers, and copper torques to take the measure of their necks, and copper bracers to take the measure of their wrists. He too made notes in a wax tablet and departed.

A girl arrived, sat them down, and then began to cut their hair with a long razor and some scissors. When she had finished Tyrion studied himself in the mirror. His hair was no longer long and unkempt. It was combed out and thick and looked much better.

Teclis's dark hair was cut close in a way that revealed his fine pointed ears and enhanced his gaunt, sallow features. He looked almost handsome, or would have if there had been more weight on him. The moon shone in through the window and in its light there was something skeletal about him, something sinister. Its gleam caught in his eyes and they seemed for a moment to burn with internal fire. Just for an instant his brother looked like a stranger. It was the haircut and the unfamiliar clothes and setting, Tyrion told himself, but could not quite believe it.

Teclis was different now. The journey, the city, the meetings with strangers, the promise of being taught magic had all changed him incrementally. Tyrion found it easy to imagine that some day the sum total of all these tiny changes would make his brother into a complete stranger. It also occurred to him that the same thing might be happening to him, in Teclis's eyes, although he himself felt no different.

'You have an odd expression on your face, brother,' said Teclis.

'I was just thinking the same about you,' said Tyrion, making a joke of it.

'I was thinking that one day all of the small changes we undergo might make us into total strangers.'

Tyrion did not need to tell him that he had been having exactly the same thought. He knew then that his twin already understood that. Teclis had always been more perceptive about these things than he.

'It will take more than a change of clothes and a change of hair-style to do that,' said Tyrion.

'Those are just the start,' said Teclis. 'They have already started trying to teach us manners, how to behave, what we must do. They want to remake us for their own purposes.'

'The trick is going to be finding out what those purposes really are,' said Tyrion.

'I am sure they will tell us in their own good time.'

Tyrion was not at all sure of that. Still, at least they were safe for the moment. It did not look like their lives were in any immediate danger.

LOOKING OUT OF the window, Lady Fayelle thought it was a lovely night. The moon was bright. The stars were shining. Unable to keep still she paced across her room. She was excited. Soon she was to be married. Soon she would be leaving her father's home forever. She was saddened by the prospect of leaving her aged parent alone in his gloomy old palace.

She had asked him to come and live with her new husband in Lothern. He had refused, saying he was too old and too set in his ways to move now. And he really loved this old place. She understood that. He had spent most of his long life here, had raised his children and buried his wife within its grounds. And it was all that was left to him, that and his pride in his ancient lineage.

Sometimes she thought he was a little too proud. He thought her new husband beneath her. His kin were merchants from Lothern and his family had been mere freeholders while her ancestors had ruled a kingdom and married into the Blood of Aenarion himself.

Her father was proud but you could not eat pride, nor repair ancient buildings with it nor pay the required number of retainers unless they too were like you, old and with nowhere else to go.

Her father understood these things, she knew, but he was too set in his ways to change. It had fallen on her to improve the fortunes of her house by marrying well, and to tell the truth, she had found it no hardship. She took out her locket and opened it and stared at his picture. Moralis, her husband-to-be, was as good and kind an elf as one could hope to meet, and he was handsome too.

More than that he brought a dash of the swashbuckling adventurer with him, for he was a sea captain and had travelled to many far places while helping make his family's fortune. She liked him, and he liked her, and there was love there, which was not something she had ever thought to find, growing up as she had in this remote place far from the centres of civilisation.

She counted it a blessing of Isha that he had bought the land beside their estate. It had proven even more of a blessing that he had taken to her when he had first seen her.

She thought she heard a noise somewhere in the gloom. She went to the window and looked out into the night once more. She could not see anything.

She was not frightened. There was nothing really threatening in this part of Ulthuan. No wolves prowled here. No monsters strayed down from the mountains. No marauders had made it this far inland in a couple of centuries. The worst things she had ever heard about were some rumours of the spread of the old cults of luxury in the area, and those were most likely just Elrion and his friends playing at being decadent, and frightening themselves with the thought of the old dark magics.

She heard a stone bang against the shutter of her window. She knew who it was without having to look. Only one elf had ever done that. She opened the shutter. As if summoned by the thought of him, Elrion emerged from the gloom. There was something wild in his appearance. He looked different although she could not quite put her finger on how and she had known him since childhood.

'What is it, Elrion? What is wrong?' she asked. She thought she heard some large animal growling in the dark behind him. Perhaps some wild thing had strayed into the area after all, and he had fled before it. That might explain the wildness of his appearance.

'In the name of Isha run down and open the door, it's following me,' he said, but he said it quietly, as if he did not want anyone to hear. Perhaps he was afraid of attracting the creature's attention. She thought about ringing the bell to summon the servants but realised it would be faster just to go down herself and open the gate as she had done when they were younger. She raced down the stairs, threw the bolts on the gate and opened it.

'Quickly, come in,' she said, peering past his shoulder to see if whatever it was was still out there. She thought she caught sight of glowing eyes glittering in the gloom. There was something terrifying about them. He stepped passed her into the courtyard. As he did so, old Peteor emerged from inside the mansion. He carried a bow in his blue-veined old hand and he had an arrow knocked and ready.

'I thought I heard the bolts being thrown,' he said. 'What is it? Who would come calling at this time of night?'

'It is only Elrion,' Fayelle said. 'Some night-stalking beast followed him here.'

'It's an odd time of the night to come calling,' said Peteor. He had never liked Elrion, and his liking had grown less as tales of Elrion's debauched lifestyle and wild parties had become common knowledge in the neighbourhood.

'I have urgent news for Prince Faldor,' said Elrion. He strode over to Peteor with his hands outstretched. 'It concerns the wedding. It's not going to happen.'

'Has there been an accident? Has something happened to Moralis?' Fayelle asked.

'What else could bring him at such a time of the night,' said Peteor. 'News brought after dark is usually bad news.'

'I am afraid Peteor is right,' said Elrion. He seemed to slap Peteor on the back. The old elf coughed and lurched forwards. Red stuff emerged from his nose and lips, and something bubbled in his chest, causing him to have trouble breathing.

'Are you sick, Peteor?' Fayelle asked. Peteor struggled to say something. He reached up and tried to grab Elrion who leaned against him and moved his arm again. Peteor bent double and more red erupted from his chest. Fayelle ran over to him 'What is wrong?' she asked, reaching out to touch him. She was shocked at how wet he was and how red her hand came away, then suddenly in a rush, she realised what was happening. 'You are bleeding,' she said. Frothy red bubbles erupted from Peteor's mouth as he tried to speak. His eyes opened wide and he slumped forward.

'He's dead,' said Elrion.

Fayelle felt sick and panicky and she did not quite understand what was going on even when she saw the red knife in Elrion's hand.

'And I am afraid everyone else here soon will be. Come now, there is someone I must introduce you to.' He twisted her arm painfully up her back and pushed her towards the gateway, seemingly not caring any more that her screams were rousing the house. Lights were coming on everywhere and she could hear retainers moving within.

From out of the shadows, a massive and sinisterly beautiful humanoid figure emerged. It was the most handsome-looking elf she had ever seen, except for the fact that its feet ended in hooves, one arm ended in a crab-like pincer and small curling goat horns emerged from its forehead. She opened her mouth to scream and took in a lungful of oddly calming, musky perfume. She was suddenly filled with the urge to reach out and stroke the goat-horned elf's naked flesh. He seemed to understand this and smiled back. It was a most winning smile.

'Greetings, Blood of Aenarion,' he said in the most thrilling voice imaginable. 'You should be pleased. You will be the first to know my vengeance. And you will be the first whose soul I offer screaming to my god.'

THE NEXT MORNING, when he awoke, Tyrion found a pile of new clothes on the table in his room. Under the table was a complete set of new footwear. In a sandalwood box was a necklace, a torque and a pair of sunstone rings. He donned all the apparel including a very fine green cloak trimmed with cloth of gold and studied himself in the mirror. He looked every inch the asur prince, he thought, but he did not look like himself.

As he studied himself, a servant entered, without knocking. 'Korhien Ironglaive requests your presence in the courtyard, Prince Tyrion. It appears he would like to give you a lesson in swordplay.'

'Please tell Korhien I will be right down.' He began to change out of his new clothes into the old ones he had used on the journey. He did not want such beautiful things ruined in weapons practice. The servant watched him uncomprehendingly for a few moments, lifted a shirt and a pair of britches and said, 'I think you will find these were intended for you to wear at practice. I was told to take away all of your old clothes and burn them.'

Tyrion laughed. 'I shall wear what you suggest but don't burn my old clothes. Have them washed and mended and brought back to me. I may have some use for them yet.'

'As you wish, sir.' The servant looked confused. He could not imagine what Tyrion wanted these rags for. Tyrion decided it was better that way. He had an idea of doing something for which they might be useful. He was not sure he wanted his relatives to find that out yet.

CHAPTER TWELVE

'GOOD OF YOU to join us,' said Korhien Ironglaive. The big elf was stripped to his tunic and looked as if he had just finished some hard sparring with wooden swords. A group of younger-looking elves stood nearby with their weapons in the guard positions.

Korhien tossed him a wooden practice blade. Tyrion caught it easily by the hilt as it tumbled through the air. 'If you would be so kind as to demonstrate your technique in the practice circle.'

Tyrion saw that a chalk circle had been marked in the centre of the courtyard. He strode into it, sword held ready. Korhien coughed. The other students laughed. Tyrion looked at Korhien.

'You don't lack for heart, lad,' Korhien said. 'I am not so sure about your wisdom but your courage is impressive.'

He indicated a stand which contained a suit of padded armour just like the others were wearing. Tyrion smiled at his mistake, strode over and laced it up. He did not need to be shown how. It was as if he was born knowing how to tie the stays in the correct way. When this was complete he returned to the circle.

Korhien said, 'Atharis! You shall spar with Prince Tyrion.'

'As you wish, sir,' said a blond haired, good looking elf, stepping forward into the practice circle. He was not as tall as Tyrion, but he was well-muscled and lithe. His nose had been broken and not badly set, and his mouth had a cruel twist to it. He looked as if he took this whole thing very seriously.

'I shall try not to hurt you,' he said in a very low voice. His tone implied that he meant to do exactly the opposite of what he said.

'That's very kind of you,' said Tyrion. He moved more slowly and clumsily than he normally would. He saw Atharis sneer, as Tyrion deliberately held the practice blade incorrectly. 'I shall endeavour to do the same.'

'Begin,' said Korhien.

Within three strokes, Tyrion had put Atharis on his back. The other student seemed very slow to Tyrion and his moves very predictable. Korhien looked at him from the corner of his eye.

'As you can see, Prince Tyrion is not quite as simple as he chooses to appear,' he said.

Korhien strode forward into the circle and spoke to the watching group of students. 'In case you are in any doubt, Prince Tyrion has exceptional gifts. You would do well not to underestimate him as Atharis did. There is a lesson here about combat in general. Don't judge your foe by what you are told about him. Don't judge him by his appearance. Don't judge him by what he says about himself. Judge him by how he fights against you. You might live longer if you do.'

He gestured for Tyrion to leave the circle and join the other students. Tyrion did so, helping Atharis up as he went. The other elf grinned at him ruefully.

'You are all here to learn to fight,' said Korhien. 'I am taking time to teach you. There are not so many elves that we can afford to lose any. Bear that in mind. Every asur life lost is a terrible blow to our people and we can ill afford such losses. It is your duty to see that you live. It is your duty to see that you are fit and that you are capable. It is your duty to learn from your mistakes and master your weapons. All of you, and I include the gifted Prince Tyrion in this statement, have a good deal to learn, but you have the time to learn it, and learn it you shall. I intend to see to that.'

'Still giving that same old speech, Korhien,' said a mocking voice from under the colonnaded arches.

'Why not, Prince Iltharis? It is a good one and there is truth in it.' Korhien did not seem to mind the mockery.

Tyrion studied Prince Iltharis as he came into view. He was a tall, slender elf, dark-haired and fair-skinned with piercing grey eyes and a languid manner. He was garbed in a very elaborate, scholarly fashion. He carried a bunch of scrolls negligently under one arm.

He sauntered over to inspect the students, smiled and bowed to Korhien. 'Indeed it is, and who can disagree with the sentiment?'

'I sense that you do.'

'Not in the slightest, my dear fellow – I just wish you would express them less pompously and with slightly more originality.'

'I see you are determined to undermine my authority with my students, Iltharis.'

'You were doing that quite well enough without my help, Korhien. I am surprised that they could keep from laughing at you.'

Tyrion was surprised that an elf as fierce as Korhien would put up with this banter, but he saw that the White Lion was not put out by it in the least, in fact appeared to enjoy it.

'Perhaps you would care to instruct them instead.'

'I am not in the least suited to being a teacher of weapons,' said Iltharis. 'Poetry or history are more my forte. When it comes to teaching, anyway.'

'That is something we can both agree upon, my friend. Perhaps you would care to leave me to giving the lessons then?'

'Indeed. Perhaps I shall remain and watch. I might pick up a few pointers.'

Korhien laughed.

'I somehow doubt that, Prince Iltharis, but you are welcome to remain.'

'Well, I am interested in your latest pupil anyway. I am writing another monograph on the Blood of Aenarion.'

Tyrion spend the next few hours sparring, losing himself in physical activity, learning everything Korhien had to say. He was aware all the time that Prince Iltharis was studying him with a watchful eye. He found that he was getting a little bit tired of being inspected so closely all the time.

Prince Iltharis eventually said, 'Your new pupil is quite exceptional, Korhien.'

'Indeed,' said the White Lion. Tyrion was annoyed at this fop passing judgement on him.

'Perhaps you would care to try a turn with the blades,' Tyrion said. Iltharis looked at him and smiled mockingly.

'It is not something I would usually do, but in your case I shall make an exception.'

He sauntered over to the sword rack, examined the wooden blades like a connoisseur selecting a bottle of wine and picked up the one that he liked the most. A moment later he was strapping on the practice armour.

Tyrion could not help but notice that for all his languid manner there was muscle there. Iltharis stretched like a big cat to get the kinks out of his muscles, saluted Korhien and then turned to face Tyrion. 'When you are ready, young prince,' he said. The rest of the students watched with interest. Some of them smiled. One or two laughed. Tyrion wondered what he had gotten himself into.

He approached Prince Iltharis, sword held ready. They exchanged two blows and his sword was out of his hand. Tyrion replayed what had happened in his mind. Iltharis had used a similar trick to the one Korhien had played when first they duelled, but had done it much faster. His speed of reflex was uncanny. Tyrion suspected that for the first time in his life he had encountered someone even quicker than himself.

'That was a pretty trick with which you disarmed me. I will wager you could not do it again.'

Iltharis raised an eyebrow. 'What will you wager?'

Tyrion felt his embarrassment deepen. He owned nothing, not even the clothes he was wearing. 'It was a figure of speech,' he said lamely.

'Prince Iltharis is also very wealthy,' said Korhien. 'Or his family is, which comes to the same thing.'

'Your plebeian roots are showing, Korhien. One would think you almost jealous.'

'The only thing I envy you, prince, is your skill with a blade.'

'Well, it's always nice to be envied for something. But I was talking to your young friend here about the terms of a wager.'

'I have nothing to offer,' said Tyrion, thinking as always that honesty was for the best. 'As I said, it was a figure of speech.'

'I will lend him a gold piece,' said Korhien.

'Are you sure, my friend? I know it is a large sum of money for you.'

'I do not want it,' said Tyrion.

'You may not have the wealth of Aenarion, but you have some of his pride,' said Iltharis. 'I can set a term for the wager that I believe will be acceptable.'

'Go on,' said Tyrion.

'If I win, you will do me one favour when I request it. If you win, I will do the same.'

'Fair enough,' said Tyrion.

'I would not be so quick to accept, doorkeeper,' said Korhien. 'You do not know what the favour might prove to be.'

'Nothing dishonourable or hurtful to your ancient pride,' said Iltharis. 'Be sure of it.'

'Very well,' said Tyrion.

They fell into fighting stances again. This time Tyrion's attack was less reckless and he watched for Iltharis to try the same disarming technique. When it came, he was ready for it. His response was swift and sure and almost successful. Instead of being disarmed himself, he almost disarmed Iltharis.

Only the other's cat-like quickness of reflex saved him. He sprang backwards, aimed a blow at Tyrion's knee, paralysing it and then knocked him off his feet with a powerful blow to the chest.

Ruefully, Tyrion picked himself up. His leg felt numb from the nerve-strike. 'I guess I lost the bet,' he said.

Iltharis shook his head. 'No. You won it. I could not disarm you with the same technique again. You were quite right.' He raised the wooden blade in an intricate salute and then returned it to the rack. 'I congratulate you, Korhien. Your pupil is everything you claimed and more.'

Tyrion glanced at the White Lion. It seemed that he and Iltharis had been talking about him in private and Iltharis's appearance was not mere happenstance.

'It is good of you to say so.'

'No, Korhien, it is honest of me to say so. Now I must thank you for an interesting morning's entertainment and bid you adieu.' With that Prince Iltharis bowed and strolled away across the courtyard.

The other pupils were looking at Tyrion now with something like awe. It appeared that Prince Iltharis was well-known and respected among the young warriors of the Emeraldsea Palace.

'Who was he?' Tyrion asked Atharis, after Iltharis was out of sight.

'Prince Iltharis is one of the deadliest swords in all Ulthuan. He has killed more elves in duels than anyone in living memory. Some whisper that he is an assassin for his House.'

'An assassin?'

'Sometimes duels are fought over more than points of honour. Sometimes they are fought to remove political inconveniences or as part of political manoeuvres.'

Tyrion stared at him for a long moment then smiled. 'I start to understand why you all take this practice so seriously.'

'It is, as Korhien said, a matter of life and death. Sometimes it has larger consequences for our House and our families. I doubt you have very much to worry about though.'

'I do if Prince Iltharis comes after me. Or anyone nearly as good.'

'There are very few that good in Ulthuan and his House is allied to our own.'

'Alliances can always be broken,' said Tyrion.

'I see you have a swift grasp of politics as well as how to use a blade,' said Atharis. 'We could be useful friends to each other.'

Tyrion extended his hand and clasped the others'. 'I can always use a friend,' he said.

TECLIS WOKE TO find Malene sitting by his bed. She looked a little worried.

'What happened?' he asked. The last thing he could remember was watching Tyrion leave for his fencing lesson. He had walked over to the table and bent over to pick something up. Then he had felt dizzy...

His heart sank. It seemed like his illness had returned.

'You were taken ill,' she said. She looked rueful. 'I think you have been over-exerting yourself recently. You have not recovered as much as you appeared to have. It seems I am not quite as good an alchemist as I thought.'

'Yes, you are. I have never felt better in my life than the past few days,' Teclis said.

'Nonetheless you must be careful not to push yourself too hard. You are still far from healthy.'

'I believe I am in a position to understand that,' said Teclis, gesturing at his recumbent form. Malene smiled. There was a knock on the door, an odd double tap that sounded unlike any knock Teclis had heard before. Malene seemed to recognise it. She made a face.

'Come in,' she said.

A tall, lithe looking elf entered. His hair was dark and his eyes a piercing grey. His skin was pale compared to the elves of Lothern. His manner was quite exquisite. His clothing had the elegance of the dandy. A faint lingering perfume billowed in advance.

'Ah, the delightful Lady Malene. I was told I would find you here,' he said. 'And this will be your new pupil. Let us hope that he is as good a student of magic as his brother is of the blade.'

'Prince Iltharis,' said Lady Malene smoothly. 'It is a pleasure to see you as always.' She did not sound as if it was a pleasure. Her expression was reserved as it normally was.

'I am Prince Iltharis,' said the elf, bowing formally and smiling. It was a very charming smile, open and friendly. 'Since Lady Malene has not seen fit to introduce us, perhaps you would do me the favour of telling me your name.'

'I am Prince Teclis.'

'Excellent. As I suspected, you are the brother of that splendid specimen down in the courtyard.'

'I heard you were teaching him a lesson with the sword,' said Lady Malene.

'News travels fast around here. He does not need too many lessons from me, or anyone else for that matter. He is a natural with the blade.'

Prince Iltharis brought a chair over to beside the bed. He carried it one-handed although it was made from heavy carved wood. He was stronger than he looked, Teclis thought.

'That is quite a compliment, coming from you,' said Malene. She did not sound convinced. She turned to Teclis. 'Korhien says Prince Iltharis is the best elf with a blade in Lothern, possibly Ulthuan.'

Teclis filed away that information. Iltharis did not look like a warrior. He looked like a scholar. There was a great deal that was deceptive about this elf, he decided.

'Korhien does me too much honour,' said Iltharis.

'You are in an unusually modest mood this afternoon,' said Lady Malene.

'Perhaps I am daunted by the grandeur of my surroundings,' said Iltharis mockingly. 'The Emeraldsea Palace is looking particularly imposing. You are spending a lot of money to celebrate this Feast of Deliverance. Is there any particular reason why?'

He looked pointedly at Teclis.

Of course, Teclis thought, if House Emeraldsea wanted to stress its ties with the Blood of Aenarion then this was exactly the time of year to remind people of them.

'It has been a good trading season,' said Malene. 'All of our vessels have returned home laden with precious cargoes. Some of the gold is being used for the entertainment of the Families.'

'So, it's not true then, you are not making a statement.'

'What statement would that be, Prince Iltharis?'

'The usual one that the elves of Lothern always feel compelled to make. That they are wealthier than the rest of us and that they have the support of the Phoenix King. And, of course, they are directly related to the most famous elf of all.'

'I doubt we are any wealthier than your family, Prince Iltharis. The House of Silvermount is fabulously rich.'

'And prodigiously ancient as well,' said Teclis. 'Its members have won renown in the service of many Phoenix Kings and the line has produced many great sorcerers.'

Iltharis tilted his head to one side and smiled again. 'I see you are quite the scholar Prince Teclis. You number genealogy among your interests?'

Malene smiled but did not say anything. Teclis was beginning to recognise Iltharis's style now. He enjoyed provoking people, getting them to say more than they intended, to reveal themselves. And he did not fear being challenged either. For all his languid manner, he seemed to have perfect poise and self-confidence. Teclis found himself torn between admiration and dislike.

'I have many interests,' said Teclis blandly.

'Rumour has it that one of them is magic, and that Lady Malene is teaching you.'

'Why are you here, Prince Iltharis?' Malene asked. She sounded almost rude. 'Prince Teclis is sick.'

'I had heard he was a scholar so I brought him some reading material.' He took the scrolls out from beneath his arm and handed them to Teclis. Despite his unease, Teclis took them and studied them becoming more and more excited as he read.

'This is an original of the *History of the Mages of Saphery*,' he said, unable to keep his enthusiasm from his voice. 'Written by Bel-Hathor himself.'

Iltharis nodded. 'It is from my library,' he said. 'You can return it when you are finished.'

'Thank you,' said Teclis, genuinely pleased and not a little troubled. 'But why are you lending it to me? You do not know me.'

'I knew your father, and your mother. They were both special friends of mine. I thought it might be pleasant to make the acquaintance of their sons. And I confess a personal interest. I am writing a monograph on the Blood of Aenarion, and it seemed like a good idea to make the acquaintance of the latest members of that line to be presented to the Phoenix King. Who knows what great deeds you and your brother will eventually perform?'

Malene was studying the prince closely now. Her face was colder than ever.

'I am sure Prince Teclis is grateful for your gifts, prince. But it might be better if we left now. He needs his rest if he is to regain his strength.'

'I am not as strong as my brother,' said Teclis, coughing uneasily. The fit grew stronger until he was almost bent double.

Lady Malene produced a small bottle of a coloured cordial which she handed to him. He drank it and the fit passed, leaving him red-eyed and wheezing. Teclis was used to elves moving away from him dring such bouts, but Iltharis did not. Teclis was surprised to see something like sympathy in his eyes.

He seemed to be about to say something but at that moment Korhien Ironglaive entered through the nearby archway. He smiled at Lady Malene and kissed her hand, then bowed to Prince Iltharis in his usual exuberant way. He nodded to Teclis. 'I see you are all enjoying yourselves,' he said.

'I suspect Prince Teclis is enjoying himself less than the rest of us,' said Iltharis. 'Perhaps we should take ourselves elsewhere.'

'Perhaps we should,' said Lady Malene.

Prince Iltharis bowed to Teclis as he departed. 'I look forward to discussing those scrolls with you at some future date. It will be nice to have someone civilised to talk to around here.'

Teclis opened the scrolls. Weak as he was, he could not stop himself from reading them.

CHAPTER THIRTEEN

ON HIS ARRIVAL home, Prince Iltharis went to his chambers. They were in the old part of the Silvermount Palace, on the ground floor. The building was extremely ancient and this part looked as if it has not undergone very much reconstruction in the past few centuries.

Two thousand-year old tapestries hung on the wall, preserved by the magic woven into them. Busts depicting the faces of elves dead millennia ago but still remembered and honoured by their descendants lined the corridors.

Iltharis looked around, smiling fondly, then locked the door. He pulled the drapes to stop any light finding its way in and then retreated deeper into his chambers, locking the doors behind him as he went.

When he reached the room deepest in his apartments, he unlocked a glass cabinet case, and produced a hookah and some incense sticks. He took a somewhat disreputable, not to mention very expensive, narcotic from a pouch and placed it in the hookah, setting it alight so that the scent would be faintly noticeable throughout his chambers and so give a suitable explanation for anyone who wondered why he had locked so many doors.

He turned the key on the final lock. It was very strong as was the door it was set in. It had been built in more troubled times and was intended to protect the occupant from assassins. It would take a group of strong elves a long time to break that door down.

Having completed his preparations, he pulled aside the wall hangings and, with the ease of long practice, pushed a pressure pad set in the wall. A section of the wall rotated to reveal a secret passage beyond. It had been intended by the builders as an escape route for the occupants of the chamber protected by that very strong door. Iltharis closed the secret panel behind him and followed a ramp that went a very long way below the city.

The air grew more stagnant and musty. The way grew darker. Prince Iltharis moved along the passage with remarkable ease considering the absence of light. Eventually his steps took him to a dead end. Here, he reached up and found another pressure plate in a place that would have been too high for anyone to find by accident. Another secret door opened. Iltharis went through it and closed it behind him, and then reached out and found a lantern hanging there and lit it. Here, deep below the earth, shielded by many spells and many tons of solid rock above him, he looked upon a potent magical artefact.

In the centre of the chamber stood a huge, silver mirror. He studied his reflection in it for a moment, smiled, swallowed his nervousness. He pricked his thumb, smeared blood on the surface of the mirror and invoked a spell.

It grew colder as he chanted. At first it looked cloudy as if some giant's breath were misting the glass, then, within its depths, a cold blue light became visible and the view in the mirror grew clearer although it no longer reflected Prince Iltharis's surroundings.

He looked now into a vast hall, dominated by a mighty iron throne on which reclined a huge armoured figure. The figure seemed out of proportion to its surroundings, an adult sitting in a child's playhouse. The armour of the figure glowed with dreadful runes but the glow of that fatal magic was no more terrifying than the glow in its eyes. Iltharis looked into them and, as ever, was shocked by the force of their owner's will.

Iltharis fought down a shudder and made himself meet the gaze of his master, Malekith, Witch King of Naggaroth.

'Well, Urian, what have you to report?' The voice was cold and stark and beautiful in its strange fashion, the same way as the frozen land-scapes of icebound northern Naggaroth were beautiful.

'Greetings, majesty, I have seen the latest of the Blood to report to the court of the False King.'

'And?'

'They are... unusual.'

'In what way?'

'They are twins. One of them very much a warrior, one of them will be a mage of some considerable power, unless I miss my guess.'

'Do they show any signs of the Curse?'

'Teclis, the one who will be a mage, is physically very weak. I do not know if he will live for much longer.'

'Then he can hardly be of much concern to us, for good or ill, can he? What of the other one?'

'Tyrion does indeed seem to be of the line of Aenarion, sire. He is tall and well-formed and very fast and strong. If he lives he will become a most formidable warrior.'

'As good as you, Urian?'

'I doubt he will live that long, sire. Word has it that the Cult of the Forbidden Blade already plans his death.' The Cult plotted the death of any they felt might be able to draw the Sword of Khaine and thus end the world. They were idiots, but they were dangerous idiots, and they numbered some very deadly duellists as part of their ancient conspiracy.

'But if he does live, Urian?'

'Then, yes, sire. It is possible he would be my match.'

'He must be formidable indeed.'

'He is, sire. And by all accounts he is quick of mind and gifted at tactics.'

'Does he bear any signs of the Curse, Urian? The Curse?'

'Not as yet, sire, but he is very young. What would you have me do about him?'

'Keep a close eye on him, Urian. If he shows any signs of the Curse, we shall let him live. If not...'

'As you wish, sire. And the other, the sickly one?'

'It does not sound like he will be a problem, does it?'

'No, sire. It does not.'

'You like them, don't you, Urian?'

As always Iltharis was surprised by the perceptiveness of his master. He did not know why that should be. It was impossible to rule a kingdom like Naggaroth for long ages without great insight into the elven heart.

'I do, sire,' Iltharis said. He always felt that honesty, insofar as he was able to manage it, was the best policy when dealing with his master. He had known too many elves suffer terrible fates through lying to Malekith.

'I do hope you are not becoming soft over there among our degenerate kinfolk, Urian.'

'I will do whatever is needed, sire. As I always do.'

'I know Urian. That is why you are my most trusted servant.'

He made a gesture and the great mirror went dark. Iltharis once again found himself facing his own reflection. He laughed out loud at his master's final words. Malekith trusted no one. Iltharis began to suspect that he himself might be marked for death.

'No one lives forever,' he muttered to himself. Not even you, Malekith, he thought but he kept that part to himself. Even down here, you never knew who might be listening. The Witch King had eyes and ears everywhere.

URIAN LOOKED AT himself in the now dormant mirror. He was not sure he recognised himself any more. He touched the long dark hair that ran down to his shoulders. Back in the beginning, before he had been singled out to become what he was today, his hair had been white. He was fairly sure of that. His skin had been pale and he had a few freckles. His eyes had been a simple green. His nose had been snub for an elf. Or perhaps his hair had been the colour of copper. He truly could not remember. His memories were twisted and there had been times when he had been less than sane. He was certain of that.

So many times now, his skin had been peeled from him and replaced with the flayed flesh of others. The bones in his face had been restructured. His eyes had been replaced by orbs stolen from someone else's sockets and kept preserved in jars of alchemical brine. He touched his eyelids now, wondering who these eyes had once belonged to; an elf, of course, but whether a high elf or a dark elf he could not tell. There was no real difference between the two, after all. Who knew that better than him?

How many hours had he spent chained to the altars in Naggarond while sorcerer-surgeons worked on him with blood-stained scalpels, peeling off his skin, magically grafting on new flesh? How many days had he spent with his brain magically altered to perceive pleasure as pain and pain as pleasure, except for those moments when the surgeons for their own amusement had chosen to let the spells lapse? How many weeks would he one day spend claiming his vengeance on those same magi?

He raised his glass and toasted himself. The wine was pallid and tasteless but he kept it here to give him something to steady his nerves after his little chats with his master. He missed the hallucinogenic vintages of Naggaroth, just as he missed the gladiatorial games and the easy availability of slave girls. He had kept a harem of them in his palace in Naggarond. They had been his, to do with whatever he wanted, to dispose of however he willed when he had done with them. That had been in another lifetime, one that seemed like a dream now. Perhaps it had been. Perhaps he had always been Prince Iltharis and he was mad, and the life of Urian Poisonblade, champion of Malekith, was some sort of deranged fantasy. Or perhaps he just wished it so.

He smiled mockingly and his reflection smiled back. He had worn so many other faces, lived so many other lives, he sometimes lost track of these things. There were times when he really believed himself to be Prince Iltharis and a loyal friend to the Phoenix King and Korhien Ironglaive. Those were not bad things to be, he thought, and then scoffed at his own weakness.

He was getting soft. He had spent too much time amid these spineless creatures that called themselves high elves and too long away from the harsh certainties of Naggaroth. He had grown accustomed to not having to carry a dozen concealed weapons and look for treachery in the faces of those who called themselves his closest friends. Now the only face he looked upon that hid treachery was his own. It winked back at him from the mirror and then it smiled sourly.

This was not what he had expected, not at all. He found he quite enjoyed living this life. He enjoyed being respected and not simply feared for his talent with a blade. He enjoyed living among people who thought of things other than their own interests occasionally.

Once, like all the other druchii, he had scoffed at the asur and their hypocrisy, the way they felt they were better, more moral. He had come to realise that in some ways they were. Even if they were hypocrites, their very hypocrisy made them better than the dark elves. The fact that they wanted to appear good, even for the wrong reasons, made them behave in a way that was better.

It did not matter that they aided each other because they wanted to be seen to live up to some ancient ideal. The fact was, that for whatever the reasons, they did. And some of them really did believe in their ideals, Korhien and young Prince Tyrion for example, unless he was much mistaken. They were fools, of course, but it was a folly that it was possible to respect. Nor were they weak – their folly gave them strength and courage.

He took another sip of wine and wished that it were laced with the ecstatic poisons made from powdered lotus. At times like these he missed them. Before he came to Ulthuan, to assume the role of Prince Iltharis that had been long prepared for him among Malekith's secret followers in Ulthuan, he had been forced to abstain for months. It had been a hard time. He had sweated through withdrawal symptoms that would have killed other druchii. He had lost the bright, mad clarity that never, ever having his bloodstream free of the drugs had given him. In some ways, he realised he really had made himself into a high elf. He had been forced to live as they did.

It was not entirely unpleasant. He was no longer given to mad rages or picking quarrels with strangers for reasons he could never quite remember the next day. He lived in a place now where that would not be acceptable. Here, elves needed good reasons to kill each other, they did not do it simply to gratify a momentary whim. Of course, he missed being able to do that sometimes. Who would not? But he found these days that he had fewer regrets.

He admitted it. He sometimes wished that he could simply forget who he was and become Prince Iltharis. He would put aside his divided loyalties and fragmented personality and become wholly one thing. For a moment, and a moment only, he allowed himself to imagine what that would really feel like.

Then he dismissed the fantasy.

There were those who knew who he was, who would not allow him to do that. And even if he killed them, there would be others, secret watchers whom he never suspected. They would bring word of his treachery to the Witch King. And Malekith was not a forgiving master to those who betrayed him. He would stretch out his cold metal hand, and a suitable vengeance would be wreaked. There was nothing more certain in this life.

No, even if he wanted to give up this life, he could not. There was no escape. There was nothing to do but make the best of it.

CHAPTER FOURTEEN

Prince Sardriane looked up. The face he saw was beautiful and reassuring. It was that of a lovely elf woman, his mother. He was surprised but he could not quite remember why. He felt as if he were awakening from a deep, languorous sleep and had not quite woken fully yet. He tried sitting up, but he could not. He tried moving his arms, but he could not. Something seemed to be restraining his hands and his legs and when he tried to lift his head something bit into his throat.

'What is going on?' he asked.

'Hush,' said his mother. 'There is nothing to worry about.'

Why was she naked? Why did she caress him so lasciviously?

There was something odd about her voice. It sounded like mother, or rather it sounded as she would have if she were in great pain while she spoke. There appeared to be something wrong with her head. Two small curling horns grew out of the side of her brow. Her mouth looked a little distorted too, as did her face.

Sardriane sniffed. There was a hideous stench in the air of burned meat, mingled with charred wood. He turned his head to one side, as far as whatever was restraining him allowed, and he saw that he was in his home, or what was left of it.

The roof had crashed in, and the walls looked burned through. A few of the more intricate carvings, of which his dead father had been so proud, were still intact, but they were soot-blackened in some places and the colour of ash in others. There was something else in the air, a strange sickly perfume that was cloying and yet thrilling at the same time. It smelled of musk and rot and hinted at other things that he did not want to think about.

'I remember,' he said, for he suddenly did. He remembered the fall of Tor Annan, the way the howling daemonic horde had come racing towards the walls, some falling to elf shafts, the daemons ignoring arrows that had not been enchanted by a mage.

The winged things had flapped down from the sky and attacked first the siege machines and then the archers. Death had come so very close to him in the opening moments of the battle. The winged furies had struck down the elves on either side of him. Daemons had smashed through the gates and clambered onto the walls, killing everybody they encountered. One had loomed over him, been about to strike and then at the last second, at the shouted command of what might have been a leader, had struck down Alfrik instead. Mad cultists had come swarming through the broken gateway, howling and chanting ecstatically as they slew.

At first the elves of Tor Annan had fought bravely. Archers had died where they stood, still unleashing their arrows at targets that ignored them. Warriors had tried to halt the monstrous red-skinned daemons. But as the fight went on it became obvious they could not overcome their foes. Some had fled. Some had tried to surrender. And some, seeing the daemonic leader of their enemies, had been overcome by a strange madness and had started throwing themselves at its feet and grovelling in ecstatic communion.

Sardriane had been one of the ones who had fled. He had raced through the streets to the ancestral home he shared with his mother and a few ageing retainers. He had told them to bar the door and to make ready to withstand a siege. Some of them, feeling that death was preferable to falling into the hands of their enemy, had taken their own lives using poisons preserved for that purpose. Sardriane had urged his mother to do so, for he feared what might happen if she were to fall into the taloned claws of the besiegers. She had refused, saying that while he lived, she would. She had as much pride as he. After all, she too was of the Blood of Aenarion.

For a while they had huddled in their chambers while the town burned around them and screams echoed down the streets. It sounded as if some hideous carnival of torture and wickedness were taking place outside. He prayed that if they waited long enough, they would be unnoticed by their enemies and escape with their lives. He hated himself for his cowardice. He hated himself for running. It seemed unworthy of his proud ancestry. The only defence he could offer up was that he was young and he did not want to die.

At last the screaming had stopped and he had dared to peek out through a gap in the shuttered windows. He had seen lines and lines of silent faces watching the building. Some of them belonged to brazen horned, crimson-skinned daemons. Some of them belonged to cultists. Some of them belonged to people who had once been his neighbours and who now gazed at his house with features dazed and numbed and subtly altered.

As if his looking upon them had broken some evil spell, they all shouted and rushed forwards, smashing in through the doors and revelling through the halls of Sardriane's home, smashing the ancient furnishings, burning the ancient tapestries, maiming and killing the retainers, howling with insatiable blood lust and something else, a primitive deep-throated pleasure that was even more disgusting than their desire to do harm.

They had overpowered Sardriane and his mother and carried them to their leader, a strange creature whose outline shimmered and shifted constantly sometimes suggesting a crab-clawed hulking daemonic thing, sometimes the most beautiful woman he had ever imagined, sometimes the most noble king. He had thrown himself towards the monster, trying to strike at it with a dagger he seized from the scabbard of one of his tormentors, and had been struck unconscious by a blow to the head.

That was the last thing he remembered until this moment of bleak consciousness, when he had come to and been confronted with this evil parody of his mother. He wished that he was not awake now. He wished that he was not seeing anything. He wished that it was all a horrible dream. He knew it was not. He had seen more elves die in the last few hours than he had ever expected to see die in his life. He had witnessed a whole small town wiped out and he was not even

sure why. The sheer malevolence of it was virtually incomprehensible. He closed his eyes again and wished the whole thing away.

'You are awake, little elfling. Do not pretend otherwise.' The voice
was impossibly sweet and impossibly malevolent and still it bore an
odd resemblance to his mother's.

'Go to hell,' he said. His mouth felt dry and it took a huge effort to
force the words out, but he felt the need to make up for his earlier
cowardice by a show of defiance now, even if it would do him no
good whatsoever.

'I will eventually,' said the thing that looked like his mother. 'Most
gratefully too shall I leave this tedious place. But there are a few
things I need to put right before I go. You shall help me.'

'Never.'

'Oh, but you will. You will help me by dying. Eventually.'

Sardriane swallowed. He did not like the sound of this at all. He
had heard tales of what Chaos cultists were capable of, and this thing
was mistress of such a cult. Judging by the earlier slaughter, the stories of their cruelty were not exaggerated.

'You are going to kill me... so do it.'

'I will at the end, but first you will beg me not to, and then you will
beg me to do so, and then when I have broken your will and your
sanity and made you worship me and love me, I shall kill you. I
might even tell you why.'

'I do not care.'

'That is simply perverse, which I admire. Don't tell me you are not
in the slightest bit curious why I have slaughtered your tiny little
town and killed all of your family and yet let you live.'

'I have had other things on my mind.'

The daemon's laughter was gentle and mocking. It reached out
with one soft hand and caressed his cheek. A thrill of depraved pleasure came from the contact, a magical spark jumping from one to the
other.

A moment later the tip of a thumb claw flipped out his eye. He did
not feel much pain, only an odd ripping sensation and then a wetness as the empty socket filled with blood. The daemon muttered
something and raised its hand and twisted. Sardriane's brain lurched
as it tried to cope with the impact of what was happening. One eye
floated in the air above him. He was looking up at it with the eye still

in its socket. A thin taut rope of nerve fibre seemed to connect it to his head. With the other eye he was looking down on himself as he wept tears of blood. The daemon reached out and put out his good eye, so that now he seemed only to be looking down on his body. His vision settled and he saw that he was lying on a pile of skinned corpses, held in place by ropes of entrails.

'Yes,' said the voice, simply malicious now. 'That is what awaits you in the end, although I confess I am tempted to animate the corpses and re-enact the Masque of the Fleshless. Perhaps later...'

It reached forward and touched Sardriane's forehead. As the elf watched he saw his own skin split and begin to part and the daemon peeled his body like a grape. He tried to swallow his own tongue but this was expected and the daemon prevented it.

'No, Blood of Aenarion,' it said. 'This game has a while to run yet.'

Sardriane was a long time dying. Everything the daemon promised came true.

THIS EVENING N'KARI wore the form of a mighty, muscular human warrior with the head of bull and the lower body of a horse. It allowed him to move quickly and he enjoyed the sensation of being a quadruped. There was something about that he had always found stimulating.

It was easier to hold the shape for longer now. He was growing accustomed to this reality and its restrictions. He was learning to use the flows of its magic almost at will.

Behind him his army awaited their instructions.

It was not as impressive a force as he would have liked but it was growing. It now consisted of a few dozen bound daemons, and several hundred cultists. Some of them had been recruited from farmers and smallholders encountered en route to Tor Annan. Many more had joined him after the destruction of their town.

The souls of those who refused to submit to the ecstatic disciplines of the Cult of Pleasure were swiftly dispatched to the netherworld, bait and sustenance for the daemons N'Kari had used them to summon. In general that had not proved necessary in more than half the cases. There was a strong pleasure-loving streak in most elves, and given the choice between death and a life of drug-fuelled, esoteric pleasure a significant number made the right choice.

The rest had provided an interesting distraction.

Sometimes the allegiance of families had been split and N'Kari had required the new recruits to prove their loyalty by sacrificing those who refused to join. Sometimes this had engendered second thoughts in the recruits, sometimes in the recalcitrant converts. In any case, it had provided a few moments of relief from ennui. He delighted in the savour of any strong emotion, and these elves were good for that, at least.

'You have orders for us, Great Master?' Elrion asked. He was beginning to look haggard as the toll of nights of pleasure and days of horror overtook him. He twitched and frothed and broke into tears at odd times. Sometimes he would rant at the other cultists, delivering terrifying if somewhat unimaginative sermons on the nature of Chaos and the goals of their master.

N'Kari enjoyed the storytelling and the embroidery of the facts and so far had seen no reason to contradict him. If anything, some of Elrion's more visionary passages had made the rest of his cultists even more devout. The elf had acquired his own small harem among the impressionable worshippers but did not seem to take much pleasure in it.

Typical mortal really. So hard to please. Give them what they claimed they wanted and they would inevitably discover it was not what they expected or desired. Even to a devotee of the Lord of Perversity this sometimes seemed a little too perverse.

He thought about those he had killed back in Tor Annan.

N'Kari felt the desire for vengeance swell within him. His desire for it grew with every death. Feeding on the souls of the Blood of Aenarion made him hunger for more. There was something about the spirits that gave him more nutriment and more power than any others he had ever consumed. He was going to need it, for his plan was approaching its most difficult stage.

It had taken longer than he would have liked to find this place due to the restrictions this reality placed on his abilities to travel. Even the strange paths of the Vortex had allowed him to move more swiftly when he had been entrapped within them, and he had become used to the freedom they offered. It was this fact that had provided the germ of his original plan, and the reason why he had chosen the place for his escape to which he had now returned.

Nearby there was a waystone and an entrance into the odd underworld that the first so-called rulers of this world had created to allow themselves swift travel from point to point. He could call upon its power and make it serve his own purposes.

'Tell my best beloved to prepare themselves. They are going to witness a miracle,' the daemon said.

Elrion's face lit up with curiosity. He knew that his master did not make such promises lightly and that something ominous and awesome was to be expected. N'Kari smiled, revealing his enormous fangs. He reached out and stroked Elrion's cheek with his taloned hand. 'Yes, little mortal, you're going to witness a mighty sorcery.'

N'Kari approached the waystone.

To his daemonic eyesight it glowed, revealing the faint seepage of energy from within the Vortex. His smile grew wider, his fangs glittered in the moonlight. He knew all about this sort of magical power and how to wield it and shape it to his purposes. He was going to perform a feat of magic here that the elves would remember for as long as they existed – which, Slaanesh willing, would not be very long even as mortals measured time.

He was going to do something here that had never been attempted before in this world and probably would never be attempted again because there was no one who could match his knowledge, magical power or skill when it came to this. There was no one else who had paid the price of being imprisoned within the Vortex for five millennia either. It had allowed him to maintain his form here in a way that few other daemons could manage without the winds of magic blowing strongly. It was going to allow him to do something else as well.

He decided that he would need to make a few sacrifices before he began. It was not that the magic required them – it was simply that he liked to begin a new venture with an offering to his patron daemon god in order to curry favour and bring good fortune. It could not do any harm, it might do some good, and at very least it would give him some pleasure, which was the main thing.

He used a waystone as an altar and offered up six choice souls to Slaanesh. If through force of habit he stole most of their essence for himself, it was only fitting because he was going to need some of the power they provided to work the spell he intended.

He drew a six-pointed star using the blood of his victims and placed a severed head at each point. Once that was done he began to chant, as much to focus his mind as to impress his followers. As he chanted, he drew more lines in a mightily convoluted hieroglyphic that represented a path between this waystone and another one, within a day's march of where his next victim dwelled.

In his mind he visualised the tunnel of light between the two points and, as he tapped the powers of magic, he forced his view of the world onto the world itself. The thing that he was creating in his mind through the power of his magic was also coming into being in the malleable substrata of reality that the waystone tapped into.

By the time he had finished his ritual, a glimmering archway hovered in the air before him, its surface shimmering like oily water reflecting firelight. With a gesture of his claw, he indicated that his followers should pass through it. Not without some reluctance the first of them did so, disappearing through the iridescent arch, as if they had dived into strangely coloured water.

Only when he had witnessed the last of them pass through did the daemon join them and do the same, plunging into a gap in reality and venturing through the strange tunnel in which kaleidoscopic sensations assaulted his senses.

TAKALEN THE RANGER sniffed the air. There was something odd about it, a smell of rotting flesh that should not have been there. The lord who owned this mansion was old but the place should not have looked so deserted and that ominous scent should not have been hanging in the air. A feeling of foreboding passed through Takalen's mind and she shivered. Overhead her companion shrieked and she knew that the great eagle was also disturbed. It was hanging in the air far above and its eyes were much keener than hers so perhaps it had already seen what was causing the smell.

Takalen moved cautiously towards the door of the old mansion. She did not like the look of it at all. She had occasionally visited Prince Faldor and his daughter Fayelle when she had passed this way previously and she had never known them to be careless. Just because this area was comparatively safe compared to the rest of Ulthuan did not mean the old noble had relaxed his guard. In the past the door had always been shut, which was only sensible, for in these dark times who knew what strange things might emerge to threaten the peace of the locality.

The door was open now, and even as Takalen watched, a fox emerged through it, carrying something in its mouth which on closer observation proved to be the remains of an elf hand. Takalen drew her sword, and passed through the doorway. She did not expect anything dangerous – the fox would not have been there had attackers still been within. It was just that there was something about the atmosphere that set her teeth on edge and made her wary.

Inside the walls of the villa was a courtyard. She saw the first of the corpses and, although she was no weak-gutted town-dweller, it made her want to heave. The bodies had been flayed and mutilated and the dismembered parts laid out in some odd pattern. The outline had been disturbed by scavenging animals but the fact that someone had intentionally laid the parts out in an ordered way was obvious. Splashes of blood and dried out strips of intestine made that absolutely clear.

There was a strong stink of magic in the air. Takalen was no mage but like all elves she was sensitive to the flows of magic. She could tell that something dark and awful had been done here. She pushed on into the main building, knowing already that what she would find would be terrible.

The air was close and foetid. Flies buzzed everywhere, brushing against her face, getting in her long ash-blonde hair, skittering across her exposed skin. There were too many of them for this to be entirely natural. The stink of dark magic was stronger here.

The old furniture was broken. It was as if a crowd of maniacs had rushed through this place, breaking everything precious they could find. Discarded clothing, blood-soaked, lay everywhere. There were odd outlines of elven shapes imprinted on the walls. It took the trained tracker long minutes to work out what had happened simply because her mind did not want to accept it. It looked like lust-maddened elves, and other things, had rolled in blood and had wild sex against the walls.

What in the name of Isha had happened here?

Takalen had heard rumours that some of the locals had been dabbling in the old rites of the Cult of Luxury. It looked like they had gone beyond dabbling here. It looked like they had taken to summoning things using the old dark magic.

Slaanesh! She deciphered another of the words crudely written on the walls, smeared in blood and excrement. Her lips curled. Her nose wrinkled. Slaanesh. The word was repeated again, mixed with other names, and curses and imprecations.

N'Kari was one of those names, an appellation almost as dreadful as that of the daemon lord of forbidden pleasures. It belonged to the Keeper of Secrets responsible for the Rape of Ulthuan in the dawn ages, a creature twice destroyed by the mighty Aenarion and thought gone forever.

N'Kari has returned.

The sentence was sometimes spelled out in crude block characters and sometimes in the graceful looping script of modern Elvish. It was repeated over and over again like the monotonous repetitions of a lunatic.

N'Kari will have vengeance.

In the great hall she found the remains of what might have been a daemonic orgy or a cannibal feast or some dreadful combination of both. Staked out in the middle of a curious ritual circle was the naked body of Fayelle, or at least something that might have looked like her, if her corpse had been desiccated and aged a thousand years.

It was a long time before Takalen could think clearly and do what had to be done.

CHAPTER FIFTEEN

TYRION PUT ON his old clothes. He stepped out onto the balcony and looked down into the street. It was late but there were people moving around down there still. Along this street he could see that the villas and mansions were all well lit but whole huge areas of the city were in darkness. Buildings loomed large in the moonlight. There was just no one in them as far as he could tell.

He felt excitement build up in him. He was really going to do this. He was going to slip out into the night and explore the city. He felt as if he were planning a prison break. It was not as if he was really a prisoner in the Emeraldsea Palace. He was sure they would let him go out if he asked. It was just that they would hem him around with guards and chaperones of other sorts and this was not what he wanted. He wanted to be on his own, to look at things at his own pace, to explore. He remembered some things about the city of his birth. He wanted to see how well it matched his childhood memories.

He considered waking Teclis to tell him what he was doing, but pushed the thought to one side. His brother would most likely want to come and that would make the logistics of the expedition so much more difficult. He would tell him about it tomorrow, when he returned. Tonight would just be a reconnaissance. There would be other nights or even days.

Plus, he wanted this for himself. He wanted to do it alone.

He lowered himself off the balcony. There was plenty of climbing ivy on the wall beneath but he doubted it would take his weight. Instead he used the gaps between the blocks of stone that made up the wall for foot and finger holds and made his way down, dropping the last ten feet to the ground. As soon as he hit, he picked himself up, dusted himself off and strolled away, whistling nonchalantly, walking with confidence as if what he was doing was perfectly normal.

As he walked he paused for a moment to study his surroundings and get his bearings. He felt certain he could find this place again. Things looked different at night but the Emeraldsea Palace was distinctive, so massive and with its towers greenly lit. He stared up at the hills above the harbour. A few lights glittered up there but not many. He knew what he was seeking was there though and he headed off, selecting a path that would take him up hill.

It was not long before the streets became much quieter, and he was alone in them. He moved more cautiously now prompted by instincts that told him in lonely places there was danger. He had his sword with him, strapped to his back for the climb. He adjusted the position of the scabbard to his waist so that it would be easier to draw, and practised unsheathing it a few times so that he could bring it forth, if needed, with eye-blurring speed. He enjoyed that. It made him feel like the hero in a story.

The buildings around him were old and gave off a fusty smell. No lights showed in any of them; they were empty. The windows of some had been boarded up. Others seemed completely abandoned. No one had lived in these places for many years. If he wanted to, he could simply pick one of these buildings and go and live in it.

For a moment he entertained the fantasy of dwelling like a castaway in the shell of one of these forgotten mansions. It made him smile to think about but then it struck him that all of these houses had once been lived in by his own people, by whole families and their retainers and cousins and distant kin. Now all of those people were gone. For the first time ever it really struck him that the elves were a dying people, were vanishing from the face of the world, never to return. Every one of these empty houses represented a great noble family that was now extinct.

How had they died? Had they been killed in war? Had they simply faded away with fewer children born every century and the old dying off? Had they died in accidents, one after the other, year after year, century after century, assassinated by chance and unlucky fate?

He supposed it did not really matter. The simple, melancholy truth was that they were gone. He suddenly understood in his gut, as he had never really understood it before, what it was that Korhien had meant when he said every elf life was precious. There were so few of them left now that each death was another small defeat for the entire people, the putting out of another candle in a vast echoing chamber that would soon be dark and empty.

It was not exactly that the thought frightened him. It made him uneasy and sad. Briefly he considered abandoning his whole expedition and returning to the palace. Doing so would be to admit a defeat though, or at very least a failure of courage, so he pushed on up the hill, following the promptings of half-remembered memories from when he was very small, until at last he found it, or at least what he was fairly certain was it; the house where he had lived when he and Teclis had been very young children.

It sat high on the hill in a row of other houses just like it. In some of these lights still shone. They had not been entirely abandoned. Their old house stood tall and old and proud. It was older by far than the Emeraldsea Palace, built in ancient days when his father's ancestors had looked down on the merchants literally beneath them. It was tall and narrow and five storeys high and each window facing outward on this side had a balcony. He could remember standing on one of these balconies as a child and looking down into the harbour. He had been too young and too small then to really understand anything that was going on around him. He felt much older than that now.

He walked to the door. It was chained. Someone had taken the trouble to lock the place up and it looked like someone visited every so often to see that it was maintained. He suspected it must be people in the employ of his mother's relatives. They seemed like the sort who would be careful about property. He supposed that he could pry open the locks or the rings of the chain if he really wanted to but it seemed a bit like sacrilege. So he clambered up the front of the building and onto the first balcony.

Memories came flooding back. He had been here before when the barrier had been so high he had to stand on tiptoes to look over it and his father and his father's friends had seemed like giants.

He knew there would be an even better view from above so he clambered up until he had reached the highest balcony and the ground was a dizzying drop beneath him. All of those hours spent clambering around in the rigging of the *Eagle of Lothern* proved their worth then. He was neither nervous nor afraid. He enjoyed the physical activity of the climb, almost as much as he enjoyed the view that was his reward.

He was very high above the city of Lothern now, and he could see all the way down into the harbour. The waves glittered silver in the moonlight. The thousands of ships looked like shadows. Their masts were like a forest floating on water.

Large patches of the city were lit up, a blaze of lights and life. Even larger parts were dead, all darkness and shadow and silence. It was as if a cancer was eating out the heart of Lothern. He was sure it had not been quite this bad when he was young, but it must have been. In the timescale of elves, a decade was an eye-blink. He had simply been young and unaware.

He saw the Foreigners' Quarter was ablaze with light. Down there, naked flames burned and torch bearers walked through darkened alleys and thousands of people went about their business in the flickering shadows. It was fascinating and attractive and he knew that at some point he was going to have to visit it. But tonight he had other things on his mind.

He went to the shuttered windows. There were no chains on the outside, and there was a bar that was easily lifted by slipping the blade of his sword through the gap in the wood. The air inside smelled musty and stale but it still had the smell of the place he remembered – waxed floors, incense, the metallic tang of something connected with his father's researches. It was dark within but he did not feel at all uneasy. He felt, in truth, as if he was coming home.

He went within and more memories came flooding back. The house was much larger than it looked from the street. It was tall and narrow but it ran a long way back from the road and it had many, many chambers. There was lots of furniture all covered in sheets and tarpaulins and there were mirrors in wooden cases that opened to reveal the glass within. He found a glow-globe and rubbed it to life. Its faint illumination was enough for him to see by. There were odd noises, bumping and creaking sounds as the wooden floors settled. There were probably rats moving around as well, although what they found to eat here he could not guess.

He strolled through the house until he came to the room he was looking for, and he found the thing he sought. A full length portrait of his mother looked down on him. She looked very lovely and very frail and there was something of Teclis in her features and appearance. Perhaps that was why Father has always preferred his twin. Not that it mattered much. He studied the portrait as he had done as a child, wondering what this woman had been like, and what she would say to him if she could talk to him now.

But she could not speak and there were no answers. He was walking through a city of ghosts, he thought. This was a place where the dead outnumbered the living and there were more mementoes of the past than people to remember events.

Sadness settled on him as he contemplated this beautiful frail stranger he had never met. After a while he got up and left, walking away from the dead and back towards the bright life of the Emeraldsea Palace. He doubted anyone would challenge him if he came in through the front door, but he went back to his room the way he had left, clambering up the walls and sliding easily over the balcony.

'Where have you been?' Teclis asked. He was sitting there, a book open on his knee, the moonlight bright enough to read by for someone with elven vision.

'I went to see the old house.'

'I always hated that place.'

'It's not so bad. I always liked it.'

'Did you see her?' There was no need to ask who was meant.

'Yes. She looked the same.'

'I would be very surprised if she looked any different,' said Teclis, rising from the chair and limping painfully to the door. 'She's been dead for a long time.'

Tyrion wanted to tell his brother that it was not so long in the elven scheme of things but he kept his silence and watched his brother go.

CHAPTER SIXTEEN

URIAN STRODE CONFIDENTLY into the audience chamber. He glanced around. Many of the Phoenix King's advisors were already present. Lady Malene was there along with half a dozen other powerful wizards he recognised. A lovely woman, Urian thought but very severe. She caught him looking at her and gave him a sour smile. He smiled back as if unaware of her dislike.

Five minutes in my harem, woman, and you would learn to smile properly, he thought.

Urian loved these midnight councils. They reminded him of being home. He had lost count of the number of times he had spent plotting late into the night with his confederates back in Naggaroth.

Of course, this was not exactly the same. The chances were that no one would be murdered because of tonight's events. There would not even be a significant change of power in the realm of Ulthuan unless something went very wrong.

No, it was the atmosphere he loved, the idea of being part of a cabal of people, meeting in secrecy under the shroud of darkness, whose decisions might affect the whole kingdom. There was an energy to such meetings that he fed on, that made his heart beat faster and pandered to his elven love of intrigue. He felt as if he really was someone, set apart from the common herd.

And, he thought sourly, in this he was like every other elf who had ever lived.

More wizards and scholars were arriving by the minute. All of them wore the worried looks of powerful people summoned in the dead of night to a secret council. Korhien Ironglaive entered, went over to his paramour and started talking in hushed tones with her.

Urian wondered what was going on here. It was not every night he was summoned to the Palace. Something big was happening. He would need to report it to Malekith.

A huge table dominated the room. On it were plates of cold meat, loaves of bread, jugs of wine, pitchers of water. There were books and scrolls and maps. It looked like someone was anticipating a long session.

'What is wrong?' Urian asked. Everyone looked shocked. No one was eating. The silence deepened and glancing around, Urian realised that Finubar had appeared. He was wearing his robes of state which made him look taller and more slender. The Phoenix King's gaze was distant but his voice was as resonant and powerful as ever.

'Do not mind me,' said the Phoenix King. 'Carry on with your discussions as if I were not here. I need to hear what you all have to say.'

'There has been another attack, sire,' Archmage Eltharik said, stroking his white goatee beard, a thing unusual in an elf male. He looked old. His skin was nearly translucent. His hair was white as bleached parchment. He was a specialist in all sorts of mystical lore, particularly that to do with summonings. 'The daemons have struck again. They completely destroyed a small town in Ellyrion.'

Malene let out a long breath. 'How did the word come in?'

'A mage survived. He performed a Sending.'

So that was what had caused Korhien to rush off earlier from their drinking party. The summons had been most urgent.

'How bad?' Malene asked.

A certain morbid curiosity filled Urian. It was obvious that many of those here knew more than he did. It looked as if some of the rumours he had picked up on were correct. There was some new threat to the realm and one the present Phoenix King was trying very hard to keep secret, at least for the moment.

'The town was burned down. All of the inhabitants had been

subjected to the most hideous torture. Their flayed bodies had been laid out in a pattern that spelled the name N'Kari in the ashes. Along with other things. Threats, warnings, promises.'

'That's the name of the daemon who led the forces of the Lord of Pleasure during the reign of Aenarion,' Finubar said. He looked at Urian, who suddenly understood why he was here. His scholarship in all matters concerning the line of the first Phoenix King was famous.

'A greater daemon, a Keeper of Secrets no less,' said Urian. This was indeed news, Urian thought. If such a creature had emerged out of legend, it was epochal. There were few more deadly creatures on the face of creation. 'A being unseen since the time of Aenarion. Is someone trying to invoke him?'

'We don't know,' said Eltharik. 'All we know is reports are coming in from all across Ulthuan about attacks by daemons and their worshippers. There have been at least a dozen so far from locations as far north as Cothique, and as far west as Tiranoc. All of them involve Slaanesh worshippers and evil magic and powerful daemons. In most of them the name of N'Kari has come up either from survivors or from inscriptions on the site.'

A White Lion appeared. He carried a map of Ulthuan. When it was unrolled on the table, Urian could see the location of all the attacks had been marked on the map in red elven runes. They were widely scattered. Too widely spaced for it to be the work of one group, he thought. The distances were too great for any one army, even one mounted on eagles, to cover in the time available.

'Why now?' Archmage Belthania asked. She was a tall dark-haired elf woman who did not look her five centuries of age. It was rumoured she kept a stable of younger lovers tired out in her bedchambers. She was known to have a penchant for all manner of hallucinogenic mushrooms as well. It did not prevent her from being one of the sharpest scholars of the Vortex alive, although it kept all manner of strange rumours swirling around her.

'We don't know,' Eltharik said. 'We are trying to find out. The Council has called a meeting of all the seers and mages in Lothern. Archmages and Loremasters are being summoned from Saphery and the White Tower.'

'What do you think is happening?' Malene asked.

'I have no idea,' Eltharik replied. 'There are a few signs that the winds of magic are growing stronger and the power of Chaos is increasing but nothing that would suggest a manifestation by dozens of such powerful daemons across Ulthuan.'

'Do any of the places attacked have anything in common?' Belthania asked.

'We are looking into that. At a guess I would say they are all close to waystones,' said Eltharik.

'The pins that hold the Vortex together?' Belthania looked thoughtful and not a little worried. 'That could be very dangerous.'

'The Keepers of the Stones have not reported any tampering with the Great Pattern. There have been no attempts to unmake it, only some strange surges of energy within it and those happen from time to time.'

'Do they?' Urian asked.

'The winds of magic blow softer or stronger. Sometimes there are storms of magic, sometimes absolute calms. The Vortex and the Pattern are intended to channel the energy of the winds so sometimes there must be fluctuations as the levels of ambient magic change.'

Urian considered this. 'The daemons are not attacking the Vortex though?'

'As far as we know, no. There has only been one broken waystone found and it seems to have been the result of a lightning strike. There were traces of dark magic visible nearby though and an aura of great evil such as you might find near where daemons have manifested.'

'Was there an attack near that waystone?' Korhien asked.

'Yes,' said Eltharik. 'There was.'

'And it was probably among the first, wasn't it?'

'Too early to say yet, Korhien, but it is possible.'

'But it is definite the daemons are not attacking the waystones.' Belthania said. 'They are attacking towns and killing elves.'

'It is strange,' said Malene. 'But who can fathom the thinking of daemons?'

'I thought someone had to summon them,' said Urian 'That's what all the chronicles say. Some mighty sorcerer raises them for his own purposes.'

'They can enter the world through the Chaos Wastes when the winds of magic blow at their strongest and most corrupt,' Eltharik said.

'But they are not doing so now. You said that yourself.'

Eltharik nodded.

Malene said, 'Who would do this? Who would summon them? The druchii? The Witch King?'

Urian considered the possibility. He had heard nothing of any such plan. Of course, his master rarely saw fit to keep him informed about such things.

'If any wizard living has the power to do so, he has,' said Eltharik. 'No dark elf armies or fleets are attacking us though, and surely there would be if this was part of one of his plans?'

'It does not sound like Malekith,' said Urian. 'It is not his way. Too random. Too messy.' He saw a number of those present including Korhien nod their heads at that.

'A renegade wizard then? A Chaos cultist?' Lady Malene asked.

'Perhaps. But the attacks are too wildly spaced to be the work of one mage summoning. The reports are coming in from all across the continent.'

'Could an army of Chaos worshippers have gathered in secret and unleashed their attacks all at once?' Finubar asked.

'The attacks did begin just after the full moon,' said Eltharik. 'That is a time of great mystical significance.'

'Yes,' said Lady Malene. 'I was at sea about that time and there was a strange storm. I thought it was tainted with dark magical energy.'

'Was that before or after the attacks began?' Belthania asked. She looked even more troubled.

'It would have been just before, I suspect.'

'Where were you?' Belthania toyed with her long black hair. It was still very dark. Urian wondered if the rumours were true about her dyeing it.

'Off the coast of Yvresse,' said Malene. 'Near where the waystone was smashed.'

'It might well have been in the storm's path.'

'It is possible these things were connected. The storm broke the waystone. The daemons attacked there or manifested there.' Malene knew it sounded weak even as she said it. Urian could tell from her expression. 'Perhaps they came out of the Vortex. It was weakened at that point.'

'Daemons in the Vortex? That seems unlikely as well.' Belthania was emphatic. She did not seem to even want to consider the possibility that it might be so. Urian could sympathise – it was a most unsettling prospect. Still, it was one that they might need to face up to.

'Perhaps the place was picked by cultists for a ritual? Perhaps the storm was merely a coincidence? Perhaps it provided them with the power they needed to summon the daemons?' Malene said.

Belthania pursed her lips. 'That is a lot of perhapses. We need to find out concrete facts. We need to know who is behind these attacks. We need to know how strong our foes are and what their goals are. It is the only way we are going to be able to stop them.'

'Let us hope we can.'

'Do you have any recommendations?' Finubar asked. 'Is there anything we can do?'

He clearly wanted to know if there was some place where he could order his troops or fleets to go. He was a warrior and he saw things like a warrior.

'We need to know what the daemon wants, sire, before we can prevent it from achieving its goals.' Belthania said.

'Then we had better work that out, hadn't we,' said the Phoenix King. 'And quickly before more lives are lost.'

Urian helped himself to some wine. It was going to be a long night, and he had better make sure he missed nothing. Malekith would want a full report on this.

'IT SEEMS MY rebellious subjects are in something of a panic, Urian,' said Malekith. His gaze burned coldly out of the great mirror beneath the Silvermount Palace. There was a certain chill satisfaction in his voice. He had listened intently to Urian's report without interrupting once, which was unusual for him.

'Indeed, sire. They are. Apparently Ulthuan is under attack by a legion of greater daemons. They have returned from the time of legends and are hellbent on destroying the entire island and sending us all beneath the sea.'

'I sense that you are not in agreement with this, Urian.'

'As ever, sire, you are correct.'

'Your simple faith in me is touching, Urian,' said Malekith, with a trace of his acid humour. 'What has been the response from the False King's court?'

'They are mustering their armies and fleets. They have sorcerers working on divinations. Scholars such as my humble self are scouring through ancient texts. They seek to ascertain the daemons' purpose.'

'Do you think they will do so?'

'Not yet, master, but it is merely a matter of time before they do. They are not without competent wizards here in Ulthuan.'

Malekith nodded. 'I do not think it is an uprising or a group of invading armies. My spies would have informed me of such a thing and I am sure that in this matter at least the False King is at least as well informed as I.'

'You think it is the daemon, sire? This N'Kari of legend?'

'It is possible, Urian. Such creatures do not age any more than I do. If it is N'Kari he will be terrible.' Urian needed to exert all his self-control to keep from shuddering. He gazed on his ruler with a feeling of something like awe. Malekith had been alive when Aenarion had defeated and banished the Keeper of Secrets. He had walked the world in that time of legend. And if he saw fit to remark that its return would be a terrible event, Urian had every reason to believe it would be so.

'This daemon, if daemon it be, is moving very quickly around Ulthuan with a very large force. Much faster than it should be able to by ship or road.' The Witch King sounded even more coldly thoughtful than usual. What was he thinking?

'Magic, sire?'

'Magic indeed, Urian and of no usual kind. If a Keeper of Secrets were simply moving itself we could assume it was being summoned by worshippers although this would speak of a level of Slaanesh worship in Ulthuan far greater than any we were aware of.'

Urian was of the opinion that Morathi was fully aware of the extent of the Lord of Pleasure's worship in Ulthuan, but whether she would share this knowledge with her son was a different matter entirely. 'You think this contingency unlikely, sire?'

'We do, Urian. Even if he were being summoned, there is no way he could bring a large force of mortals with him. There is some other form of magic at work here, one that interests me greatly.'

Urian could understand why. Anything that might allow the movement of large bodies of troops around Ulthuan so swiftly would be of great interest to the Witch King. His eventual goal was nothing less than the unification of the two elven realms under his own legitimate rule.

'You wish me to investigate this matter, sire?' Urian said, risking much. It was always dangerous to assume you knew what Malekith wanted and always dangerous to speak to him when he had not asked you a direct question.

'Precisely so, Urian. I want you to keep your ears open for even the tiniest scraps of information about this thing. Nothing is too unimportant to report as far as the daemon N'Kari is concerned.'

'I will pay scrupulous attention to all I hear concerning this. I will gather all the information currently available and hunt down every shred of rumour.'

'Diligence will be rewarded in this matter, Urian. Failure...' Malekith let the word hang in the air. There was no need whatsoever for him to spell out the penalties of failure in his service. 'Concerning the matter of the twins, do nothing at the moment. This takes precedence.'

'As you command, sire,' said Urian.

Malekith placed his hands together and the mirror went dark. The audience was clearly over. Urian was glad. He wiped cold sweat from his brow and helped himself to some wine. He had his work cut out for him.

CHAPTER SEVENTEEN

'It looks like they are preparing for a feast here,' said Tyrion to Liselle. The morning sun shone down on the courtyard, illuminating the bustling activity all around them.

His cousin was dressed in another expensive gown of green Cathayan silk and watching the retainers hang more lanterns on the trees in the courtyard. Twigs of oak and wreaths of oak leaves were being placed over doorways. Trestle tables were being placed in the courtyard. Carved wooden statues of treemen guarded every entrance.

'It will be the Feast of Deliverance soon. My grandfather is giving a ball to celebrate it, and the fact that you and your brother are among us.'

'You are certainly doing it in style,' he said. 'Making a statement, I suppose.'

'Yes and yes,' said Liselle smiling.

The Feast was a celebration of the return of Aenarion's children, Morelion and Yvraine from the heart of the Forest. They had been believed dead even by their father when in fact they had been under the protection of the Treeman Oakheart. He had saved them from the forces of Chaos and hidden them in the depths of the forest, thus preserving the life of the future Everqueen and her brother. Tyrion was descended from Morelion as was every other surviving child of the Blood of Aenarion save Malekith, the Witch King of Naggaroth. He could see that House Emeraldsea was reminding everyone of their connection with the Blood by ostentatiously giving this feast. If it turned out that he and Teclis were judged accursed it was a potentially very risky move.

'It looks like it is going to be a very big party,' said Tyrion. 'When exactly will it be?'

'In less than a week, on the night of the Rejoicing.' That was the traditional night when balls and parties were given and offerings made in temples. 'Although there may not be much to rejoice over this year.'

'What do you mean?'

'Word is that Ulthuan is under attack. Outlying mansions have been ravaged by worshippers of the Dark Prince of Pleasure. A whole town was sacked by an army headed by a daemon.' She sounded a little worried as she said it, but not as if she was taking it entirely seriously.

'How do you know this?'

'A messenger brought word to my mother last night. She was summoned to the palace. A ranger found bodies at a mansion in the mountains. It seems a mage survived the attack on Tor Annan and managed a Sending. Other places have been attacked. The Phoenix King called a council to discuss what happened and decide what to do about it.'

'A town sacked by daemons – that sounds very serious. Perhaps he will have no time to attend parties.'

'You obviously have not had much experience of life in Lothern, Prince Tyrion. The social round would go on if the world was ending. It is the life blood of this city. Anyway, I doubt Finubar is about to strap on a sword and go hunting daemons himself. That's what he has people like Korhien for.'

Tyrion paused to think about what she had said. Cultists attacking outlying mansions. Towns destroyed by daemon-led armies. It all sounded very unlikely standing here in this bustling courtyard in the bright light of day. And yet he supposed that was how these things must always seem to those not directly involved in them. This was nothing to do with him. Of that he felt sure.

'I hear you have been slipping out at nights,' said Liselle. She smiled. 'It did not take you long to find a secret lover.'

Tyrion smiled back. He should have known that his comings and goings would not be unobserved. There were other observers than guards watching over the mansion.

'There is no secret lover,' said Tyrion. 'I merely wanted to see the city without an entourage of retainers.'

'Use the front door,' she said. 'It's the easiest way.'

'I have the elven passion for secrecy and intrigue,' he said.

'Good,' she said. 'That always makes things more interesting.'

Before he could ask her what she meant by that, she strode away, pausing in the doorway to turn and smile at him. It looked posed but she was still lovely.

Life in Lothern was certainly interesting. There was no mistaking that.

TYRION HAD NEVER seen a place quite so crowded, dirty, smelly and wonderful as the Foreigners' Quarter. He was glad he had put on his old clothes and snuck out of the Emeraldsea Palace again.

He was free and just for this evening, he felt like his old self again. It was not just wearing his old clothes. It was not being hemmed in by endless formalities and the rituals of life in the palace.

He was already starting to be bored. Weapons practice was fun, but the endless lessons in protocol were not. He had enjoyed the dancing lessons and flirting with his pretty relatives but he had not enjoyed being told how to behave. He felt like he was somehow on probation, less than a guest, something of a prisoner.

Servants watched his every move. Bodyguards followed him everywhere, supposedly for his own protection. Tonight he had climbed down from the balcony of his chambers into the street and slipped off where no one would dream of looking for him. He knew he was being childish, that he should simply have taken Liselle's advice and used the front door, but he liked doing this.

This was the sort of adventure he had dreamed of ever since he was young.

For the first time ever Tyrion was seeing beings of a different race, and lots of them. They bustled through the Foreigners' Quarter as if they owned the place, and they paid less attention to him than he did to them. He supposed they must be used to seeing elves. He was not at all used to seeing humans.

They were smaller than he was, shorter than almost all elves, and yet heavier, bloated with fat and muscle. They looked clumsy and graceless and their voices sounded like the squawking and bellowing of beasts in a jungle. There were so many different types of them: tall, pale elaborately dressed men from Marienburg and the Empire; dusky hawk-featured, scimitar-bearing Arabyans from the lands of the south; Cathayans clad in silk robes.

He understood why some elves affected to despise them. There was a coarseness about them, a brutal directness of speech and gesture combined with a grubbiness and stench that was off-putting. And yet he was not put off – he found the differing accents and voices and clothes and body language exhilarating, as entertaining as any book or poem he had read.

Their clothes were coarsely made and their foods smelled of fat and salt and spices. Sausages of some indescribable meat sizzled on spits. Fish blackened on braziers. Sellers stomped everywhere with trays of savouries strapped to their chest, small but vicious-looking dogs snapping at their heels.

These humans were a long way from their homes but somehow they had made themselves at home here. The architecture of the quarter had taken on a humanish look. Brick buildings leaned at crazy angles against the remnants of much older elven structures. Ancient palaces had been turned into vast warrens and mazes of dwellings and shops and merchants offices.

There was none of the courtliness or formality of elvish culture. Men bumped into each other in the street and either backed away swiftly, hands reaching for swords, or grinned and nodded and passed on their way.

Merchants argued prices. Harlots led drunken sailors into side alleys and in pairs they humped and groaned against the walls. In quiet corners, men played chess on odd-looking boards with carved wooden pieces of strange design. He stopped to watch a game and just from a few moves he could tell the rules were not so different from those he was used to.

When the humans noticed him, they stopped and looked at him as if they anticipated him saying something. He gestured for them to continue but they just stared until even he felt a little uncomfortable and a little rude for distracting them from their game, so he sketched a bow and moved on deeper into the great bazaar.

Carpets hung overhead, draped over wooden racks intended to display them to best advantage. Perhaps it would have worked as intended if the skylights had not been blackened with soot and grime and the shadowy interiors of the corridors lit only by lanterns and flambeaux.

From the gloom he saw smaller, bearded figures peering and he was astonished to see dwarfs. Despite their long beards and squat builds these dwarfs were garbed more like humans than the heavily armoured warriors he expected. Had the race really changed so much since the times of Caledor the Second or were these some strange new hybrid of dwarf and human? He remembered Teclis telling him once that several clans of dwarves had gone to live among the humans of the Empire. Perhaps these were such.

He passed pawnbrokers and factors' offices and doorways where lurked small groups of armed men who appeared to have no business there. These looked at him with a real sense of menace. At first he thought they were simply as curious about him as he was about them, but after a while he realised that there was a different quality in the glances they gave him.

One of them, more elaborately dressed than the others, with a peacock feather in a slouched hat, strutted up to him and walked around him, inspecting him and all the time glaring at him.

'What you want, elfie boy?' he asked, mangling the elvish language with his teeth and tongue. His pronunciation was poor and his grasp of the subtleties of grammar non-existent, but it was still astonishing in its way, like listening to a dog that had learned to talk. It made Tyrion smile.

'What you grinnin' at, cat-eyes?' the human asked and his companions laughed. For the first time Tyrion realised there was a note of disrespect in the man's voice. He was more astonished than angered. It was like being mocked by a monkey.

He kept quiet because he could not think of anything to say and his silence seemed to encourage the human. His companions egged him on. As he came closer, the stench of coarse strong alcohol from his breath hit Tyrion with the force of a blow.

The man was drunk, Tyrion realised, and looking for a fight. Tyrion had never had any great need to learn the human speech and he greatly regretted that deficiency now. Perhaps if he had been able to speak to the man in his own tongue he might have been able to defuse the situation.

At the same time as the thought crossed his mind, another realisation hit him. He did not really care. If this monkey-man wanted a fight, he would get it. Tyrion had never backed down from one in his life and he did not intend to do so now.

It occurred to him that perhaps this was not the most sensible attitude – he was alone in the Foreigners' Quarter and there were none of his own kind to help him. This human had a whole gang of friends and it was perfectly possible all the other humans within earshot would aid him out of solidarity with their kind. Still, Tyrion decided, even taking all of these factors into account, he was not about to back down.

'What you lookin' at?' the human demanded in his pidgin gibberish.

'I don't know but it's looking back,' Tyrion responded. He did not know whether the man understood his words, but he certainly understood the tone of contempt. The man went for his sword. Before he could draw it, Tyrion struck him, the force of the blow smashing him to the ground. His friends rose swiftly, reaching for knives and blades.

'That was a good punch,' said a voice from behind him. From its tone and timbre, Tyrion could tell it belonged to a human but the words were not mangled or slurred. They could almost have been spoken by an elf. 'So fast I did not see anything but a blur.'

The owner of the voice said something in their own tongue to the gang of warriors. They sat down again as quickly as they had risen.

The speaker came into view. He loomed over the fallen bruiser and berated him. Tyrion's victim lay on the ground, abashed, a stream of blood running from his nose, and a dazed expression on his face. He seemed to grow smaller and smaller and less and less confident as the newcomer's tirade went on. Eventually he pulled himself up and slunk back to his friends, and they vanished through the archway they had at first appeared to be guarding.

'What did you say to him?' Tyrion asked. The newcomer turned to look at him. He was tall for a human and broad, running to fat. His face was ruddy but it had an open, honest quality that even Tyrion could read on a human face.

'I told him he was an idiot.'

'You seemed to tell him a lot more than that, or is idiot such a long word in your language?'

The stranger laughed. 'I was explaining to him exactly why he was an idiot, like his father and his father's father before him.'

'And why would that be?'

The stranger cocked his head to one side and inspected Tyrion for a long moment. There was nothing sullen or aggressive about that stare and Tyrion felt no resentment of it.

'You really don't know, do you?'

'I really don't,' Tyrion agreed.

'And you are much younger than you look.'

'How old do I look?'

'It's hard to say. All elves look the same and they could be a thousand years old.'

'Most do not live that long.'

'Yes but mostly you die through misadventure or violence. You don't age the same as we do.'

Tyrion thought about all of the humans he had seen in his wanderings through the Foreigners' Quarter. Some of them were more decrepit than any elf could ever be. 'We age more slowly and perhaps differently. I do not know enough about your kind to say.'

'Nor I about yours.'

'You seemed to have avoided my question, sir,' said Tyrion. 'Why was that man an idiot?'

'Because he was drunk and because by attacking you he could have gotten all of us banned from Ulthuan and that would be true idiocy, for there is a power of gold to be made in trading with elves, too much to be risked by the drunken stupidity of one ignorant fool with a chip on his shoulder.'

'That makes sense,' said Tyrion.

'Most assuredly it does, sir,' said the newcomer. 'Most assuredly. I try to make sense whenever I speak, I would like to think I am a sensible man, sir elf.'

'You seem so to me.'

'Thank you, sir. It is a compliment indeed that you should say so.' Tyrion noticed that the man had been almost imperceptibly guiding him out of the labyrinth of the bazaar as they walked. He found it amusing to have been so neatly manoeuvred and to his own advantage. Clearly the man did not want to say there was the possibility of Tyrion's presence creating another disturbance deeper in the bazaar, and just as clearly he was trying to avoid the possibility arising. It was handled most adroitly. Tyrion realised that he would have to reassess his opinion of the humans. They were clearly cleverer and capable of greater grace than most elves gave them credit for.

He could not wait to share this information with Teclis. He knew it would amuse his brother.

'AND THEN WITH the greatest of ease, he led me out of the marketplace, and to the gates. He was saying farewell in such a natural and easy manner that it seemed only natural that I should pass through them and come back into Lothern proper.'

Teclis laughed but there was something else written alongside the amusement on his thin face, a wistfulness that made Tyrion realise just how much his twin envied him this little adventure.

'Who would ever have thought you could have a sitting room like this?' Tyrion said, to change the subject. The chamber was impressively furnished. The table was massive, worked from rich aromatic wood from Cathay and inscribed with intertwined nymphs and godlings. Over two walls hung heavy tapestries of the richest sort. There was crystal in the windows and they had no shutters, only a thick pair of curtains capable of cutting out any draft.

On the wall opposite was a picture depicting merchant ships at sea, the source of their relatives' great wealth. Near the table was a freestanding mirror in which Tyrion could see his own reflection and that of Teclis. He stood in the light of the lantern, Teclis was partially concealed in shadow.

'I think the servants have chambers as good as ours,' Teclis said, his tone caustic.

'I do not care,' said Tyrion. 'I have never seen a room as sumptuously appointed as my own.'

'That's because you have so little to compare it to. There are other houses in Lothern as rich as this one and with rooms ten times as well furnished.'

'How do you know so much about this place already?'

'Because I read, brother, and because I quiz the maid who comes to make up my room and see to my needs.'

Tyrion could imagine his brother's questioning and felt a little sorry for the maid. Teclis was blunt to the point of being almost human, and he had a most un-elven way about him.

'I do not care if anyone is much richer than us. I, for one, intend to be happy here.'

'You would be happy anywhere. It is your disposition to be so, disgracefully, bright, optimistic, sunny.'

How could I not be, when I have this great city to run around? Tyrion was about to say, but he realised that would only make Teclis more bitter and envious. It came to him then, and he was astonished at his own slowness of mind, that the reason why his twin was being critical of their cousins was because he was angry at Tyrion for having his adventures but could not bring himself to say so.

Teclis was making his anger felt in other ways, unfair to their kindred and unworthy of him. Tyrion felt almost guilty for a moment, but pushed the feeling aside. He was who he was through no fault of his own, he was not going to apologise for it to his brother.

'And it is yours to be bitter, brother,' said Tyrion. 'Although I can understand why...'

'I honestly doubt that, Tyrion. You have no idea what it is like to be stuck here, knowing that out there life is going on and a great city is going about its business while you are trapped and can do nothing... nothing.'

'I can try,' said Tyrion weakly. And behind all the other bitterness he sensed a deeper one. Teclis had briefly enjoyed a few weeks of good health before his relapse. It was a cruel blow to him. No wonder he was angry.

'Yes, and you do.' Teclis said.

'What is that book on the bedside table?' said Tyrion to change the subject again.

'It is a book of conjurations. Lady Malene has a whole library of such things here.'

'You've visited this library then?'

'Mara, the maid, told me of it so I had to see it.'

Tyrion could imagine his brother limping along the corridor to reach such a prize. He had gone through all of the books in their father's house except the ones their father kept locked in his magically sealed cabinet because they were too dangerous for any but a skilled sorcerer. Tyrion could well remember his brother's obsession with that cabinet. It looked like nothing was locked here. He supposed the spells must be harmless, otherwise they would be kept under lock and key.

'And you... ah... borrowed this one?'

'Yes.'

'Does Lady Malene know?'

'Take a look at this,' said Teclis, going from bitter and caustic to excited in a flash. He opened the book and Tyrion saw lines of words separated by multiple straight lines marked with what looked like musical notes.

'It looks like music with words,' said Tyrion. 'Is it a song?'

'No, it's a spell. The words are the incantation, the first line of symbols below shows right-hand gestures, the line below that left-hand gestures, the last line shows inflexion.'

'Inflexion?'

'It's a sort of twist of mind that you must perform to touch the power of the spell in the right way – violent, sad, passive and so on.'

'Like a mood?'

Teclis made a face which showed what he thought of his brother's suggestion.

'In a way, I suppose.'

'They are just squiggles on a page to me.'

'Trust me they are more than just that. Lady Malene has told me enough of the theory for me to know.'

'I'll take your word for it.'

An urgency came into Teclis's voice. 'It all just fits together. There is a unity to it and when you understand that you can do almost anything. You change your own internal state, you touch the winds of magic, you tap their power, you change your state again, and shape the forces with your mind, your words, your gestures and all the time what you are really doing is altering the world.'

'In all honesty, I can't say I follow you.'

'I will show you, look. Put a chair in front of the mirror and help me to it.'

Tyrion was not sure he liked the way this was going but he did as his twin asked. It was good to see him so animated and for once not touched with bitterness. Teclis sat with the book in his hand, and then made some odd gestures, fingers rippling, hands twisting as he crooned words in an archaic version of the elvish tongue.

A chill touched Tyrion's spine. He felt uncanny forces flow around him. He looked into the mirror and saw concern on his face. Teclis's features had become a mask, and his gaze was fixed and staring. Even as Tyrion watched, the mirror misted as if someone had breathed on it, although no one had. Their outlines became shadow and blurred and then vanished altogether. The surface of the mirror rippled and settled and became normal again.

'It looks just the same,' said Tyrion. 'I don't know what you were trying but it did not work.'

Teclis smile was a ghastly rictus. He made a gesture with his left hand as if he were spinning a top. The image in the mirror turned. At first Tyrion wondered if Teclis had made him dizzy with his magic but then he realised that he was perfectly stable and so was the room. It was the point of view in the mirror that was changing.

Teclis made another gesture and he was looking at the two of them from behind. It was as if the mirror had become the eye of some great roving beast and they were looking out from behind that eye. Tyrion laughed at the wonder of it and Teclis joined in, obviously enjoying the feeling of power, and the use of magic.

The view in the mirror shifted again, moving through the door and out into the corridor. It flew along now as fast as Tyrion could run, and Tyrion guessed his brother was enjoying the vicarious experience of running at a speed he would never achieve in life. Tyrion wondered if the point of view could fly. That would be truly a wonderful thing.

Even as that thought struck him, he saw Lady Malene running along the corridor towards them. She reached a point just in front of the eye and gestured. The mirror went suddenly dark. Teclis gasped as if stabbed. A few moments later, the door in the room opened and she entered.

'What is going on?' she demanded, in a tone of utmost urgency.

She gazed around the room as if seeking some threat, a faint nimbus of light played around her hands. Tyrion realised she was prepared to work magic at a moment's notice, and he guessed from her expression that it would be a spell of a potent and deadly sort. 'Did something try to break in here?'

He could hear the sound of many running feet now. Armed warriors poured into the room as if in answer to some unheard summons. They gazed around the room too, obviously as baffled as Lady Malene. They looked like soldiers who having nerved themselves up for combat were disappointed to find no foe awaiting them.

'It was me, lady,' said Teclis.

'What was you?' she said.

'I worked a spell.'

'You are not a mage yet, boy. I sensed the presence of an awful power. I thought we were attacked, that you were attacked because the focus of the power was here.'

'I worked a spell,' said Teclis stubbornly. He indicated the open book on his knee.

Lady Malene came over and snatched it up. 'You cast this?' There was naked disbelief in her voice. 'Impossible.'

'My brother does not lie,' said Tyrion rankled by the tone their aunt was taking. He would have been more annoyed at her tone had he not sensed that she was angry as much from concern about their well-being as annoyance at what Teclis had done.

She looked at the spell again, and then at the mirror. Her hand moved through a small circular gesture. She spoke a few words in the archaic version of Elvish that Teclis had used to invoke the spell. The surface of the mirror shimmered brilliantly and then faded. She turned her gaze back upon them.

'Look at me,' she said. 'This is no joke so don't smile. Answer me and answer me true. Did anything enter this chamber? Did anything breach the wards on this palace?'

'No,' said Teclis with utter assurance.

'Did you cast the Spell of the Invisible Eye?'

'Yes.'

'Who taught you how to do that?'

'No one.'

'Don't lie, boy. What did your father teach you?'

'Nothing, witch,' said Teclis just as annoyed, and seemingly completely oblivious to the way armed elves reached for weapons when they heard his tone. 'My father taught me nothing. The basic procedures were all in this book. I worked out the rest for myself from what you have already taught me.'

'You worked out the rest for yourself? Do you seriously expect me to believe an untrained lad could derive from first principles the knowledge to cast a third order spell of transvisualisation?'

'I don't care whether you believe me,' said Teclis with superb arrogance. 'I did it. I could do it again.'

Lady Malene stared at him for a very long time. 'You are either a wonderful liar or the greatest natural mage who has ever lived.'

Later Tyrion was to remember that her words had the force of a prophecy.

CHAPTER EIGHTEEN

'WHAT AM I to do with you?' Lady Malene asked. She sounded as if she did not really know. She looked as if she had not slept since last night. Teclis had, the most peaceful and natural sleep he had enjoyed in many days.

'I am not yours to do anything with,' he said. Her manner made him nervous. He was glad Tyrion was not here in his room to witness this. He was not in her power exactly but she had something he wanted, knowledge, mastery of technique. It would be possible for him to teach himself magic based on what he had seen in the grimoires but she might well forbid him access to any more books. If that happened he would find a way to get them if he could, but they might stop him. In any case it would be a much longer and slower route to learning, and he wanted to learn magic the way an elf lost in a desert craves water.

'Your life is,' she said with some certainty. 'At this moment.'

'Is that a threat?'

'No. I mean your path in life. I can teach you or I can report you to the Phoenix King's palace and you will be restrained until after you have been tested.'

'That is not fair.'

'Life is not fair, Prince Teclis. I regret that you should have been introduced to this concept so young, but you are wise beyond your years so I am sure you will have no difficulty grasping it.

'I do not require platitudes or irony.'

'No. You require teaching – that much is obvious. You will experiment on your own if you do not get it or are not actively restrained. And to one of your power that could be very dangerous.'

'I am not unaware of the dangers of magic.'

'Fire will not hurt me, says the child who has never yet put his hand in the grate.'

'I am not a child.'

'Then do not behave like one and do not sound so petulant. You know nothing of the dangers of magic... Nothing! One of your power can so easily do so many things and do them wrong.'

'Like what?' He was more curious than angry now.

'You could overdraw your power and burn it out forever. Believe me that is not a fate that anyone born to the Art would want. Death would be preferable.'

Teclis could see how that would be true, but he sensed a hesitation in her manner. There was something she was not telling him and did not want to. Of course, he had to know.

'And?'

'And what?'

'What else could go wrong?'

'Is that not enough?'

'There are other dangers you are not mentioning.'

'And should not, not until your studies are far more advanced than they are now.'

'How can I avoid a danger when I do not know what it is? You say you fear what I might do. Help me avoid that.'

She looked at him warily and with something more like respect. To her, until that moment, he had been nothing but a gifted adolescent. She had never considered the possibility of treating him like an equal although she must have known she was going to have to one day. She seemed to come to a decision.

'Very well. For your own good I will tell you. Heed my words and heed them well – for not just your life but your soul might depend on them.'

He felt a thrill then, and not the one she expected him to feel. He was on the verge of dark and secret knowledge and he felt its unrelenting tug. It was something he knew had power over him and likely always would. Perhaps he thought this was how the Curse of Aenarion worked on him.

'Speak,' he said.

'There is something about working the Art that draws the attention of daemons. There is something about the souls of those who can use magic that attracts them, something daemons desire the way an epicure craves larks' tongues in honey. If your soul is not properly warded, if you cast a spell unthinkingly and without protecting yourself, you can draw their evil to you.'

'That is the sort of superstition that humans believe,' Teclis said.

'It is nothing less than the truth. When you work the great high magics you will know it. You will sense the presence of Chaos and its minions around you. You will sometimes sense their hunger and their rage even when you work the slightest of spells. It is the way of things.'

'You are saying this to frighten me.'

'Yes, I am. And you should be frightened! For there are magics you will never work without placing your soul and the lives of everyone around you in peril. That is why what you did today was foolish and wrong. You risked not just your own being but that of your brother. You put me at risk and the guards who came to investigate. If something had reached out from the great abyss and taken possession of you, it could use your body and your talent to wreak great evil. The more natural power a mage has, and you have more of that than anyone I have ever encountered, the greater the prize they are going to be for the powers of Chaos.'

She spoke calmly and with authority and with utter conviction, and much to his surprise Teclis began to feel ashamed of himself. 'I will not do it again,' he said at last.

'That would be wise. There will be many temptations placed in your path, Prince Teclis, some of them very subtle. It is best to be wary when you are a student of the Art. Always remember that. Always!'

'I shall.'

'Do so. There is something very strange happening in the world today. Daemons have come to Ulthuan once more and I would not like you to draw them to you.'

N'KARI FELT STRONG. For the first time since he had escaped the cursed Vortex he was starting to feel like himself. He had fed well on blood and souls and agony and ecstasy. He had bathed in the blood of the Blood of Aenarion and feasted on their hearts and eyeballs then used their corpses for his pleasure.

His followers had grown to be quite an army. Cultists from all over Ulthuan had come to join them as word of what they were doing spread, a company of renegade dark elves had come to do homage, and a crew of shipwrecked Norsemen had been seduced and broken to his will. He had summoned more daemons and drawn more monsters to him. His legions could face an army in the field, but he was not quite sure that was necessary yet.

Of course, there had been the problem of food. The perennial problem of supplying an army on the move had arisen. N'Kari had solved it in the traditional way. Some of the captives had been used as pleasure slaves, some had been taken as recruits, others had become cattle to be devoured by his soldiers.

He had taught his followers the exquisite epicurean pleasures of the Dark Feast and he suspected that now they would have trouble going back to lesser foods, even if he let them. He had imbued the spiced elf-meat with some of his own dark magical power and was well-pleased that some of the mortals were starting to show the stigmata of mutation. They were well gone down the path of Chaos and would go much further before their adventures were over.

'There are magicians within,' said Elrion. The chief of his followers looked demented. His sanity had not been improved by the fact that his skin had started to harden on his arms and chest, providing him with some natural armour at the cost of some diminishment of his personal beauty. N'Kari rather liked the effect of his wild, staring eyes, and the crack that came into his voice whenever he tried to pronounce certain words. His teeth were becoming fangs and something was happening to his tongue and throat. N'Kari could hardly wait to see what.

'Yes,' said N'Kari. So much was obvious from even a cursory examination of the tower on the hilltop before them. It was wrapped in powerful protective spells and had a number of sophisticated wards in place. A few of those who waited on the walls surrounding it were mages. He could tell easily enough from the way they wrapped themselves in shimmering spells of illusion and battle. Their weapons too had enchantments placed upon them, as did the weapons and armour of the warriors. 'And their flesh will taste all the sweeter for being spiced with power. Trust me there is nothing quite like the savour of a wizard's soul when you devour it.'

'I think the master of the tower is expecting us,' said Elrion.

Of course, he would be expecting them, for he was a mage. He had probably seen their approach at leagues of distance through his scrying crystal. It was a pity the tower was not closer to the entrance to the elder paths; then they could have taken him completely by surprise. Then again that would have deprived N'Kari of much of the pleasure of battle and slaughter. One always had to take a balanced view of these things.

N'Kari doubted being forewarned would do the defenders much good in the end. His forces were too numerous now and there was no chance of reinforcements reaching the elves unless they used the same means as N'Kari did to transport their forces, and they had not the knowledge or the courage needed to do that.

Some of his troops possessed the wit and the skill to begin to construct crude siege machines – catapults and covered battering rams. They had cut down the trees from sacred groves to make them, and one or two of the cultists had even managed to imbue them with magic to improve their utility. It would only be a matter of time before the gates or the walls surrounding the tower were breached and his followers were within. All he had to do was give the order and the battle would begin.

N'Kari paused for a second to savour the moment. As he did so a tall figure appeared on the battlements and began incanting a spell. It was an order of magnitude more potent than anything being woven by the apprentices. The master of the tower had decided to take a hand. A ball of pure magical energy arced towards the nearest siege machine, blasting it to blazing fragments, searing the flesh from its crew and leaving only vitrified bones standing there for a heartbeat before they collapsed.

N'Kari was not amused. He had been about to give a rousing speech to his followers, to act the part of the great leader. It would seem their opponent for the day did not intend to give him time to play that role. So be it. He would find his amusement in other ways, by tormenting the soul of the one who had robbed him of that fleeting pleasure.

'Attack,' N'Kari shouted, shifting his form to something like his natural and most beloved one. He was rewarded by screams of terror from the walls. You could usually rely on magicians to recognise a daemon when they saw one. It seemed like some of those on the walls had some idea of N'Kari's capabilities. Perhaps he would spare a few of the most abject of them, if they grovelled enough.

Then again, perhaps not.

'YOU'RE VERY GOOD, doorkeeper, and you're getting better all the time,' said Korhien. He was actually breathing heavily from the workout. He leaned on the practice sword and he stared at Tyrion. 'You have made a lot of progress in the past weeks.'

'I'm pleased to hear you say it,' said Tyrion. He glanced away. More and more porters were arriving, bringing decorations and food for the upcoming ball. 'I feel like I am getting better but I have nothing to judge my progress against.'

'I have,' said Korhien. 'And you can take my word for it – there have been very few warriors who have learned how to use a sword as quickly or as well as you have. You have an uncanny ability with weapons. It's as if you were born to use them.'

'Maybe I was,' said Tyrion. 'But I think that is true of most elves who live in these times. We are all born to use weapons whether we like it or not. It is an age of war.'

'That it is, doorkeeper. Although I doubt that you have much of an idea of what that really means just yet.'

'I'm sure that I will have before much longer,' said Tyrion.

'I hope not,' said Korhien. 'You're a bit young yet to be going to war.'

'It is what I have dreamed of since I was a child.'

'You will find that the experience does not bear much relation to what you have dreamed about. These things never do. It is one thing to read about them in stories or to hear warriors tell tall tales around a campfire. It is another thing entirely to chop an elf into pieces or stick a sword through his body.'

'You have done these things,' said Tyrion. 'And you do not seem to be any the worse for it.'

'I have done these things and there are times when I wish I had not.'

'And there are times when you're glad that you have,' said Tyrion. 'I can tell.'

'It is a complicated thing, doorkeeper.'

'In what way?' Tyrion asked.

'Killing someone in combat is a complicated thing. It is not how you imagine it to be. It is wonderful and it is terrible and it is not at all what you expect.'

Tyrion looked at the older warrior. Korhien's face was thoughtful and Tyrion could tell that he was choosing his words with care. He stared off into the middle distance as if remembering something that was important to him and which he wanted to communicate exactly.

'It is like this,' Korhien said. 'When you kill someone in battle you have proven your own superiority over them. You are alive and they are dead and there is no more definitive proof than that. It is thrilling in a dreadful way. It is horrible and it is terrible but it is also thrilling. You feel more alive than you ever have before or quite possibly ever will again. You are very aware of the presence of death and how close it has come to you and that lets you know that you are alive in a way that nothing else ever will. Do you follow me?'

'I think so,' Tyrion said. 'But what is so terrible about it?'

'At that moment, nothing. But later you will find yourself thinking about what happened and about how you felt and about how the other person feels now.'

'They won't be feeling anything,' Tyrion said.

'Exactly,' Korhien said. 'They won't be feeling anything at all and you will have ensured that. You will have made that happen. And after a while you'll start to wonder about what you have done – was it justified? What right did you have to kill that person? Would it perhaps have been better if they had killed you?'

Tyrion could see that Korhien was not just talking in the abstract here. He had someone specifically in mind. He was thinking about things that had affected him deeply in his time. It was not so much what the older elf was saying that affected Tyrion. It was the way he said it.

Tyrion could not imagine ever regretting killing someone who had been trying to kill him. In a case of his own life or that other person's, he would feel entirely justified in his victory. And yet something in Korhien's tone gave him pause for thought. If the older warrior had found something in all of this that had affected him so deeply, at very least Tyrion felt it deserved his deepest consideration.

'Do you wonder about such things?' Tyrion asked.

'All of the time,' Korhien replied.

'Why?'

'I wish I knew. When I was younger they troubled me not at all but I have found that over the centuries I have thought more about them and I have found the easy answers harder to find.'

'You are a warrior,' Tyrion said. 'It is your duty to kill the enemies of the Phoenix King.'

Korhien smiled. 'I wish I was young again and everything seemed so simple to me.'

Tyrion resented that. 'Have you heard any more about these attacks everyone is talking about? The servant girls seem to think Lothern itself will be besieged by an army of daemons any day now.'

Korhien shook his head. 'It will not come to that. Not yet anyway.'

'Then there have been more attacks.'

'Yes. And many of them. Not a day passes without reports coming in by messenger bird, sending spell or word of mouth. The whole island-continent seems to be under attack by an army of daemons. And yet when our troops investigate, they find nothing. It is as if the attackers have vanished into thin air.'

'The daemons are using magic,' said Tyrion.

'I see your genius for understanding military matters was not understated, doorkeeper,' said Korhien sardonically. 'Of course, the daemons are using magic.'

'Why are they attacking the places they do? What do they want?'

'No one knows and no one can see any pattern to it. Not even the cleverest of mages. The daemons appear out of nowhere, they attack, they slaughter like maddened wolverines and then they depart, taking nothing. It is a kind of madness, or so it seems.'

'It is what you would expect from daemons,' said Tyrion. 'Who knows why they do what they do?'

'Not I, that is for sure,' said Korhien. 'Nor anyone else at the moment. Nothing like this has happened for centuries. Panic is spreading everywhere.'

'Perhaps that is the intention,' said Tyrion. It seemed absurd to be thinking this way, watching tradesmen bring flowers and lanterns for the ball, and chandlers bringing in provisions for a great feast.

'You are not the first to suggest that, doorkeeper.'

'At least we are safe here,' said Tyrion. 'Lothern is the best defended city in Elvendom.'

Korhien nodded. 'It galls my heart to remain here doing nothing while our land is ravaged,' he said.

'I am sure the time will come when you will be called on to fight,' said Tyrion. He rather envied Korhien that chance.

Korhien smiled.

'I will see you tomorrow night at the ball,' he said. 'I understand it is going to be a special one.'

'No training tomorrow?' Tyrion asked. He was disappointed.

'The Phoenix King has called another council to discuss these attacks. I must be there. Some things take precedence even over your training, doorkeeper.'

'Apparently balls are exceptions.'

'Believe me, after one of these councils, we will all need a party to cheer us up.'

CHAPTER NINETEEN

Floating spheres of spell-woven light illuminated the great hall of the Emeraldsea Palace. An orchestra of the finest musicians played on a raised dais at one end of the room. Huge fans swirled in the high ceiling propelled by unseen magic. Hundreds of beautifully garbed and noble-looking elves crowded the room. They stood at the edge of the chamber in the shadow of alcoves housing enormous statues or round the tables on which a buffet of the finest elven viands lay. They chatted in dark corners or drank wine from carved crystal goblets or danced in the centre of the floor, performing the steps of the vast intricate ritual quadrilles demanded of this sort of social gathering.

Teclis had never seen anything like this. It was his first ever ball in one of the palaces of Lothern and it was, to say the least, impressive.

Tyrion stood on the balcony, watching everything and smiling easily and amiably at all who passed. He looked perfectly at ease in his beautiful clothes. His natural charm and good looks made up for any lack of formal courtesy in his manner. Teclis envied him all of these things. His own clothes felt too loose for his tall spare frame and no matter how often the retainers adjusted the cut and flow of them, they could never seem to make him look like anything but a gangling scarecrow.

Back home, Teclis had been the one favoured by their father and Tyrion had been the outsider. Here it was obvious their roles were always going to be reversed. Tyrion was the one who was the centre of attention and Teclis knew beyond a shadow of a doubt that it was going to be that way from now on.

He felt a touch on his elbow. Lady Malene stood there in a sparkling blue dress of some mage-woven cloth that shimmered with cosmetic glamour-spells. Her hair was piled high on her head and held in place by jewelled pins. Long diamond rings depended from her pointed ears.

'You are not enjoying this, are you, Prince Teclis?' she murmured.

'How can you tell?' he asked sardonically.

'You hang back from the gathering. You have not talked to anyone or asked anyone to dance. Your brother does not seem to suffer from any such restraint.'

'Tyrion is the soul of charm. People like him. He knows how to put them at ease.'

'It's unsurprising. He is good looking, poised, confident – he is not shy.'

'You think I am, lady?'

'You are not easy with yourself or with other people. Perhaps you never will be.'

'If you are trying to bolster my self-confidence with this little chat, you are failing.'

'These are not uncommon failings among practitioners of the Art. We have a reputation for eccentricity, reclusiveness and a lack of social skills.'

'I have not noticed that you possess any of these qualities.' He said it because it was true. She was a very lovely woman and capable of being quite charming despite her severe manner.

'I have had several centuries to gain some polish. Hopefully you will get the same opportunity.'

'Do you think what people say about mages is true then?' Teclis was curious.

'In some ways, yes. It's hardly surprising that mages should be reclusive. Ours is a life that requires study and a great deal of time spent alone with books. We need a lot of specialised knowledge that can be of no possible interest to the layman. It also requires that we be strong-willed and self-centred.'

'I follow you. Where does the eccentricity come from?'

'A lot of time spent isolated will make even the most balanced seem eccentric and give them a chance to develop strange notions and habits. And I think there is something about exposure to the winds of magic and the practice of the Art itself that lends itself to mental instability.'

'So I can look forward to even more isolation in the future,' he tried to make it sound like a joke, but he was feeling somewhat sorry for himself. Tyrion had enthusiastically thrown himself into a quadrille and was dancing with a group of smiling young elves. He said something that made them all laugh.

'No – you will find comradeship with other mages, if you do not alienate too many of them. They are the ones you will have most in common with – shared interests, shared knowledge and shared needs.'

'Well that is something to look forward to at least,' he said.

'There is no need to mock, Prince Teclis.'

'As if I would ever do that to you, Lady Malene.'

Tyrion was dancing with their cousin now, the lovely Liselle. He said something. Liselle smiled. She said something. He smiled. How effortless he made it look, and yet when Teclis tried such things, it never worked. People did not respond to him the way they did to his brother.

At moments like this, Teclis thought he would be willing to give up the Art to be able to make a girl smile the way Tyrion could. The feeling never lasted more than a moment though. The Art would make him master of his world eventually. He felt sure of that.

TYRION DREW LISELLE away from the dance floor. Her bare arm was warm beneath his fingers and he felt the erotic spark pass between them. She smiled at him, glanced at the direction of Lady Malene and Teclis and said, 'Your brother is watching us most intently.'

'He is watching you most intently,' said Tyrion. 'He is captivated by your beauty. As what elf would not be?'

'He is very odd.'

'In what way?'

'The way he stares so. He is intense and cold and calculating. You feel as if he is measuring you and finding you wanting.'

'I have never found him to be like that.'

'He thinks he is cleverer than us.'

'He *is* cleverer than us. Take my word for it.'

'You always stand up for him, don't you?'

'He is my brother.'

'And that is reason enough to take his part? Against anyone?'

'If I do not take his part, who will?'

'My mother will. She likes him, I can tell.'

'Then I like her,' Tyrion said, hoping Liselle would take the hint.

'Your brother is a cripple. Has he always been so?'

Tyrion did not like the direction this conversation was taking at all. 'Would you care to dance once more?'

'They say that among the dark elves cripples are exposed upon the mountainside as babies, to prevent them being a burden on the rest of the community.'

Tyrion stared at her. 'And you think that is a good idea?'

'Our ancestors used to do the same, before the Sundering.'

'Those were crueller times. They had just fought a war against the forces of Darkness. In many places they still were doing so.'

'I have heard people say that we are becoming weak and decadent.'

'You think that becoming more like the dark elves will make us less decadent?' He smiled, hoping she would see the joke. 'Perhaps we should try being more like dwarfs to make ourselves less stubborn.'

'There are some who say we became decadent during the reign of the last Phoenix King. They hope that Finubar will bring back elven boldness and elven strength. He is a seafarer and an explorer, not a decadent conjurer.' She spoke with obvious pride. Finubar was of Lothern. He exemplified the virtues of her people.

'It is not necessary to denigrate one person in order to praise another.'

She laughed at his serious words as she had not laughed at his joke. 'There are times when I think you cannot be an elf, dear cousin, but some sort of changeling. There does not seem to be much malice in you.'

'I don't think you need to be malicious to be an elf either.'

'Then you have a lot to learn, my dear Tyrion. You are in Lothern now. It's a nasty, vicious place.'

He glanced around at all the rich people, in all their fine clothes, eating their fine food and drinking their fine wine. 'Yes, I can see that. It's really cut-throat.'

'Do not be deceived,' she said. 'Many of these people would stick a knife in your back if they thought it would get them ahead in the world. And in some cases, I am not just speaking metaphorically.'

'Are you always this cynical?'

'I am a realist,' she said. 'I grew up here. I know what they are like.'

'I have always heard it said that the high elves are the noblest people in the world.'

'And I am sure you have always heard it said by high elves. We are not ashamed to praise ourselves, are we?'

'Should we be?'

'It would not matter if we should. It would not stop us. Oh dear, it looks like Lord Larien has noticed us.' She made a small grimace but he thought she was not really so displeased.

'Why is that a bad thing?'

'He has been paying court to me for some time. He can be quite jealous.'

Tyrion had noticed the tall, athletic-looking elf earlier. He had not appeared to be so jealous. He had been surrounded by a coterie of admiring beauties to each of whom he seemed to be giving a portion of his attention. All of them appeared to be flattered to receive it too. He strode closer, straight backed, head held high. He smiled at Liselle, nodded curtly to Tyrion.

'Ah, the delightful Liselle,' he drawled. 'And this would be your cousin from the mountains we have heard so much about.'

Tyrion smiled at him. 'I only see one of you. Is that the royal we you are using?'

Lord Larien looked at him a little more closely, as if he had not been expecting any rejoinder from Tyrion.

'I am Prince Tyrion,' said Tyrion, to make the point that he did have royal blood. He bowed. 'I am pleased to make your acquaintance.'

Liselle laughed. This did not please Larien. 'Larien. Delighted,' he said, his expression making it very clear he was anything but. 'It has been a pleasure. Lady Liselle. I hope we can expect a dance later if your cousin does not insist on monopolising your time.' His tone made it clear how boorish he considered this.

Gracefully, Larien bowed to them in a way that made it clear he was only really bowing to her, and then he backed away to his coterie of admirers. Liselle laughed and smiled at Tyrion admiringly.

'There is more to you than meets the eye,' she said. He smiled back but he was not happy. He sensed she was playing a game here and he was a counter in it. Her real interest was in Larien and he was being set up as a potential rival to generate a little jealousy and interest.

Larien said something to his female admirers. They all looked at Tyrion and laughed. He waved at them gracefully as if delighted to be the centre of attention although he knew he was somehow in trouble.

A VERY PRETTY young elf maid detached herself from the laughing group orbiting Lord Larien. She glided closer, a picture of grace in her long ball gown. 'Lady Liselle,' she said. 'Why do you not introduce your beautiful companion to the rest of us? We are all ab-so-lute-ly dying to make his acquaintance.'

'Prince Tyrion, Lady Melissa,' said Liselle. He bowed. She curtsied. Lady Melissa looked up at Tyrion through very long lashes. Her eyes were a very pale grey.

'You do not look much like your brother,' she said. 'It is hard to believe you are related. One so fair, the other so... interesting.'

'We are twins,' said Tyrion. 'I am the older by a few minutes.'

'Twins. That is so unusual. Twins are very rarely born to high elves,' said Melissa.

'They are very rarely born to any sort of elves,' said Liselle.

'Indeed. That is what I meant. It's very, very unusual. Perhaps your parents used certain occult fertility rituals.' She placed a strange emphasis on the last two words, and Tyrion could not help but feel that he was being insulted although he had no idea how.

'I don't think so,' he said. 'My father was a mage, of course...'

Melissa sniggered. Liselle looked torn between embarrassment, anger and a desire to laugh herself. He did not see how what he said was funny. He kept smiling smoothly though, unwilling to let them make him uncomfortable. If they wanted to play games, that was fine. He knew that once he had worked out the rules, he would win. He always did.

'I have said something amusing,' he said. 'Perhaps you would care to explain to me what it was.'

They were discomfited by his response. It was not what either of them had expected. He smiled easily and stepped forwards, invading Melissa's personal space. He was aware of exactly the effect his physical presence had on women. He leaned forwards, intimately and whispered in her ear, 'Tell me what was so funny.'

She stepped away a little flustered. He smiled at her friends as if they had been sharing a confidence. He saw that they were all looking in this direction now. Melissa looked down over her left shoulder and then back up at him, and he was suddenly aware that he had changed the dynamic between the three of them completely.

'I meant nothing at all,' she murmured and retreated to her circle of friends.

Tyrion looked at Liselle and raised an eyebrow. 'I think Melissa was hinting, rather indelicately, that your parents might have used certain forbidden magics,' said Liselle 'Or been involved with certain forbidden cults. Just as she was at first hinting that twins might be rare among high elves but not among dark elves. She likes to think she has a subtle wit.'

'Why would she say that?' Tyrion asked, genuinely puzzled. 'About my parents.'

'There are certain rumours,' said Liselle. 'There always are. It's that kind of city.'

Tyrion decided he would need to take this matter up with his brother. Teclis always knew more about this kind of thing than his brother. 'If you will excuse me for a few moments, I will be right back.'

He walked over to Teclis, passing Melissa and Lord Larien and their little clique. He smiled as he passed, as if there was nothing more delightful than their attention.

'An animal,' he heard one of the women say, as he walked by.

'But a rather beautiful one,' said somebody else. He thought it was Lady Melissa.

* * *

'SHE SAID WHAT?' Teclis sounded annoyed. Tyrion smiled as if his brother had just made a joke. He glanced around. Lady Malene was involved in a discussion about seafaring with Iltharis and Korhien. No one was paying them any attention.

'Hush, brother,' said Tyrion. 'Do not let them upset you. I suspect that it is what they want. They seem to take pleasure in that sort of thing around here. In this game it appears to be the way you score points.'

'They are talking about our parents, Tyrion. They are hinting that they were members of the Cult of Luxury, a forbidden cult, associated with the worship of daemon gods. With the Lord of Pleasure, the One Who is not Named.' Teclis had lowered his voice now. This was not a subject anyone wanted to be overheard talking about. This was a thing mentioned only in whispers, talked about obliquely, never confronted directly.

'I cannot picture our father being involved in such a thing,' said Teclis. 'Can you?'

Tyrion tried to imagine his father anywhere else but in his workroom or reading a musty tome of magic. It was impossible. There was no way to picture him being involved in forbidden rites. It was as easy to imagine him captaining a slaving ship from Naggaroth. 'No.'

Teclis became thoughtful. 'And yet we are here, twins. And twins are indeed rare among elves.'

Tyrion remained quiet. He could see his brother was giving serious thought to the matter. He had always been one to try and see all sides of an issue.

'I do not think it is possible,' he said eventually.

'I am glad we are in agreement then,' said Tyrion. 'Why would anyone spread such rumours?'

'Malice,' said Teclis. 'You know what elves are like.'

'Surely there are better targets for such malice,' said Tyrion. 'Our father is an old, poor elf living in seclusion in the mountains. No one gains anything by saying such things about him.'

'Everybody always has to have a reason with you, don't they, brother? Has it ever occurred to you they might do it for the simple pleasure of the thing.'

Tyrion could not see what that pleasure might be, but he was starting to realise that he might be unusual in that last respect.

'You have a good heart,' Teclis said eventually. He said it as if it was an accusation of weakness. Tyrion did not take it personally.

'Be that as it may, I think it is safest to assume someone somewhere has a motive for spreading this rumour now. If it is not aimed at our father, it is most likely aimed at our dear, rich relatives.'

Teclis nodded. 'Possible. Or it may just be that we are the topic of discussion of the moment and people are throwing mud in the delightful elven fashion.'

Tyrion laughed. 'You are probably right. I may be taking this too seriously.'

'Frankly I am surprised that you think about these things at all, brother. If it's not to do with war or battle, you are usually not interested.'

Tyrion inclined his head in the direction of Liselle and Melissa and the small faction of extremely lovely young elf maids around them. 'I am starting to realise there are all sorts of battlefields and all sorts of ways to compete for glory.'

'Are you sure it's glory you are interested in?'

'The span of my interests is wider than you believe.'

'I should add girls to war and battle, should I?'

'Girls were always included. I am starting to think about politics.'

'The reason why wars are fought – according to one of our more ancient philosophers.'

'When diplomacy fails, wars begin,' quoted Tyrion.

'So you have taken to reading other things than histories of battles and legends of heroes.

'No. Korhien told me that.'

'Perhaps you should emulate your mentor and start reading more widely.'

'Lady Malene told him that. Or so he said.'

'At least he listened.'

Tyrion did not tell him he suspected Korhien was lying about that. The White Lion read much more widely than he wanted anyone to know. It suited him to be seen as the bluff and not-too-intelligent soldier but he was actually something more.

It was not surprising when he considered it. Korhien was a companion and a bodyguard to the Phoenix King. He went on diplomatic missions for him. He acted as a go-between between Finubar and the great houses and the princes. Of course, he was more than a simple soldier.

Tyrion could also see the advantage he gained by having people underestimate him. It was not too difficult to understand the advantages Korhien gained from the role he played. Perhaps he should consider doing the same.

'You are thinking too hard about something again,' said Teclis. 'There is a nasty smell of burning wood.'

'You know me too well, brother,' Tyrion said. 'Now if you excuse me I must return to the ladies.'

'They look as if they are getting lonely without you.'

'I will see what I can do to change that,' Tyrion said. He walked back over to Lady Liselle smiling pleasantly, the very picture of a simple, true-hearted, lusty young elf with only one thing on his mind.

CHAPTER TWENTY

T YRION WALKED BACK into the lion's den. He smiled amiably at anyone who looked at him, giving no indication that he felt embarrassed or flustered by the gossip circulating about his parents, his brother or himself. There was no reason to. He had no quarrel with any of those present, unless they chose to make one. In that case, he would not back away from a fight.

The Lady Melissa glanced at him and smiled again. Larien stared rudely. It seemed like a deliberate attempt at intimidation. Tyrion shrugged and walked over.

'I trust running to your crippled brother and your frosty aunt has put your mind at rest,' said Larien. His face was a little flushed although whether with wine or anger or something else Tyrion could not tell.

'About what?'

'About your dubious parentage.'

There was a moment of silence. This was not the sort of thing said in polite elf circles. Even those nearby were quiet now, waiting to hear Tyrion's response.

'There is nothing dubious about my parentage,' said Tyrion calmly.

'I am sorry, perhaps I should have said your dubious parents,' said Larien.

Definitely drunk, Tyrion decided. The goblet in his hand was empty, and Tyrion could recall seeing it refilled more than once.

'Hush,' said Lady Melissa. 'This is not the time or place for this. You are a guest of House Emeraldsea.'

She shot Tyrion what looked like an apologetic look, but he could not miss the glitter in her eyes and the faint twist of her lips. She was enjoying this.

'Yes, hush, Larien,' said one of her friends. 'You are embarrassing yourself.'

Nothing could have been better calculated to goad Larien than pointing this out, Tyrion thought. Perhaps that was the intention.

'I am not the one who should be embarrassed. I am not the one who was conceived at some Slaaneshi orgy.'

'Nobody here was,' said Tyrion.

Larien gave a cruel laugh that was all the more shocking because of the note of pity in it. 'You really don't know, do you?'

'Larien,' said Lady Melissa. The warning in her voice was obvious. Larien paid it no more attention than a drunken dockman would pay an ant.

'Know what?' Tyrion asked. He knew that he really should not, but he was curious.

'You and your brother were conceived in the Temple of Dark Pleasures. That is why your brother turned out the way he did...'

'How would you know?' Tyrion asked pleasantly. 'Were you there?'

'Are you implying that I am a member of the Cult of Luxury?' Larien asked. He looked a lot more sober all of a sudden. His words were said very loudly, as if he wanted everyone to hear them.

All around was silence. All eyes in the room were on them now. Tyrion understood what was going on but there was no way he could stop it. It had all happened so quickly.

Out of the corner of his eye, he saw Korhien moving across the room towards the disturbance. He would not get here in time to intervene.

'Well, are you?' Larien was almost shouting now. He cocked his head to one side as if Tyrion had already replied. 'How dare you imply such a thing?'

Tyrion decided he might as well make the best of a bad situation. He smiled mockingly at Melissa and her friend and then at Larien. 'I was merely astounded that anyone could claim such familiarity with Slaaneshi ritual as you did. If anyone implied such a thing, it was you.'

Larien's hand shot out towards Tyrion's cheek. He obviously intended to strike the blow that marked the formal challenge to a duel. Tyrion had been expecting it. He stepped to one side and struck Larien hard in the stomach. The goblet fell from his hand.

When he had regained his wind, Larien said, with some satisfaction. 'You struck me.'

'It seemed better than allowing you to strike me,' said Tyrion.

'There can be only one redress,' said Larien. 'The Circle of Blades.'

'As you wish,' said Tyrion, ignoring the way Korhien was shaking his head.

Larien pulled himself upright and glared around.

'Leave now,' said Korhien. 'You've got what you came here for.'

Larien smirked at him.

'And I would not smile like that if I were you,' Korhien said. 'If this young elf does not kill you, I most assuredly will.'

That took the smile off his face, Tyrion thought. He grinned and then the thought struck him that the only circumstances that Korhien would be taking vengeance for him, was if he himself was dead.

'You cannot do that Ironglaive, duelling is forbidden to White Lions,' said Larien. His smirk had returned. Surrounded by his clique of adoring ladies he made his departure.

The air seemed suddenly very chilly.

'THAT WAS VERY foolish, doorkeeper,' said Korhien. He had led Tyrion into a side room. Outside, the hall was in an uproar.

'Listen to the commotion,' Tyrion said. 'Apparently challenges to duels are not as common at Lothern parties as this evening's experience has led me to believe.'

'This is not a joking matter. That elf intends to kill you and he is quite capable of doing it. Sober he is one of the best blades in this city.'

Korhien's seriousness communicated itself to Tyrion. 'I wish you had told me that before I hit him.'

'Go ahead! Joke your way into an early grave, doorkeeper.'

'I did not start it.' It was the sort of thing a child might say and Tyrion was conscious of it as soon as the words left his mouth.

'I am sure you did not.' Korhien expression was bitter. 'I should have seen this coming.'

'Who would have expected anyone to be so boorish as to start a brawl at a Lantern party,' said Lady Malene. She had just entered the chamber. Teclis was beside her, his face pale.

'The question is who put him up to it and why?' said Korhien. 'We need to know who it is so we can put pressure on them to make him withdraw.'

'What?' Tyrion asked. He had never heard of such a thing. Or read about it. 'No one withdraws challenges.'

'It happens all the time,' said Lady Malene. 'Larien will lose face and have to leave the city for a few years.'

'If we can make whoever set this hound on Tyrion call him off,' said Korhien.

'We are going to have to,' said Malene. 'I do not think he is ready to kill his first elf just yet.'

She was wrong. After what Larien had said about his parents Tyrion was more than willing to kill Larien. In fact he would enjoy it. It was the first time he had ever realised such a thing about himself. It was not a pleasant thought.

He was disturbed to discover that Liselle had been wrong earlier. There was malice in him. It was just more deeply hidden than it was in most elves. And there was a terrible anger too although most times he hid it from everyone, even himself.

TYRION HEARD A knock at the door. Cautiously he padded over on his bare feet and answered it. He could hear someone just outside. He was not too worried but he slid the bolt back cautiously and pulled the door open. He was surprised to see Liselle standing there. She was dressed in a night robe which clearly had nothing underneath it.

'What do you want?' he asked.

'I'm sure you already know,' she replied.

'Then I suppose you had better come inside,' he said. He pulled the door fully open and gestured for her to enter. She strode inside and looked around.

'My room is just down the corridor,' she said. He reached out and pulled a strand of hair from behind her ear. He leaned forward as he had done earlier, and whispered into that ear, 'That is very fortunate.'

She leaned forward and kissed him on the lips. It was a long kiss and it started experimentally, tentatively but it ended up being very passionate.

'Yes,' she said, 'it is. Let us both make the most of that fortunate accident of geography.'

She led him by the hand towards the bed.

N'KARI ROARED AS he raced through the streets of Tor Yvresse, killing as he went. He was strong now. He had eaten many souls and supped on many pleasures, his own and others. He felt almost as mighty as he had been on the day he had faced Aenarion millennia ago.

His army was an army now, no longer a mere raider band or an ill-organised group of cultists. It was a force strong enough to take even an ancient walled city like this one.

Hundreds of partially altered warriors had joined him. He had found more humans, shipwrecked mariners from the Old World. Groups of beastmen who had somehow survived in the high mountains and kept to the old ways had been drawn to him. Decadent elves had responded to the summons of his magic. Souls offered up in sacrifice had multiplied the number of daemons bound to his will. All of them rampaged through the streets of the city now, maiming, killing, raping, torturing, pillaging.

Terror and pleasure and hatred and fear pulsed through the air around N'Kari. It was like a banquet to him. He drank it all in.

A company of elf soldiers formed up in the square ahead, moving in a disciplined phalanx to repulse a company of his beastmen. The brutes threw themselves against that steady line with simple-minded ferocity that might have worked if they had been facing tribesmen as primitive as themselves but which had no chance of success against these foes.

Briefly N'Kari considered aiding his followers, of using his own power to break the bodies and spirits of the enemy but he sensed the opposition to his presence was growing and he still had a task to perform here. Somewhere out there a cabal of wizards was using its power to strengthen the ancient wards against his kind that had been built in ancient times. These were spells that could hurt him. They were already making him uncomfortable and they had the potential to banish him from this place if he was not careful. He was not going to take the risk of that happening, not until he had completed his vengeance on the Blood of Aenarion.

He could sense the nearness of the prey he sought. His nostrils flared in response to what his spiritual senses detected. Saliva filled his mouth and dripped onto the ground. Elrion leapt forward and grovelled in the dirt, licking it up, moaning in ecstatic pleasure that contact with N'Kari's secretions always gave to mortal things. N'Kari trampled on his back, leaving great talon marks on the writhing acolyte's flesh, forcing Elrion face down in the puddle of drool as he strode forwards.

Ahead of him was a small tenement house, inside of which a few warm bodies huddled. The ones he sought, two elves half-garbed in their militia gear who had obviously been trapped here en route to joining their unit, were being menaced by a group of beastmen. They bore the spiritual scent of the Blood of Aenarion.

N'Kari shifted his form, becoming an elf of spectacular beauty, goddess-like. He blasted his own beastmen in the back with a bolt of purple lightning and raced up to the elves. They stood there bemused by his loveliness and the narcotic cloud surrounding him.

'Quickly, follow me,' said N'Kari in a voice at once seductive and commanding. 'I will see you to safety.'

The elves looked at him, grateful for being saved, bemused at the appearance of a powerful sorceress they did not recognise. N'Kari reached out and stroked the cheek of the nearest one. He quivered with pleasure. 'We do not have any time to waste. Follow me. I will weave a spell that will get us out of here.'

He opened a portal and without giving the elves time to think, shepherded them through it before following him themselves. The elf he had touched was already looking at the other with insane jealousy. N'Kari chuckled, thinking of the sport he would have with this pair.

Behind him his army battled on. It would take them some time to realise they had been abandoned by their leader and begin a fighting retreat. N'Kari did not care. He had found what he had come for. Soon there would be two fewer of the line of Aenarion left.

There were not many more now. Soon his vengeance would be complete.

CHAPTER TWENTY-ONE

LORD EMERALDSEA LOOKED up from his telescope. He had obviously been studying the ships in the harbour. He gestured for Tyrion to join him on the balcony. Tyrion walked over, curious why he had been summoned into the august presence this fine morning.

'It took us a thousand years to put Finubar on the throne,' said Lord Emeraldsea. His words took Tyrion off guard. He had expected to be lectured about the events of the previous evening, about challenging other elves to duels at family parties.

'A thousand years?' Tyrion said, just to see where this was going. He was exaggerating. Finubar was not that old.

The old elf obviously sensed the current of his thoughts. 'He was the first Phoenix King ever to come from Lothern. You have no idea how difficult it was to make him that. The work began long before Finubar was born.'

Tyrion wondered why his grandfather was telling him this. Perhaps the old elf was lonely and just wanted someone to talk with, to go over old triumphs with, but somehow he doubted it. Lord Emeraldsea did not strike him as someone who did anything without a purpose.

'Why was it difficult?' Tyrion asked, because he felt he was expected to.

'The princes of the Old Kingdoms objected to it, of course. They have had a monopoly on the throne since before the time of Caledor the Conqueror. Aenarion was the only one they never had a say in the choosing of.' He glanced at the huge statue of the first Phoenix King in the harbour with something like admiration. From up here all they could see was his back. 'It's always been one of their own they made ruler.'

'Why did they object to Finubar?'

'Because he was from Lothern.'

'Because he was not of ancient blood?'

Lord Emeraldsea laughed bitterly. 'Finubar's house is as ancient as that of Caledor. So is mine for that matter. We have been here since the Kingdoms were founded.'

'But you are not of princely blood,' said Tyrion. He did not really care about that himself, he was just trying to understand the argument. Lord Emeraldsea looked hard at him, as if attempting to discern any trace of mockery or pride in his own ancient lineage. Apparently he was satisfied with what he saw.

'No, we are not. But nowhere is it written, nowhere did the gods dictate, that our rulers must be of that blood. In the past, some of them were not, some were simple scholars or warriors.'

'But they were chosen by the princes.'

'Indeed. They were chosen by councils of princes, selected from candidates put forward by them, usually because the princes felt they could control them, or because they were in the debt of one prince or another.'

Lord Emeraldsea was tampering with his faith. Tyrion had always liked to believe that Phoenix Kings were chosen from the best elves available with the best interests of Ulthuan at heart. This all sounded rather sordid. He said as much.

'All the workings of the machinery of power look sordid when you see them from close up,' his grandfather said. 'And they are. But that does not mean they are a bad thing. At least we do not have Malekith as our ruler like the dark elves. And that is the point. It is why he is not our king and we still fight wars with the druchii.'

Tyrion understood at once. 'You mean because he wanted to be the single absolute ruler like Aenarion, and because the princes would not let him be. They chose one of their own to make that point.'

His grandfather seemed gratified by the quickness of his understanding, which pleased Tyrion. He was not used to being appreciated for that. 'In a way. Malekith wanted more power than Aenarion ever really had. Aenarion was a war leader, accepted as such because in times of danger it is necessary to have a clear line of command. Any ship's captain can tell you that. Malekith wanted the same power as Aenarion held in war in peacetime, or rather his mother wanted that for him, or so it seemed at first. Our system is as much about preventing that sort of tyranny as it is about the exercise of power. The dark elves have a different system. You can see what it has brought them to.'

'Surely they have a bad system because they have a bad ruler,' Tyrion said. 'What has happened there merely reflects the personality of Malekith.'

'Or perhaps they have a bad ruler because they have a bad system,' his grandfather countered. 'There are no checks on the power of the Witch King. He does what he wants. He rules by fear and terror with a fist of literal iron. He does not need to consult with anybody, or take the interests of anyone except himself into account. I think that sort of power would make anybody mad, and believe me I have had some experience of wielding power in my life.'

'I do not doubt it,' said Tyrion.

'It's a very seductive thing,' said Lord Emeraldsea softly. 'To stand on the command deck and issue orders. To know everyone has to listen to you and obey and that their lives depend on it. Even when you are not on the command deck, it distorts life around you.'

'What do you mean?'

'Sit at a captain's table on a ship. Watch his officers and his crew as they eat. They laugh at his jokes, acknowledge his wisdom, burnish his pride. They have to because their own assignment of duties and their own prospects of promotion depend on his assessment of them. Power exercises its own magnetic field. Never doubt that, Prince Tyrion, and remember it if you exercise power yourself.'

'I will,' said Tyrion, and he meant it. He was glad of the circumstances that had forced him from his father's house at times like this. He felt he had a lot to learn from elves like his grandfather and Korhien and Prince Iltharis. He could never have learned it if he had stayed at home.

'I know you will, which is why I am telling you it.'

'You were telling me about the election of Finubar,' Tyrion said. 'Of how difficult it was and how much it cost.'

'It was and it did. We needed to convince a large number of the old princes that we were serious. We extended loans to some, bought up the debts of others. Gifts were given to those who could not be pressured. In the end, we still could not have done it, if it had not been Finubar's time.'

'What do you mean?'

'The princes recognised that the world had changed and we needed a new style of leadership, one that engaged us with the younger races and the world beyond Ulthuan. They saw that we needed allies and those allies would need to be made by someone with an understanding of those far lands. That's one advantage that Finubar had and one advantage that we have. We tend to get the leadership we need when we need it because in the end all of our interests are conjoined. Your idealistic view of the world is not so far from the truth as it may sometimes sound, lad.'

'Why are you telling me this?' Tyrion asked.

'Because I was thinking that the day will come when we might need a leader like you could become, a warrior who thinks.'

'Who also happens to be a member of your family?'

'That would be a bonus. You have everything needed, lad. An ancient line, the look of Aenarion, connections. You could go very far.'

Lord Emeraldsea paused to let his words sink in. They did, far and fast. Tyrion understood what his grandfather was offering and why. Right now, he was very far from being a Phoenix King but he had the potential. Once his grandfather was certain Tyrion understood he spoke relentlessly on.

'Of course, you have put any chance of that at risk by allowing yourself to be provoked into this foolish duel.'

'Larien insulted my father and my mother.'

'He insulted all of us, and he would have been dealt with in time, trust me on that.'

Tyrion did. He realised that he would not like to be subject to any desire for vengeance on his grandfather's part. 'Revenge, Tyrion, is a wine which improves with age. It's one of the things you will need to learn, if you live. If you are to end up where you deserve to be.'

'I cannot stand by and let my father be insulted.'

'You will need to learn how to deal with such provocations better. Even if you live, this will not be the last such you will face.'

'I will do my best.'

'See that you do, lad, and one last thing...'

'Yes, grandfather.'

'Rest assured that if Larien does kill you, my vengeance will be one of which elves will talk for a thousand years.'

'That would almost make it worth being killed,' said Tyrion sardonically.

'No, it would not. Go now and rest and practise. I want you to live. You have a lot to live for.'

Tyrion departed, feeling as if he had just been offered the world, and did not quite know what to do with it.

'ARE YOU PROUD of yourself for having provoked this brawl?' Tyrion looked at his brother, then sprawled in the chair of their shared sitting room. Tyrion could see that he was worried, and that was what was behind his brittle sarcasm.

'No,' said Tyrion. 'I am not. I would have avoided it if I could. I should have avoided it. I can see that now. But I lack your quick wits.'

'That is not true,' said Teclis. 'You are sharp enough when you want to be. I think perhaps you wanted this fight. I think you want the glory of being a famous duellist. I think you are making an early start on a career of violence.'

Tyrion laughed, not least because his brother was right. He could see that now. He did want this fight. He was looking forward to it.

'It might be a very short career,' Teclis said. 'Larien is, by all accounts, something of an expert with the blade. He has killed almost as many elves as Prince Iltharis.'

'You have been asking around, have you?'

'Lady Malene told me.'

'It seems I have become almost as much of a topic of conversation as these daemonic attacks.'

'Don't let it go to your head. It most likely will though. There is nothing in that vast empty cavern to stop it.'

'I am touched by your concern,' said Tyrion, stifling a yawn.

'Do not let cousin Liselle keep you awake too long. You are going to need your rest, if you are to survive this thing.'

'I will survive it, brother, never doubt that.' It seemed to Tyrion that he was the only one who thought that way.

TYRION LAY BESIDE Liselle on the bed. He stroked her naked back with a feather that had come loose from the pillow during their love-making.

'That tickles,' she said, turning to face him and looking long and hard into his face.

'You are going to have to fight Larien tomorrow, you know,' she said. Tyrion looked at her. She had obviously heard something he had not.

'I already knew that,' he said. 'I knew it when I struck him.'

'He cannot be bought off. He cannot be intimidated. He seems to want to go through with this fight almost as much as you do.' She sounded thoughtful. Tyrion tickled her once again. She squirmed away.

'You should take this very seriously,' she said giggling. 'My grandfather has brought a lot of pressure to bear and it has not worked. That is not usual at all. Usually what he wants, he gets.'

Tyrion did not wonder that his grandfather had not tried to dissuade him. If Tyrion withdrew it would besmirch his reputation and that of his family. He would no longer be a potential candidate for the Phoenix Throne and would become useless as far as his grandfather's plans were concerned.

'You do not sound unhappy that this is not the case.'

'It will not do the old megalomaniac any harm to discover he is not a god. My concern is that you will have to pay the price for his self-knowledge. I do not want anything bad to happen to you.'

Tyrion smiled at her, sensing the insincerity of her words. She was saying them because she felt she had to, because the role she was playing in this drama demanded them. There was no real concern there. She was as self-obsessed as most elves. He could not blame her for this. They had only really known each other for a few weeks. It saddened him. He began to have some idea how lonely a place a city like Lothern was going to be.

'Rumour has it that Larien belongs to the Cult of the Forbidden

Blade,' she said. 'They are sworn to kill the Blood of Aenarion to prevent one of them from drawing the Sword of Khaine and ending the world.'

'Maybe they should start with Malekith. He is a more likely candidate for that than me. I find this world quite appealing.'

'I don't want anything bad to happen to you,' she said. Again, she sounded like an actress playing a role.

'Nothing bad is going to happen to me.'

'Death might,' she said.

'Well we are alive now and if I am soon to die I want to sample some more of life's pleasures.'

He reached out for her once again.

CHAPTER TWENTY-TWO

IT WAS AN odd sensation, rising on what might be his last day of life. Tyrion dressed with care, inspecting himself in the mirror as he did so. He was not pale. He did not sweat. His hands were steady. His heart did not race or pound in his ears. The only thrill he felt was excitement. He considered his response, observing himself dispassionately as an outsider would. He was definitely not afraid. He doubted that whatever happened he would disgrace his family or his famous ancestor. That, at least, was good.

He was aware of the possibility of death, perhaps even its likelihood, but he suffered none of the symptoms of fear or nerves he had heard or read about. He was merely curious as to his own reaction or lack of it.

If he was honest with himself, he was looking forward to the Circle of Blades. It would be his first real test as a warrior. He felt as if he was finally getting to do something he had always wanted to. His curiosity extended to what it would be like to have a life or death combat and how he would perform.

Perhaps this excessive calmness was a reaction to the situation. Maybe his mind was trying to deal with the danger by minimising it. He had read that such things happened. He did not think it was the case for him. Something told him that he would always be this way on the morning before a battle. If it was abnormal then he was abnormal. He was of the Blood of Aenarion, a descendant of the first true elf warrior.

When he came downstairs to breakfast, he could see that others were not taking it quite as well. Teclis looked pale and afraid. His eyes looked huge. Tyrion could tell that he had not slept at all. Lady Malene did not look any better. Her expression was filled with foreboding. Liselle looked wan and pallid.

Tyrion grinned at them as he sat down at the table. He helped himself to water and a slice of bread and butter. He did not want to eat heavily for it would slow him down but he wanted to make sure he had some energy.

His grandfather merely smiled his chilly smile, apparently pleased by the way he was going to meet his fate.

The servants moved quietly around him as if afraid to say anything, as if he were an invalid or a ghost. It was as if some vast formal ritual were taking place, as if they wanted to show support or say farewell. Most of them looked at him curiously as if he were a rare specimen the like of which they might never see again. Many were sympathetic. Some looked jealous or disbelieving, as if they were watching a poor performance by an actor.

Why would that be, he wondered? Did they resent him being the centre of attention? Were they envious of his supposed bravery? Did they secretly dislike him and wish him ill? He felt sure that some did. It did not matter to him. He smiled at them all alike.

Korhien and Iltharis entered. They were formally garbed. Korhien wore his lionskin cloak. Iltharis was garbed in sombre black.

'Ready?' Korhien asked.

'Ready,' Tyrion said. His voice sounded calm and normal. He wanted to tell everyone not to worry, that it would all be all right, but that did not seem like appropriate behaviour. Instead as he passed Teclis he squeezed his shoulder. Then he was out of the dining room and into the courtyard where the horses were waiting for them. Thirty armed retainers were there as well. They would be needed to make up the circle.

It occurred to him that he might just have seen his brother for the last time. As a thought it was troubling but he felt no emotional response. It came to him then that he really was behaving differently. This calmness and clarity of thought were unnatural. So was the retreat from emotion. They were his body and mind's response to the danger of the situation.

He was absolutely aware of everything around him, the faint sheen of the sunlight on the horse's skin, the animal smell, the bulk of it. When he vaulted into the saddle he felt his body's movements and the interplay of his muscles with the horses as he had never done before.

This intensity of perception continued as they rode through the city. He saw the cracks in the pavements and the plasterwork of the buildings, the feathers on the gulls that perched on pillars. The streets were busy as merchants set up shop and farmers drove their flocks into the city for market. Workers were already making their way down to the docks. Other riders moved through the streets on their own errands. Tyrion drank it all in, noticed everything, smiled at everyone who looked at him.

They rode through the north gate of the city and along the Sea Road, pushing through the late arriving drovers and early arriving travellers as they moved towards Lothern. Korhien took the left-hand path up the Watch Hill. It was traditional that the other protagonist would arrive by the right-hand one. Idly Tyrion wondered who would be first to arrive. Some people made a lot of that. Some chose to arrive early to show they were not afraid, some to come late to unsettle their opponent. For him, it did not matter. The fight was the thing. He was looking forward to it.

They rode to the hilltop and he could see his opponent and his two seconds were already there along with the thirty warriors of his part of the circle. They stood ready, looking at Tyrion with contempt graven on their faces. Tyrion smiled at them with the same friendliness he had shown everyone else this morning. The two seconds looked away. Larien shook his head as if Tyrion had committed some kind of faux pas.

Tyrion turned to look down from Watch Hill. He had a fine view of the Inner Sea approach and the Northern Walls of Lothern. It was not as impressive as the view of the Great Harbour coming in from the ocean but it was still striking. From the hill, you could see over the walls and notice the slate roofs of the buildings, the layout of the streets, the size of the largest statues. The waters of the Inner Sea were a calm mirror.

The sun had fully risen now and the morning was already warm. The sky was a very clear blue overhead. Gulls cawed. In the distance tiny figures made their way along the road. It was curious that they still had everyday business. Down there in the city, merchants bought and sold, lovers held hands, families were sitting down to breakfast. Up here two elves prepared to settle a matter of life and death.

It was the way the world worked. Always somewhere someone would be going about their daily routine while elsewhere mortals fought for their lives.

He rolled his shoulders and stretched his muscles and became aware that the others were looking at him curiously, as if they could not quite understand how he could be so calm. He knew they thought he was young and inexperienced and he supposed they expected him to show nerves. He did not feel any. He was enjoying himself. In a way he even took pleasure in being the centre of attention here. He would have smiled again, but this was a serious business now and deserving of a serious response.

He focused his attention on Larien. His opponent did not look so relaxed. He looked tense but not in a way that would be bad for a fighter. His movements crackled with nervous energy. His pupils seemed very large. All of his attention was focused on Tyrion. When their gazes met, he turned his head and spat, sending a gob of spittle to land at Tyrion's feet. It was a very grave insult.

Tyrion merely shrugged. This was all posturing, an attempt at intimidation, to unsettle Tyrion and put him in a frame of mind where he would make a mistake. Tyrion looked at Korhien who nodded, and Iltharis who was studying him closely in the way a gambler might study a horse before a race. Tyrion wondered if Iltharis had made a bet with someone and whether it would be for or against him.

It would have to be a bet for me, Tyrion decided. The odds against me would not make risking gold worthwhile. You could get good odds on me winning. That was the decision he himself would have made at least.

'For or against?' he asked. Iltharis seemed to understand at once what he meant. He smiled ruefully.

'For,' he responded.

'How much?'

'Ten gold dragons.'

Tyrion whistled. It was a hefty sum.

'Your confidence is inspiring,' Tyrion said.

'I got excellent odds.'

'I thought you would. What were they?'

'You sure you want to know?' Tyrion understood the question. It might damage his confidence if he knew how little was expected of him.

'Absolutely.'

'Fifty to one.'

'I wish I had known. I would have asked you to put something on for me. It would be a good bet. If I win, I get to spend the winnings. If I lose, I don't care.'

'You will not lose,' said Korhien. He did not sound entirely confident of that, but it was heartening that he cared.

'You are right,' Tyrion said, with sudden absolute confidence. 'I will not.'

Iltharis said, 'Larien has a tricky feint. He will mount a strong attack high and right and then will stab for the stomach. He will try to get you into the rhythm of defending against the flurry and then switch when you think you see an opening yourself.'

'I will bear that in mind,' Tyrion said. He would too, but he would not put too much faith in it. He preferred to study his opponent for himself and work on his own observations.

'He will use the early parts of the fight to feel you out,' said Korhien. 'He will pretend to be slower than he is, so he can take you off guard with the killing strike.'

Tyrion smiled at them both. 'I thank you for your advice.'

'But you have had enough of it,' Iltharis said. 'I recognise that tone.'

'I will win this for myself.'

'Never refuse any advantage you might get in a fight,' Korhien said. 'It can make the difference between life and death.'

'Even if it's dishonourable?' Tyrion asked.

'Especially if it's dishonourable,' Iltharis said with a grin. Korhien shot him a warning look. The other seconds were coming forward now. The duel was about to begin. All sixty warriors were forming in a circle, presenting their blades, points towards the centre. The duel would take place within a ring of sharp steel. The warriors would strike down any contestant who tried to flee from the battle.

The formalities were already gone through. Larien was not willing to retract the insult. Tyrion felt that honour must be satisfied. The seconds had done their best to make sure the quarrel had been settled amicably. Duty was done. The fight could begin. Both participants stripped to the waist and took up their weapons.

'I shall kill you slowly and painfully,' said Larien, as they walked down into the depression and took their places in the flat space below.

'The way you think,' said Tyrion and smiled brightly.

Larien looked hard at him.

'Slowly and painfully,' Tyrion said, to make sure Larien got the point.

Things were obviously not going the way he expected. Tyrion's nonchalance had evidently surprised him. He had come expecting to kill a nervous boy. He had found someone more self-possessed than he was. Tyrion decided that in part this fight was to be won in the mind. He suspected that most individual combats were. It was as much about the attitude of the fighters as it was about skill.

'I am of the Blood of Aenarion,' said Tyrion, simply, as if he were explaining something to someone slow of mind. It was an attack designed to increase Larien's unease and make him less sure of himself.

'I will soon see what that looks like,' said Larien. 'I am guessing it is the same colour as anyone else's.'

It was a good response and Tyrion smiled at it as if hearing a joke he enjoyed particularly.

'Shall we begin?' he asked, looking from Korhien to Larien's chief second. The two of them nodded. They stepped back to take their places on the edge of the ring. They too presented their blades. There was no way out of the circle now. All of the gaps were closed. Anyone trying to get out would be impaled upon a blade.

Larien sprang forward as lithe as a tiger. Tyrion parried easily enough and stepped forward. Blade strokes blurred between the two of them for the moment. Tyrion kept his guard up and made a few ripostes. He was content simply to ride out the fury of the initial attack and take the measure of his opponent.

Larien was quick and he was strong and his technique was excellent. Tyrion did not need Korhien's training to know this. Something in his mind was aware of it, in the same way as he was aware of the strength and weakness of a chess position. He doubted Larien had the same quickness of reflex as he himself possessed but he decided not to act on that assumption until he had more proof of it. Larien could, after all, easily be faking it, hoping to make him overconfident.

A few more passes of the blades told him this was not so. The elf's personality was reflected in his blade work. His swordplay was intricate and deceptive but the deception was in the technique. Larien relied on that and his natural strength to overcome his opponents. He was much better with a sword than most elves ever would be. He smiled at Tyrion, teeth gritted.

'I see what you mean about killing me slowly,' said Tyrion as they stepped apart. 'Are you trying to lull me to sleep?'

'No,' said Larien, springing forward. His blade was aimed high. An elf less quick than Tyrion might have had his head split. As it was Tyrion merely stepped backwards, parrying as he went, noticing that the rain of blows Larien had unleashed did indeed have a rhythm, and one most likely intended to lull the opponent into parrying the pattern of it.

He found himself falling into the pattern almost automatically, as an elf might sometimes find himself tapping his fingers in time to a drumbeat. He could see the danger of what Iltharis had predicted happening. It came as no surprise when suddenly the blade was not where it should have been according to the pattern of strokes. Tyrion had already predicted where it would be and parried it. He brought his left fist crashing into Larien's face.

Cartilage broke under the impact. Larien went reeling back, blinded by pain and tears. Tyrion leaned forward to full extension, ramming his sword into Larien's stomach. He felt the impact all the way up his arm. There was a scraping sensation as his sword hit bone. Larien screamed like an animal being pole-axed. Blood gouted forth, covering Tyrion's sword and hands, spraying onto his naked chest. Some of it got in his mouth. He caught the coppery taste.

Part of his mind was aware that this should be horrific. It was certainly not beautiful or glorious. There was a stink of blood and entrails, of things that should normally be inside an elf's body but now were not.

He did not mind it, just as he did not mind the screaming, or the sight of the light dying in another elf's eyes. The main thing was that, at some point, the sword had left Larien's hand and was now lying on the ground. His own life was no longer in danger. He had wiped out an insult to his family's honour and he had forestalled an attack on his clan by their enemies.

He felt a twinge of sympathy for Larien's pain. Korhien had been right in one way. It was hard to watch another elf die, but that too was a problem easily solved. He struck again, aiming for the heart, and silenced Larien's screams forever. He looked around at the other elves present. They stared at him in wonder and something else; it might have been horror.

'Unorthodox and inelegant,' said Iltharis. 'But effective.'

Korhien nodded. 'The main thing is that you are alive.'

He stepped forward and hoisted Tyrion into the air, laughing. He seemed more relieved than Tyrion felt and suddenly it struck him why. Korhien had not been looking forward to explaining to Prince Arathion how he had led his son to his death. Tyrion looked down at the corpse of Larien. Already it looked different. The face looked stark and all animating spirit had left it. The eyes were glazed.

Larien's two seconds were covering his corpse with a cloak. Tyrion contemplated the shrouded form for a moment, only too aware that it might so easily have been his own. He felt no rush of reaction, no urge to scream or shout or sing with joy. He was keenly aware of his triumph, that he was alive and he had proven the victor and that was enough for him. He had a sense of satisfaction and pleasure though.

'By all the gods,' Iltharis said. 'You are a cool one.'

TYRION WAS BARELY aware of his surroundings as they rode back towards Lothern. He kept going over the fight in his mind, replaying every move, reliving every blow, remembering every small detail lovingly. He was excited, not disturbed. He had never felt better or more alive.

Larien had tried to kill him, for reasons that Tyrion was still not very clear about. He had never done anything to hurt Larien and, as far as he knew, he hadn't given the elf any reason to pick a quarrel with him. Larien was dead through his own choice. Tyrion had merely been his chosen means of execution.

He was sure that Larien would not have looked at things this way. He was quite certain that Larien had expected to be riding away on his own horse while Tyrion lay cold on the ground. He imagined that no one ever thought that they were going to be the ones who died when they picked these quarrels but it was inevitable that somebody was and Tyrion was glad it was not him.

He was more than glad – he was pleased and proud. He had demonstrated his skill against one of the most famous duellists in Lothern. He had beaten Larien fair and square and he knew that in some ways he was going to inherit the elf's reputation. Now he was going to be famous. Now he was going to be the one that people studied when he walked down the street and he was going to be the one that they whispered about in taverns and salons.

He glanced around him and saw the way that his companions were looking at him. Korhien looked troubled. Iltharis looked pleased. The rest of his companions looked at him admiringly and enviously. He could tell that some of them wished they were him and that was a heady feeling. They were all basking in the reflected glow of his victory.

Tyrion glanced around at the road and his surroundings. He had not been really aware of it before. He had been too lost in his own thoughts. Now he could see everything with an almost perfect clarity. He was aware of the greenness of the grass and the brightness of the sun and the caress of the wind against his flesh. He knew that food would taste better and that kissing a girl would be much more pleasant.

Korhien rode up beside him. 'How are you feeling?'

'Never better.'

'You are taking it very well. I have seen some warriors be sick after their first kill, some of them after many kills.'

'I don't feel sick,' said Tyrion. 'I feel great.'

'That is because you are a natural,' Prince Iltharis said. He had ridden up on the other side and Tyrion found himself sandwiched between the two. 'A natural killer.'

Korhien grimaced. He did not like the sound of those words at all. Tyrion was not sure he liked the sound of it himself. It made him sound like a murderer. Iltharis could tell that he had given offence. He smiled coldly. 'I did not mean that as an insult. It is a compliment in its way. You are like me, Prince Tyrion, you do not feel any remorse when you kill someone who deserves it.'

'You're always very certain that the people you kill deserved death,' said Korhien. Iltharis's smile widened and he looked even more sardonic than usual.

'If they had not deserved death, I would not have killed them,' he said. He laughed and there was a genuine humour in his laughter that chilled Tyrion a little.

This was not a subject he felt that one joked about. It was a serious matter, a matter of life and death. On the other hand, he did feel closer in his attitude to Iltharis than to Korhien. He did not really see why he should regret killing Larien. After all, Larien would have had no regrets about killing him.

'I don't think everyone I killed deserved death,' said Korhien. He seemed to be taking the matter seriously too and Tyrion liked him for that even more than usual. He felt like he had something in common with both of these elves and that was not a bad thing. They were equally great warriors in their way and he could learn something from both of them. He was going to have to if he was going to become the fighter he wanted to be.

'You think too much, my friend,' said Iltharis.

'I don't think you can ever do that,' said Korhien. 'Too many people kill without thinking in this world.'

'You and I are in agreement about that, at least,' said Iltharis. 'But come. Let us celebrate the fact our young friend is alive. We can all agree that is a good thing and raise a glass to it.'

'Let us not get too drunk. There will be another council this afternoon. You would not want to embarrass yourself in front of the Phoenix King.'

CHAPTER TWENTY-THREE

Urian took another sip of the very fine wine the Phoenix King had provided for his advisors. There was some subtle narcotic in it, something that sharpened the wits and blunted the edge of fatigue. Of course, it was not nearly as potent as the equivalent vintage would have been in Naggaroth, but that was not necessarily a bad thing. If these elves had been drinking that wine they would most likely have been at each other's throats by now. He set the goblet back down on the highly polished table and listened to the equally polished debate.

By this stage of the proceedings, it was not so much about deciding what was to be done or what the problem really was. It was more about who would get to make the decisions, who would make his rivals look foolish or weak or lacking in knowledge, who would get the credit if there was any credit to be had and who would be apportioned blame in the event of anything going wrong.

It did not matter where elves came from, Naggaroth or Ulthuan, in this their councils were always alike. Of course, in Ulthuan the stakes were not as high as they were in Naggaroth. Here, the worst that was likely to happen to anyone coming out on the losing side in a debate was that they might lose face or some fractional increment of prestige. In Naggaroth, where the stakes were in favour of Malekith, there was always the stimulating possibility that death might await the loser. The Witch King did not tolerate failure and he did not love bad advice.

Listening to some of these windbags, Urian thought they might benefit from the lash of Malekith's iron discipline. It would certainly stop them from rambling on and on and on. One thing he could safely say about the wizards of Ulthuan was that they loved the sound of their own voices.

It made him almost nostalgic for those councils where the Witch King would execute those who bored him. Like all tyrants, Malekith loved only the sound of his own voice and was intolerant of those who would steal away some small fraction of the attention that he craved. That was his rightful entitlement, Urian corrected himself ironically.

At the moment the archmage Eltharik was laying markers on the maps of Ulthuan spread out on the great table of the council chamber. He was making the point yet again that all of the attacks had taken place near waystones. He was also placing the names of those who dwelled in areas that had been attacked and were known to have been killed.

As he listened to the long list of casualties, Urian almost sat bolt upright. For a moment he thought he perceived the pattern and he listened carefully to what was being said. As the evening wore on and Eltharik continued to bore with a list of names that he had so lovingly compiled for this purpose, Urian again and again heard names that were familiar to him from his studies.

He wondered if anybody else had seen the pattern, and decided that they had not because they did not share his fascination with the heritage of his master Malekith and his very potent father.

He wondered whether he was really correct. Perhaps it was simply seeing something random. It was the nature of the mind to try and make order out of chaos, to try and see patterns in everything. That was a danger that he was well aware of. And yet, the more he thought about it, the more what he saw made sense.

He cast his mind back over the research he had been doing for his monograph on the descendants of Aenarion. Every single one of the places that had been attacked was a place where one of the Blood had dwelled and would most likely have been dwelling still had not the daemon attacked. And it seemed very likely that a creature as malicious as N'Kari would seek revenge upon the descendants of the Phoenix King who had caused him so much inconvenience as to slay him twice.

Yes, he thought, I have it. The Keeper of Secrets is killing the descendants of Aenarion one by one. He intends to wipe out the line. Urian smiled a secret smile, knowing that for once he really was ahead of every other elf in the room.

The question was, what was he going to do with this knowledge? It would be a very dangerous thing to keep this from his master. If N'Kari was killing all of the descendants of Aenarion, the Witch King himself must surely head the list of potential victims. It would be interesting to see what happened when an ancient and powerful daemon clashed with the mighty ruler of Naggaroth.

For Urian the question became whether the reward his master would give him for finding out this information would be of greater value to him than the amusement to be gained from letting the struggle happen.

Lady Malene noticed him smiling. She looked at him sourly and said, 'Prince Iltharis, perhaps you would care to share the joke with us. I do not really see anything to smile about in this long list of the dead.'

'Forgive me, Lady Malene, my mind is full of butterflies tonight. I was merely pleased by the taste of this fine vintage. There is indeed nothing to smile about in this catalogue of horrors. Now if you could excuse me, something has just occurred to me and I must beg leave to return to my mansion and consult with my books.'

'YOUR HYPOTHESIS IS an interesting one, Urian,' said Malekith. Even over all the long leagues between the two communicating mirrors, Urian could hear the anger in his master's voice. 'And it concurs with some information my mother has seen fit to pass on to me.'

'She has had one of her visions, sire?' Urian was suddenly glad he had chosen to pass on his information to Malekith. Not to have done so and then to have the Witch King even suspect he had behaved in this fashion would be inevitably fatal.

'Precisely so, Urian, or so she would have me believe. It is also true that my mother has her own sources within the Cults of Luxury in Ulthuan, some of them hidden even from me.'

It was typical of Malekith to speak that way, Urian thought. It implied that he knew a very great deal even as he admitted he did not know everything. Knowing his master it was most likely an accurate summation as well. Malekith was only imprecise when he wanted to be.

'What would you have me do, sire?' Urian asked. This was the nub of the matter.

Malekith was silent for a long moment. Urian could almost feel the force of his thoughts, the titanic brooding immensity of his calculations. He was looking at the matter from all sides, weighing advantages and disadvantages closely.

'I think it would be useful if you were to share your theory at the next council. It would redound to your credit. And if perchance our misguided kinsfolk should teach this arrogant daemon a lesson then so much the better.'

'As you wish, sire,' said Urian, feeling certain as always that his master had kept his real purposes hidden and his real reasons obscure. It certainly could not be that Malekith was frightened by the possibility of the daemon coming for him.

Nothing frightened the Witch King. Urian was very certain of that. Still if anything might, the possibility of a Greater Daemon of Chaos coming to seek vengeance would surely head the list.

URIAN LOOKED AROUND the chamber. His expression was grave but inwardly he was enjoying the commotion he had caused. He was also feeling secretly smug. It was he, after all, who had divined the daemon's intentions, not these clever wizards, or proud scholars or even the Witch King himself.

'I do not believe this, Prince Iltharis' said Eltharik.

Urian smiled at him. 'Perhaps that is because you did not think of it yourself.'

The wizard's mouth fell open. He was obviously not used to being talked to this way, except perhaps by other archmagi.

'It fits the facts as we know them,' said Lady Malene. 'And so far it is the only theory we have that does.'

'That does not mean it is correct,' said Belthania.

'But if it is correct,' said Finubar, 'then every surviving descendant of Aenarion is in danger.'

'Perhaps that is why Eltharik quibbles with my theory,' said Urian. He kept his voice reasonable. 'Perhaps he sees a way to end the problem of the Curse for all time.'

It was a possibility that had almost certainly occurred to most of the elves in the room, even if none of them had dared mention it. He thought it best to get it out into the open, and if by doing so he could cast a slur on this haughty archmage, so much the better.

'That was not my intention at all. I merely think we should not accept an untested hypothesis without proof.'

'How do you intend it should be tested?' Lady Malene asked. 'Shall we wait until every descendant of Aenarion is dead and every place where they dwell is ravaged?'

There was anger in her voice. She was obviously concerned for her nephews.

'I can assure you that the facts are testable. I have access to all of our genealogies and I have talked with many of the people killed,' said Urian. 'If you check the records you will find their names and places of abode are all stored by the Priests of Asuryan and the Loremasters of Hoeth.'

Urian looked around the room. This was indisputably his area of expertise and no one was prepared to challenge him on it. He could see that many of those present were coming around to his point of view. It would indeed be too bad, he thought, if Eltharik was correct and all he was doing was projecting an imaginary pattern onto the course of events.

He looked at Finubar. The Phoenix King's face was bland but there was something about his manner at that moment that reminded Urian of Malekith. The Phoenix King too was making his calculations, and they were not all about preserving the lives of the Blood of Aenarion. They were to do with enhancing his prestige and strengthening his position.

Finubar's eyes snapped open and Urian found himself meeting the Phoenix King's gaze. For a moment he felt that something else was looking out at him, something that could see into his very soul and plumb all of his secrets. He told himself that could not be so, for if

Finubar really could do that, he would be ordering his White Lions to cut Urian down where he sat.

'I think Prince Iltharis has spoken to the heart of the matter,' Finubar said. 'We cannot allow any of our subjects to be terrorised by this daemon, nor can we take the risk of the descendants of Aenarion being wiped out. After all, the Everqueen herself is counted among their number.'

Urian could see that got everyone's attention. None of the elves of Ulthuan wanted to risk of anything bad happening to their beloved spiritual leader. None of them wanted to be the one who spoke out in favour of doing anything that would cause it to happen either. Urian knew his point was carried.

'What shall we do, sire?' Lady Malene asked.

'The descendants of Aenarion must be protected. There is only one place we can be certain they will be beyond this daemon's reach. The Shrine of Asuryan itself. Not even N'Kari would dare attack that place.'

Urian shot Finubar an admiring glance. He was a deep one, like Malekith. There was more going on here than met the eye, Urian felt sure of that. Finubar was using the crisis to strengthen his political position using both politics and religion. An attack on the shrine was the only thing more likely than an attack on the Everqueen to unite the whole nation behind him.

'What about the Everqueen?' Urian asked.

'We cannot command her, nor will she leave Avelorn. But she must be warned so that she can take steps to protect herself.'

'What about my nephews, sire?' Lady Malene asked.

'They must be summoned to our presence without further delay. I must decide whether they are in need of protection too.'

Urian already knew the answer to that.

CHAPTER TWENTY-FOUR

'YOU HAVE BEEN summoned to the Palace,' said Lady Malene. 'An escort awaits you.'

'To see that we do not run away,' said Teclis.

'Do not even joke about that,' said Malene. 'I suggest you treat this interview with the utmost seriousness and the utmost circumspection. Your lives may depend on it.'

'Surely our lives depend on whether Finubar believes we are under the influence of the Curse of Aenarion?' said Teclis. 'I doubt our behaviour has anything to do with it.'

Tyrion wondered at the obtuseness of his twin. Could he not see that Malene was worried about them, and that she was trying to say something, anything, that might let her believe they had some control over their fate. Not that it mattered. Teclis was a realist in this.

'Run along and put on your court clothes. Do not do anything to disgrace us,' said Malene.

Teclis smiled. 'So that is what you are really worried about.'

Tyrion wondered how anybody so clever could also be so stupid.

'Yes,' said Lady Malene. 'That is all I am worried about.'

Her tone gave the lie to her words and even Teclis saw it then.

'I would do nothing to disgrace you, lady,' he said with a

courtliness that compensated for his earlier tactlessness. Tyrion smiled. His brother was still sometimes capable of surprising him.

AS THEY APPROACHED the throne room, Korhien came towards them. He was all seriousness, and very impressive in his court uniform and his lionskin cloak. He stood before them, barring their way with his axe. He looked grim. Tyrion suddenly had a sense of what it would be like to face him on the battlefield. He would be a terrifying opponent.

'I must ask you to remove your weapons, princes, and place them in my keeping. On this day of all days, you may not enter the royal presence armed.'

It was what they were expecting. Teclis had even been given a sword for the occasion; otherwise he would have nothing to surrender. They placed their weapons in the racks that Korhien indicated as he stood watching them.

'You will enter the presence one at a time, in order of age. Prince Tyrion you will go first. Prince Teclis I must ask you to be seated in the attendance chamber over there.' Korhien opened the door to attendance chamber first, and Teclis went within.

Then he opened the door to the audience chamber and Tyrion was ushered into the presence of the Phoenix King.

TYRION FOUND HIMSELF facing a tall, powerful-looking elf, narrow of face and keen of eye. He was dressed in what at first appeared to be a simple robe of Cathayan silk but which when studied revealed itself to be woven in patterns of subtle complexity.

The elf smiled in a friendly fashion. His manner was open and relaxed but there was something different about him. He seemed somehow distanced from the elves around him, much more remote. And he seemed larger, although not in any physical sense. It was as if he was somehow more real.

Tyrion stood there caught in a web of complex emotions and reactions. He was face to face with the Phoenix King, in the presence of someone who was more than merely an elf, who was not quite mortal.

Something looked out from behind Finubar's eyes. It was not unfriendly, bore him no malice, was even concerned for his welfare in a very distant fashion, but it was not something like him. It was an entity of an entirely different species.

Finubar smiled and the spell broke. Whatever had looked at Tyrion was gone, swift as the flickering dance of a flame. Now he was facing a friendly-seeming, young-looking elf who studied him with an unfeigned interest.

'You would be Prince Tyrion,' he said. The voice was rough and much deeper than Tyrion had expected. It had odd accents in it, a twang picked up in distant places and an air of authority of the sort you picked up on the command deck of ships.

'Yes, sire,' said Tyrion. 'I am. I am here to be tested for the Curse of Aenarion.'

Finubar laughed. 'I do not do the testing myself, Prince Tyrion. The priests and the mages do it. My part of the process is simply to look at you and recommend a course of action. It is one of the gifts of the Phoenix King. I can see when certain elves are of... consequence. I can tell for example that you are very strongly of the Blood of Aenarion and I will need to send you to the seers. I suspect the same will prove true of your twin.'

Tyrion felt some unease, facing the tranquil gaze of the Phoenix King. Once more he got that sense of remoteness, but it was of a different type. Finubar seemed unaware of the fact that he might well be condemning Tyrion and his brother to death. Or perhaps he simply did not care.

Was it passing through the flame that had done this, Tyrion wondered, or was it simply the responsibility of kingship?

'May I ask how you can tell, sire?'

'You may ask – but I am damned if I can tell you.' Finubar laughed and the simple sea captain was back. 'I just know, or rather the part of me that was touched by the flame knows and it deigns to communicate its knowledge to me. I can see that there is something about you that is different from others. I could tell you were of the Blood. It was the same in the old days when I was a captain on my father's ships. I could tell when a storm would be a bad one or whether the wind was about to change suddenly.'

'I can see patterns on a chessboard that tell me how the game will play out, most of the time.' Tyrion did not know what it was that made him say that just then. He just felt the urge to communicate with this remote but not unsympathetic figure. He sensed they had something in common and it was something to do with his gift.

Or perhaps he was simply trying to let Finubar know that in him the Curse had come in a harmless form.

'That must be a very useful gift. I wish I had it. I would not lose nearly so much gold playing against my White Lions.'

'You lose gold playing against your bodyguards?' Tyrion was so astonished by the confession that he forgot to use the honorific. The Phoenix King did not appear to notice or to care.

'Oh yes. I bet on their play sometimes too. Korhien tells me you can beat him. That is quite unusual. You and I must try a game or two sometime. I am curious about this gift of yours. I understand it is not the only one you possess. Korhien tells me you are a natural with weapons, and by this he does not mean merely gifted.'

'He is very kind, sire,'

'No, he is not, Prince Tyrion. He is a warrior and a killer and that is not something you should ever lose sight of.'

'I meant it as a figure of speech, sire.'

'I know you did. I chose to misunderstand it to make a point.' Finubar smiled as he said it, but Tyrion was suddenly on guard. He sensed that there was more going on here than he understood, that he was in deeper waters even than he had thought.

'Good, Prince Tyrion. You have a brain as well as a gift for the blade. That is a useful combination of talents in a warrior. I can always use elves who possess them in my service.'

Tyrion wondered if he was being offered future employ as a White Lion or whether Finubar had something else in mind. Perhaps Tyrion was merely misunderstanding him.

'Assuming I pass the tests your priests put me through, sire.'

'They are not my priests, prince. They serve Asuryan.'

'You are his chosen representative, sire.'

'I fear you have a lot to learn about politics and elven priestcraft, Prince Tyrion.'

'I am sure you are correct, sire.'

'I wish more of my subjects shared your belief,' said the Phoenix King. Again he smiled, but Tyrion sensed that he was not entirely joking. Of course, there were those who opposed him. There always were. It was the nature of asur politics.

'What do you think of the rumours of this new terror besetting our land?'

The sudden change of subject threw Tyrion. He considered for a moment.

'You mean that the daemon N'Kari, Aenarion's enemy, has returned to take vengeance on the elves?'

'Precisely so.'

'I thought the daemon slain by Aenarion, sire.'

'You think it unlikely to be it then?'

'I do not know enough about these matters to venture an opinion, sire.'

'And you are unsure why I have asked you for one and are too polite to say.'

'Something like that, sire.'

'You must never be slow to voice your opinion to me, prince. A Phoenix King needs those around him who speak the truth as they see it. It is the only way he keeps any grip on reality at all.'

'I will bear that in mind, sire.'

'Well, bearing that in mind, what do you really think in answer to my original question?'

'I think it unlikely that anyone would call himself by the name of Keeper of Secrets as a jest, sire, although there are some who would take the name of one of our ancient enemies merely to frighten us.'

'And yet...'

'And yet my heart tells me that it is not the case. I believe it quite possible the daemon has returned to take vengeance on the elves, sire.'

'I am afraid my advisors agree with you, prince. N'Kari has returned to slay all of the Blood of Aenarion. He has already made a very good beginning.'

A thrill of horror and concern passed through Tyrion. 'What about my father, sire?'

'A messenger will be dispatched to warn him. One he will trust and hopefully listen to.'

'Korhien Ironglaive, sire?'

Finubar nodded. 'They have been friends for a very long time.'

'And what of myself and my brother, sire? What is there we can do?'

'Stay alive, Prince Tyrion. And to that end you will be dispatched to the safest place in Elvendom. The Shrine of Asuryan. If there is any place that we can put you beyond the reach of the daemon, it is there.'

'It is the holiest spot in Ulthuan. Do you really need to send us so far, sire?'

'You were going to have to go there anyway, Prince Tyrion. You are of the Blood of Aenarion and that is where you will be tested for the Curse. We are killing two birds with one stone, you see.'

'I understand.' A courtier approached the Phoenix King and murmured something in his ear.

'If you will excuse me, Prince Tyrion,' Finubar murmured.

Tyrion understood that he had been dismissed.

TECLIS STUDIED FINUBAR with just as much interest as the Phoenix King studied him. He might never get another chance of doing it so he might as well make the most of the opportunity.

He saw a tall, athletic elf with an air that reminded him of every other Lothern merchant or captain he had so far encountered. Finubar had that air of command they all had and that air of brisk informality. His garb was much richer, of course. His robes were luxurious and formal, subtly understated but the finest in the lands. They were in keeping with this chamber.

Finubar was armed, even though Teclis was not. There were other White Lions in the room, at a discreet distance, just out of earshot of a murmured conversation, close enough to spring to Finubar's rescue in the unlikely event of Teclis attempting an assassination. They were taking no chances. He understood why. There had been numerous attempts on the lives of Phoenix Kings in the course of asur history, all of them blamed on Malekith and the Cults of Luxury. Teclis was inclined to wonder whether that was a convenient fiction that covered up other conspiracies.

It was not just the external appearance of Finubar that interested Teclis though. It was the fact that he had been touched by a Power. Teclis could sense that about him. It was well concealed, hidden deeply in fact, but it was there. Finubar's whole body was saturated with magical energy of a very particular kind. Teclis did not doubt for a moment that if he entered the chambers of the Sacred Flame at the Shrine of Asuryan he would sense the same power there.

He was not entirely sure what the magic of the Flame did for Finubar. It was, of course, a measure of the god's blessing, but it seemed unlikely that so much energy could have been imprinted on him for only that effect. He warned himself to be careful and not make assumptions.

Who knew why the gods did anything?

'You are very quiet, Prince Teclis,' said Finubar. His voice was friendly, his manner open, and yet Teclis sensed something strange here. It was as if Finubar were acting a part of someone attempting to put somebody else at ease without really having a connection with them at all.

'I am sorry, Chosen One,' said Teclis.

'I trust you are not going to tell me you were overwhelmed by my presence,' said Finubar. There seemed to be genuine warmth in the smile now.

'No, Chosen One, I am not.'

'You see the Flame, don't you? And please spare me the title. I do not often have private conversations these days. Call me Finubar at least while we are in this chamber or sire if you must.'

'Yes, I see the Flame,' Teclis said, wondering how Finubar knew. 'It glows through your flesh.'

'Loremasters and archmages and those very sensitive to magic see that. You are not yet one of the first two so I must assume that you are the latter.'

'I always have been.'

'So I have been told. I have also been told you are extraordinarily gifted at magic. Perhaps after you return from the shrine you will have the chance to study it.'

'I am going to the shrine then, to be tested for the Curse?'

'You and your brother both.'

'You think we may be cursed then?'

'The Flame thinks you need to be tested. I merely relay the message.'

'What is it like?' Teclis asked. Another elf might not have dared ask, but he was curious.

'It is not at all what I expected before I passed through the Flame,' said Finubar. 'It is not entirely a comfortable thing to spend your life in the presence of a living god. More I am not allowed to say.'

Teclis did not ask who did not allow him that. Finubar had already answered.

'When do I go the shrine, sire?'

'At once. Your relatives have been notified. A ship waits for you at the docks. It will take you to the shrine at once.'

'Is it so urgent we be tested?'

'You are being sent there for your own protection. We have reason to believe a daemon is hunting you, for all the Blood of Aenarion.'

'Is that why N'Kari has returned?'

'My advisors think it likely. I see no reason to doubt them. It is unlikely even a Keeper of Secrets will seek you out within the reach of the Flame. It will find its fires very hot if it does. Believe me I have had some experience of the process.'

'I thank you for your kindness, sire,' said Teclis.

'You have my blessing and my leave to depart,' the Phoenix King replied.

CHAPTER TWENTY-FIVE

'Oh no, another ship,' said Teclis. The twins stood on the dock at Lothern's northern harbour. It was neither as busy nor impressive as the Great Harbour. It lacked the variety too – the only ships in view were asur vessels. No others were allowed on the waters of the Inner Sea.

'I sometimes doubt you are my sister's son,' said Lady Malene. 'She was a true daughter of Lothern, as at home on the water as on land.'

Teclis looked oddly at her. He did not seem to know quite what to say or quite how to take this parting. Tyrion suspected that he had become accustomed to her company and that, unusually for his twin, Teclis trusted her. 'I take after my father. He always preferred the mountains.'

'I know,' said Malene. There was a world of wistfulness in her voice. Tyrion suspected she was thinking of the distant place in which her sister had died.

Tyrion was surprised when his twin walked forward and with great awkwardness hugged her. She hugged him back.

'We will come back,' Teclis said.

'Be sure that you do,' said Lady Malene. 'You still have a great deal to learn.'

'When you come back we shall see about making a warrior out of you, not a duellist, doorkeeper.' Korhien said. His manner was joking and jovial, a soldier who had said many goodbyes. Tyrion could see he was champing at the bit to get away as well though. He needed to bring a warning to their father.

'What do you mean?'

'There will be armies in the field this season. This business with the Cult of Pleasure has got everything stirred up. We will be sweeping the mountains of vermin. There will be raids on Naggaroth too.'

'The world must be shown the might of Ulthuan,' said Tyrion.

'Your quickness of understanding is gratifying, doorkeeper,' said Korhien.

'That's the first time anyone has ever told my brother that,' said Teclis. Korhien looked at him and smiled. He understood Teclis's joking manner.

'Be grateful he is your brother, otherwise he might call you out for insulting him.' There was an edge to the White Lion's words. Korhien was unhappy about the duel with Larien or something it had revealed about Tyrion. It was a matter he would have to take up with Korhien on his return.

If he returned.

'You had better get aboard,' said Lady Malene. 'You sail with the tide and the captain will want to get under way. Best not keep him waiting.'

'Blessings of Isha upon you,' said Korhien.

'May you live a thousand years,' the twins responded in unison.

TYRION STOOD ON the bowsprit of the ship, balancing there, watching the dolphins surge through the water alongside. They were keeping pace with the vessel, leaping high and landing in the water, frolicsome as children at play. The coast of the Inner Sea was visible in the distance, a soft-looking land in this light, rising away to the distant mountains.

'Stop showing off,' said Teclis. He sounded a little peevish. Perhaps he was more affected by their departure than he wanted to let on. Realising his harshness of tone, he made a joke, 'I could do that if I wanted to.'

Tyrion performed an elaborate courtly bow to him, still balancing on the bowsprit, ignoring the rise and fall of the ship.

'If you were not so seasick, of course,' he said. He too felt odd. He missed the bustle of the Emeraldsea Palace, the feeling that he was standing at the centre of the world. He even missed Liselle a little.

It felt like he was alone with his brother now, among strangers. There was a time that would not have bothered him. He had been changed by his time in Lothern. Of course they both had other things on their mind – the upcoming test, being hunted by a daemon.

'I don't feel quite so bad,' said Teclis. 'Perhaps it's the medicine Lady Malene gave me. Perhaps it's the sea itself. It feels somehow different from the wild outer ocean.'

'They say the storms are not so bad here, and there are not the same ocean currents,' said Tyrion. 'Maybe that makes a difference.'

They were talking around something. His brother would get to it sooner or later given time. 'Would you like to take my place here?'

'No. You make a better figurehead for a ship,' Teclis said. 'After all, your head is made of wood.'

A dolphin erupted from the water. It came almost level with Tyrion. He could have reached out and touched it if he wanted to. Its skin was slick with sloughing water. Its eyes looked oddly merry.

'The audience appreciates your jokes,' said Tyrion. He bounced on the bowsprit a couple of times to build up momentum then used its springiness to propel him into the air. He backflipped onto the deck, landing beside Teclis.

'It's sad you've been reduced to competing with dolphins,' said Teclis, but the pain in his eyes showed that he understood who Tyrion was really competing with. No amount of magic would ever allow him to do what Tyrion had just done, or enjoy the ease his brother had. As soon as he did it, Tyrion felt guilt mingle with a natural elven malignant satisfaction.

'Would you like to tell me what is really bothering you?' Tyrion asked.

'I am worried about our father. What if the daemon has already found him?'

It was a disquieting thought, imagining their old home besieged by an army of daemons. Even more disquieting was the idea that it might already have happened and they would not know about it. 'Me too,' said Tyrion.

'You have another idea in that thick skull of yours, I can tell. Spit it out!'

'I think we are being used as bait.'

'You think that we are being sent to one of the safest places in Ulthuan to tempt N'Kari to attack us.'

'No, I think we are being sent there to tempt N'Kari to attack it.'

'Go on.'

'What would happen if N'Kari attacked the Shrine of Asuryan?'

'He would be destroyed.'

'What if he was not? What if he escaped to try again?'

'He would be hunted down and destroyed.'

'And how would that affect the population?'

'I see where you are going with this – they would unite behind Finubar. They would be outraged and they would demand action. They already are. Congratulations brother, you have been using your head for something else other than to block blows.'

'The princes will have to unite around Finubar. His position will become stronger. Theirs will be weaker. For a time.'

'Lothern has made you cynical, brother.'

'No. It has merely showed me how our rulers think. Now why don't you tell me what is really bothering you?'

Teclis looked at him for a long time. It seemed like he was not going to answer then, eventually, he gulped and said, 'We will be tested soon. What if I am cursed? What then?'

Tyrion could see that his brother was afraid and he could understand why. He wanted so badly to be a mage, to have a life, and that might well be denied him by the decision of the priests at the Shrine of Asuryan. They would not even have to put him to death. Interring him would be just as bad.

'You are not cursed,' Tyrion said.

'Look at me. Who would believe that?'

'Being the way you are means you were unlucky, not cursed.'

'Let me tell you something, brother,' Teclis's voice dropped so that only Tyrion could hear. 'I knew I was doing wrong when I took that spellbook from Malene's library. I did it anyway. I would do it again. I want the power and I am drawn to it, no matter what the cost. If that is not a sign of the Curse, what is?'

Tyrion smiled coldly. 'Then let me tell you something, brother. I was not horrified when I killed Larien. I enjoyed it. I enjoyed killing another elf. What does that say about me?'

They stared at each other in silence for a long time. Eventually Teclis said, 'I would have enjoyed killing him too. If I was able.'

'I am, brother, that is the difference. And I very much doubt Larien will be the last elf I kill.'

'Being a killer is not such a bad thing. In the world we live in it counts as a useful talent.'

'I think I enjoy it too much.'

The words hung in the air for a long time.

AFTER THREE DAYS and nights of sailing, a small island rose out of the Inner Sea ahead of the ship. It looked volcanic. Palm trees covered some of the slopes. Caves and terraces dotted its sides. On the highest point of the island was a large stepped pyramid. It must have been massive indeed, Tyrion thought, to be visible at such a distance.

In spite of everything, his worries and his fear for his father's safety, Tyrion was glad that he had come here, and seen this. It was one of the most sacred sites in all elvendom.

This was the place where Aenarion had first passed through the Flame of Asuryan and became Phoenix King. This was the place where, ever since, every Phoenix King from Bel Shanaar to Finubar had made his own ascension to the throne. It was the place where Malekith had made his doomed attempt to wrest the power of the gods from its rightful wielder.

It could be said that elven history began in this place. Before Aenarion had shaped them into a warrior people, the elves had been peaceful farmers and herders. They had lived in harmony with their land in the eternal springtime of their devotion to the Everqueen.

After Aenarion had passed through the Flame everything was different.

Aenarion had taught the elves how to make war, to follow kings, to fight and to conquer. They had become a different people after that day. He had remade the elves in his own image, into what they needed to become in order to survive. Peaceful farmers could no longer survive in a world from which the old gods had fled and through which the evil powers of Chaos marched. Aenarion had made them into something that could.

The ship moved ever closer and the island loomed ever more massive until they entered a small harbour. Statues of the Phoenix Kings lined the entrance. Images of the gods looked down from the cliffs overhead. The crew brought the ship in and moored it and soon Tyrion found himself on dry land again.

An escort of Phoenix Guard, proud in their distinctive uniforms waited to greet them. The ship's captain exchanged silent greetings with their leader in hand sign and soon the twins were walking up a long pathway on the side of the island towards the shrine, surrounded by twenty of its proud guardians.

Tyrion found his thoughts drawn inevitably back to one of the reasons why they were here.

N'Kari was looking for Teclis and himself. In a way it was like being told Aenarion himself had summoned them to an audience. A creature had stepped directly out of ancient myths and into the modern world and it was seeking to kill them. Tyrion had often dreamed of taking part in stories like the ones he and his twin had read as children. It seemed as if his dreams had come true.

He was not frightened exactly. It all seemed too strange. Walking here on the slopes of this ancient island, passing vineyards and flower gardens as the sun beamed down, the very idea that a daemon was looking for the two of them seemed a mad fantasy. Birds sang, huge butterflies almost as big as the songbirds moved from hedgerow to hedgerow and flower to flower. This was not a world in which things like daemons could possibly exist.

And yet his brain told him otherwise. Why else was he here? Why else were these heavily armed elves marching in regular pace beside him? Was not this island itself a place of legends and dreams? Was this not a place where the gods reached into the world and spoke to their chosen people? Even an elf as insensitive to most forms of magic as Tyrion could tell that this was a mystical place. Power charged the atmosphere all around them. He could feel it as he could feel the presence of a fine cool mist on his skin on a winter morning.

The Phoenix King himself had ordered them placed under guard here, which argued that he at least took the threat of the daemon seriously. And if Finubar did so, could he and his brother do anything less? No. The daemon was out there and soon it would come looking for them, and when it did he had better be ready, although he was not entirely sure how that was possible.

And tomorrow they would be tested. The Keeper of Secrets was not the only thing they had to worry about. It seemed that very suddenly his short life had become very dangerous.

THE TEMPLE OF Asuryan rose above them. The stones were ancient and weathered, covered in an ochre moss. It was difficult to tell the real scale of the place. It seemed as if it was part of the cliffs, a mountain that had been partially sculpted by the ancient builders. It was as if the gods themselves had placed it there.

Even he could tell that there was a power contained within this place. He could sense the energy pulsing out through the very stone and he was sure that his brother, who was far more sensitive to these things than he was, was even more aware of it. Teclis stared as if he were looking at some natural marvel: a mountain landscape, a perfect beach, a glorious sunset. His face was transformed as if he were looking upon a wonder.

'A god dwells in this place,' he said.

'What gave you the first clue?' Tyrion asked. 'Was it the fact that it is the Temple of Asuryan? Or was it something more subtle like the religious symbols carved into the cliffs? Perhaps it was the smoke rising from the Sacred Flame at the top of the temple.'

'I can see the Flame burning through the cliff.'

'You can see it through the rock?'

'Perhaps see is the wrong word. I can perceive its energy. This is a place where a power from Outside touches our world. Something vast and slow and terribly ancient.'

There was a mixture of awe and something else in his brother's voice. Tyrion could not tell what it was. He looked at the temple again.

'It does not look like it was built by elves, does it?' he said.

'It is not in a typically elven architectural style, that's true,' said Teclis. 'The ziggurat echoes the patterns of ancient cities of the slann. Some think it was they who first contacted Asuryan and taught his worship to the elves.'

'Aenarion was in this place,' said Tyrion. It was a strange thought – the first Phoenix King had not yet been touched by the power of

Asuryan when he first looked upon the spot. He could have walked away and the whole course of history would have been different. There would never have been any Phoenix Kings. Perhaps the forces of Chaos would have engulfed the world and there would be no Tyrion standing here to look up at the temple with wonder and unease in his heart.

He noticed the Phoenix Guard seemed to be paying attention to them now. He was tempted to ask them what they thought but he knew he would get no answer. These warriors were sworn to silence and he did not know the hand signs they used to communicate. They guarded sacred mysteries and it was said they knew their own dooms.

'Malekith was here too,' said Teclis. 'He tried to emulate his father. He tried to walk through the flame. He failed and was damned.'

How like his brother to concentrate on the dark side of things, Tyrion thought. But Teclis was correct. The Witch King of Naggaroth had once walked here too. He had gone forth from the spot, a wretched, scorched cripple, twisted by the experience. And yet, for all that, he had left. He had survived for far longer than his mighty father.

'Every Phoenix King who was ever crowned has stood near where we are standing now. From this small island, a great deal of our history was shaped.'

'Well, brother, now our history will be shaped. The course of our lives will be decided here,' said Teclis.

CHAPTER TWENTY-SIX

A PRIEST OF Asuryan awaited them at the entrance to the walled temple complex. The Eye of Asuryan worked into the surplice of his robes mirrored the symbols set in the wall. It gave Tyrion the feeling that he was in the gaze of the god.

They passed through a small postern gate and into the grounds around the great ziggurat. Within the cool shadow of the massive stone walls a host of smaller stone structures waited attendance on the mighty stepped pyramid of the temple proper.

The priest led them through courtyard after courtyard.

Ominously, the temple was full of elf soldiers, warriors of the levies hastily dispatched to increase the garrison camped in every courtyard and open space. There were hundreds of them, and Tyrion gathered that more were due to arrive soon. It seemed the Phoenix King was taking this threat very seriously.

Tall, grim elves in the uniforms of the Phoenix Guard moved everywhere. They said nothing, merely glanced warily at the twins, assessing them for any threat and then moving on.

They came to a small refectory and were offered food then showed to monastic cells. After the luxury of the Emeraldsea Palace, the size of the chambers and the sparseness of the furnishings came as a shock to Tyrion. Somehow small cabins had been easier to accept on a ship.

'Spit it out,' Teclis said. 'I can see you have something on your mind.'

'This place is a fortress,' said Tyrion. 'But there are not enough warriors here to defend it against a really powerful enemy. It is too big and the guards are still too few.'

'It is a temple not a fortress,' said Teclis, 'which might explain that. Also it is defended in other ways, my magic-blind brother.'

'How so?'

'There are extremely ancient and powerful wards woven into the walls. And there is a mighty presence here. It is not exactly chained, but it is constrained in some way. I can feel it.'

'Asuryan?'

'The same thing as touched Finubar, so yes.'

Tyrion smiled. 'We are here. In the same place as Aenarion once walked. Who would have thought this a season ago?'

'I wish it were under happier circumstances,' said Teclis. 'I wish we were at home with Father.'

'What could we do for him if the daemon comes?' said Tyrion. 'He is a wizard. He can look after himself.'

'The daemon has killed other wizards. Some of them vastly more powerful than our father.'

'There is nothing either you or I can do about that now, Teclis. I wish there was but it is not so.'

'I do not like being hunted,' said Teclis. 'One day I intend to be powerful enough to destroy a daemon like N'Kari if he troubles me or mine.'

'You do not lack for ambition, brother. I will settle for a good sword, nothing too ambitious, say Sunfang or the Sword of Khaine, then I will be able to do the same thing.'

'Hush, brother, that is not something to be joked about in this place, at this time.'

'Then I shall bid you goodnight and retire to my cell. Tomorrow a lot of things will be decided.'

Looking out through the window, Tyrion saw clouds scudding across the face of the moon. It looked like there was a storm coming. He wondered whether it was an omen.

* * *

278

N'KARI STOOD AMONG the rubble of another destroyed town drinking in the emotions of fear, misery and disgust along with the adoration of his worshippers. He laughed as the buildings around the central square finally collapsed into a charred heap. In the distance he could hear the sound of his followers destroying the last few standing structures and rounding up the last of the terrified survivors.

It was time for the next phase of his plan. He was strong enough now to bargain from a position of power with those he needed. He had gathered enough sacrifices to begin the ritual. So far, his triumphs had been almost too easy but he was going to attack the Shrine of Asuryan and for that he would need allies of enormous power.

He looked at the assembled captives milling around like sheep in a pen. They had the eyes of those who had known defeat and enslavement and who knew that their fates were only going to get worse. N'Kari ensured they knew this by wearing his true battle form. He was not doing this just for their benefit. There were others he was going to have to impress more.

With the claw that tipped one of his four arms, N'Kari drew the symbol of Tzeentch in the ground, digging out channels with the talons of his fingers. By the time he had finished the sacrifice the channels were filled with blood. With a word he set the blood alight and with another twist of his magic he sent the scent drifting through the hole his ritual had punched in the fabric of reality and downwards into the uppermost Hells.

He let his spirit drift along behind it, following strange paths into the realms of Chaos that were his natural home. For a moment he was almost overcome with nostalgia. He considered giving up his quest for vengeance and returning to this malleable reality that would respond to his every perverse whim. It was a temptation, and as a servant of Slaanesh he felt almost obligated to give in to it, but he resisted, not least because this was a place where he needed all his wits about him.

The dark miracle of the burning blood had attracted the attention of something and in this place, it was massive and powerful. N'Kari recognised it for what it was immediately, an old enemy and an old ally, a potent servant of the Changer of Ways, the daemon god Tzeentch. It sensed his presence and approached warily, as if it suspected a trap. Under the circumstances N'Kari could hardly blame it for this. He made the signs and ritual gestures that among their kind showed that he wished a truce and that he had come with offerings. The Lord of Change responded in kind and soon they were in discussions.

By the end of the negotiations, N'Kari was well pleased with the outcome. He had gained a potent ally and in return he had given up very little that meant anything to him. All he had to do was provide the Lord of Change with a way into this world and the souls of several scores of elves to devour. He did not care about that. They were not his souls.

He sent his spirit hurtling back to mortal reality. He had other rituals to perform, other mighty allies to gather. By the time he was finished he would have a force the likes of which had not been seen since the time of Aenarion. They would respond to his summons. They would come to this world. They would kill and maim and destroy if not exactly in obedience to his commands then at least in accordance with his plans.

'THERE IS NO need to be nervous,' said Teclis. 'They are not going to find anything wrong with you.'

'I am not nervous,' said Tyrion. In truth his brother looked more nervous than he felt. Tyrion had come to terms with the fact that he was going to be tested. Whatever the results were, he would deal with them.

An acolyte entered the cell and gestured for Tyrion to follow him. He bowed to the priest and clasped Teclis by the arm after the fashion of a comrade.

'Good luck!' Teclis said. He looked very young and very vulnerable and Tyrion could see that he was scared.

'And to you,' he replied.

The priest led him deeper into the temple. They came to an archway guarded by warriors of the Phoenix Guard, who gestured that the acolyte should come no further. Tyrion nodded and walked through the archway. Another priest led him to a robing chamber. His clothes were taken from him. The priest indicated a pool that was obviously fed from a bubbling hot spring.

'Purify yourself,' he said. Tyrion walked down into the water. It was hot, almost unpleasantly so, and had a faint sulphurous stink. He washed himself and emerged from the pool.

The priest waited, arms outstretched holding a simple robe with a belt of cloth. Tyrion took it and put it on. It smelled faintly of incense. He noticed that a small corner of the cuff had been patched.

The priest led him deeper into the temple. Slowly the downward sloping corridors of the building gave way to the walls of a cavern. He was deep beneath the earth. Lanterns lit the way. He passed walls carved with glorious scenes from the life of Aenarion. Here he was passing through the Sacred Flame. There he defeated hordes of Chaos monsters.

As he strode deeper into the caves it came to Tyrion that all of this had happened not far from here. He had a sense of passing backwards into history as he walked. This was a holy place and the power of the gods was strong here.

The priest brought him at last into a large cave far beneath the ziggurat, lit by flickering flames that surged and roared from a great pit. Enormous statues inhabited shadowy alcoves. A great altar flanked each side of the volcanic maw. It looked like a bridge that had been broken. It came to Tyrion that during the ritual in which the Phoenix King ascended he would pass from one of those altars to the other. This was the deepest and most sacred shrine on the island. He was closer to the presence of a god than he had ever been.

A group of masked elves waited there. They indicated that he should disrobe. They walked around him and inspected him minutely.

'No blemishes,' said one.

'No stigmata of Chaos,' said another.

'No visible taint,' said the third.

They chanted together and a glow gathered around each of them and then to Tyrion as the spell took effect. He felt tendrils of magical power pass through him, aware of it in the elven way even if he was not aware of what they were doing.

'There is no taint in this one,' said the first masked figure.

'There is no taint,' said the second.

'There is no taint,' said the third. The flames suddenly surged and roared and it seemed to Tyrion that they twisted for a moment into a gigantic robed figure. The eyes of the priests suddenly glowed, mirroring the dancing flames. Their voices became clearer, more distinct and far less elven. They seemed filled with a transcendent presence that even Tyrion could sense. He wondered if they were about to make the sort of prophesy that his father had talked about.

'This one will bear the weapons of a Phoenix King,' said first.

'This one will wear the armour of a Phoenix King,' said the second.

'Weapons and armour both,' said the third.

'Pass from this place and walk free, Blood of Aenarion,' they said in unison. The flaring flames died down. The sense of god-like presence vanished.

'I am not cursed,' said Tyrion. His voice sounded loud and awkward.

'All of the Blood bear Aenarion's curse, even if only to pass it on to their children. You do not bear the taint of evil and Chaos,' said the second priest. He felt sure from her voice that she was female. She sounded tired now and certainly nothing more than mortal.

'Yet,' said the third.

'You are pure in the gaze of Asuryan. Pass on into the Light of his Flame,' said the first. Tyrion walked out through the exit and took a flight of stairs upwards. He emerged onto a ledge that looked out onto the sea. The sunlight seemed blinding after the gloom of the caves. Gulls fluttered away from him and came to rest on a great stone banister.

He smiled. He had passed the test. He would have a life among the elves. And he would bear the weapons and armour of a Phoenix King, if they were correct.

What did they mean by that? Was he to be Phoenix King? Or did they simply mean he would wear gear given to him by a Phoenix King and be a White Lion like Korhien? In any case, it did not seem like a bad destiny.

He stood a little taller and it came to him that he had not even felt the weight of the knowledge of doom pressing down on his soul until it was removed. He laughed out loud and performed a cartwheel on the ledge. He felt fairly certain it had never been used for that purpose before.

He looked up at the sun, and then he wondered what was happening to his brother back down there in the gloom.

* * *

THE OLD, PATCHED robe was scratchy and uncomfortable on Teclis's skin. The air was close, humid and warm. There was a sulphur stink in the air, doubtless from the volcanic springs deep below this place. The carvings on the walls were ominous, disturbing scenes from the life of Aenarion, battle and warfare and bloodshed.

Teclis felt like a prisoner forced to walk a path of doom to his own execution. He did not like this place. He did not like the reason he was here. He did not like being this deep underground.

He felt like he had to force air into his weak lungs. He was having difficulty breathing. The walls pressed down on him. The weight of old earth was heavy. At the same time he was uncomfortably aware that all it would take would be for the ancient volcanoes below this place to stir into life and those walls could easily fall in on him. Or hot lava could come gushing up from the depths and flood these corridors, burning him alive. If the ancient philosophers were right though, he told himself, that would not happen. The poison breath of the volcano would kill him first. It was not a reassuring thought.

He was aware of the enormous flows of magical energy around him. This entire site was a nexus of enormous power, of a very specific, sacred kind. This temple was not just located on a fault line in the earth's crust but on a fault line on the surface of the universe. The god or extra-dimensional entity or whatever Asuryan was could reach into the world of mortals here.

Aenarion had made his ascension here for a reason. This was the only place in the world where he could be invested with Asuryan's blessing. There must be other places in the world like this, he thought, where other Powers could reach in.

Vaul's Anvil would be one, which would explain why so many artefacts had been made there. It was a certainty that the Chaos Wastes must be like this for the daemon gods. There must be other shrines where elf, human and dwarf gods could touch the world. There must also be ways in which that magical energy could be tapped, if only a wizard could find a way.

The sudden insight lifted Teclis out of himself for a moment, and took away his fear and uncertainty. If he could only find a way to do that... It was a blasphemous thought but one that came naturally to him.

The fear returned, redoubled as the priest led him into a dimly lit cave where three masked and shadowy figures waited. He knew he had reached the shrine itself. Titanic statues of all the old elf gods were suddenly visible as flames leapt from the great central pit. They vanished back into shadow as the fire died down.

A glance told him that the three were all wizards of great power but the most potent presence by far dwelled within that pit flanked by twin altars. He walked towards the priests. Their hands moved in what might have been a blessing but which instinct told him was the beginning of a divinatory spell.

'Disrobe,' the first told him. He did so slowly and uncomfortably, aware of how weak and unfit his body must look to them. He coughed, in spite of all his efforts not to. He did not want to show weakness here of all places. He felt sure that they would hold it against him. They were elves and elves were like that.

The three circled around him, inspecting him minutely. He thought he sensed their contempt and their mockery. It took all his strength of will to avoid covering his private parts with his hands.

'No blemishes,' said one. 'But he is very infirm. His muscles are wasted.'

Teclis felt ashamed of himself. He knew he had been judged and found wanting.

'No stigmata of Chaos,' said another. 'He may not live. His lungs are weak.'

That comment made him angry. He was well aware of how precarious his grasp on life was. He did not need these three to rub his face in it. Who were they to pass judgement on him?

Presumably very well qualified indeed, the calmer and more sardonic part of his mind observed. Otherwise they would not be here.

'No visible taint,' said the third. 'It is not Chaos that has made him this way. If he is cursed it is with ill-health.'

The three stopped and looked at each other and began to commune as if he were not present. 'It is too early to pass judgment on that,' said the first.

'I concur. With such a one as this the taint will not be visible. It will be spiritual and connected with power,' said the second.

'I stand corrected,' said the third. 'Let us proceed.'

The three of them began to work a ritual magic of great power and sophistication. Teclis watched fascinated as they wove the spell. It was divinatory magic of awesome complexity. He followed every part of the weave even if he did not understand all of its functions.

If he had possessed any doubts about the skill of these wizards, their ability to work this spell would have removed them. It was part ward, to contain any inimical magic that might be unleashed, and part revelatory spell designed to inspect his body and soul for the effects of the curse and the taint of Chaos.

The number of wizards present had been carefully calculated. No single mage could stand against three wizards of such skill. Even if he was tainted, and had been fully trained, there was nothing he could do here against the three of them. And he was not a fully trained wizard, merely a sixteen year-old elf with some stolen scraps of knowledge.

He felt the spell invade his form, passing along nerves and blood vessels, touching chakras and soul lines. He felt tiny flares of energy within his body respond, blazing up like a stoked furnace.

'He has the Art,' said the first.

'He has worked magic,' said the second.

'Interesting,' said the third.

'If he lives this one will be mighty indeed,' said the second.

'The seeds of greatness are in him.' Suddenly a huge jet of flame erupted from the pit. Gigantic plumes of molten magma formed themselves into the image of a huge, robed figure. Flames flickered in the eyes of the priests. Teclis saw the lines of force connecting them to the thing in the pit.

Teclis realised that the spell had joined not just the mages and himself. It had joined the mages at least in part to the power this shrine was sacred to. They were receiving wisdom from somewhere outside of normal space and time.

'He sees us. He senses the presence of the god,' said the third.

'Mighty indeed,' said the first. 'And perhaps wise.'

'This one will commune with ghosts,' said the second.

'This one will bear a crown,' said the second. Her voice was altered. It seemed as if something else was speaking through her. 'And a staff.'

'And confront the greatest daemons,' said the first. His voice sounded exactly the same as his comrades now.

'And stand at the centre of creation.'

'And face the Ender of Worlds.'

'And fight against his own blood,' said the third.

'Against his own blood,' all three of them said in one terrible voice. Then all of them slumped, like puppets whose strings had been cut, and the spell ended abruptly. The power went suddenly out of them, and they seemed less like threatening and mighty wizards and more like soul-weary ancient elves.

All of them looked at each other as if shocked, and Teclis wondered what they had seen, what visions of his future had passed through their mind. Fight against his own blood? Did they mean that he was to fight Tyrion? Surely that was not possible. It was something he would not do. He wanted to demand answers from them, but the part of him that was a wizard already knew that they would not answer and he could not compel them.

'There is no taint in this one,' said the first masked figure.

'There is no taint,' said the second.

'There is no taint,' said the third.

'Pass from this place and walk free, Blood of Aenarion.' All three of them spoke in unison. Weak, and sick at heart, Teclis limped up the stairs. It took him a very long time to reach the light of day emerging out onto a stone ledge. The smell of the sea assaulted his nostrils and made him feel sick.

Tyrion waited there for him. His heart started to pound. His head started to spin.

'I passed,' said Teclis and collapsed.

CHAPTER TWENTY-SEVEN

BY THE LIGHT of the two moons, through the curtain of pouring rain, N'Kari looked upon the Shrine of Asuryan and gloated. The portal shimmered closed behind him as the last of his followers emerged from its glowing surface. Ahead of him, the misty outlines of a huge ziggurat were visible through the gloom.

N'Kari studied the walls with eyes that saw more than light. He inspected the great patterns of magic swirling around the shrine. Potent spells woven by great mages in the days of high magic were there, but they were old. There were areas where Time's endless entropy had frayed them. There were places where the physical foci had gone and the spells were worn so thin that they were vulnerable.

He looked at them, seeing the patterns of magic superimposed on his vision of the world. He saw the souls of his own army, purple and sickly green cultists, bright blood-red Khornate daemons, lilac and lime for the Slaanesh daemons. He saw the sun-gold souls of the elven defenders.

His current force numbered in thousands with scores of daemons. They would have troubles of their own on the sacred soil within the shrine. Its very purity would make it difficult for them to maintain their present forms in the material world. Still, what was that to him.

They would serve his purposes anyway. He knew he could maintain his own form even down there. He was still imbued with the energy he had stolen in the Vortex.

He gestured with his great claw. His followers responded. Sticks of bone thrashed drums skinned with elf flesh. Flutes carved from the thighbones of still-living maidens wailed dire tunes. Brazen war-horns sounded cacophonously. The stormy weather did not trouble his force. They revelled in it.

He was going to need all of his magic and all his followers to achieve his goal. The Shrine of Asuryan was a place where something akin to his kind and yet opposed to them made contact with this world, communicating with its followers, feeding off their worship, touching this plane with its magic. It was a mighty enemy.

It would oppose him every step of the way once he stepped on its sacred ground. More to the point it had the strength to oppose him, could cause him great pain, banish his daemon followers, twist the minds and destroy the bodies of his mortal worshippers. The core of this place was protected by spell walls that would make it difficult to work magic until he was within them.

But the shrine was not without weaknesses. Spell walls would be useless without warriors to protect them. The stones in which their magic was embedded could be battered down, swarmed over, destroyed in a dozen physical ways. Destruction of their physical housing would disrupt the spells themselves.

There had been a time when there had been enough elves to hold a place like this, but their numbers were fewer now than in Aenarion's time. There were weak points where he would concentrate his attacks, forcing the elves to defend them and throw away life after life, giving the elves the choice of guarding their outer defences or retreating within the Inner Shrine.

Either suited N'Kari's purposes. If they stayed he could use magic more easily against them. If they withdrew, they surrendered access to their inner defences without a fight.

Elrion looked up at him with mad, adoring eyes, his rain-soaked clothes clinging to his skin. He was like a hound now; he lived only for N'Kari's approval. It would be amusing to teach him hatred, so that he adored and resented at the same time. N'Kari resolved to do it when he had the time.

'Once I give the signal, order all the forces forwards. Attack the point where the walls are weakest. Draw the elves into combat at every point.'

'Yes beloved master.'

'We shall devour these elves.'

'The Dark Feast will be celebrated.'

Saliva dripped from the corner of Elrion's mouth and vanished amid the raindrops running down his face.

THUNDER BOOMED OVERHEAD.

Teclis woke from a nightmare with the sense that something was terribly wrong. He looked around at the rough stone walls of his small cell. They seemed to be closing in on him. Tyrion looked up from the book he was reading. He sat cross-legged near the door. The last thing Teclis could remember was talking to him before he collapsed. His brother must have carried him back here.

'You are awake then,' Tyrion said. 'That's good. I thought you would sleep forever.'

'There is something wrong. Can't you feel it?' Teclis said.

Tyrion looked serious. 'Feel what?'

'There is something very powerful and very evil very close.'

'The daemon?' Tyrion asked.

Bells began to sound, stridently.

'He's here,' said Teclis.

'Then let us go and take a look,' said Tyrion. 'You can get a fine view from the top of the temple.

Teclis shook his head. 'I do not have the energy. I will remain here.'

Tyrion shrugged and departed.

BANNERS BEARING THE rune of Slaanesh and the symbol of N'Kari unfurled. Beneath them demented cultists cavorted deliriously. Lust-maddened elves paused to steal a kiss from dancing, lascivious daemonettes. Gargoyles took wing through the buffeting winds. Mutated berserkers raced towards the walls bearing ropes and grapnels and makeshift ladders made from magically fused bones.

Arrows darkened the sky in response, descending on the oncoming horde in a shower of death. Deadly spells woven into their tips allowed them to pierce the magical flesh of daemons almost as easily as they parted the armour of cultist and skin of mutant. It seemed that there were more elves left alive within than he had thought and their mages had somehow managed to shield their essence even from N'Kari's magical vision.

Good, N'Kari thought. It would be more stimulating this way. It would lend a little piquancy to the conflict. Opposition would provide a little relish.

Things were going well. Vengeance would soon be his.

THE ELVES WERE proving troublesome. A storm of arrows had descended on N'Kari's troops, along with a hail of spells. His warriors had been thrown back again and again. The greater daemons in his retinue, loath to be the first forward in case it was a trap, were holding off from the attack. The lesser ones were not powerful eough to clear the walls on their own. It was time for another tactic. He called his army back and ordered them to cease attacking, to give their foes an hour to rest, to snatch sleep, to dream...

He breathed deeply and exhaled, emptying his lungs in a cloud of narcotic perfume that all but stunned Elrion and the other cultists who watched him with bright, mad eyes. He extended one of his claws and inscribed runes in the dirt. He indicated to a cultist that she should bow her head, and took it off with one clean sweep. He breathed in again as the huge jet of blood spouted into the air. All of the crimson fluid was sucked into his chest, bringing with it the faint taste of its supplier's tainted soul.

Swiftly N'Kari worked his spell, changing the blood within him, adding some of his own eternal essence, drawing corrupt phantasms from the Chaotic netherworlds. He added visions of sin from his extensive memories and lustful dreams taken over the centuries from the souls he had devoured.

He breathed in again through his nostrils, drawing on the winds of magic and adding power to the witch's brew he exhaled through his mouth. An army of phantoms emerged in his breath, beautiful elf maidens and boys, translucent, dancing seductively.

His worshippers reached out and tried to embrace them but N'Kari shooed them away. These things were not for them. These wraiths were half-formed, malleable, responsive to dreams and whims. He did not want them shaped by the demented drives of his worshippers. These were meant for other beings. They would offer temptation to the guardians of the wall.

N'Kari aimed a coruscating bolt of energy at the weakest point in the spell walls. Even weakened the defences were still powerful. It took effort to blast even the smallest chink in them, but that small gap was all he needed to create. The wraiths flowed through the gap like water seeping in through a small hole in a ship's hull, carrying within them a freight of dreams, desire and demented horror.

CHAPTER TWENTY-EIGHT

THE SKY WAS dark with thunderclouds. Rain poured down. The heavens themselves seemed angry. Lightning split the night.

From the top of the temple, a soaked Tyrion looked down on the onrushing horde illuminated by the sudden stark light of the thunderbolt. This looked bad. The attacking force was far larger than anyone had ever imagined it would be, and it had arrived far sooner than anyone had expected.

Tyrion was not frightened. He was rationally aware that there was a very strong possibility that he was going to be dead before this day ended but that did not scare him. He was fascinated. Below him were creatures out of legend – daemons the likes of which had not been seen since the time of Aenarion.

If the stories were true, the howling horde of attackers throwing themselves at the walls were led by N'Kari, a being who had commanded the attack on Ulthuan in the dawn ages of the world and who had twice faced Aenarion himself. He thought he could make out a monstrous four-armed figure that might be the Keeper of Secrets ordering his troops forward.

He had certainly seen with his own eyes a Lord of Change's fire blasts of multi-hewed Chaotic energy directed at the archers on the walls. Its magic carving through the protective enchantments and then the flesh of the defenders. Its raptor-screams of triumph echoing across the battlefield, their very sound freezing the weaker-willed in fear.

He wished Teclis were here to see this. He felt sure his brother would be at least as fascinated by the sight as he was. Tyrion did not need his brother's gift to see that there was powerful magic at work here on behalf of the elves as well as the daemons. Elven weapons harmed hell-things that ought, according to the legends, to have been invulnerable to them. Something shielded the defenders from many of the daemon's spells. He felt sure that the greater daemons were holding back because of the presence of something they feared although he was not sure for how much longer they would do so.

All night the daemon worshippers had attacked in waves, and then at last, as the defenders had tried to snatch some rest, that horrific cloud of sorcery had come. Tyrion had no idea what had happened within it, but screams of agony and delight had echoed over the battlements and when the cloud had finally dispersed the ground around the exterior walls had been littered with the half-naked bodies of fallen elven troops. The Chaos worshippers had come surging over.

There simply were not enough elves to hold the shrine against the force assaulting it. The speed with which such a huge attack had come had thrown the elves off guard. They had never imagined such a force could set foot on the sacred soil of the holy island so quickly.

What had been intended to be a safe refuge for himself and his brother had turned out to be a death trap. There was no way off the island without passing through that daemonic horde. Perhaps reinforcements would arrive soon but if they did not come in force, they would be destroyed piecemeal as they tried to leave the harbour.

In the distance brazen horns sounded. Winged furies descended from the sky, falling on the defenders with terrible rending claws. Down there people were dying to protect him and the sacred soil of this most holy place. Part of him wanted to leap into the fray and aid them but that would not be wise. Needlessly exposing himself would make the defenders' task harder and perhaps even make a mockery of their efforts if he were to be killed.

The most sensible thing he could do was to retreat into the deepest and best protected parts of the shrine and pray that the battle turned out well. He already knew that it would not. He could see what would happen quite clearly. The daemons would clear the last few defenders from the outer walls, and force them to fall back.

Tyrion heard feet on the stairs behind him. The rain-soaked cowl of a priest of Asuryan rose into view. He was breathing hard, his face was pale and he was obviously frightened.

'There you are, Prince Tyrion,' he said. 'We have been looking all over for you. The abbot has ordered me to take you the inner shrine. You will be safe there along with your brother... if you are safe anywhere. The god will protect you.'

He did not seem at all sure of that.

TECLIS KNEW THE battle was going badly. He did not even have to look at the faces of the messengers bringing reports to the captain of the warriors guarding the innermost shrine to know it. The news had been bad ever since the priest had come to lead him to this sacred sanctum deep within the shrine. There were a few wounded warriors here in the shadows cast by the great fire pit and twenty Phoenix Guards. The warriors looked worried. The Phoenix Guards stood as impassive as the massive statues surrounding them.

Teclis could sense there were many daemons, some of enormous power, outside the shrine and drawing ever closer. He felt their presence like an evil shadow lying on his heart. It made him want to howl with terror. Only by an enormous effort of will could he keep himself from doing so. When mortals faced daemons the evil ones usually had the advantage in power and magic and morale. They need not fear for their infinite lives. Mortals did. The mere presence of daemons was enough to ensure terror.

The daemons were not the only supernatural entities making their presence felt in this hour. He looked up at the great flame burning in the centre of the chamber. It roared like a city on fire. Its heat was enormous. At any other time he would have felt privileged to witness this manifestation in the most sacred heart of elvendom, the chamber of the Flame of Asuryan.

He was more aware of the flows of power around him within the shrine than he ever had been in any other place and at any other time. He sensed the presence of the god as it leaked out of whatever realm Asuryan dwelled in and into this world. It was visible to his magesight all around. The air seemed full of glittering sparks. His skin tingled where they touched and the hairs on the back of his neck rose.

If he reached out with his own senses, somewhere infinitely remote and yet so close he could almost touch it was the presence of Asuryan. Being here and being a mage was like swimming in murky water as a leviathan rose from the depths beneath. He sensed the imminence of the god as a massive displacement of energy from one world to another.

If only there was some way to tap into the power of the Sacred Flames and use it as a weapon, he felt sure that the daemons could be defeated. The mighty mages of old could perhaps have managed such a feat. Others had mastered the art of bending the Flame to their will too. The priests who protected the Phoenix King as he passed through it must know some way. That showed it could be done by mortals in this age of the world.

Of course they were shaping the energy in a completely different way, or perhaps they were merely shielding someone else from it, but the thought gave him hope. There might be a way to use the power of the Flame to save himself and Tyrion and the warriors who were trying so valiantly but fruitlessly to protect them. All he needed to do was work out how that could be done.

He offered up a prayer to Asuryan for guidance. Somewhere far off he thought he felt an answering call. Something out there would aid him, if only he could find a way to contact it and make his prayers clear to it.

Tyrion entered the chamber, his clothing soaking wet. His brother looked torn between wonder and unease, but he did not look afraid. His unbounded bravery astonished Teclis.

'How is it going?' Teclis asked.

'Not well,' said Tyrion. 'The priests don't think they will be able to hold off our attackers much longer. I expect we shall be seeing the famous N'Kari soon.'

His idiot brother did not even sound troubled by the prospect.

TECLIS TOOK HIS brother to one side. None of the soldiers were paying any attention to them. They had their own worries.

'The guards will not be able to stop N'Kari,' he said.

Tyrion nodded. He had already made his own assessment of the situation, and doubtless, as in all matters military, it would be an accurate one.

'There is nothing we can do about it,' Tyrion said. 'The Phoenix King's advisors miscalculated. We are not safe here. The reinforcements will not get here in time. Perhaps we would not have been safe anywhere. Who would have thought our foe could become so strong in so short a time?'

'The soldiers cannot stop the daemon, but perhaps I can.'

Tyrion's eyes widened in surprise at Teclis's words. He tilted his head to one side. At least he was not showing outright disbelief in the fact that one barely trained sixteen-year old was claiming to be able to do what an asur army and its contingent of wizards could not.

'How?'

'I may be able to tap into the power of the shrine here.'

'That sounds sacrilegious. Dangerous too.'

'Believe me, I don't like the idea any more than you do but it may be our only chance. I am of the Blood of Aenarion. I may be able to touch the power of the Flame and live where others could not.'

'You are not planning on walking through it?' Tyrion did show some alarm now. The last person who had tried that unprotected was Malekith and his fate had been awful. He had been a mighty warrior too, not a sickly child.

'No. I am planning on begging for aid. Perhaps the power behind the Flame will respond. Perhaps not. If it does not we have lost nothing but our lives, which are already forfeit.'

'What can I do to help?' This was the part Teclis did not like at all. He was going to have to ask his twin to risk his life, perhaps even sacrifice himself so that his plan might work.

'If I have not completed my spell by the time the daemon gets here, you must distract it for as long as possible. Keep it away from me at all costs.'

'I would do that anyway,' said Tyrion immediately.

Teclis looked at his twin with wonder and admiration. He had always known Tyrion was brave but never realised exactly how brave. He asked no questions, made no excuses, did not prevaricate. He was ready, instantly, to go into battle, to give up his life if necessary. He did not even seem to realise how courageous he really was. Teclis wanted to say something to his twin at that moment, but he knew he was wasting time.

'Just be ready,' he said, knowing that Tyrion would understand how he felt. He always did.

Teclis picked a place behind the altar, by the flame pit, that would hide him from view from the doorway. He took a deep breath and concentrated as hard as he could. He was not simply praying. He was working magic as best he could. He pulled power purified by the sacred flame from the air around him and wove it into a structure that would suit his purpose. He created a thin filament of light that he could extend down the well that connected the Flame in this world with the being known as Asuryan in the other. In some ways it was a spell very similar to the one he had used on the mirror in the Emeraldsea Palace only instead of the mirror, he was using the Flame as a focus.

With invisible fingers of magic, he probed the rent in the fabric of reality until he could find the place where it was holed. Once he had done so, he pushed the line of energy through and extended it as far as he could.

He was like a fisherman dropping a line into deep, still waters. He was not sure what response he would get to his efforts but he knew Asuryan could not be pleased to have his sacred space invaded by his ancestral enemies. Over all the millennia the elves had known of him, Asuryan had hated Chaos and warred against it. Teclis held this thought firmly in his mind. There was aid to be had here, if only he could reach it.

He kept extending the line of energy and still he did not make contact. The strain mounted. Mortals were not meant to reach too deeply into this place. He could feel that. There was a power here that only the most rugged could wield, and he was very far from that.

His head spun and his stomach heaved. He felt himself getting weaker and weaker as he extended himself more. It was possible that all life would be drained from him by his efforts. Or something else even more terrible might happen – his soul might be drawn from his body and flee into the depths of the well, never to return.

He felt as if he were drowning. He could not breathe. His chest felt as if it was being crushed. He remembered the flying fish on the deck of the *Eagle of Lothern*, drowning in air.

At this moment, he knew that was him.

He was going to die.

INSIDE THE COOL depths of the shrine everything seemed calm. No screams had so far penetrated the rock walls. No tainted footsteps were heard echoing within. Tyrion knew it was only a matter of time. His blade felt heavy and useless in his hand. He longed to be outside, in the fighting, doing his part to beat back the attackers. Inaction did not suit him. He was a fighter.

Be calm, he told himself. The time for blades will come soon enough. You will have your chance at combat and you will most likely die of it, in a place where no one will see you fall and no one will remember your fate.

One of the Phoenix Guards came over. His face was as impassive as if it had been hewn from stone. He looked at Tyrion and then at the door and nodded his head. His expression was peculiar, as if he recognised something. He squared his shoulders and let out a long breath. His face was calm, as if reconciled to something.

Teclis suddenly shrieked and spasmed, as if he was having a fit. Over and over again, he repeated the name of Asuryan. It looked as if something had gone terribly wrong. Tyrion rushed over to his brother, feeling helpless, for once not knowing what to do.

N'KARI STRODE INTO the shrine. Behind him the gate was broken and corpses lay strewn everywhere. He was alone. The other daemons would come no further and the mortals were distracted by pillage and rapine. The air crackled with inimical energy. The light of Asuryan was strong here but not strong enough to keep him from his goal, not saturated as he was by power stolen from the Vortex. He was enjoying using the full power of his battle form. It had been a long time since he had given full and free rein to his lust for combat. His only regret was that even with the backing of their god, these elves were barely worthy of death under his claws.

He raised his great sword in one hand and swept it down, cutting two of the Phoenix Guard in two with one blow. He snipped off the head of the first bisected corpse with his claw just to enjoy the expression on its face. The brain still lived and thought for seconds even after it was cut off from the body.

Ahead of him were a set of stairs leading down into the depths of the temple. He sensed the presence of his prey down there where Asuryan's power beat most strongly. The presence of that old god was all around here. The Flame blazed strongly as if trying to hide those N'Kari sought within the shadows its light created.

Given time, Asuryan himself might even manifest himself and deal with the interlopers. That would be a sight worth seeing. Unlikely though. It took long ritual magics to get the god's attention. Beings like Asuryan moved and thought in different timescales from their little elf puppets. An eye-blink to a god could be the lifetime of an elf. N'Kari reckoned that he could easily be finished his work here before Asuryan even realised there was a threat to respond to. Unless very powerful magic was used of a type that was beyond the high elves now.

The elves had thought that placing them here would put his prey beyond his reach. He would enjoy showing how useless all of their efforts were. Once he had done that, he thought he would consider finishing the work he had begun five millennia ago and turn Ulthuan into his personal fiefdom.

Laughing with joy, basking in the adoration of those elves who looked at him longingly, even as he killed them, N'Kari made his way down the stairs towards the innermost Sanctum of the Shrine of Asuryan.

THE CONTACT WAS sudden and shocking. Teclis felt something ancient, ageless and terrifyingly powerful. It inspected Teclis as Teclis might inspect an insect. The mind was not mortal. It bore no resemblance to elven consciousness. It operated on a different level entirely, one that Teclis knew he had no chance whatsoever of comprehending.

He sensed the presence was waiting for something but he had no idea what. He concentrated with all his mind, asking for help, for power, for aid against their mutual enemy. Something vast and slow responded but he was not sure it was responding in the way he wanted it to. It was too alien and immense.

There was something, a sense of recognition that might have been an image, a rune, a name. *Aenarion*. Whatever it was, it knew Teclis was connected with the Phoenix King. It must be his blood. Or perhaps it remembered him from his trial. Now he had to make the being understand that he needed help and the nature of the help he needed.

He pictured the daemons. He pictured the shrine. He pictured what was going on around him. Nothing happened. Perhaps the being the elves knew as Asuryan worked on such a timescale that it would take hours for it to respond. All of the rituals concerned with contacting him had taken time and had been performed by elves who were his priests and presumably thus already had established some link with the entity. Teclis had never done so. Perhaps all of his efforts would be in vain. He felt the contact slipping and tried desperately to re-establish it.

A spark of enormous power passed into him so painfully strong that Teclis almost passed out. He knew that if this kept up the force of the magic would kill him. Asuryan was trying to help but seemed unaware that his colossal strength might be too much for the one he sought to aid. He thought again of himself picking up the flying fish. He had never even thought to wonder what had happened to it. Had he crushed its gills with his fingers, killing it even as he tried to save it?

Would that happen to him now?

THE SCREAMS OF the dying and the dreadful roars of their killer were audible now even through the thick walls of the shrine. They echoed through the corridors like notes within the cone of a trumpet. Tyrion waited, loosening his muscles, breathing deeply and letting the tension seep out of him. He looked over to the shadow of the great altar.

Teclis's face was pale and Tyrion could sense his twin's fear and agony. Its distant echo made his stomach churn and his muscles tense. Teclis's brow was knotted in intense concentration. His eyes stared off into the far distance as if he was looking out on things others could not see. His thrashings had stopped and he seemed to have regained some control over himself.

Images of what might be happening outside intruded themselves into Tyrion's mind. He pictured elves being torn apart by ravening daemons, and the hordes of Chaos rampaging through the most sacred shrine of the elves.

He realised that he was not afraid. He was angry. He was angry about the desecration of this holy place, of the threat to his brother's life, about the strange twists of fate that had brought him to this place to die.

Anger and fear are two sides of the same coin, he told himself. Both can get you killed. He forced himself to breathe deeply, to remain calm. Now was not a time when he could afford any emotion-driven mistakes. He saw one of the wounded soldiers looking over at him with something like admiration.

'I wonder that you can remain so calm, Prince Tyrion,' he said. The effort of keeping his voice steady showed in his speech. His voice seemed about to crack when he mentioned Tyrion's name.

'We are in the keeping of Asuryan,' Tyrion said, gesturing to one of the massive statues. He was remembering the way Lady Malene and Captain Joyelle and the officers of the *Eagle of Lothern* had stood on the deck in the storm and given their confidence to the crew.

'Your faith is inspiring,' said the soldier, with only the faintest hint of irony. What he obviously wanted to say but did not dare do in this holy place and in earshot of his comrades was that he did not share Tyrion's faith.

Tyrion smiled at him and the soldier squared his shoulders and gripped his weapon tighter. As Tyrion had suspected he was not about to show himself less brave than an untried sixteen-year old. Tyrion looked away. He had been glad to deal with the soldier's doubts, they had distracted him from his own dark thoughts. Deep in his breast he felt a titanic rage building once more, an anger that could consume him if he let it, the sort of rage his ancestor Aenarion might have felt when he confronted the hosts of Chaos.

Is this how the Curse manifests itself in me, he thought? Am I a child of rage, like those elves who followed Aenarion in the dark days after he lost his wife and children? Is that why I can kill without conscience? Am I chosen by Khaine in that way?

He knew he might not live to find out. The leader of the remaining Phoenix Guards gestured to the warriors present. The Guards and the wounded alike moved to place themselves between the twins and anything that sought to get at them. Tyrion knew they had no chance of doing it, but he was touched by their bravery anyway.

Something enormous bellowed outside the door.

'Whatever you're going to do, do it soon,' Tyrion told his twin.

Teclis stared sightlessly at the ceiling.

THE GREAT WOODEN doorway of the sanctum crashed open. A four-armed form stood there, brandishing an enormous greatsword in one oddly delicate arm. A huge claw clicked at the end of another. With its remaining two arms it wove potent spells. The last twenty of the Phoenix Guard faced it.

Tyrion wondered if there would be any of the order left after this battle. It was said that each of the Phoenix Guard was granted knowledge of his own death during the intricate rituals performed when they were raised to the status of member. He wondered if the proud warriors around him had always known that this moment would come.

He studied their faces. All of them were grim. None of them showed fear, even in the face of the horror confronting them. Tyrion looked back at N'Kari. He had always known the daemon was going to be massive, what he had not conceived of was how oddly beautiful it would be. It was not that the creature's form was lovely, rather it was that it moved with the lithe grace of a dancer and the beckoning, seductive movements of a high-class courtesan. It should and did look obscene, but it was also fascinating.

Magic, he told himself. The daemon's aura was working on him. He shook his head and was surprised how easy it was to throw off the spell that had even the steel-willed Phoenix Guard standing quietly before the monster like rabbits before a serpent.

For a moment that seemed as long as eternity, the spell held, and all stood, seemingly frozen. Then the first of the Phoenix Guard sprang forward to strike at the monster. N'Kari parried and cut the elf in two with his return stroke. Silent as stalking cats, the remaining elf warriors threw themselves into the fray.

CHAPTER TWENTY-NINE

I am going to die.

The knowledge beat against Tyrion's brain with utter certainty as he watched N'Kari rip one of the Phoenix Guard asunder with his great claw. There was no way he was going to survive this. He simply was not a match for the daemon, even weakened as it was by the magical radiance of Asuryan's flame.

I am going to die.

N'Kari beckoned with his hand and some of the wounded soldiers abased themselves before him. N'Kari sprang forward walking on the backs of his newfound worshippers, the great claws on his feet tearing flesh and shattering bone with every stride.

Tyrion was not afraid. He was not angry. He was simply struck by the futility of any action he might perform. He knew in part this was a reaction to the languid vapours the daemon emitted and in part it was his own mind responding to the hopelessness of the situation.

I am going to die.

The remaining Phoenix Guard threw themselves forward to meet the daemon. Its blade reaped their lives like wheat. It laughed with soul-flaying mockery. Blood and brains splattered everywhere, hitting Tyrion on the face. Calmly he wiped them away to clear his sight.

It was all just information. His death was one of the rules of this game. Accepting the truth of it, he could still win. The goal was to distract the daemon until Teclis cast his spell. It was now simply a problem of tactics.

I am going to die.

The daemon gestured again. Polychromatic lightning surged from its extended claw. It hit one of the defenders and consumed his flesh even as he groaned in what might have been agony or ecstasy. The flare of the bolt cast the huge statues of the old god into stark, blasphemous illumination.

N'Kari was huge and very fast and enormously strong. Its claw was capable of shearing a fully armoured elf warrior in half with as little effort as a seamstress cutting thread. It could fire bolts of magic at its targets. It was all but invulnerable to mortal weapons.

I am going to die.

Blades shattered on N'Kari's flanks or passed through flesh that knitted behind them. Whatever protected the daemon seemed random but it was effective.

The invulnerability did not matter. It was not his goal to kill the daemon. Only to waste its time. To draw its attention. His task was to keep himself alive as long as possible. To hold its attention. To save the life of Teclis until he could cast his spell. If he could cast his spell.

I am going to die.

The pitifully few remaining defenders threw themselves forward. The daemon pounced to meet them and rend them asunder.

Time was passing. Every second he did not do something was a second that brought N'Kari closer to victory and Tyrion closer to defeat. He needed to act soon if he was going to act at all. He raised his sword. His hand was steady. He considered wasting an instant to turn to Teclis and wave goodbye but that would merely draw N'Kari's attention to the one he was trying to keep it from.

I am going to die.

He smiled. He had never expected to live forever. His life was going to prove a lot shorter than he would have wished.

Why was he hesitating?

There were things he still wanted to do and would never get the chance to and once he started he never would. No matter. It was too late for that now anyway.

'Face me, daemon, and meet your master,' Tyrion shouted. His voice was as steady as his hand.

TECLIS FELT THE electric thrill of contact with the presence of the god. Knowledge surged into his mind, showing him where to put his hands, how to move his fingers, which words to say. He did what he was told, binding the power and shaping it into a weapon that he knew would prove inimical to the daemon.

He moved in the patterns shown, spoke the words he was told, adapted his mind to the sorcerous inflections demonstrated. The power flowed into him like wine poured into a cup. It thrilled him and it pained him. His life and soul were in danger, for mortal forms were not intended to act as conduits for god-like power. He was filled with so much magical energy that any elf who was not a sorcerer would already have been fried to a crisp. He wondered at how much he could bear. He knew it was going to have to be a lot more if he was to have any chance of harming the daemon.

THE VOICE WAS the same, N'Kari thought. He paused for a moment in something that was almost shock. The face was the same. It might have belonged to Aenarion himself although a younger, less stern, less time-ravaged Aenarion. The scent was the same, flesh for flesh. The spirit was almost the same. It did not blaze so bright. It did not burn with the Flame of Asuryan. It was not corrupted by the Sword of Khaine. It was not dimmed by the shadow of that all-devouring blade.

Astonishingly, it was not afraid. It had not yet learned the meaning of fear as Aenarion had, even when he had his fears most under control.

This was indeed a bright tender morsel to offer up to Slaanesh. The spirit burned bright but it was not the only one of the Blood that N'Kari detected. There was another nearby. No matter. This one would do. It would give N'Kari the greatest of pleasure to teach this foolish mortal the meaning of terror before he killed it.

He would torment it as a cat torments a mouse.

He sprang forward, aiming just in front of it. The elf was quick indeed. N'Kari had intended to do no more than scratch it but the elf was already gone. A pinprick in his left side, near where the heart would have been in an elf told him his opponent even had the temerity to strike back.

N'Kari smiled. This might prove even more amusing than he had hoped.

'I will start with your fingers and toes,' he said. 'I will snip them off so delicately you will not even miss them at first.'

The blade flicked at his eye. It stung. It did not really hurt. It merely interfered with vision for a moment until it healed.

N'Kari struck again, faster this time, certain that this time he would connect. The elf was no longer where he had aimed. Once again it eluded with a speed much greater than N'Kari had anticipated.

'I thought daemons were to be feared,' said the elf with the sword. 'You cannot even hit me.'

It was already backing away though, as if it sensed that on the third attempt N'Kari would unleash his full fury. Tempting as it was, N'Kari resisted. He struck again and thought at first he had connected but then realised his claw had only hit the elf's blade. It was not exactly a parry. There was no way the elf had the strength to either hold or deflect N'Kari's blow. He had simply managed to evade.

It was only a matter of time, the daemon thought. Nothing mortal could defeat him.

TYRION MOVED AWAY as fast as he could. N'Kari was fast, faster than anything Tyrion had ever faced and he sensed that the daemon was not even exerting itself. It was over-confident. It knew it was going to win and that it had time.

Up close the creature was fearsome. It bulked much larger than him. Its hide was armoured. Its massive claw looked too heavy even for its mightily muscled arm but somehow was not. The scent of the thing was odd, musky and spicy and oddly disturbing. Aromatic sweat or some other secretion glistened on its armour.

That was wrong. Flesh sweats. Armour does not.

He pushed aside the thought as a distraction and aimed a blow at where the skin and armour joined, at a point which on any living thing would have been vulnerable. He ducked a blindingly fast claw sweep and lashed out with his blade. It pinked the daemon where he had aimed but the flesh knit behind the blade almost as soon as it was pierced.

N'Kari struck again, aiming low, trying to hamstring Tyrion. He leapt forward, feeling the wind of the displaced air below him, careering off the daemon's side. He hit the ground rolling, let his momentum carry him to his feet and turned to face his foe again. N'Kari was already reaching for him.

Tyrion was glad that he had entered this fight with no illusions as to his chance of survival. It would have been very discouraging otherwise to discover just how fast and strong and powerful the daemon really was. He was outclassed completely. He began to have some inkling of just how mighty Aenarion had been. He had triumphed over this creature and others just as powerful.

Discouraging, he thought again. There was an understatement. Somehow the thought made him laugh.

This offended the daemon. It bellowed in incoherent rage then its surprisingly beautiful voice said, 'Chortle all you like Blood of Aenarion. The last laugh will be mine.'

Tyrion did not doubt it. He kept fighting. He might not have any hope of victory but he did have a goal and it appeared he was achieving it.

He aimed a blow at the daemon's eyes once again. It expected it this time and its riposte was so swift it took Tyrion by surprise. He ducked just in time. Its claw snapped shut just where his head had been. At first he thought it was trying to behead him but then he realised it was trying to grab him. If that happened, he knew things would go very badly for him.

TECLIS BURNED. HE felt sure his flesh was crisping and turning to ash but when he looked it was still intact. His hand glowed with a strange white light. The aura radiated out from his body. His vision had changed. He saw everything wrapped in shimmering auras.

Tyrion stood out golden and bright as the sun, fearless, unafraid, fighting calmly and methodically against an opponent he could not hope to beat, simply to give Teclis a chance.

N'Kari glowed lascivious purple and sickly green and radiated colours there were no mortal words to describe. There was a strangeness about the daemon's aura. In a way he resembled a mobile version of the great well of power here in the shrine. His form somehow extended out of this world and was yet connected to it. It was as if the thing that was N'Kari was merely a finger-puppet on the end of a claw that had been poked through the walls of reality by some much greater being.

That was what daemons were, he realised. The mighty things we think we see and against which we were vain enough to imagine we fight were not the daemons themselves but the merest fraction of vast cosmic entities, constructs made from a tiny portion of their power and sent into this world to work their will.

He had no idea why it should be so – he was like an insect trying to imagine the motivations of an elf. These things operated on a different order of intelligence in a different scale of reality. It was a humbling thought but not, at that moment, a useful one.

Mighty as the thing was, he needed to sever its contact with this reality, break its link with its extra-dimensional creator. If that could be achieved the mortal shell that remained could be cracked and broken and killed.

He focused the energy that was flooding into every cell of his body, shaping it into a weapon. As he did so, every nerve burned with agony. His weak heart raced. The air filling his lungs burned. He unleashed a bolt of energy at his foe.

N'Kari DECIDED THAT this little battle had gone on long enough. He had enjoyed toying with his foe but it was time to get on to the real meat of the experience. He had a mighty soul here to offer up to Slaanesh, one which he would have taken great pleasure corrupting into the ways of pain and pleasure, making it love and adore him before he offered its screaming spirit to his patron daemon god.

It was a pity he simply did not have time for this. The presence of the accursed Asuryan was making it more and more difficult for him to maintain his form here and somehow that presence was increasing.

There was another descendant of Aenarion present here and he was going to have to kill it before the pain became too great for him to endure. Of such little trials is life made up, he thought, and laughed.

He lunged forward with all his strength, catching the elf even as he tried to dance away from the blow. A moment later, N'Kari's claws were on either side of the elf's neck. The warrior looked up at him with a defiance that was amusing, and then spat in N'Kari's eye.

'Great and loving Slaanesh, I offer up this soul to thee,' said N'Kari, twisting the currents of magic around him with his mind. The power thrilled through him. He felt an immense sense of satisfaction. His vengeance was almost complete.

All he had to was close his claw and twist and another descendant of accursed Aenarion would be gone. He paused for a moment to enjoy the sweet sensation of victory. After all there was going to be only one more opportunity to enjoy such a delicious sensation today.

He would make his last offering to his patron special he decided, something so depraved and unspeakable that the elves would remember it for the few paltry centuries their race would continue to exist. Yes, he thought, vengeance would be ecstatic indeed.

A wave of fire crashed into him and he screamed in agony. His claw spasmed open. The elf dropped from his grasp.

THE POWER OF Asuryan blazed through Teclis. It crackled like lightning, burned like volcanic flame. It struck N'Kari like a tidal wave. The daemon's anguished howl was deafening. Its carapace blackened and cracked, greenish-purple pus leaked out and was consumed.

N'Kari turned his jewelled gaze on Teclis and beckoned lasciviously, using some sort of spell of compulsion and seduction. Filled as he was with the power of Asuryan it barely touched him.

Twin blazes of power emerged from his hands. The daemon howled and burned but it still lived. It moved towards Teclis, pushing against the blasts like a man pushing upstream against a strong river current. His great claw clicked together menacingly. Clearly, it intended to do with physical force what its magic had been unable to achieve – end Teclis's life and cut off the source of the god-like destructive power aimed against it.

Teclis concentrated as hard as he could on burning it down, but he knew that he was too slow, and that he did not have time to achieve his goal.

Death came closer, step by step.

* * *

ONE MOMENT, TYRION knew he was doomed. The daemon was through playing cat and mouse with him. It was going to kill him.

The next moment the daemon was surrounded by a blaze of incandescent energy, screaming orgasmically in agony. It turned away from him towards Teclis. Its flesh was crisping, its carapace cracking like that of a crab baked too long in an oven too hot.

Tyrion took a moment to recover himself and assess the situation. Teclis had somehow conjured enough power to harm the daemon, if not to kill it, if such a thing was even possible. But something had not gone quite according to his twin's plan. Perhaps he needed more time, which meant Tyrion was not done trying to get the daemon's attention.

He sprang towards its back, aiming his sword at one of the cracks that had appeared in the carapace. This time the blade plunged home. He felt as if he were carving through flesh. The daemon was vulnerable.

N'KARI FELT THE sword blade slam into the gap in his armour. It hurt, but not as much as the magical flame did. He concentrated his mighty will on keeping himself moving forwards. The mage was the main threat. He could see that now. He had been duped into thinking only of one of the Blood of Aenarion while the other sought a way to destroy him.

This mage was another of the accursed descendants of the Phoenix King. Only one of them could channel so much of the god's power unscathed. No other mortals could have endured such a divine contact for so long.

Perhaps this one would not survive it either. Mortals were so fragile. N'Kari could not risk the wait.

There would be no time to slay this one elegantly. Asuryan was using the mage as a vessel for his wrath, outraged as he was by N'Kari's desecration of his shrine. The god would not care whether the mortal lived or died, only that his vengeance was fulfilled.

Five more steps, he told himself, and he would destroy the wizard and then take special pleasure in destroying the warrior to make up for the loss.

* * *

THE DAEMON LOOMED over Teclis. Its great claw was wide open. Within moments it would lunge forward and snap him in two.

He would not survive that but it did not matter. He saw a way to save Tyrion. Swiftly he wove a knot of power and sent it arcing over the daemon to wrap itself around Tyrion's blade, turning it temporarily into a new focus for Asuryan's power so that even if he died, the god would be able to use it.

Tyrion's sword glowed as if it had just emerged from the forge. For a moment, Teclis feared the surge of power would prove too much for it, that the metal would melt, that the blade would prove useless, but it was a good blade, of ancient elven make, and it endured.

The thing was done.

TYRION'S SWORD BLAZED like a weapon of legend, like Aenarion's Sunfang in the tales. He did not know how it had happened and he did not care.

He drove it down between the daemon's shoulder blades. It burned through N'Kari's flesh, scorching it. A sickly sweet stench of corruption and narcotic incense filled the air. Tyrion drove it home again with all his might, aiming towards where the heart would be in an elf.

He had no idea whether even this blade could kill a daemon, but he was going to find out.

SEARING AGONY BURNED between N'Kari's shoulder blades. He had thought the pain could not get any worse. He was wrong. The mage had done something new and terrible.

Even as the power of his onslaught decreased, he had transferred some of the god's force to the warrior. N'Kari could kill the mage now but if he did so all the god's power would flow into the sword. It already held more than enough to destroy this physical form. If he turned to defend himself, he might be able to slay the warrior but only at the cost of giving the mage a chance to escape.

It was a hard choice, to forgo part of his vengeance and wait for the time to recreate his form. The one good thing about the situation was that his victims were elves. If one of them survived it would most likely live through the hundred years it would take N'Kari to return to this world. He could take his vengeance then.

N'Kari decided to kill the mage. It was better to be certain under the circumstances.

THE DAEMON DID not turn. Tyrion knew why. It was going to slay his brother. It was determined to kill one of the Blood of Aenarion and that was the option most likely to succeed.

He leapt over the daemon, using its shattered shoulder carapace as a springboard, twisting in the air to bring himself down in front of the daemon, between it and Teclis. With his free hand he pushed his brother away even as he turned to strike.

He felt fast, faster than he ever had. The blade seemed to move of its own will in his hand. He drove the blazing sword forward, striking the daemon with the power of a thunderbolt. He struck it again and again. The daemon reeled back, howling and cursing, great chunks torn from its flesh by the power of the blade, wounds cauterised by the cleansing flame.

The twins drove N'Kari from the chamber of the sacred flame, through the long corridors until they emerged on a ledge in the side of the ziggurat, looking down upon the sea. Tyrion recognised it as the place he had come to after passing the test of the priests of Asuryan. It seemed appropriate. He felt as if he had passed another test.

The daemon seemed to be fading in the sunlight, mist emerging from its charred skin. Perhaps it sought to escape.

Tyrion kept pushing forward, smiting as he went. Teclis sent more bolts of magic crashing into the daemon. N'Kari staggered away, making for the great balcony overlooking the sea.

Tyrion struck again and again. N'Kari turned at bay, claw held high, bellowing defiance. He seemed to have given up on thoughts of escape. He was going to make his last stand and now he would be at his most dangerous.

Tyrion brought his blade down in a thunderous arc. The force of the blow, combined with the daemon's enormous weight, drove it through the banister. It tumbled headlong towards the sea below, disintegrating like a meteor hitting air, burning up like a falling star and disappearing even before it had hit the waters far, far below.

Tyrion let out a long sigh of relief. Teclis limped into place beside him. He looked exhausted and his hair and clothing were scorched.

'I think it's over,' said Tyrion.

'IT'S NOT OVER, you know,' said Teclis. The two of them stood at the very top of the temple. The clouds had blown away and the sky was a clear, brilliant blue. Below them, the elves had begun to clear away the debris of the battle. With the demise of N'Kari, the will that had bound the remaining daemons to this world was lost, and they had vanished, unable to bear any longer the holy air of the shrine. Without their daemonic patrons the remaining cultists had proven no match for the elves. The battle was won.

'You think the daemon will return?' Tyrion asked.

'Aenarion himself could not kill it. I don't think we did. It will be summoned into this world again before too many years pass; and gain a new body, and it will return to finish its vengeance on us.'

Tyrion nodded. 'He certainly seemed a very persistent fellow.'

Teclis laughed. 'You are in remarkably good spirits for an elf who has just been told that he will have to spend the rest of his life being the object of a Keeper of Secret's desire for revenge.'

'I am happy enough just to be able to watch this sunset. I did not expect to see it.'

Tyrion laughed with the pure pleasure of being alive. Teclis leaned against the broken banister and wondered how long it would be before N'Kari returned.

ABOUT THE AUTHOR

William King's short stories have appeared in *The Year's Best SF, Zenith, Interzone* and *White Dwarf*. He is the creator of the Gotrek & Felix novels and the author of four Space Wolf novels starring Ragnar Blackmane. He lives in Prague.

COMING DECEMBER 2012

WILLIAM KING

WARHAMMER

SWORD OF CALEDOR

A TYRION & TECLIS NOVEL

THE SECOND BOOK IN THE TYRION & TECLIS TRILOGY

An extract from Sword of Caledor
by William King

WET LEAVES SLAPPED Tyrion in the face, obscuring his vision. Something heavy and scaly and rain-slick slammed into him. Its momentum bowled him over.

Instinctively, he let himself go with the flow of the motion. Landing on his back in the soggy mulch, he kept rolling and kicked out with his feet, pushing the thing off.

Fang-filled jaws snapped shut in front of his face. Something slammed into his leg with bruising force. He caught sight of something green and vaguely humanoid. He continued his roll and somersaulted upright.

On his feet now, blade in hand, Tyrion sought enemies.

His attacker disappeared into the undergrowth. It looked like a big humanoid lizard, running upright, balancing itself with its long tail. The head was something like that of a dragon with enormous powerful jaws and massive teeth that looked easily capable of tearing flesh right to the bone.

It was one of the legendary servants of the slann. A warrior of some sort although very primitively armed. In one scaly hand it clutched a stone axe tipped with coloured feathers. Only luck had stopped the thing from braining him. As he watched, the thing's skin changed colour, scaly patterns altering so that it blended in with its surroundings. That chameleon-like camouflage was what had allowed it to get so close.

Tyrion's heart beat faster. His breathing deepened. He had a sense that he was lucky to be alive. Judging from the crunching noises nearby some of his own people had not been so lucky.

He looked around to see how Teclis was doing.

The glow of a protective spell surrounded his brother. A group of the lizardmen circled him, snapping at him with their massive jaws and striking at him with their axes. His alchemical gear lay discarded at his feet. His fire was scattered. So far, Teclis's spells had warded off their blows but it was only a matter of time before they managed to do him some harm.

Tyrion sprang forward, lashing out with his sword. His first blow separated the head from one lizardman's body. His blade caught another in the chest. Greenish blood flowed. The air took on an odd coppery tang.

The lizardman shrieked, the sound of its voice like the hissing of a boiling kettle until the note went too high to be audible to his ears. Tyrion twisted his blade, turning it until it grated against rib. He leaned forward, hoping to hit the heart but not sure of the layout of the internal organs that a lizardman might possess.

Of one thing he was certain – he was causing his victim a great deal of pain, judging by the way it screeched. Its tail curled around threatening to hit him with the force of a bludgeon. He leapt over the blow, even as two of the lizardman's companions closed in from either side.

Tyrion caught one in the throat with his sword, where the windpipe ought to be. Something crunched under the blow and the lizardman fell backwards, mouth open in a silent scream, no sound being emitted from its broken voice box, then the pommel of his blade connected with the snout of the other lizardman with sickening force. It too halted momentarily, stunned.

Tyrion split its skull with his sword and then wheeled to stab the other one as it clutched at its slashed throat.

With the force of a striking thunderbolt he smashed into the melee, dancing through the swirl of combat with impossible grace. Every time he struck a lizardman fell. Within heartbeats he had turned the course of the battle and slaughtered half a dozen more of the cold-blooded ones. The rest of them fled off into the undergrowth, shrieking and bellowing like beasts.